KAA

KT-426-187

WITHDRAWN

B000 000 011 7519

ABERDEEN LIBRARIES

TURNING
the
STONES

TURNING *the* STONES

DEBRA DALEY

HERON
BOOKS

First published in Great Britain in 2014 by Heron Books
an imprint of
Quercus Editions Ltd
55 Baker Street
7th Floor, South Block
London W1U 8EW

Copyright © 2014 Debra Daley

The moral right of Debra Daley to be
identified as the author of this work has been
asserted in accordance with the Copyright,
Designs and Patents Act, 1988.

All rights reserved. No part of this publication
may be reproduced or transmitted in any form
or by any means, electronic or mechanical,
including photocopy, recording, or any
information storage and retrieval system,
without permission in writing from the publisher.

A CIP catalogue record for this book is available
from the British Library

HB ISBN 978 1 78206 989 8
TPB ISBN 978 1 78206 990 4
EBOOK ISBN 978 1 78206 991 1

This book is a work of fiction. Names, characters,
businesses, organizations, places and events are
either the product of the author's imagination
or used fictitiously. Any resemblance to
actual persons, living or dead, events or
locales is entirely coincidental.

10 9 8 7 6 5 4 3 2 1

Printed and bound in Great Britain by Clays Ltd, St Ives plc

Typeset by Ellipsis Digital Limited, Glasgow

To Chad,
and to Finn and Beau

Contents

PART FOUR

The House of Kitty Conneely, Connemara

April, 1766

Do you know what I am going to tell you? This is it now: a vision of the missing child has come to me.

How did the vision arrive, you will want to know. Lookit, as I have grown older my powers have amplified. You would not know me now to look at me, I have withered in the face and there is a head of hair on me as white as foam, but the goings-on inside my mind are so full of wonders you would not credit. How else may I talk to you, friend of my heart, save through the marvels of the mind, for we have long been parted?

You could say that in my own way I have migrated to the deep, just as you have. I see things behind my eyes as if reflected in water. I send out invisible feelers from the sprit of my head like a lobster into the currents around me and from time to time I receive a transmission.

In that way, last night, I saw the child. She was in a place far from here. She is grown now, but hang me, Nora, if I did not recognise her.

I must tell you that she is frightened and in danger. She has been ill-used and by the blood of Brigid I will not stand for it. When I saw her plight I was swept anew by fury. Indeed that vengeful tide has been long rising to its occasion.

Seventeen years have passed since that terrible afternoon on the strand and the loss it left behind. I have had a poor time of it since then with only bitterness and wrath for company. It was my wish to bind a curse on those villains at that time, but I feared that it might by chance harm the child. And to tell the truth, my powers were weak then. I had lost the force of them. I suppose you may be surprised by that. You always knew me as a sure woman who had many people cured with herbs, and I could talk well-shaped stones out of their hiding places under the earth. Many a neighbour man came to me for help in that regard when he was building a house.

But you will remember, Nora, how I suffered for my ways of knowing. People in the parish said I would pay a price for my knowledge and God help me, I did. They say that a woman with powers must sacrifice something to them, and so it was.

I found I could not conceive a child. Sure though, you knew that. But what you do not know is this: I made a promise at a holy well to give up making cures. In return I asked the well to let me get a little babe.

I put away my herbs, Nora. Yet no child came to me.

But now that I have entered my late years, I find my powers are renewed. Perhaps God has taken pity on me for all my years of emptiness, sure that is it. There is nothing I cannot do these days, my friend, once I set my mind to it, bar flying up in the sky. And so those sinful people must watch out for me! Had they cherished the girl, in spite of what they did, I might have thought to stay my hand.

But what am I thinking to let them off the hook? I have

brooded too long on the greediness of those who believe another's life is theirs to spend. And I have felt every class of despair at the desperate want of justice in this world.

I know, Nora, that dark ways were never to your liking, but I declare in all sincerity that strong measures are called for to punish those who harmed us.

I myself, Kitty Conneely, am able for the task. That woman there and that man there will pay for the past. They must pay a penalty. I will bring back our girl, if I can do it, and take their daughter away from them. In that way, the grief will be put off me and cast on to them. Sure, it will not be an easy thing to bring off. A soul of iron is needed for such work. I know right enough that the words that are used to bind a curse are violent and irrevocable.

But God forgive me if this is not deserved three times over.

PART ONE

Mayfair, London

April, 1766

With brutal suddenness my mind wakes from its stupor and surprises a girl in the looking glass. Her face is as white as paste, her black hair unravelled.

She stares at me with eyes that are dark pools.

Her shift slides from one lascivious shoulder, gaping open at the front, nakedness beneath. I see that her pockets are still securely tied around her waist, a detail that strikes me as absurd given the air of desecration that hangs over her. There is a string of tiny teeth, or pearls rather, at her throat. She raises her hand to the necklace – which I recognise, it belongs to Eliza Waterland – and my own hand touches the pearls.

Oh, God. *My own hand.*

The wretched reflection belongs to me.

I am shocked to find myself in such a state, my brain un-tethered, my senses at a stagger. Do I even know where I am? In a closet, evidently. It belongs to a gentleman, I see. Shaving brush, soap, cologne laid out on a silver tray in front of the looking glass. A pitcher and a basin. I reach with shaking hands for the pitcher.

Because I must wash away the blood smeared on my chest and on my forearms and on one of my feet. I seem to have trodden in blood.

In a wild movement I dash myself with water. As I scrub my skin with the hem of my shift, the numbness begins to lift. Many parts of me inside and out are hurting. I cease my foolish laundering. Because now I understand that I am in a place of danger and I must make an escape.

Quitting the closet, I rush to a door at the far end of – of, I see it is a bedchamber. There is a bedstead. Rumpled linen shows behind ponderous velvet hangings. I do not care about the bed. I want the door.

But the door is fast. *Who has locked me in?*

I tug at the handle, a sob trying to scramble up the walls of my throat. It threatens to burst from my mouth with a howl that will bring servants running. I swallow it down, but still, panic flops around in my stomach looking for a way out.

I turn to face the chamber. I do so with extreme reluctance as if there is something there I do not wish to see. The light is dim – the candles have consumed themselves – and the air is stale and sickening. The window curtains are drawn, but blades of light show between them. The sly gleam of a steel chimney piece catches my eye. Could he have left the key there? (And who is this he? I do not know.) Alas, there is no sign of a key on the chimney piece or on the hulking bureau. But my search brings me in proximity to a couch.

I cannot avoid noticing that my clothes are lying in a distressed strew on the floor and that, oddly enough, someone has dropped a bloody razor on the tangle of my stockings. My gaze fixes on the blade and then insists, against my will, on travelling towards the *thing* over there between the couch and one of the windows.

Oh, dear God. There is the *he*. Lying face down where he

fell. He must have been there for some time because the blood that spurted out of him has turned black upon the carpet like a monstrous blot. I swear that I did not kill him. I do not believe I did. I couldn't have. I do not even recognise him. I cannot say that I know who he is. I cannot admit that I know who he is.

But now I am awake to my predicament. It does not take a genius to foresee how this picture will be interpreted when the door is cracked open by constables. They will make a connection between the dead man and me that will bind me as a murderess and the thread of my life will end in a noose or transportation.

I need the door-key.

There is a coat here, tossed over the back of a chair. Reaching into the slit of its pockets in search of the key I am overwhelmed by a sensation of disgust and then suddenly I am burning, inexplicably, with shame as if it is my own fault that I have come to this. I snatch away my empty hand. Oh, Lord, the key, where is the key? Did it fall from his pocket to the floor? My hand, floundering about, brushes against something beneath the couch that feels like a dead mouse. With a choking cry I draw back – and the abruptness of my movement sweeps an object into view. It is a suede moneybag. A glance shows the glint of a guinea or two and a few shillings and pennies. I shove the bag into one of my pockets and now I think to step into my crushed gown and petticoat. Tie the petticoat clumsily. Where are my shoes? Here they are near the bureau. Was I wearing a hat? My mantle is missing, too, and my hairpins are lost. I cannot put up my hair. No matter, it really is of no matter at all to go abroad with my hair undressed. And my bloodied stockings – I will leave them off.

Suddenly, a noise comes to my ear and with it a wash of horror. I freeze, the nape of my neck prickling, and eye the door. Someone is tapping at it.

As the tapping sounds again, a whimper of fear escapes from my mouth. I stand, rigid with tension, waiting for discoverers to burst in and drag me away.

Tap-tap, tap-tap.

And then it dawns on me that the sound does not come from the door at all, but from quite the opposite direction.

I tread a line of watery light towards one of the window curtains and heave it to one side. The tapping comes from a sycamore that is scratching at the glaze with its fingertips as if it is trying to attract my attention. On throwing open the window, I find that I am on the third storey of a house in an unfamiliar street of handsome townhouses. The street lies half in shadow. The pavement is unattainably far below. Craning my head to look towards the roof of the house, I see no way out in that direction either. The sky seems lower than usual as if it has been crammed into a space too small for it. There is a cloud directly overhead threatening rain.

I can feel hysteria gathering itself for an assault on my reason, but before it can pounce, the sycamore comes to my assistance. The young leaves in the topmost branches begin to rustle loudly, which draws me to stare into the green crown. With my ear alert to the excited whispering of leaves and the murmur of branches, a thought sparks in my mind.

And all at once, I am inspired to a course of action. There *is* a possibility of escape!

Withdrawing from the window, I scan the chamber for the

material I need. My gaze slides over the bloodied shape on the floor and rests on the bedstead. I dash towards it and seize one of the velvet bed-curtains. The thing resists me at first, but it is easily defeated by the rage that surges through my arm and it dives with a wrench from its fixings, its brass rings clanging against the bedpost.

But as I flounder with the bed-curtain, I hear a muffled metallic groan. The handle of the door is moving. Someone in the hall is trying to enter.

Fear flutters in the pit of my stomach. In the deathly silence of the bedchamber I have the impression that the lurker at the door is straining to make out, as closely as I, what is happening on the other side. Then there is a vague sound, which I take to be a receding footfall. Surely it is a servant who has gone now to fetch a key and a superior. In a cold sweat I spring to my task, dragging the curtain to the window. I struggle to wind the velvet around my torso, leaving my arms free. I wriggle on to the sill like an insect half-emerged from its cocoon and without thinking, and yet with an arm flung across my forehead to protect my eyes, I throw myself out of the window into the void.

I feel, for an instant, gloriously light and liberated.

Though it is a harebrained hope, I have placed my faith in the tall sycamore growing by the window. It may just possibly break my fall, but I will not be surprised if instead I should meet the paving stones below with a crash and be struck dead. That, too, would be a form of escape. It is a fate that seems likely as I pitch into the sycamore's up-reaching arms. The tree fumbles its catch and the scrabbling branchlets in the canopy fail to detain me. With a cracking, snapping, down-rushing sound, I slither through the branches in a blur, my hands grasping futilely at sparse leaves and springy green twigs. Fortunately the tree grows more dense towards its lower branches and the stuff wrapped around me snags on them, slowing my fall – and then all at once my tumbling ceases and I find myself lodged about twenty feet above the ground in the sycamore's twisted arms. For a few minutes I am afraid to move.

A gentle rain begins to patter among the leaves.

Footsteps approach and fade in the street and there is the clip-clopping of horses' hooves and the thrum of wheels, but I remain unremarked. No one turns their gaze skyward to discover what has littered the footpath with vegetation. I reach for the branch above and manage to depend from it, my feet groping for a foothold below. My velvet casing collapses in folds beneath my knees and I kick free of it, wriggling through the branches. There is a drop of about ten feet to the ground. I wait for a passing chaise to quit the street – in fact the postilion spots me, his mouth falling agape, but he must ride on – and then I let go first my shoes and then myself.

The fall knocks me off my feet and jars my knees, but I am in order, I find. I suppress my jubilation, because I must armour myself against emotion, absolutely, and I retrieve my shoes and the bed-curtain, which I drape from my shoulders to serve as a cloak.

Where should I go? What shall I do?

I stare through the drizzle at looming houses with smooth facades the colour of curds. They are much grander than Mr Paine's house in Poland Street. Even if I could find my way back to Soho from this unknown quarter, there is no going home for me. I must accept that fact.

Suddenly I sense movement from behind a tall ground-floor window and glimpse a shadowy figure in the house in front of me. God's teeth, how could I be so stupid! Here is the dwelling from which I have only now escaped. You fool, Em! Someone in there has seen you loitering in the street. Run for your life!

I dash towards the nearest corner.

As I round it at a scurry, a glance over my shoulder shows a person in livery emerging from the house, his head turning in my direction.

I break into a sprint up a street with a slight ascent, searching urgently for a way to duck my pursuer. I plunge into the narrow entranceway of a mews – and at once someone paws at my arm. It is a cadger, after a coin. I cry, 'A shilling for you if you will show me shelter from the rain!' The cadger points vaguely towards a door that stands ajar and I run towards it. The door admits me into a dismal hall that smells of ashes and mould. I have the impression of household offices at the rear of a dwelling. Pulling the door to, I shoulder past a threadbare curtain. There is a flight of stairs ahead, ending in a closed door.

Through the flimsy door I hear the sound of footsteps striking the cobbles in the mews. They come ever closer. Surely they must belong to the servant of the house I have just fled. The footsteps stop and I listen with bated breath to the burble of men's voices. I can hardly hear them over the drumming of my heart. Doubtless the cadger will give me away if he is offered money. My hope is that the footman, who has left his post in haste, will not have a coin to hand.

Silence falls. Then the creak of the opening door. As a figure darkens the doorway I form my hands into puny fists, determined that I shall not be taken without a fight.

It is the cadger, with his hand outstretched. Is there anyone with him? No, he only wants my shilling. He snatches the coin I offer without meeting my eye. In a whisper, I ask if he will tell me my whereabouts, since I am practically a stranger to London, but he affects not to hear me. Instead, he lifts an arm and gazes in consternation at a stain on the sleeve of his grimy pink suit, as if he had just noticed this taint on an otherwise spotless ensemble. Strings of damp hair cling to his pate and he has the air of a man beyond all hope. He looks nervously over his shoulder and says that he will escort me outside so that I may be on my way. But that jumpy glance has told me all I need to know. Behind the door, my pursuer lies in wait.

I push past the cadger towards the stairs. As I reach the bottom step, the gloom in the hall fluctuates. The back door has opened and the sound of violent footsteps turns my stomach to water. Up the stairs I rush and fling myself through the door into a parlour. There is a glimpse of startled faces. I tear through a grand vestibule and out the front of the house and sprint away.

I reach a street corner, gulping at the air. But I cannot get my breath, because I am confronted by a sight that causes me to gasp anew. I have arrived nearly exactly where I started: in the thoroughfare of well-bred pale stone houses. There, some fifteen yards away, is my friend the sycamore tree.

With a cry of despair, I spin on my heel and race off in the thickening rain without the slightest idea where I am going.

As I hasten onwards, my hair drooping under the influence of the rain, it occurs to me that I do not have my makeshift cloak. I must have lost it during my wild charge, but I have no recollection of its falling from my shoulders. How unreliable is memory. Mine has locked away the events of yesterday evening and refuses to show them to me. Have I somehow brought this forgetfulness to bear on myself because I lack the moral fibre to admit to a crime? Well, here is something I will admit: I feel, somehow, guilty. As I slope along in this fading light I expect at any second to feel a heavy hand grasp my arm. I expect to be detained under suspicion.

Just now I almost cannoned into a gentleman stepping out of a print shop. He barely acknowledged the collision for his head was lowered over a news sheet that claimed all his attention. No doubt he will soon be riveted by my story, which is that of a bolting lady's maid and a body slashed to ribbons at a patrician address. The printers will junket with my likeness and my name and no one will care for the truth — whatever that should be — or even listen to my part. If only I had the protection of the Waterlands. If only they could stand up for me and vouch for my good character — but I cannot drag them into this. Imagine the publicity. The embarrassment of it.

I am dodging and diving now among constricted streets and evening is coming on. The public lighting here is very scant and I fear that the cloaked figures appearing at the mouths of the dark entryways around me cannot be other than villains and wild-bloods. The thought of being abroad in this hard town at night adds weight to my already considerable burden of fright. It is with some relief that I discern the rumble of heavy traffic nearby and I head towards it in search of the security of a crowd.

I find myself on the edge of a manic thoroughfare watching a whirligig of carriages, carts and unstoppable sedan chairs. I hover at the kerb, shivering and panting. A long minute passes before my eye falls with a start of recognition on a red brick building on the far side of the road.

I believe I know this place! Is it not Piccadilly?

Eliza and I came here the other day with Mr Paine – it already seems a lifetime ago – to visit his peruke-maker, who keeps a shop in that building. I remember we were almost mown down by a coach coming out of the inn next door. The inn has a substantial frontage, cleft by a covered archway. As I gaze at it my heart suddenly lifts. For here is my way out of London.

In a second I have struck out, dodging pats of dung and riders who insist on bringing their steeds to a canter even in the jam of traffic. The inn is called the White Bear, I see. The schedule inscribed on its door tells me that coaches and diligences depart from here daily at five o'clock in the morning for the port of Dover. There is also a night coach at seven for Bristol and all points west. In a flash, patting at the moneybag in my pocket, I resolve to take the night coach. Dover would be more convenient for France – without an explanation for the scene I awoke to this afternoon, what can I do to save my life but flee from England? But I cannot delay until morning for the coach south. I will try for a passage from Bristol.

And yet I hesitate to enter the yard of the White Bear. Should I return to Eliza in Poland Street and tell her what has happened – or rather that I do not know what has happened? She would never take me for a murderess, would she? And perhaps Mr Paine could help. But I know it is pointless to entertain such a notion. It is beyond their skills to smooth over such an unholy mess. Mrs Waterland could do it, perhaps, but she is two hundred miles away in Cheshire. And besides . . .

It gives me a queer feeling to say this, but a shiver comes over me at the thought of Poland Street and intuition tells me to stay away.

I pass under a covered entranceway into a long yard made gloomy by the rain and by dilapidated wooden dwelling houses that rise three storeys above the stables and coach houses and hinder the light. There is a straggling crowd standing at shelter in a doorway.

A voice cries, 'Looking for a seat, missus?' A crone in a frayed mantle and a cross-barred petticoat jerks her thumb towards a door set in a crook of the wall.

It leads to a vestibule and a booking office. Huddled up on a stool at a sloping desk in a corner of the office, next to a window glazed with imperfect glass, the book-keeper has just lit an evening candle. The atmosphere is pungent with the stink of rancid tallow. There is a large plan of London affixed to the wall with a red line running through it like a knife cut.

The book-keeper raises his head with a sideways glance that gives him a shifty look. He is a swarthy man with many chins and a twisted wig cut as close as a lawn. He says at once that he can offer me nothing, neither for Dover nor for Bristol.

I am aware that my appearance must present a slatternly sight and I fear the book-keeper does not believe I have the funds to buy a seat. But perhaps he sees my desperation, because he offers me a constrained smile and says that an outside place is available on the night coach, but only as far as Reading. At the George Inn in Reading I may hope to connect with a morning coach to Bristol.

The inept X that I make on a page of his ledger is quite convincing, I believe, and so is the lie regarding the name I give him. 'Ann Jones' slips easily to my tongue.

The night coach west has turned out to be a disreputable piece of work. There are ten of us heaped up here on the roof like human baggage: an apprehensive woman with red, gummed hair under a white cap, holding a child tightly to her chest; a whiskery, oblong-shaped couple; and a cluster of rough men talking out of the sides of their mouths. 'Last night was a belter, all right,' says one of them. Another blows out his cheeks with a hoot of laughter, 'You're right there, Frank. Blow me tight if it weren't.' The inside of the coach is swarming with drovers and their dogs. They are staging up to Swindon, I hear, after selling their beasts at Smithfield. Our coach is aptly named the *Demon* – certainly it seems to possess an unclean spirit. Two enormous lamps on each side of the body and another on the hind boot show up the deficiencies of the turn-out – the unkempt horses in cobbled-together harness, the driver in a tatty greatcoat, and the lack of a guard. The boot is packed with bags of wool, apparently. 'Or so they say,' one of the men remarks with a tap on the side of his nose. I cannot make out his meaning exactly, but there is an unsavoury air about the entire enterprise and I have the feeling that our journey is likely to be exposed to every possibility of mishap.

I am riven by the fear of capture. The half-hour I was obliged to wait before the coach departed felt intolerable. I hung about in an agony of nerves, trying to keep out of sight in the stables. But even though we are on our way now, staggering through the western precincts of London, I expect at every stage to find us flagged down and myself arrested. What a pathetic dodge it was to give a false name to the book-keeper at the White Bear. That will not fool a determined hunter for a second.

My memory still refuses to disclose the sequence of events that brought me to that bloody bedchamber, and this amnesia makes me suspect myself. Shall I wake up tomorrow to find that I have killed a man? I will admit that, like most people, I have a capacity for anger and animosity, but does that make me capable of taking a life? Will you believe me when I say that I am innocent? I yearn for that understanding.

The light has gone and our surroundings are as dark as a bag now. It suddenly occurs to me to wonder: who is this *you* to whom I plead my case?

At the village of Hammersmith we changed horses and a knave in a mashed hat and a sour coat took a seat by my side. I am frightened of him. His head lolls on his shoulders with the reeling of the coach like something unhinged. He keeps pestering me with a black velvet scarf, which I am sure he has stolen. 'Come now, wench,' he wheedles, 'only pay me a little florin for this lovely scarf.' The harassment continues as we cross a heath in a descending fog. The road is a queasy one and the darkness intensifies my fear.

'Give us a florin then.' The nagger dangles the scarf in my face. He grins at the fellow sitting on the other side of him, who is similarly ragtag and sinister. 'She won't pay up,' he sniggers. 'What do you say, shall we make her?'

Fortunately for me, his neighbour chooses that moment to vomit over the railing of the coach. By the time the ensuing commotion has settled, there are dull spots of light visible ahead. The presence of an inn must not please my tormenter at all, because he seizes his chance, as soon as the *Demon* slows, to make a hurried departure. In fact he scuttles with such haste on to the packets piled in the boot and thence to the road that he leaves behind the scarf. And now it is mine.

I wrap myself in the scarf's soft velvet. What a boon it is in this sharp night air. And its blackness offers a fleeting sensation of invisibility. Nevertheless, I eye with anxiety the arrival of a new passenger. He is a well-upholstered individual carrying a pannier – the coach sagged quite significantly as he came aboard – but as he settles among us with a genial expression on his big face, my tension slightly eases. The pannier contains a brace of leverets, he announces. They have hung for twenty-four hours and he does not expect them to raise a stink. The woman with the child looks up and observes that there is nothing worse than a green leveret. She ducks her head suddenly as if regretting her remark and presses her lips to the forehead of the sleeping toddler in a flutter of kisses that seem to have the effect of reassuring herself as much as the child.

She is not alone in her need of comfort. My own longing for solace is so grievous, I have begun to pour out my woes to a phantom auditor. To *you*.

The horses that have been put on at our last change are wretchedly used up – an old piebald with swollen hind legs and a couple of nags that can scarcely stand, with bald patches on their coats where the harness has rubbed – yet somehow we lurch on, hour after hour in the black night, occasionally shifting our haunches on the hard roof. I continue faint and cold and worrying at things that are beyond my understanding. Why, for instance, am I dressed in my good gown and petticoat? For I have suddenly recognised them as such – is not the gown my best blue lustring satin and the petticoat the peach taffeta that Mrs Waterland gave me to wear in London? I have stared a hole in my petticoat this past hour, but I cannot bring to mind in any way the occasion that caused me to put on this attire.

This coach is fiendishly uncomfortable and yet I am so tired I almost dozed off just now despite the cold mist and the jouncing about. But I forced myself awake. I should not like to lose my grip on this brass rail and crash overboard. On my journey down to London with Eliza, the driver set off so precipitously from one of the inns – I think it was the Cock in Stoney Stratford – that a woman fell from the roof of the coach. I remember glimpsing a cinnamon petticoat spilled on the cobbles. There ensued an altercation between the coachman and the woman's husband, the coachman shouting that it was not his fault the passenger had not secured herself, and since she was not dead he had nothing to answer and must get on. The other outsiders threw down the couple's luggage and a bundle, which turned out to be a small child. With a crack of the lash and a hi-ho, we set off, abandoning the injured family in the yard.

I have learned my lesson in that regard. Here I cling securely to my perch, not daring to get down even to stretch my legs between stages. In any case, now that we are in full night, there are watchmen stationed at the yards of the inns. They are well rewarded, I have read, for apprehending suspects of felonies. And so I imprison myself on the roof of the *Demon*, afraid most of the time even to catch the eye of my fellow passengers. Above, black clouds sail across a black sky. Below, the wheels thunder.

To whom do I make these observations?

It is to you: my mysterious, nameless mother.

Of course it is you to whom my story is addressed. It is you whom I desire to convince of my truthfulness.

I have nothing at all of you save for the knowledge that you gave birth to me. But this stark fact, that I am connected to you by an unbreakable bond of blood, is the only prop I have in my hour of need. How strange and rare and potent those words: *my mother*. The thought of you at this bleakest of times makes my soul feel less forsaken, even though you are dead.

Because I am sure you must be dead – you are, aren't you?

Well, I will not let that be an obstacle. You seem very real to me now. Often unseeable things seem real to me. I have always been prey to torrents of sense impressions. It is as though none of my doors is ever quite closed. Is that a tendency I inherited from you? Perhaps you might have thought, too, as I do, that there is more to the world than meets the eye. I will even go so far as to say that the human mind might have a capacity for communication that has not yet been entirely revealed to us. That possibility excites me. It brings me to wonder if you could even actually hear me now or read my thoughts, in a manner of speaking, from some other plane of existence.

Well. You see I go too far with these notions. I will admit that I am fanciful.

It is such a comfort to talk to you.

I beseech you with all my heart to listen to me – for if not you, who else?

The Cursing Stones, Connemara

April, 1766

A soft day it was today, wasn't it, with the sun shining in and out behind the rain and a little gathering of clouds late in the afternoon. I waited until twilight came on and then my two feet brought me to the place of the stones. I suppose, Nora, you might have seen me from your high perch, going about my mission.

Few things can be more terrible than the words 'The devil bless you', but say them I did as I stood before the cursing stones. I made nine circuits around them, walking against the direction of the sun. At the end of each circuit I called out, 'Your souls be damned for what you have done!' I felt myself tremble in the core of my body and a blast of wind arrived that made me wonder if someone from the other side had come to see what I was up to. But they would have known I had a right to be there. I told the wind to go back and so it went.

Each stone I petted like the head of a darling babe and then I whispered in its ear the penalty that must be paid by those people. Hard though it was, I turned the stones leftwards. Lookit, those stones there are not much larger than a child's ball but it is a business to move them. They make you work at it. There is a reluctance, Nora, on their

24

part. But if it were easy the curse would not be worth a tinker's dam.

As I wrenched the last stone in the direction of the devil, didn't it seem to me that it let out a groan – but whether of horror or of sorrow I could not say. But I will tell you that it frightened me to hear that cry. Impossible it was to know if the stone was in sympathy with my loss or if it lamented being brought to such vindictive work.

Night Coach to Reading, Berkshire

April, 1766

We have arrived at the Saracen's Head, a few furlongs, I am told, out of Slough. As we passed beneath the inn's swinging sign, I caught a glimpse of a forbidding image painted on its boards, an Arab whose turban was pinned with a sickle moon, before the sign knocked off the leveret-keeper's hat. The rest of us were obliged to duck before we turned into the yard to avoid a braining. Peeping over the rail, I see no sign of a burly overcoated watchman with his lantern. I am thankful to note that the further we travel from London, the less prevalent are these apprehenders, but I do not come into the yard of an inn without flinching.

Two lads have run out from the dark tavern to cheer our change with a tray of cold sausages and a bucket of spirits. I sacrifice one of the pennies in my moneybag in order to purchase a cup of gin. I hope that it will help to soften the bolus of anxieties that is jammed in my chest, but I have swallowed only a mouthful of it when someone jogs my arm and the gin spills in my lap. A youth begs my pardon. Where has he come from? I don't remember his climbing on board at the last stage. He seems to feel the heat of my stare, because he turns up his collar, pulls down his hat and pretends to fall into a doze.

As I am about to throw down my cup to the lad in the yard, my line of sight is drawn to two men some yards behind him, who appear on horseback from under the covered entranceway. Fearfully I shrink down on the roof and draw my scarf over my head. The men dismount and turn their pale faces towards the coach and it seems to me that they are watching the two or three disembarking passengers. Then the men lead their horses to the water trough on the perimeter of the yard. Is it possible for me to say at this distance that one of them is similar in build to the footman who pursued me in London?

But if he were the footman, he would have had me brought from the coach at this pause. Or do they mean not to have me arrested at all, but to take me off at a lonely spot on the dark road and, and . . . ? You see how I go spinning into a helix of conjecture and consequence that brings the sweat to my armpits and a lurch to my heart, while forgetting that this is entirely my own speculation.

But now one of the watching men *does* begin to make his way towards the *Demon* and my panicked thought is that I must get off this coach! But how? The way is blocked by the gasping leveret-keeper, who is climbing ponderously aboard by way of the hind boot, where the wool bales are stacked. He swings around and plumps down his huge arse so that he is facing the rear of the coach and settles his pannier on his knees again. And suddenly, with a resumption of our jinglings and creakings, we are off!

There is a shout from below. The footman, if it is he, has missed his chance.

I crouch behind the great slab of the leveret-keeper's back, grateful for his bulk. And rolling on into the blue night, I allow myself to sneak a look at the receding road. I have every expectation of an approach by those cloaked horsemen, but the *Demon* continues on its rickety way with no one in pursuit. At length I begin to breathe more easily. I turn to gaze at the quiet beauty of the sky – it is thick with stars and wads of silver clouds. Soon I will be on a fast coach to Bristol and away on the tides to freedom.

But all at once the wretched *Demon* lumbers to a stop.

We have arrived at the foot of a sticky rise that resists our progress and we are called to get down in order to relieve the horses. They stand mud-spattered in the moonlight with a spectral glow rising from their steaming coats, while the driver orders the men to form up and push the helpless machine. I hang back from the other women as we climb the hill, listening to the coach being manhandled behind us and the skitter of the drovers' dogs. One of the passengers does all the urging, while skidding and unskidding the brake, and the driver calms the galled horses. There are no hedgerows here, only the fields and a great swathe of woodland like a frontier.

The coach arrives at last at the crest of the rise and the driver stands up in his box to call us to come aboard. But he hesitates – and my pulse starts to quicken. He has swung around to stare with obvious strain in his bearing at a bend that lies in the road ahead. Then we all become aware of the reason for his alert – the reverberant hoof-beats thudding towards us. Not highwaymen, surely? Why would anyone bother to hold up a ramshackle night coach? Still, I tear into the field at the side of the road, although it is only a feathery sea of young barley that gives little cover. The woodland being too far to reach, I throw myself down and burrow into the soft, damp crop. The hoof-beats come closer. I press into the cold earth, peering through the grassy veil of barley to see who it is that runs upon the coach.

I can make out three horsemen. One of them, wearing a visor on his face, is pointing a pistol at the driver, and two others have come up on the rear of the coach.

A muffled voice cries out, 'Throw down your cargo, man!' They are highwaymen after all.

To my surprise, the driver decides to risk a flight. At a crack of the whip, his team leaps forward and the robber in front must yield to them. A shot rings out, but there is no stopping the coach, which takes off at a rattling pace. The highwaymen in turn spur their mounts onward and the drovers must call the dogs to heel. The dogs watch in a sulk as the pistol-men disappear over the brow of the next rise in pursuit of the *Demon*, and I clamber to my feet and brush down my damp skirts, feeling giddy with euphoria at my reprieve.

My fellow passengers are flocking together on the road in indignation. An old man eventually makes himself heard. He insists, his words carrying in the stillness, that the coach was transporting cash concealed in bags of wool, placed on the run-down vehicle for disguise. This news delights me for now I see the mysterious men at the Saracen's Head in a different light. They were interested in the *Demon*, not in me. At any event, the coach has disappeared with everyone's luggage. The passengers set off in its wake, their strident review of the hold-up gradually receding into the night. I have no intention of being among their number when they totter into the next hostelry on the road, where an alarm will be raised, witnesses sought and questions asked. How far it is to Reading I can only guess, but I hope that I will reach an inn before daybreak and find a coach to take me onwards to Bristol – and to France.

As I make my way along the hushed highway, I try to picture myself undertaking successful employment as a seamstress in an enchanting French town with cooperative weather. But this exercise only reminds me how scanty is my knowledge of France. I can conjugate a handful of verbs. I have read Montaigne's essays in translation. I know that the currency is the livre. It does not seem very much to go on.

My shoes begin to pinch and my stride shortens to a trudge. With only the sound of my breath for company, a feeling of desolation begins to creep over me. The signs of life in the air – a cock's crow and the smell of chimney smoke – make me nervous. I imagine local yeomen rising for the day with a stamping of feet and a rubbing of hands as if to say, let us get on with the task of bringing miscreants to book.

I pine for Sedge Court, even though my life there was dogged by insecurity. I miss the assurance of its routines and the everyday tasks whose banality once irked me so. I can see in my mind's eye the little flock bed in the corner of Eliza's dressing room, where I slept. How could I have ever found it cramped and uncomfortable?

And I wonder whether I ever had any insight into Eliza at all.

Is she really as blind as she seems to the distancing effect that she has on her mother? Or does she employ incognisance as a tactic to protect herself from rejection? Everyone at Sedge Court sees the gulf between Mrs Waterland and her daughter.

Apparently it has been present since Eliza's birth. Hester Hart, our parlourmaid, says that Mrs Waterland had been long foiled in her attempts to hatch another child to follow Johnny, the heir. It was ten years before she managed to bring a second infant to term and then she was sorely disappointed at the outcome of her travails. Hester says that Eliza came into the world as a bawling babe with a face as red as a tomato and a persistent case of colic. Her squalls succeeded very quickly in driving Mrs Waterland from the nursery. Eliza never did master the art of sweetness. I, on the other hand, divined from the day I passed through the portal of Sedge Court, that my presence must always be a boost to the company.

The wind has risen. I can hear it moaning on the upland to the north like some phantom that has lost its way. Now it is bothering the new hawthorns in the hedges and their white blossom is set swirling like a flurry of unseasonal snow. There are times when things like the movement of shadows through tall grasses or a grief-stricken gust of air seem so vivid to me, almost alive, that I could take them for the shades of long-passed souls roaming among us. Do you think it possible that we might continue to exist in the universe in some form after we have left our bodies?

I wonder this, because it seems to me that I can sense you. I feel you flowing all around me. It is an apprehension that lifts my spirits and gives me a sudden desire to shake off my self-pity and to acknowledge that Sedge Court is not Eden any longer. It is likely, in fact, that the people of that house are waking this morning to their jeopardous situation. Were not the affairs of the Waterlands badly bungled? I am

31

remembering now that the recent news was very bad. Exceedingly bad. I am scrabbling for the details, but they won't yet quite come to mind. Is it a collapse of financial means, though? Perhaps the servants have already been sent away and the fires are dead in the grates and the pantry empty of its victuals. I seem to feel that it may be as bad as that. In which case I am not the only one who is stranded. My heart trembles for Eliza.

Birds are in flight now against the skimming clouds and there is a feeling in the air that all things are shifting and changing. Soon labourers will be abroad, and other travellers.

I swerve from the road and make my way towards a stand of woodland on the crest of a hill. On reaching its shelter, I crawl under the skirts of a wide shrub. I have just enough strength to suck dew from its leaves to quench my thirst, and then nothing, not the bellowing of my empty stomach or the shivers of cold, nor my anguish, can prevent me from plummeting like a stone into the well of sleep.

I wake much later in the deep of the afternoon without any sense of being refreshed. My petticoat smacks of the gin that was spilled on me at the Saracen's Head and my hair is horribly stale and my bruises ache. Just now a cowherd came to the field nearby, and when he was at its far end standing at piss I stole a slice of bread and a lump of cheese from the napkin that he had left tucked under a log away from the prying tongues of the cattle. I can only eat the food in tiny bites, because my throat is swollen; but that small amount of sustenance has lifted the fog from my brain and energised my legs. I will walk to the coast if I must. What can I do but see this course through to the end?

★

32

I have had a stroke of luck. I encountered on the road an old skinner, who was taking hides to market, and he gave me a lift in his cart. It was drawn by sluggardly mules, but I was glad to be off my feet and thankful, also, for his blighted eye. I uttered a silent hurrah when he turned his afflicted gaze to me and I saw that he would make a very poor witness.

That's how I am now, heartened by another's ill fortune if it should turn to my convenience. The skinner offered to drive me all the way into Reading, but I excused myself on the outskirts before we passed through the turnpike. I diverted through trees on a rise that gave me a view of the road and the town – Reading seems to be built on a low ridge between two rivers – and settled down to wait for the night to unfold. I found a dew pond nearby and scooped handfuls of water into my parched mouth and slept again. On waking I saw that the moon had passed to its downward journey and I judged it an apposite hour to depart. My intention now is to locate the George Inn and try to connect with the early-morning coach to Bristol.

I made my way to the highway on a chalk path glowing in the moonlight. It brought me out at a curve in the road, just as a herd drove past a gaggle of geese. I joined their train and followed them across a bridge, then leftwards on to an unpaved, unlit thoroughfare lined with burly buildings. Now up ahead I sense light and movement.

A complicated black-and-white frontage turns out indeed to be the George, its yard already bristling with business. But my exultation at this discovery is short-lived. The book-keeper here has informed me, after allowing himself a pause to brush the front of his waistcoat, which is spoiled with snuff, that the day coach to Bristol is full inside and out. Can this be true? Does my tattered appearance tell against me? Or am I simply riddled with suspicion and mistrust?

I have dragged myself to a seat in the inn's vestibule and sit staring in a glazed manner at the foxes' brushes fastened on either side of the entrance. Above the lintel hangs an arrangement of horns and crossed swords. My recent assertion that I would stride to the coast if I must is nothing but empty bluster, of course. I am so weak I could barely cross the yard.

A boy pushes past bearing a tray of hot, sliced ham and disappears through curtains that must lead to the dining room.

Am I really capable of living like this from now on? Scrambling along muddy fields under cover of night, endlessly on the move, edging around the perimeters of civilised places to the constant drone of fear and hunger, with every fibre painfully alert to exposure?

Oh, Lord, how shall I proceed? The only certainties are that I cannot sit on this bench for ever; and that I was right to dread the loss of Sedge Court, for without it I have nothing and I am nothing. The waiter reappears with his empty tray. I am tantalised to the point of giddiness by the savoury aroma that lingers in the vestibule. I have money to pay for scrapings of ham, but it seems foolish to squander even a farthing of it while I do not know how far my limited funds must stretch.

But so unbearable is my hunger, it drives me to seek the dining room. It is a low-ceilinged place tarnished by tobacco smoke where busy lads pass to and fro with trays of tankards and pipes. Breakfast has been set up on a long table that is already under assault by ravening travellers and their clashing forks. In my frantic condition of body and mind, I struggle to stay on my feet, but somehow, in one swift movement, I abscond with several slices of ham clutched in my hand and flee into the vestibule.

I blunder up a flight of stairs, jostling travellers descending from their chambers, and press into the dimness of the landing's return. I expect to be apprehended by servants of the inn, but nothing will deter me from gobbling the greasy ham. The meat tastes heavenly. Were my mouth not stuffed I would laugh out loud in triumph, for I find there is a thrill in carrying off this theft without a consequence.

The landing overlooks the vestibule and I have a useful view of its activities. It is filling now with passengers preparing for departure, but no one runs from the dining room on behalf of the ham.

So intent am I on guzzling, it takes perhaps a minute or two for me to realise that I am not alone in my hideaway. A lad of about thirteen or fourteen has crept to my side. He grins at me and whispers from behind his hand in the style of a conspirator, 'How are you, *madame*? All right?' He has a pasty complexion with a downy smudge on his upper lip and bright eyes. His scrunched-up face looks familiar to me, but I cannot place it. He widens his eyes in wordless entreaty, and I offer him the remaining slice of ham.

He crams it into his mouth and the two of us stand in silence, chewing.

He wipes his fingers on a gaping coat that is dark blue with a hint of the military about it and doffs his shaggy high hat, at which his wild hair springs free. He says, 'Your humble servant, *madame*,' and describes with the hat an intricate arabesque. As he bows, an odd pendant falls free of his neck and dangles on a leather thong. It looks like a rusty nail.

A self-important clamour out in the yard announces the arrival of the coach.

The lad asks, 'Do you take the Bristol stage, *madame*?' I explain that I would if I could, but the day coach is full. He sighs, 'Ah yes, that too is my difficulty,' and smoothes the nap of his hat with gnarled, thin fingers that look like they have already worked through three lifetimes. His voice is familiar to me, too. Is not this the youth who sat next to me for one or two stages before the highwaymen came and, in fact, caused my gin to spill when he came aboard the *Demon* near Slough?

A servant has thrown open the George's main entry door to accommodate the flow of passengers, those departing and those coming in with faces creased and costumes crumpled from the journey. A bell begins to toll dolorously to mark the hour. The Bristol coach will soon depart. The boy is speaking to me, but I cannot make out his words.

Because there is a roaring in my ears. It is caused by the blood rushing through all my channels to the aid of my heart, which has nearly stopped dead. Is this what it feels like to be hit by a thunderbolt? The pain of a jumping fire followed by stone-cold shock?

Advancing into the vestibule below is terror made flesh. I am too horror-stricken even to whisper his name. The sight of him produces in me an overwhelming desire to evacuate my bowels like a sheep being driven into the killing shed.

I was right to be so frightened at every turn in the road. He was always coming after me. He will enjoy bringing me before the watch, he will have made it his personal business to do so. But most of all he will lap up the spectacle of my hanging, I know that without a doubt.

In he saunters, pulling off his hat, and looks about, oozing confidence, and turns to usher someone forward . . .

My God, has the shock of seeing him robbed me of my senses? I could swear that Eliza Waterland has followed him into the vestibule. There she stands in her three-cornered hat and her blue riding habit. Eliza!

I am too far distant to make out the expression upon her face, but she seems the picture of misery. Her arms are wrapped around herself as if she is very cold or is trying to hold herself together. What is she doing here? It perplexes me utterly to know why she should embark on this chase. Is it to satisfy her curiosity regarding my disappearance? How I wish I could run to her now and reassure her and bring her away from the monster at her side. It anguishes me to see her with him. But I cannot reach her without signing my own death warrant.

A voice penetrates my daze: '*Madame!* Do you hear me? I know a way to ride that Bristol coach, full or no. I could be putting you on to it for only a little shilling.'

I struggle to tear my gaze from the friend of my childhood.

'Sixpence then,' the lad says. 'I would have a poor time of it if all the world were as hard as you, my lady.'

'Very well,' I manage to reply in shaking tones, 'but I must sidle out of here unobserved.'

'Nothing easier, for you have a casement at your disposal.' The lad pivots on his heel and darts towards the landing window. 'The window opens, *madame*, do you observe, and we are small enough to slip through.'

I clamber after him over the sill and down to the outdoor promenade of the first-floor gallery. While the driver and the guard are bustling up on to the box of the coach in their crimson coats, my rescuer and I descend fleetly the side stairs into the yard. Just as the coach makes its wallowing start, the lad jumps up quickly on a hind wheel, which raises him so that he may grasp with one hand the boot. He beckons me with the other. Following his example, I step up lightly without pause on an ascending spoke of the wheel and gain a purchase with my foot on the iron rim.

'*Allez, madame, allez!*' The lad catches my arm and then we are the both of us dangling, but only for an instant. We flop over the side of the boot onto its cargo.

As we balance on hands and knees upon swaying boxes and barrels, I glimpse a familiar silhouette in the doorway of the George. Has my escape been noticed? I scramble to hide among the roof passengers, but they resist us.

'Spongers!' one of them shouts.

'Cheating dog!' another growls. 'We will throw you off!'

But the lad forces a place for us at the rail even as a woman screeches in the direction of the driver, 'Hie, we've intruders among us!' To which the lad returns, 'Have a heart, *madame*, we will pay directly.'

In any event, the driver is not inclined to pull up now, since we have passed on to the High Street and the coach is gathering speed. Reading's half-timbered dwellings and crooked chimney pots rattle by at a clip.

'Keep your wits about you,' the lad advises, 'in case these rogues try to tip us over.'

But it is a dank morning with scraps of mist still clinging

to the trees, and the outsiders sink down once more into their mufflers and coats. They lack the energy to sustain their cavils.

'I am very much obliged to you, young man,' I whisper. 'What is your name?'

'Madden it is. Terry Madden.' He offers a bow. 'And to whom do I have the pleasure of speaking, *madame*?'

I bring out my thin lie. 'Mrs . . . Mrs Ann Jones.'

Madden eyes me sidelong and gives me a wink of amiable complicity. Is my lack of truthfulness so transparent? I turn to look out on the countryside. The mist is lifting, revealing wave-like hills and fields of undulating corn. My mind is full of Eliza. The amazement at seeing her. And the panic of seeing *him*. Instinctively my hand reaches into my petticoat and pats my pocket for reassurance. My escape money. I gaze down upon the blur of the coach wheels. They throw up pale chalk dust that settles on the wildflowers growing on the verge of the road. I urge the wheels to go faster.

I think I may have misinterpreted the tone of Eliza's appearance at the George. I thought that she seemed frightened and confused, but isn't that what my imagination wished to see? She might have been, rather, determined to witness my capture. There is a reason for that but I cannot get at it exactly. It is like looking for something that has rolled underneath a bureau; I know the reason is there but I cannot reach it.

We have come upon a grasping clay road now, which sucks the life from the horses and defeats our pace. The slog has stretched out this stage and everyone is complaining that we will arrive late in Bristol, if we will get there at all. I am in an agony of impatience at the slowness of our progress. To distract myself I ask Madden how he came by his words of French. He tells me that he was put as a child under the command of a master who sailed him to France.

'Where are you from?'

'A little village in Ireland, *madame*, which is not an easy sort of place.'

'Where is your master now?'

'Our crew put up at Bristol on this run, but we were laid up on the mud and the stranding hurt our boat. It's a fine cutter that I belong to. The *Seal* she's called. While we were in repair, it came to me that I might nip up to see London and be back quick as you like, since never did I lay eyes on the golden streets of that town.'

'You must have been disappointed then.'

Madden heaves an eloquent sigh.

'Will not your master punish you for your absence?'

'It is likely, *hélas*. That he will not sail without me is my great hope.' Madden touches the nail hanging around his neck.

'What is that charm you wear?'

'It is a fierce sort of interrogator you are, my lady, if I may say so.'

'My questions signify nothing. I am only trying to keep myself awake.'

Madden tucks the talisman inside the placket of his shirt and says, 'It is only a nail against the other crowd. It's well known they will have nothing to do with iron.'

'What crowd is that?'

Madden's brow buckles in a frown. 'I will not name them, *madame*. They do not like to hear their names bandied about.'

He aims his gaze at the surging downs. A river gleams in

the distance beneath the dull shine of a white windmill, whose sails are slowly turning. We are under a determined whip on a noisy road. We shift our backsides, irritated by the effrontery of the stones that fly up from under the wheels as though determined to strike us.

The shock of seeing Eliza – and him – has jolted my memory and loosened one of its shutters. The whole of the picture eludes my remembering, but now I have got a glimpse, through a dark glaze, of the death scene.

Flaxen hair matted with blood. Violet coat soaked in blood. I feel sick. My hands fly to my mouth to stifle a cry. It hits me with sudden and terrific force: the identity of the victim in that chamber.

Oh, dear God. The shock of it.

My stomach turns over. It cannot be true. But it is.

Johnny Waterland is dead.

Eliza's brother. There could be no greater catastrophe in her eyes. She adored him extremely and constantly. Now I understand why she appeared at Reading. She believes I killed him and she is on my trail. She has come to hunt me down.

Madden is shaking my arm. 'Do you hear? We must stay on the roof during the change, Mrs Jones, otherwise we shall lose our places.' Seeing my stricken expression, he adds, 'Do not disquiet yourself, *madame*, we will win the tussle up here. I am used to it. In my experience, seldom is there a day that there is not a fight in it.'

Johnny Waterland. Dead.

I can't –

I did not –

The Port of Bristol

April, 1766

Something jogs me awake, an elbow grazing against my cheek. There is a tang of salt and fish in the air and I feel a stab of homesickness. I was dead to the world, dreaming of a sun-filtered chamber where I was far from trepidation. I have had this dream before. The distant beat of waves, sequins of light scattered on the sea . . . Nothing occurs or perhaps something has already taken place.

Oh, God. I am awake. And something *has* taken place. Johnny Waterland is murdered and I had something to do with it.

What *happened*?

I feel disgraceful. A coward as well as a fugitive. Don't I owe it to the Waterlands to confess that I was there . . . Only I cannot tell them how he came to his death because I do not know. At the same time, is there not something awfully self-serving about my forgetting? The convenience of it.

Where am I?

I peer groggily over the railing and find that the coach is shoving its way through heavy traffic. I turn to Madden to ask if we are at Bristol, but to my surprise there is a young woman sitting in his place. She has a pockmarked face and a baby tied to her chest. The coach leans into a narrow cobbled street and then pitches itself at an inn, whose sign shows a square-rigged ship rocking on the waves. I suppose Madden might have secured himself an inside seat while I was dozing. He is enterprising enough to manage such a thing.

While my neighbour struggles with her howling infant and a bundle of belongings, I disembark with caution from the coach, for I have not paid for a single stage since Reading. I slip through the crowds milling in the yard to an out-of-the-way spot under the gallery and draw my scarf low over my head. The coach empties, the boot is unloaded and the horse-keeper takes the team off the pole and walks the tottery off-wheeler away. There is still no sign of Madden, and now his disappearance begins to confound me.

I will not go back on my plan to flee England. Knowing that the dead man is Johnny Waterland does not alter the danger to me if I stay. I am pragmatic about that.

I wish Madden would turn up. This waiting makes me anxious. He has offered to show me the way to a ship bound for France, or even America. He said that two guineas would easily pay for my passage —

My heart falls from a great height.

I clap my hands to the sides of my thighs, where I expect to confirm the presence of my pockets, although I think I already know in that split second that the one holding the moneybag is gone. Plunging my hand into the slit in my petticoat, I bring out only the pathetic strings, neatly cut by Madden, I have no doubt, while I slept. My eyes glaze with useless tears.

Now I have not a farthing to my name and only the clothes I stand up in, and those are fast turning to rags.

I hang my head in despair. A buckle, I notice, has vanished from one of my shoes and the discovery of this paltry deprivation on top of the critical loss of my funds enlarges my misery to the point where it overflows. Oblivious to the stares of passers-by, who must find my soiled, flittered and rat-tailed appearance a telling advertisement for the decline of my circumstances, I sob like a child.

Do you know what is so very wearying about adversity? Well, I am sure you must know, and far better than I, but recent bitter experience has shown me that repeated misfortune not only undermines material resources, but acts even more insidiously as a drain to the soul. As I stand in the yard of the Ship Inn with my empty hands, I wonder: when all of the hopefulness has finally leaked from me, what will happen then? It is likely I will find myself alarmingly altered, transformed into a person who has become capable of remorseless actions. I see that possibility quite clearly. Would not one do anything — deceive, steal, even murder — to avoid slipping from the precarious perch of existence?

I cannot bear this loss! But fear, that great predator, snarls at me from a corner of my mind and I am obliged to set off on the run again, stumbling away under the arch of the inn's entrance.

I am shaking with anger, too. I am angry in the extreme. I could kill Madden, I could, I could . . . You could what, Em? Stab him through his treacherous heart? Then a new fear bubbles up. Will Madden tell tales of me to others and thus lead them to me?

There is a wharf here, in front of the inn, with many vessels at anchor. Their masts and rigging stick up like giant reeds from the slop of the water. The view to the east shows substantial houses built on an eminence, their windows winking in the flare of the setting sun. A small crowd stands about in the foreground with quantities of luggage. I take in this scene with a quick, harried glance, looking always all around me for the slightest sign of followers. Mingling among the passengers for cover, I gather that a sailing has been delayed. A packet-ship has been grounded downstream.

A minuscule woman lost in the folds of an enormous capuchin moans, 'We will not get away until tomorrow now,' and a gentleman shaped like a bag pudding remarks in my general direction, 'Take my advice. Never pay for your passage until the moment you set sail, because all sorts of obstacles may prevent your embarkation.'

'Do you know,' I ask without hope, 'of a cutter hereabouts by the name of the *Seal*?'

If I could discover Madden's ship among the multitude of vessels in Bristol, I should challenge him for the return of my guineas or at least throw myself on the mercy of his master, who might – now I am plainly tumbling into fantasy – recompense me for the theft and offer me a passage to France.

The becloaked woman examines my appearance and finds it wanting. Her companion shrugs. 'The *Seal*? I've no knowledge of it at all.'

The wind blows cold off the leaden water and the disgruntled would-be passengers shiver and pull their coverings closer. Disappointed, they begin to call for porters. I watch bleakly as they gradually disperse. I see no way out of my predicament. At my back looms a row of hard-faced warehouses, their steps occupied by squatting, ragged figures. Before me there lies a channel of water, like a line ruled under my story bringing it to a close. I comprehend now how the union of many small currents of feeling and thought under duress may cause a powerful perception – that there is no way out but death – to burst forth and overwhelm a person. I am thinking of Miss Broadbent, of course.

At last I shift myself, spurred by the possibility that my pursuers will arrive at Bristol on the next coach. As I trudge towards the landward end of the wharf, I sense a displacement of air nearby, accompanied by an awful thudding sound, and I glimpse a tall black entity bearing down on me. At a bellowed command of 'Mind yourself, hussy!' I cower, looking up fearfully from under my chaotic hair, and find that I am almost run down by a sedan chair. It rushes by, all thumping footfalls and squeaking leather walls, pumped by the engine of the chairmen's rhythmic breathing, which comes in snorts like that of a horse. The chair shuffles to a halt in the shadow of one of the massive cargo winches that line the wharf and discharges a passenger. With one hand clamped on his hat and the other lugging a portmanteau, he hurries away. I steal closer to the chair. An animal odour emanates from it, arising, I suppose, from the glue that holds the conveyance together. The smell takes me back to the summer house at Sedge Court, where I undertook shellwork for Mrs Waterland. The glue I used there had been rendered from quills of rabbit skin and gave off the aroma of winter stew. That was the morning of the day that he stalked me and brought me down.

I hear myself call out, 'Hie, sir!'

The chairman, a burly individual, with the typical slabby shoulders of his ilk and a balding dark yellow velvet coat, turns a broad, thick-featured face in my direction and regards me with

46

indifference. My grubby appearance does not suggest a potential customer.

'Sir . . .' I edge still closer, 'I should be obliged if you would take me to the berth of a cutter called the *Seal*.'

The chairman turns his head from side to side like someone rueing the foolishness of a child, and says, 'Only show me your shilling, madam, and the chair shall be yours.'

I career into an account of Terry Madden's thieving. If I could only arrive at the cutter and reclaim my funds, I should be able to pay for the chair at that point. I add lamely, 'I believe the culprit is Irish.'

The chairman hoots, 'An Irishman is he? Then ye've only a few thousand to choose from in Bristol town.' He shouts over his shoulder at his partner, 'Did you hear that, Kev? Lass here is hunting for an Irish lad who cut her purse. And she expects to find him, too.'

Now it's the hind chairman's turn to chortle. 'What're the odds he's already drunk up her coin in a tavern?'

Their mirth nettles me and I shout, 'Give me the name of a likely tavern and I will hound him down myself and be damned!'

My outburst further piques their amusement. 'You will be wanting the Breeze and Feather, I warrant.' The front-man grins. 'That's a place kept by Irish people and attracts a lad with more money than sense.'

The hind chairman calls, 'We are going that way and you may trot behind.' The chair is wheeled about and the men set off without further ado. I assume that they are trifling with me, but no alternative presents itself, and so I scurry to catch up to them.

We rush through a tangle of streets and arrive in short order at the head of an oppressive thoroughfare, where houses with protruding gables lean over a row of shops and alehouses. The cluster of black chairs at the corner of the street reminds me of the crows that I saw on our way to Weever Hall last summer. It was a golden afternoon and we stopped to dine alfresco. I see Eliza dozing under a walnut tree with one arm draped across her face, unconcerned that her marriage prospects were dimming by the day.

Oh, Eliza, do not think ill of me. I should like to believe that sympathy and loyalty do obtain as a result of a long connection, but I have been proved grievously mistaken about people's characters. I wanted things – people – to be true that weren't true. The thought of Mrs Waterland pricks my heart.

Have you ever had the experience of being blasted by blandishments? It is elating to be the object of flatteries, but they level your defences and leave you exposed to devastation when betrayal strikes. I want to say more, I own a powerful desire to purge myself of this story, but I am afraid that dwelling on the past is likely to keep offences alive.

Thank heavens, we have come to a stop. I must recover my breath, but the chairmen, having set down their conveyance among the others at the rank, are flexing their arms with little sign of exertion.

One of them jerks his thumb at the street. 'There's your mark, down there on the right.'

I set off diffidently, pressing against the walls of the buildings to avoid a couple of drunks. But the berserkers swerve into my path, making a what-have-we-here clutch at me. A roar sounds from the rank of chairs: 'Another step nearer her, lads, and you'll be in danger of a slap!' The sots leave me alone then, and I cast a backward look at the chairmen with a pang of regret. I wish I were not passing out of the orbit of their protection – but onward I must go.

The Breeze and Feather is a low, smoky tavern with patrons to match and a note of threat humming in the background. A ship's wheel fastened to the chimney piece and rigging that droops from the dark beams bespeak a nautical theme, which is not entirely jaunty. There is a hint of wrecks and drowned sailors in the rusted anchor, the crumbling cork life-preservers and the solitary oar fixed to a wall. At the pewter counter a sandy-complexioned publican in soiled shirtsleeves is filling mugs with a dipper from an anker whose fumes cause my eyes to water. Or perhaps the miasma produced by the patrons' pipes is responsible. I dash the tears away with the heel of my hand. The atmosphere, however, remains misty and unreal.

The publican flicks a dead-eyed glance at me and continues his laborious transfer of liquor from one container to another. There is a blurry chequerboard pattern inked on one of his forearms and a constellation of stars on the other. He offers no response to my salutation, but I launch into a tale, regardless, claiming to be a relation of a ship's boy called Terry Madden, whom I describe in great detail. The publican hands mugs to a barmaid who bears them away. Without any acknowledgement of my presence, he turns to a customer and I am jostled out of place.

I battle through the crush to a far reach of the room, where I must puzzle out my next move. No doubt I look ripe for some offensive by one of the voluptuaries of this tavern. Boozy laughter erupts from the drinkers huddled over their cups and a wench insists on singing to her swain while making the most of her bosom.

The barmaid approaches and plonks a platter of crimson salt beef in front of a trio of balladeers. Turning away, she says to me out of the side of her mouth, 'People will not talk to you here. They do not know you.'

'I am looking for a ship's boy called Terry Madden,' I blurt. 'He is about thirteen or fourteen years of age.'

'You his mother?'

'No. His sister.'

She pulls in her chin with a curled lip to indicate that she does not believe me.

'He is on a cutter called the *Seal*, but I do not know where it is berthed.'

'The *Seal*?' The barmaid's eyes widen.

'Do you know it?'

Her expression becomes guarded. I am about to relate a long and winding lie-story about why I must find my brother, but I am exhausted by the thought of it. Instead I say, 'The boy of that ship robbed me and I wish to speak to him about the matter.'

The barmaid lets loose a shout of laughter and claps me on the shoulder. 'Hah! I am always happy to inconvenience a plaguey rogue, although I have no argument with the master of the *Seal*. He is a man of repute, you know, among certain circles.' She flashes an impish eye and seems to expect me to understand her meaning. 'The berth is not close by and it is difficult to tell the way, but if you give me sixpence I will call a lad to lead you.'

'There I am stuck, since I am bereft of funds.'

'I will give you sixpence for that pretty necklace.'

My hand flies to the little string of pearls at my throat. I had forgotten that I was wearing Eliza's necklace. I am surprised Madden did not pilfer it, but as it did not come easy I dare say that is why he left it behind.

'These pearls cost fifty pounds!' I cry. In fact I do not know what Mrs Waterland paid for them, but they are certainly worth a great deal more than sixpence – I would be a fool to give up too cheaply this unexpected resource.

The barmaid shrugs. 'Fifty pounds? I think not. They are only seed pearls.'

Her eye catches the upraised hand of a patron and suddenly she is wading through the crowd to take his order, leaving me marooned. Might I find a pawnbroker who will give me a better price for the necklace and more than cover the loss of the moneybag? But that is an outcome by no means certain and, moreover, I quail at chancing my arm in the alarming streets of this town. I decide to try the barmaid again. I offer the pearls to her for the sum of five pounds. A wretched break in my voice betrays my desperation.

She enjoys a rueful chuckle at my expense. 'Sixpence,' she says, 'and there's an end to it.'

'All right then, I will let you have them for half a crown.'

The barmaid winks. 'They are worth what they are worth in the circumstances, lovey. I will give you sixpence and you may bestow it upon Billy.'

She holds the upper hand and I have no other card to play. I sigh my agreement, and with a furtive look at the publican, who is probably her father – the freckles and the powerful forearms betray a family resemblance – the barmaid shows me into a narrow passage punctuated by several doorways – the tavern is a hive of rooms. She brings from her pocket a coin and displays it in the palm of her hand, although in the gloom I cannot make out its authenticity. Since I have no choice, I give over the pearls, expecting to emerge from this exchange the dupe, but she whistles up a lad of perhaps ten years with a frizz of yellow hair and a wiry frame and briefs him from behind her stubby hand.

I hasten to keep up with the boy and his bobbing torch as we lope through the docklands. In these dark, greasy lanes I fall prey to the terrors of a dozen different possibilities of kidnapping, rape and murder. Bristol is famously thick with slavers and I fear they trade in women as well as Negroes. Surely it was a snare at the Breeze and Feather that I walked into, laid by the chairmen who directed me there and the barmaid . . . Won't this boy get a great deal more than sixpence if he brings me to a lair? How long can my poor heart pound at this rate before it bursts with fright? I would turn and run, but we are crossing a long bridge and at my back there comes a handcart, which traps me into moving forward.

We are free of the bridge now, and the cart has gone. The boy has come to a halt and I look around suspiciously, but no one else appears. It seems this is our destination.

It is a quay on a narrow, sequestered stretch of waterway where few vessels are moored. I can make out in the distance two or three men in smocks who are coiling ropes. One of them looks our way, but they go on with their work. The boy wordlessly palms the sixpence and I watch him leave with a familiar feeling of abandonment and anxiety.

There are two small cutters moored upstream on the other side of the quay. I will have to find another bridge in order to reach them.

As I walk along the quay's edge I notice that the slop of the water begins to sound more insistent. A boat is approaching.

Voices carry through the air together with the creaking of ropes and the *crump* of canvas. Sails show rust-red in the twilight as a vessel glides towards me. The fore-and-aft rig and single mast, and the rakish lines, define her as a cutter. We see many of these economical vessels at Parkgate.

The long bowsprit draws level, giving me a close view of a side-whiskered seaman on the foredeck unlashing the jib. The depth of tide has brought the cutter nearly flush with the quay. The gunwales are hardly six feet from where I stand. As the cutter slinks by, a lean fifty or sixty feet in length, I note the swivel guns mounted on the deck railings. The boat is so near I can make out the detail of the helmsman's appearance, his dark hair curled all around, the red-and-white checked shirt under his short jacket, his tarpaulin trousers and low shoes. A rowboat dangles from curved davits beneath the vessel's high transom stern – and underneath the rowboat the name of the cutter is picked out in white on the black hull.

It is the *Seal*.

'Wait!'

At my cry the helmsman looks up. He sees nothing but a girl diminishing on the quay. He turns away and attends once more to his course.

I begin to run then, gathering momentum. Without pausing to argue with myself about it, I spring from the very edge of the coping.

I rise into space, and time slows, allowing me to come at my leisure to the realisation that my jumping stratagem will not succeed a second time — and why should it? To do so would offend the laws of chance. As I float aloft, feet pedalling the air, watching my target of the cutter's deck slipping away beneath, I recall in fitful flashes a bargeman at Parkgate . . .

He misses his footing and pitches seaward.

The master's cargo sinks in the beer-house hole.

A skiff sails away on the horizon.

I am grieved to find this body of mine plunging towards the sombre surface of the water, but I hold no reproach against myself for trying so very desperately to prevail.

The House of Kitty Conneely, Connemara

April, 1766

I have lost sight of the child, Nora, but do not fret. Since I turned the stones I sense their mighty influence within me and I do not doubt I have the strength in it, the ferocity of will, in fact, to bring her back now before my days on earth pass for ever. My face I have turned to the past, friend. That is where our girl was left – I will even go so far as to say that the past is where she has been imprisoned. But the turn of the stones has opened that portal. All kinds of scenes are floating towards me now.

I can see Josey O'Halloran as large as life saluting into the house of the Mulkerrins. And the coat being taken off and himself being offered the chair. And your brother Colman watching with arms folded high on the chest in that spurning way of his, and a curdled face on him. They brought in the writing apparatus then, didn't they? And Josey drew in a mighty shuddering breath as though the Holy Ghost itself had inspired him and next thing he had a sentence sprinting across the paper like a hound after a hare. There was not a hint of hesitation in it. A tremendous hush fell on the crowd while Josey worked the pen. And yourself could not take your eyes off him. Very moonstruck by him you were then and always.

And do you recall Martin Lee, God rest his soul? You can't imagine the number of times I have gone over that night when he came to your house. Don't I wish we had listened to him. But he was as old as a field and well known for rambling talk that did not add up to much. And strong was his inclination for drink. Sure, as soon as he stopped in that night he asked if there was a drop in the place at all. You were bound to bring out the jar and invite him to pull into the fire, but you were not glad about it. You thought Martin took advantage of Josey's generosity. It means the food and drink out of your own mouth, you would say to Josey. But Josey used to say he wouldn't recognise himself if he refused a guest.

I can see Josey pressing Martin to take a drop and Martin saying, I will do the same so, Josey, right. He said that his own jar had been taken and he knew who was to blame for that. It was the good people up to their mischief. It's well known, he said, that they like a drop. They come down from Sligo, so they do, and steal my drink. People say you see them strolling around as if they owned the place.

And then he warned us not to stay at home on the following day. Everyone was going to the saint's island to pray at the well, which had begun to flow for the first time since ages past.

Nor will I forget this: as you were seeing me out that night, we noticed a queer little breeze swirl under the covering of the doorway and nudge it a little. A thickening of the air like that was supposed to be a sign. It meant that the other crowd was near at hand. We ought to have stayed out of their way, Nora. We ought to have gone to the saint's island.

PART TWO

Sedge Court, Cheshire

February, 1758

I think of Mrs Waterland as a fateful figure. In fact the idea of fate weighs on me. You must think me quite a blasphemer, but when I compare the powers of our Christian God to those of the Fates, I find him less compelling. Is he capable of putting events into play or of altering their course? It seems to me that he only watches, and judges, and punishes. It is fate that makes things happen. Certainly it seems to have played a primary role in the story of the Waterlands – the family that reared me. I am not the only one to believe that.

Our scullery maid Abby Jenkins says that the Waterlands are so thwarted you would nearly think that a binding had been laid on them, although that is the kind of thing she is prone to say, since she is from Wales and they are known to be fanciful, the Welsh. You should have seen Abby when she first arrived at Sedge Court off the ferry from Flint. Her raven hair was wild and loose in the Welsh style and she wore a scarlet cloak and a round black hat like a man's. Ten days passed before our housekeeper, Mrs Edmunds, could get her to lay that hat aside.

I wish I knew whether there was a difference between fate and a random concatenation of circumstances. And who is it that drives us forward? I should like to believe that we ourselves, not God, nor the Fates, have the capacity to influence the actions of our lives, but I do not know how to explain persistent bad luck. For instance, many contrary events have occurred at Sedge Court and you could even say they had produced a pattern of misfortune – but is it possible to attribute them, as Abby insists, to an impost made by an unknown force upon the family?

There was a heavy atmosphere in the house during the winter that Abby came into service, which may have set the tone of her thinking. It was an atmosphere that pressed on the nerves of everyone except Mrs Waterland, whose sangfroid was unalterable in those days. Sedge Court has its share of cooped-up, squally temperaments. The master is a snappish man, who is never easy in the house, and Downes, it goes without saying, is always as cross as a sack of cats. But everyone was jumpy that winter, even Mrs Edmunds. It was an action of hers that causes a particular day from that time, late in February, I recollect, to linger in my memory.

As I came into the servants' hall in the morning, bent on an errand for the mistress, Mrs Edmunds happened to be lugging a crock of milk from the still-room. At the same moment I glimpsed the kitchen cat, which was black and panicky, make a late decision to cut across her path. Our housekeeper is usually as unflappable as a fire shovel, but when the cat shot in error under her petticoat, she gave a shriek and let loose the crock of milk. The crock seemed to hang in space for a very long time before plummeting to its doom on the flagstones. The kitchen rang with a stunned silence.

Mrs Edmunds cried, 'In God's name how did that happen?'

as if it had taken a supernatural force to wrench the crock from her grip.

We stared in disbelief at the shards and spillage on the floor. In the background a joint at roast on the spit faintly seethed. Then a gob of fat fell into the dripping pan. I can still hear its hiss of disapproval. Mr Otty, who is otherwise the pattern of affability, cuffed Rorke's ear and bellowed, 'What in blazes are you gaping at?' and Hester Hart burst untypically into tears. The cat, too, was confounded and dared not take advantage of the slowly dilating puddle of milk. Evidently overcome by the tension in the kitchen, she slunk into the scullery.

I think we were all of one mind about the incident: it was an affront to the accustomed order and somehow even ominous. Now that I am at a distance from the event, it is clear to me that my life was never the same afterwards. I did not absolutely understand at the time – I was not yet fourteen years old – that my position at Sedge Court was not entirely secure, but I believe I sensed even then that the long fuse of childhood was burning down to its annihilation.

I came out on to the driveway on that February morning in a state of sudden anxiousness, wondering why everyone was so on edge, and I recall looking back at the house a little fearfully, like someone fleeing a building rigged with gunpowder. Needless to say, Sedge Court simply sat there indifferent to my imaginings, calmly regarding its reflection in the lake. The house is built from the soft red sandstone that abounds in that part of the country, and if not as tremendous as Lady Broome's mansion, Weever Hall, it is certainly substantial enough with its three storeys, a courtyard and many offices out the back. I will say, though, that the house always struck me from the outside as looking surprisingly small or, rather, smaller than my experience of it. The interior, on the other hand, seemed to go on for ever in order to accommodate within, I supposed, the ballooning cargo of our lives and their accompanying emotions. I once relayed that observation to our governess, my dear Miss Broadbent, and she remarked in her quietly astute way that I had too much the sensation of things that are not there. There is a lake on the right-hand side of the drive as you look towards the gates. Well, Mrs Waterland called it a lake, but actually it is an old marl pit, one of the many meres and sloughs of our perforated countryside. We are very watery in our offshoot of Cheshire, you know. Waves lap at us continuously from the Dee in the west to the mighty Mersey at our backs in the east. From the north, the Irish Sea delivers any amount of storms and wrecks.

It was a chilly day and as I walked along I had the sense of being squeezed between petered-out winter and locked-up spring. Save for their trunks, which were smothered by dark creepers, the oaks and alders were bare – you could see the blotches of birds' nests high in their branches. Last year's grasses and brambles lay withered at the feet of leggy hedgerows and the daffodils seemed to be stuck, their points hardly showing above the ground. The only yellow in the world belonged to the French shoes that I was wearing. They had formerly belonged to Eliza. Their supple leather the colour of butter, their mannerly heels and winking buckles made me feel puffed up and important.

I walked westwards until I came to the intersection of Wood Lanc, where the rolling fields decline towards the shore a quarter of a mile away. From that vantage point I could see the vague outlines of several tall-masted ships congregating at anchor downstream on the lacklustre waters of the Dee. Miss Broadbent once told me that our ancestors worshipped the rivers of this land – but if the Dee is a god, then it must have been offended in some way, because it shrinks from us and prevents us from flourishing.

The hush of the morning was disturbed by a gang of big black-backed gulls. They came swaggering up from the estuary, elbowing finches and warblers out of the way, and wheeled low over my head, screeching their usual prophecy of bad weather. The sky, however, looked quite harmless except for a dirty cloud loafing above the Welsh hills on the far side of the river. Then I remarked the source of the gulls' hubbub. There were several buzzards approaching from the north. They sidled up to the field on the corner of the lane, where drovers sometimes park their animals before taking them to the market at Great Neston, and hovered in a sinister manner. I parted the branches of the hedge to see what had attracted them and discovered a sheep felled by the burden of itself. Its wool had become waterlogged for lack of grease and the poor thing had keeled over in the mud.

The remainder of the daggle-tailed flock lurked uselessly in a corner of the field, their heads turned away as if embarrassed by their fellow's plight, chagrin their only weapon against the buzzards. I guessed that the drover was probably taking his ease in the beer-house at Parkgate. The sheep exuded helplessness. I was sorely vexed at it for slumping there under its fatally heavy fleece, which meant I must ruin my shoes in order to set it to rights, if that were even possible. At that moment a sparrowhawk fluttered on to a nearby sycamore branch and perched quietly, waiting, and I thought, well, I must try.

I removed my shoes and stockings, hitched up my skirts and squelched across sloppy grass pockmarked with the imprints of hoofs. As I approached the inert animal, a foul miasma climbed out of the wool and rose to welcome me odiously to its host's death – for I saw as I came closer that I was too late to be of any assistance. Froth was bubbling at the corner of the black mouth and the bleary eye oozed dark liquid. Before my gaze the creature's life leaked away and the flank fell still beneath the dun-coloured coat. The eye filmed, the lower lip subsided into an awful grimace that exposed brown teeth. I shouted at the buzzards, waggling my arms at them like a bugbear, but they continued lazily to circle the field, laughing under their dark-fringed wings, I imagined, at my futility.

I hastened downhill towards Parkgate and swung past the master's storehouse and granary. The pens behind the beer-house were empty. They usually heave with cattle swum ashore from the Irish boats, but there had been no landings for nearly a fortnight. The conditions were still light, I recall. The beer-house's sign barely creaked and a backlog of passengers was hanging around outside the booking office. Parkgate is the terminal for traffic to Dublin and people are always twiddling their thumbs there, awaiting the caprice of the winds. The beer-house stands hard against the shore on a projection. The sight of it at full tide looking like a ship on the waves always makes my heart swell. I get the impression that it is trying to launch itself seaward, in spite of its landlubberly nature, as if yearning to be other than what it is.

I followed the road past the pawnshop and its embarrassment of riches – the casualties of slack air are always having to give over their valuables for the price of another night at the inn – past the fishermen's carts piled with sacks of shellfish. Parkgate's shops and merchants' houses form a barricade between the sea and the hinterland. The buildings are tall and high-shouldered as though tensed for an onslaught that must arrive sooner or later. Which, of course, it does. In bad weather waves charge up on a high tide, hurl themselves across the road and pound at doors and windows.

The thoroughfare hugs the shore as far south as Moorside Lane and the herring house. There tend to be excited gannets and terns down at that extreme, flapping around after scraps, and straggly girls hoping for work gutting and salting the fish. At the customs house, where they register imports, the road heads inland, but I do not like that turn-off. A gibbet stands there. Last summer Eliza asked Mr Otty to take her to watch the remains of a wretch being cut down, hanged for robbing the customs house. He was a local lad, too. But Mrs Waterland would not allow her to be seen gawping.

All at once I came to an abrupt halt. Some half-dozen yards ahead a familiar figure was emerging from a doorway. There was no mistaking the shape of the master. He is as longitudinal as a pair of tongs. He was wearing a coat the colour of snuff, his breeches tied over his knees in a countryman's style above black stockings, and that repugnant wool wig that Mrs Water-land used to beg him to leave off. He would always defend it, saying it was durable and a roof against the wet. He had come out of the shop that Theo Sutton kept beneath his house then. Folks said that Sutton sold goods under the counter that had been confiscated by the customs man, rum and suchlike, and hair powder and soap, but I can't imagine that the master ever had any interest in those things. He has never been a man for luxuries or jaunting. He is a very separate kind of person. I don't believe he likes human company at all unless you count a murderously prolific wildfowler from Burton called Georgy Bird with whom he used to go out hunting.

His boisterous gun dogs, two liver-and-white springer spaniels, were jumping around on the edge of the strand dismaying the birds. He adjusted the grip on his cane, shoved his hat under his arm in that twitchy manner he has, called the dogs and began grimly to walk in my direction. I could picture the fierce gaze under the shaggy balcony of his eyebrows, and the working of his mouth, which he tightens like a person biting a lemon or someone trying to suppress a bout of weeping.

I retreated along a weint – that is, one of the narrow lanes that run between the big houses and lead to the maze of backstreets where the sea-folk live – and found myself in a noisome clearing. The sea breeze that drives the worst of the herring-house stink from the parade does not reach the jumble of shoddy cottages in the hindquarters of the town, their half-bald, mostly rotten thatch adding its own note of decay to the general stench. Dingy barefoot children in flitters sprawled at every door and a couple of hungry-looking curs crept towards me with their ears back and haunches up. The faces of the children were wild and sharp and the older ones leaped up and grinned at me with a sly glint. I fancied that they took me for an opportunity on which they were prepared to pounce.

Someone threw a stone. It hurtled from a dark aperture in

the scaly wall of one of the hovels and banged against a herring barrel. Stifled laughter sounded from inside the hovel and then a chute of grey water, a pail emptied by an unseen hand, shot from a door and landed *splat* at my feet like a challenge. I fled the way I had come, one of the mongrels snarling at my heels, until a squawk-voiced fisher-child called it off. I bolted past the Sutton house with my head down and fetched up outside the haberdashery, from where I directed a furtive look back along the thoroughfare. To my relief the master had vanished. As I recovered my breath, I noticed that my shoes had suffered a sorry loss of allure, marred by mud and water-splash.

In her customary manner the haberdasher, Mrs Ladykirk, was roosting at her counter under a feathered cap with two winged protuberances above the ears that suggested a hen surprised on its nest. She regarded me with indifference as I stirred boxes of hairpins and false flowers, flipped through cards of trims and tickled bouquets of plumes dyed violet and madder. In the awful stillness of the shop, with its flaxy odour of the linen-press, cabinets scaled the walls nearly as far as the ceiling, their innumerable drawers and compartments containing multitudes of miniature items, pins, needles, threads, thimbles, bobbins, buttons, hooks, measures, scissors, in relentlessly ongoing allocations. The cabinets lorded it over sectioned tables, where ribbons, ruchings, fringes, flounces, nettings and knots vied for attention.

I had left the door open and I could hear the rustle of waves across the way subsiding dreamily upon the shore. Spotting at last a spool of velvet ribbon that answered to Mrs Waterland's instructions, and a frill of Belgian lace, I bought the trims in a silent transaction.

I set off along a dark border of damp sand above the receding tide, wending my way among the shrimp boats beached on the shingle and the fishermen repairing their nets and their pots. Curlews and oystercatchers feinted at the waves and the breeze buffeted my hat and bloated my mantle. Mrs Waterland makes pretty things out of pretty things and I scanned the sand for some little treasure, an intriguing shell or a hank of shapely seaweed, in an effort to please her. Although I searched the shore with extreme intent, I came all the way back to the precinct of the beer-house without finding a single item that might pique her interest.

I looked up with a sigh and, Lord love me, but there was the master again.

He stood stiff-necked with his head pulled in like a buzzard's and one hand on his hip, the other resting on the knob of a tall cane that he had planted in the streaky green sea-mud. The long-legged spaniels were romping in the shallows, but he did not pay them any attention. He was looking out to sea in the direction of a laden barge. It was attempting to meet a punt that was coming out from the slip below the beer-house to offload the cargo. I was shy of the master, not only out of the deference natural to a gentleman of his standing, but because he always struck me as a sort of harrowed figure.

In fact, I found it quite painful even to be in his presence. Have you ever had such a sensation in proximity to another person? I mean where you simply cannot abide to be near them, because they depress your spirits so.

Downes, of course, inspires such melancholy in me, and Mrs Ladykirk in the haberdashery, too, and – who else? I have a strong aversion to Sutton, although I have hardly anything to do with him. It is as though they press on my soul until it is bruised and smarting. Or perhaps it is only that I do not like these people because they do not like me and I reach for an overly abstract explanation to cover up the hurt I feel at that rejection. The master, for instance, has always held an antipathy for me despite my efforts never to cause offence.

At any event, in order to avoid him, I skirted around the back of the crowd of transit passengers who had gathered on the strand to watch the barge strive against the tide. I intended to climb up to the beer-house and set out on the path home, but the way was barred by a tall man swathed in a cloak, who was in conversation with one of the fishermen. He wore a three-cornered hat low on his head – it was a chestnut colour, I think – and boots of a style that we did not see in those parts. Were they French? I wonder. I might have asked the stranger to step aside so that I could go past, but I did not. I was very taken by his presence.

I heard him say in an unfamiliar accent, 'What an awkward business. The punt goes at that barge like a drunken partner in a longways dance.' The fisherman sucked on his pipe and said, 'Aye, we are often troubled to bring cargo ashore. We have no quay here, sir, for we are not deep enough.'

I remember the stranger's hair hung down in a long, wrapped queue, which seemed somehow soldierly. Standing at his back, I felt as protected as a defender behind a battlement and it seemed to me that he bore out my theory that people somehow project invisibly the essence of their nature. Just as the master had about him a rather sad little threadbare aura, this stranger shimmered with strength, and although I had not the slightest idea who he was, I felt drawn to him – or, should I say, charmed by him in the sense of an operation of magic. To be near him aroused such interest in me that when he moved a little further down the strand, away from the general focus of the barge, I found myself at once trailing him.

I had the impression there was something definite on his mind that he meant to accomplish and that he was acting against the grain of the scene, which was something that appealed terribly to me. He struck me as an individualist. Perhaps I found that attractive because of my disposition to aloneness. In any case, I remember blushing violently as he turned. It seemed for a second as if he might notice me. Even now in the recollection my cheek feels heated. He seemed to be someone of experience, but I suppose he was not yet thirty years of age, perhaps even younger. He was somewhat dark in the face, like a man who spends his time outdoors – and he had not shaved that day. I hardly need to mention that he gave no sign at all of remarking the short, scrawny girl lingering in his wake. He was looking towards the southern end of the strand.

I watched him intently: the way he lifted his head with dawning interest to meet the puff of a breeze as it came off the waves, as if a useful idea had struck him. He had a game-some aspect about him and at the same time he brought to mind stillness, not moribund haberdashery-stillness but a well of calm, while all else, the master, the frustrated passengers, the labouring cargo boats, was under pressure. Is that why I was drawn to him so?

A burst of applause sounded as the punt managed at last to clinch with the barge, the crew putting out grappling hooks to steady the two craft alongside one another. The master attended closely as the boatmen went at their work handing chests from the barge to the punt. I suppose I was vaguely aware of rumours that the master's business had become scattered and was not up to much, but I was too young at the time for them to signify, for I believed the Waterlands to be of infinite means. My gaze searched for the stranger again and found him in conference with the fisherman beside a skiff pulled up on the tide-line. The stranger then bent to the boat and helped the fisherman to haul a net from it.

All at once I felt a chill – something was amiss – and I cast a speculative glance around me. I expected to see trouble approaching. And there it was.

At the southern end of the strand I spied a trio on horseback and my keen eye recognised them even at that long reach. My immediate impulse was to warn the stranger of the approach of the customs man and his constables. I divined that this intelligence would concern him, but he was already absorbed in a course of action, making a beckoning gesture in the direction of the gawkers.

As the fisherman pulled up the hood of his holey jersey and stole away across the sand, I heard a shout of warning on the wind. Three men detached themselves from the crowd, which was still riveted by the fraught transfer of the cargo on the big swell, and ran to the skiff. In a trice, the stranger and his men hoisted the fisherman's boat over their heads and with strong arms bore it away to the breakers. The stranger did not look away from his task, not even to see that the customs man and his constables had put the whip to their mounts. I dare say he judged that the heavy going would not permit the horses to come on at a gallop. He did not give the shore another glance.

I retreated to the crowd and watched the skiff push off, its occupants rowing strongly away, aided by the outgoing tide. The bystanders were not interested in the skiff. All eyes were on the punt and its imminent ungrappling – 'I do wonder at the bearing of that weight upon yon punt,' I heard someone say. ''Tis looking desperate burdened.'

Even as the customs man drew level with the churned sand that indicated the skiff's launching spot, no one paid any heed. The pursuers were armed with pistols and I wondered if they would aim and fire, but the onlookers had pressed forward and a safe bead could not be drawn on the retreating men from among the crowd. As well, the heavily laden punt lolled on the swell like a floating hillock, providing cover for the escaping skiff. The customs man and the constables were further hampered by a contretemps, which occurred as a stout party on the barge made to transfer to the punt. As he raised his leg, the waves made an unfavourable shift and the bargeman landed awkwardly. In the vicinity of a spot we call the beer-house hole, which is the only deep water in those parts, his weight threw the craft off balance, allowing the sea to rush on to the punt. The boatman lost his pole and he and the bargeman both pitched overboard, followed by the master's chests. At that moment, an oversized wave happened by, turned over the punt and ran away to the shore, leaving the men and the chests to flounder. It was a stroke of great bad luck for the master.

My gaze slid towards the customs men. The soft sea-mud had forced them to dismount. While the crowd shouted encouragement to the two men in the water, who were clinging to cork floats thrown from the barge, the chests were faring less well. They seemed determined to sink themselves.

I shaded my eyes to look downstream and saw that the skiff's mast had been raised and a lug-sail was set. I remember hearing the rasp of the beer-house sign up on the promontory as the freshening breeze set it to swing. My heart lifted as if on a huge wave as the skiff disappeared behind a merchant brig anchored in the channel. When it appeared again as a receding smudge on the water I felt a sort of sorrow as if I, like that foolish, swamped punt, was in danger of overturning.

The breeze must have carried my scent to the master's spaniels, because their muzzles went up and they bounded from the water. They lost no time in flushing me out from among the onlookers. Mr Waterland, sensing something close to hand that displeased him, tightened his shoulders. He spun round and fixed on me a stare that was in equal amounts frightening and frightened – as though I had rendered him aghast – before he turned abruptly away.

That evening, after Eliza had retired to her bedchamber, I came downstairs with her hat, thinking to trim it in the servants' hall so as to keep it out of her sight until our birthday. My date of birth being unknown, Mrs Waterland has given me Eliza's to share as a convenience. The ribbon and lace were still in Mrs Waterland's parlour on the ground floor, where she had inspected them that afternoon and showed me how the ribbon must create a careless, trailing effect as though it had sprung loose during a game of high jinks and had been left unheeded.

I knocked timidly on the connecting door between the back stairs and the parlour. Finding no answer I was about to steal into the room to retrieve the trim, when I heard the mistress's voice cry, 'Do not pursue me, sir! I have stopped my ears against you.'

At once I blew out my candle and held my breath in the darkness. I could tell by the approach of her voice and her footsteps that she had marched across the parlour and was standing close on the other side of the door. I longed to rush away, but I was afraid that the squeak of the floorboards might find me out for an eavesdropper.

The master shouted in a voice that was harsh and breaking, 'You *will* attend my words, madam! Nothing has gone right since you brought that child here! Don't you see how she causes our misfortune?'

'A pox take your ravings!' the mistress retorted. 'She is nothing to do with it. How could you injure so grievously an entire shipment, and in front of the whole town, too?'

'I tell you, she stood at my back and willed it to happen. The loss was designed!'

'You mean like the fortune you promised me on our marriage. Gone, gone and never the fault of Bernard Waterland.'

'God's blood, Hetty, I have ordered you over and again to rid us of her. Now I will not—'

'You may give me orders, Mr Waterland, when your account book warrants it.' Mrs Waterland's tone was haughty. 'It is my money that keeps the wolf from our door. Your obsession with the past is an excuse for your own failure. Praise God we have a son to be man of the house.'

I stood in a wash of moonlight by the long table in the servants' dining hall with the extinguished candle in my hand, my workbox under my arm and the master's *Rid us of her!*

74

resounding in my ears. His exhortation detonated in me the cold dread that lies dormant in the depths of any found-ling: the fear of a return to the void. He brought that fear to the surface that day and ever afterwards I was to feel the precariousness of my position in the house.

Truth to tell, I was bewildered by this flaring-up of his dislike of me, since I was as a rule so much out of his way and I could not think what I had done to cause offence.

I could hear Abby in the scullery banging pots around and then she appeared with a stack of plates and began slotting them into the racks of the sideboard. She gave me a squinty look and asked why I was standing there like a stunned rabbit.

I rushed away to the butler's pantry without giving her an answer. In the pantry I found Mrs Edmunds seated at her accounts and Hester Hart bent over a piece of green baize on the table, cleaning cutlery. Mrs Edmunds looked up irritably, the lappets of her old-fashioned cap dangling like a beagle's ears, and told me to make haste with my work. I placed the hat on the table and slid into a seat next to Hester, who gave me one of her unintentionally baleful smiles. It is the lack of eyelashes that gives her such an air of hostility. The smallpox took them and left behind lumps on her cheeks like pellets embedded in the skin. Sometimes she bridles when you speak to her, even if you are only after the time of day, as if you have commented on her scars for your own amusement. But her hair is lovely. It likes to escape the confines of her cap. On such occasions Mrs Edmunds says that Hester ought to be ashamed of going about like such a trollop. But that fall of hair like honey syrup is the only portion of her beauty that the pox has left to Hester and it is determined to show itself.

I opened my workbox and brought out the yards of ribbon. As I guided a thread towards the eye of my needle, I glimpsed a shadow that made me start and my hands trembled and defeated my second attempt to thread the needle.

Hester said, 'Yer making a right mess of that an' all.'

Mrs Edmunds eyed me sidelong as if she had caught me sneaking a pie from the oven. She is as tough as an old boiling hen, and about the same size, and we are all cautious around her.

I threaded the needle at last, but then the strangest thing occurred. I had the impression that the velvet tangles had begun to rise and subside of their own volition as if they were slopping about in a laundry basin. But of course it was a trick of the senses. I was tired and the candle flames were wavering.

Mrs Edmunds said, 'God almighty, what is it now, wench?'

I shook my head. The ribbon reminded me of something, but I could not remember what it was. It was like having a word on the tip of your tongue that will not utter itself. I found it awfully upsetting not to be able to plumb the deeper meaning of these yards of ribbon.

Then something rose in me like a big bubble coming up from under water and I burst out with, 'The master does not like me! He wants to send me away.'

Hester said, 'Huh. Ain't we all waiting for the axe to fall.'

'Shut it, Hart,' Mrs Edmunds said. 'And, Smith, stop wasting the light of a good candle and get on with it.'

I pushed a wary finger towards the velvet. How could it be anything other than a snarl of ribbon? Feeling ashamed of my outburst, I bent over my stitches with a brow as stormy as Eliza's. As I sewed on, by the light of a guttering flame, I wondered what Hester meant by the falling axe.

The Schoolroom and the Parlour

March, 1758

Eliza put on an habitual scowl as she set about trimming her nib. She loathes essay writing. We are always told that a young lady should present a serene aspect, but Eliza is not a person disposed to mask her feelings. I am far more proficient in that regard. She has the strength of character to be a plain-speaker, too. After minutes of the rowdy mouth-breathing that tends to indicate powerful concentration on her part, she flung away in disgust the goose quill she had successfully mutilated. A crescendo of hoof-beats rising from the driveway three storeys below brought her to her feet.

She cried, 'That is Johnny. I know it!'

Miss Broadbent, who was at the window, answered that it was only Croft on an errand and ordered her to sit.

Eliza said, 'I wish he would hurry and arrive. We are waiting for him to bring home bags of coin to salvage us, since Papa cannot. I heard Mama say so to Lady Broome.'

My ears pricked up at that and I thought of the master's cargo that had fallen into the sea. How the economy worked at Sedge Court I did not know exactly, but I was old enough to grasp that money – the want of it and the need for it – was a powerful governor of actions and atmospheres. People hung from a gibbet for it and left their families behind for it – I am thinking of Hester and Abby, for instance, and the herring girls, all of them exported from their homeland in return for their wages – and I had heard bankruptcy spoken of in the shops at Parkgate in the same tone of voice used to report a death or a sin.

Miss Broadbent said, 'It is unkind to speak of your father so disrespectfully, Eliza, and you are indiscreet as well, which is almost worse.'

Eliza puffed out her cheeks with a noisy expulsion of air. She has a tendency to deploy a range of tics and gestures – huffing sighs, a jabbing finger, an eye rolled back in her head as if to preface a fit – as a point of emphasis or assertion. I do not mean to disparage her, although I admit I sometimes felt a twinge of pleasure when she made a gaffe in front of her mother. That had the potential to make me look more attractive to Mrs Waterland by comparison and reinforce the possibility that she might regard me as a de facto daughter, which was always my covert desire. At the same time I was troubled by such lapses in loyalty on my part towards Eliza. Regardless of the difference in our rank, she and I had a connection that I may call sisterly, and I cared for her as much as I cavilled about her.

Eliza said, 'Do you know that Johnny once saved me from drowning?'

'You might have told us such a story once or twice, my dear, or one very similar,' Miss Broadbent replied, and returned her gaze to the window. She pressed her hands into a steeple and turned the steeple upside down and inside out. The vertical crease between her eyebrows seemed to deepen slightly.

'I shall tell the story to Em, while she shaves me a nib.'

You see Eliza's mettle? She ploughs on undeterred, although it requires dragging out a dog-eared tale that Miss Broadbent and I both had heard often before in several inconsistent versions. The gist of it was Eliza's unexplained fall into a river followed by a heroic rescue by her brother. The story ends with Johnny wringing his hands with concern, while she hovers between life and death in his rooms in Cambridge, wrapped for comfort in the skin of a lion, or sometimes a tiger, that he happened to have ready for just such an occasion.

Eliza had a fund of preposterous accounts of things that never happened between her and Johnny. You were bound to feel sorry for her, because even a lugworm could see that her brother did not give a fig for her. By the time she was born he was gone away, at first to Charterhouse School and then up to Cambridge, and if he ever wrote an actual letter to her no one has laid eyes on it. She, however, sent him frequently her thoughts from the nursery, written in a blotchy hand. Whenever he sojourned at home we saw little of him except for a blur of blondness and lanky limbs striding by in a hurry, pockets jingling, while Eliza and I dropped our crooked curtsies. He was inclined to reckless driving and to going abroad in a blaring way with firearms and dogs, reports of which I had gleaned from the servants' hall. It seemed unlikely that he had ever decided, 'Let me leave off this jigger of gin and interest myself in the musings of my juvenile sister.' He lived in Rotterdam at that time and what his undertaking was there I did not know and neither did Eliza, for all her pretence that Johnny was her zealous correspondent.

It would not surprise me if you found these observations to be somewhat tart in nature. I have to confess that my compassion for Eliza, which is heartfelt, is at the same time flawed by a dark little seam of envy that runs through it, for she was born to the house and is entitled to the security that I lack. Perhaps I was so dismissive of Eliza's fantasising because I saw in it something of my own woeful neediness.

She had a habit of wrapping her arms around herself and I can see her now in that self-embrace, complaining, 'Bah! This fire gives out scarcely any heat. I wish I had Johnny's lion skin now. Em, fetch my waistcoat!' To which I am sure that Miss Broadbent would have replied something like, 'Eliza, you may fetch your own waistcoat. Either that or sharpen your nibs. Em cannot undertake two tasks at once.'

Eliza must have gone into her dressing room then with a lot of groaning and sighing in order to convey the onerous nature of life, because I remember we heard her galloping across the floor as she used to do with her hobbyhorse, when she was little. She was a great one for bashing and crashing and games of skittles, hoops and diabolo.

As soon as we were alone, Miss Broadbent offered me one of her amiable, leaning-forward-to-help smiles and said, 'You do not seem to be yourself this morning, child.' I got up and joined her at the window. She liked to position herself on the margins of a room. She made a point, you know, of taking up very little space. There was hardly anything more to her than to the bundle of slender sticks and pleated silk that was Eliza's folded-up kite. She had quite a knack for invisibility, in fact. Whenever she brought Eliza and me to perform for Mrs Waterland, she seemed able to disappear even while remaining in the room. I suppose that facility owed something to the gowns of drab linsey and light-sucking bombazine that she wore, which blended easily into the back-ground.

Her looks too were fugitive – hair not exactly brown and not exactly dark blonde, nose and mouth neither large nor small. What colour were her eyes, do I recall? Hazel, perhaps, or the grey of a drizzly sky. Yet the interior of Miss Broadbent was another prospect altogether. If you looked into her, you would find a bold panorama, and not even an English one, in my opinion. Her inner landscape had sweep – it extended halfway around the world, as far as I could see.

I told her about the altercation I had overheard the evening before, how the master wished I had never come to Sedge Court and believed that the sinking of his cargo was my fault, and that if it had not been for the intercession of the mistress, he would have had me evicted from the house.

'Dear girl,' Miss Broadbent said, 'do not agitate yourself over things the master says at the minute. He has been dogged by bad luck and it has put him on edge. It is a great respon-sibility, you know, to have the burden of a large household on one's shoulders.'

'But why is everybody else on edge as well? Do not you feel it, Miss Broadbent? The house is laced through with anxiousness.'

'That is what happens when people dwell at close quarters, Em. Mood is infectious, which is why we must guard against it.'

I am thinking of those shrewd covers on the chairs that flank the fireplace in the library at Sedge Court. Why do they stick in my mind? Certainly Mrs Waterland had worked them cleverly, raising the needlework above the linen ground to resemble cut velvet. If the master were not at home, Miss Broadbent would sometimes bring us to the library for instruction. It seemed always to be chilly there and in winter the light was so dim it was like peering through a veil. Eliza and I would shiver in our quilted waistcoats while Miss Broadbent scurried on whispery feet to the chimney piece to light candles. We were surveilled by mounted antlers, turtle-shells and sombre Dutch paintings. The shadows cast by the antlers looked like branches so that it seemed we were crouched in a forest surrounding the dark green sward of the billiard table, and the forest in its turn was enclosed by the leathery palisades of books in their presses. There, if you can imagine it, is Miss Broadbent carrying the brass candelabrum to the map table. Beneath its jittery light, Eliza and I are hunched over an old map of Wirral looking for the inscription that says 'Sedge Farm'.

The estate is still a farm. Beyond the woodland in the east there are three cottages in rather a sorry state of repair where the farm labourers live with their families. That is where the odd-job boy, Andy Croft, comes from and the laundress, Mrs Heswall. You see the labourers in the fields harvesting the corn with their sickles and the women raking it into rows ready to huddle up in sheaves. In the back-end of the year you might discover a man trimming a hedge or mending a fence and he will tip his hat and greet you with deference because you are from the house even though he knows you not, but otherwise the labourers go about unseen. The corn is cut, the cows milked and the pigs fed by the hand of spectres, it seems. Mr Otty says that when his father was a lad Sedge Court was little more than an overgrown farmhouse, but the master's father crowned it with an additional storey, where Eliza's apartment and the servants' garrets are now, and he built extensions at the back to form the commodious inner court, where a chaise may circle with ease, and garnished the facade with a perky little porte cochère. He planted the lawns and the copses, which screen the pastures for the milk-cows, and he aggrandised the name of the house.

Eliza said, 'Why must we get cross-eyes over a map of the Dee, when we could drive to Parkgate and ogle the Dee itself? Surely that would be geography?'

'No, young lady, that would be an excursion.'

Eliza squinted at Miss Broadbent. 'When you were a girl, were you a Parliamentarian or one of the King's men?'

Miss Broadbent tilted her head to one side, a finger to her chin, and said with an amused smile, 'Do you know I can hardly remember. After all, the war *was* more than a hundred years ago. Fortunately, I still have my own hair and teeth in spite of my amazing age.'

'Well, I am bad at dates,' Eliza said sweetly. 'Em remembers them for me.'

'Perhaps you won't always have Em as your proxy.'

'Of course I will. She has nowhere else to go.' Eliza's truth-telling struck me a forcible blow as it so often does, but I kept my expression calm. She rested her chin on my shoulder, and said, 'What is that broken line by the Welsh shore?'

I said I knew it to be a long trench called the New Cut and Miss Broadbent asked, 'Why do you think such a trench was dug?'

'To force an entry through the sand?'

'Exactly, Em. Our Dee is a troublesome river, girls. It ebbs more than it flows, which causes its tides to create prodigious shelves of sediment. Three hundred years ago mighty vessels of trade could sail all the way to Chester, can you imagine? But then the silt rose and blocked the passage of the ships and the only solution was to move the quay downriver to Shotwick.'

Eliza said, 'Shotwick has no quay now.'

'That's right, poor old Shotwick gave way to sludge and salting as well and its quay was abandoned. There was nothing for it but to retreat further north to Great Neston. Of course the inevitable happened and the relentless sediment choked that port, too. Now ships may only advance as far as the anchorage at Parkgate.'

We stared down at the map. The banks of the Dee were shaded by thousands of tiny dots that gave the impression of mould. They represented the creeping silt that would shrink the river until it was reduced to little more than a trickle.

Eliza cried, 'But what will happen to us and to Papa's granary when the Dee bungs up Parkgate, too?'

Miss Broadbent spoke softly. 'I dare say we will be stranded and no ship shall be able to reach us at all.'

Downes was waiting in the dressing room with what looked like a failed blancmange oozing over the crook of her arm. She turned her crimped face to us, mouth as thin as a crack in a piecrust, eyes like currants, small, black and unblinking. She said, 'Smith, I haven't got all day,' and thrust the pale pink stuff at me. While Eliza fidgeted in her stays and shift, Downes fastened side-hoops to her waistband and adjusted them to sit evenly. I helped Eliza into a petticoat and stomacher and then she contended with the gown, which was not very lenient across the back or in the arms. By way of encouragement I said, 'The pink looks well against your complexion.'

Eliza said, 'Oh, fiddle,' and goggled her eyes at her reflection in the glass.

Downes showed me how to tie the muslin handkerchief on Eliza's bosom without the knot bulging out like a frightful tumour, and when that was settled I went at Eliza's limp hair with a brush. Where Mrs Waterland's hair is silvery blonde, Eliza's is ash, which is regarded as a misfortune by those who admire her mother. There is also only a faraway echo of Mrs Waterland's slight figure in Eliza's low stature and shortness of limb. But Eliza does not care. She is robust in her indifference to beauty.

I twisted her hair into a tail and bound it with ribbon. 'It will have to do,' Downes said. She swatted away my attempt to situate a lace cap on Eliza's head. 'You must perch it up so that it is high on the crown,' she growled, manipulating the thing until it looked less like an object discarded from the sky by a passing bird. I retained my morning ensemble of a mouse-coloured gown, not very handsome, faced with a narrow ruffle.

The mistress of Sedge Court was absorbed in her work and seemed not to notice our arrival, despite having called us to enter. She was poised at a drawing board, supported on a drop-leaf table in the centre of her ground-floor parlour. Eliza and I bade her good afternoon and she looked up with an expression of glad surprise as though we had suddenly materialised from the ether, although it was she, with her shimmering hair, complexion of pearl and frosted taffeta gown who had the quality of a vision. Even now, regarding her through the more discriminating gaze of my adult years, I still find Mrs Waterland to be a dazzling proposition. Throughout my girlhood, I revered her desperately. To me she was the lamp in the dark, the spark in the void, the omphalos of Sedge Court, and I worshipped at the cult of her.

She had come across me, the story goes, among a swarm of rickety foundlings in a London hospital, while making her charitable rounds. My inability to recover that day from my memory has always been a source of great frustration to me. I can only imagine the elation I must have felt when her limpid eye fell on my cot and she plucked me from the fate to which I had been originally assigned.

How casual is the line between misery and salvation, between letting an impulse pass and taking an action that alters a life for ever. She might easily have passed on, but she did not.

I hasten to say that I hold you in no blame for the place in which I stewed before the advent of Mrs Waterland. How could I, when I know nothing of you except that you must have been badly let down by the man who fathered me and left you in circumstances where you were forced to a decision that would appal any mother's soul. You must have agonised about the fate of your child. I wish you could have known that I was carried away to a fine country house, where I have enjoyed more privileges than any poor orphan has a right to hope for.

In autumn and winter the Wirral peninsula, where we live, is sometimes rocked by savage gales that break ships to pieces on the sandbanks. But even under the most unnerving conditions, rain and wind lashing the windows, thunder crashing overhead, Mrs Waterland's parlour remains a beacon of brightness. The play of light there is managed by the use of ingenious refractors – spangles and sequins, prisms and lustres – and it seems as though every surface is on the brink of alteration. There are sheets of looking glass fastened to the walls in frames of golden boiserie, reflecting broken bits of sky and vegetation from the garden, and a fantastic mirrored edifice on the marble chimney piece which multiplies the glitter of the collection of rock crystals. The profligacy of the gilt chandelier has always annoyed Mrs Edmunds, who complains whenever candles must be brought to feed it. But the flames create enchanting upside-down pools of light on the ceiling, and tiny fiery fingers at the ends of the chandelier's long curved arms reach up to them in adoration.

Mrs Waterland approved of Eliza's dressing in the pink tulle gown, but Eliza could never make anything out of a compliment from her mother, possibly for lack of practice, since they were expressed only rarely.

She scrambled to upright from her curtsy, saying, 'Well, I do not care for pink, Mama. It reminds me of a pig.'

Mrs Waterland sighed. 'Must my advice fall very completely on deaf ears, Eliza? I beg you not to launch a conversation so. No one wishes to hear swine mentioned in polite company.' She shared an irked smile with me and straight away I presented her with my praise-seeking alternative to Eliza's blunder. 'Madam, if it pleases you, may I study your drawing?'

The delicate forefinger that Mrs Waterland raised to her lips hinted at a demurral, before giving way to assent. 'How very kind of you, Em.'

'I am sure my interest will be amply repaid.'

Eliza expanded her considerable eyebrows in my direction and I knew what she was thinking. Once when Lady Broome visited Sedge Court she brought with her a confection made by her French man-cook, a hard froth of pounded sugar all airy light in a paper coffin, and a pretty creamy colour. It was called a meringue. Eliza said that the meringue reminded her of me whenever I was in the proximity of her mother – so sugary it made her teeth hurt. True, I can be overly delightful around Mrs Waterland, but as I explained to Eliza, since I lack her entitlements, there is nothing for it but to render myself damnably adorable.

Mrs Waterland said, 'Can you guess the subject?' Her design showed kinked lines that I took to be waves and fronds of seaweed and branches of coral. I identified it as the underneath of the sea.

'You have hit it exactly. The design is meant for the mosaic in the summer house and I hope that you will help me with the application, my love. I shan't be able to do it without your keen eye and nimble fingers.'

As I sank into an acquiescing curtsey Mrs Waterland said, 'You know, Em, you are growing into quite a beauty. Let us hope that those freckles will fade in time. I wager you could snare a husband of the first water, all things being equal.' She laughed merrily, and I could not tell if she had made a joke or not.

The object of our visit lay spread out on a low table in front of the couch: a tea equipage and a kettle of hot water positioned on a trivet above a spirit lamp. Eliza was to practise her service. The potential for disaster – the horribly fragile bowls, the simmering kettle, things balanced on top of other things – seemed great to me. I envy Eliza her obliviousness to such potential hazards. Far better to be knockabout and a whirligig at one's ease than to be a slinking charmer, who must extort commendations night and day in order to survive. Mrs Waterland patted the couch next to her chair and invited us to sit down.

Eliza said, 'Mama, have you heard from Johnny? Will he soon be home? I am unbearably dying to see him! I do hope he will be here for my birthday.'

'You shall be the first to know when I have word, my love. Now let us rehearse the tea. When we have next the pleasure of Lady Broome's company I should like you to make a good impression, if that is not too dizzy an ambition.'

Eliza gave no sign of noticing her mother's sarcasm, but she did eye the tea service with a certain amount of wariness. Mrs Waterland commenced then to speak in low, sweet tones of warming and steeping, while the tall Delft flower stands on either side of the fireplace looked down on us like a couple of corpulent fops. Their midsections were studded with pockets sufficient to hold an entire garden's worth of blooms.

A knock came at the door and Rorke was admitted with a letter. He carried it in on a salver, which he gripped like a man at the reins of a mettlesome horse. Mrs Waterland rose to standing and her chin went up as Rorke approached with his large head and beaky nose thrust forward and bendy legs lagging behind. He looked like the outline of a question mark. After offering the salver to the mistress with stiff arms, he delivered a departing bow with the air of an individual who had done us a favour.

Mrs Waterland invited Eliza to pour the tea and then

turned away to a window that overlooked the garden. From my seat I watched her reflection in the glare of one of the looking glasses as she unsealed the letter. Even the offensive clang of teaspoons which accompanied Eliza's ham-fisted management of the service did not distract her. As she read, she began to twist one of her ringlets around a finger to restore its bounce.

And then I noticed, as I shifted in my seat, that I was also reflected in one of the panels of gold-framed glass. The compliment that Mrs Waterland had paid me was still uppermost in my mind. I smiled at myself rather nervously. I was elated of course that my appearance pleased the mistress, but I felt troubled too. I wondered if there was not something dangerous about beauty – I mean in the way that it could set one apart and attract harmful attention. But I am sure that Abby does not think such a thing, and she is lovely in my opinion. She, like me, has the look of winter, I would say, with cold white skin and sea-coloured eyes and black hair. And we are both small and wiry with a lively way of moving.

'Why are you simpering at yourself in the glass?' Eliza asked in a loud voice.

I jumped up, mortified at having my conceit exposed, and straightaway trod on the hem of my gown. I stumbled and fell to my knees. My face flamed with embarrassment, my vanity well and truly punished.

Eliza burst into laughter. I looked anxiously in Mrs Waterland's direction. I couldn't bear for her to see me look a fool.

But she was completely absorbed in her letter. She was gazing at the page in her hand with an expression of deep satisfaction or even a kind of euphoria.

The Servants' Hall

March, 1758

For months Mrs Edmunds had guarded our store of candles with such ferocity you might think the world was running out of tallow, but from the moment that Mrs Waterland unsealed that letter, the moods and interiors of Sedge Court grew lighter. There was a fizz in the air as if great changes were abroad. In fact, that very evening Eliza was invited to dine with her parents, which was a noteworthy event in itself, and Miss Broadbent and I were asked to take our dinner downstairs.

We arrived in the servants' hall to the merry sight of candle flames in abundance, reflected in the glass of the water bottles set upon the table and in the copper pots hanging on the wall, and there was a hearty fire flourishing in the grate. Even Downes looked more or less thawed. Miss Broadbent appeared below stairs infrequently – we usually dined in Eliza's dressing room – and I wondered if there might be some demurring at her company, because she did not properly belong to the basement, but Mr Otty welcomed her with bonhomie, saying, 'Draw yourself up cosy, Miss Broadbent, for it is crisp out tonight.' He was the picture of informality with coat flung aside, neck-cloth untwined, and paunch liberated by an untrammelled waistcoat. I am not sure of his age. His whiskers are white and he has a face that has been blasted by all kinds of weathers during his career as a driver – it is as rubicund and wrinkled as an overwintered beetroot – but he is sprightly on his legs for an old man. Actually Miss Broadbent seems to carry a greater burden of years, although she is probably scarcely in the middle of her thirties.

At the head of the table, Mrs Edmunds was carving a joint. With something very close to a smile she said to me, 'No need to stare like a throttled earwig, wench,' and, pointing her knife at Downes, 'Ease up, missus, and make room for the lass.' Rorke arrived with a plate-basket of dirty dishes and said that they were drawing out their dinner upstairs. Then he winked at me and said, 'They won't begrudge us our junketing down here tonight. After all, it has passed more than a twelve-month since we were given our wages.'

This was not the first time I had heard of the wages being long delayed, but since I myself was not paid in coin, I had not appreciated the seriousness of this state of affairs.

'Abby!' Rorke shouted. 'Come now and bustle off these plates.'

Abby was making conversation with Andy Croft, an ungainly, good-natured boy with big-knuckled hands and a speckled complexion, but she followed Rorke into the scullery, and I did as well, for I was keen to know what was afoot in the house.

Rorke said, 'It has been stark bad right enough. The master was well nigh jigged up and we were all feared for our situations.'

'What do you mean, jigged up?'

'Near to bankrupt. Has Miss Broadbent taught you the meaning of that or is it all dancing and folderol upstairs?'

'I know that bankruptcy is a miscarriage of money.'

'You are not wrong there. The prospect of it has put the terrors on us.'

Now I understood the cause of the house's anxiety. The rumours of the master's languishing income were true. Miss Broadbent had been right to attribute his prickliness to the worrisome responsibilities associated with this and I felt abashed at having mentioned my fear of eviction to her. Recalling the overheard exchange between the master and mistress in the light of this news, I began to see that I had leapt to conclusions. The master had spoken of a child, yes, but was I indeed the child in question? Mulling it over again, I wondered if he had been referring to one of the servants — Abby, perhaps? In truth, I am so minor as to be beneath remuneration, my position as Eliza's companion being compensated for in perquisites rather than pay. How vain of me to think that Mr Waterland gave any thought at all to my existence. Of course Miss Broadbent had been too kind to observe that only a nonentity with a runaway imagination and an altitudinous opinion of herself would presume that she, and not his debts, had rattled the master's composure.

'But we are all safe now, don't you know,' Rorke said, and sallied out with his platter.

I took my place at the table next to Miss Broadbent, and Hester hastened the pease pudding towards us, and the gravy boat. Mr Otty asked Croft to fetch more beer. 'And cork the barrel well,' he shouted after him, 'else all the virtue will go out of it!'

'Thank you, Hester,' I said, helping myself to pudding. 'I am glad to dine here. It is much jollier than in Eliza's apartment.'

Downes said, 'How fortunate that you feel that way, miss, for I wager you must get used to the servants' hall. The mistress will be looking to put you out of the way, I warrant.'

'What do you mean by that? I wonder,' said Miss Broadbent. 'The child knows full well that Mrs Waterland finds her very obliging.'

Downes pursed her lips. 'I am only saying that if this young lady is not careful she will vex the mistress by showing up Miss Eliza's wants.'

'Ah, here is Croft,' said Miss Broadbent, making a point of ignoring Downes. 'Shall we raise a toast to the young master, Mr Otty?'

I could not help feeling unsettled by Downes's remarks and resolved to be on my guard against any inadvertent eclipsing of Eliza. Everything about my conduct – whether I stepped forward or hung back – was qualified by Mrs Waterland's opinion.

We stood then and cried the good health of Johnny Waterland and when we had sat down again, Mr Otty made a rather rambling speech. I gathered that after a long and nerve-racking delay, the mistress's uncle, Sir Joseph Felling, had agreed to sponsor Johnny for a future at the bank of which he was a principal and there was even hope that Johnny might be favoured as Sir Joseph's heir. This was the news imparted in the letter Mrs Waterland had received, although the servants seemed already to know most of it. The intelligence, I later found from Hester, was owed to the combined efforts of the servants, their individual differences notwithstanding – Downes, for instance, poking into the correspondence tucked away in Mrs Waterland's secretary-desk, Rorke doing likewise with the master's, and Mrs Edmunds and Mr Otty drawing on a network of connections developed over their long years of service in the respective families of the mistress and the master. They worked together for the common good in this regard, since their fates were, naturally, bound up intricately with their employers'.

Croft charged our cups again. The beer was sour and tasty and made me feel as if I were leaning slightly to one side. Another toast was made, this time to Sir Joseph. Abby asked, 'Now but who is he, though?' and Mr Otty explained, 'Sir Joe is the spigot who augments the flow of cash. He is the uncle of our mistress, head of the Felling family and a man bowlegged with brass.' Mr Otty speared a flap of mutton and used it to emphasise his remark that it would be a strange thing if young Johnny did not get a legacy when Sir Joseph shuffled off. 'A handsome one it will be too,' he said, 'and when that comes to pass not a cloud will darken Sedge Court never no more.'

'I would not count your chickens, Mr Otty. The Fellings were always right snooty about the Waterlands.' In response to Miss Broadbent's enquiring gaze, Mrs Edmunds added, 'The Waterlands come from millwrights, but the Fellings on the other hand have always been much further upstream, if you get my drift. They were right flummoxed when Henrietta Felling condescended to Bernard Waterland, but it wasn't such a surprise to me. Her branch of the Fellings had very dry pockets and it seemed he had a fortune.'

'That is not so unusual, is it?' Miss Broadbent observed. 'A pedigree in exchange for cash.'

'Leave something for the poor footman!' Rorke slogged into the dining hall with another basket of used plates. 'It's all right for you lot; I'm the one obliged to be in and out like a fiddler's elbow, but I will dip my beak now, if I may.'

'Go on, man –' Mr Otty poured Rorke a foaming draught of the beer – 'take a quick sup on the wing.' Then he turned to Miss Broadbent and said, 'The master's father, Jack Waterland, was a terrible canny man. My dad was a ploughman time back on Sedge Farm and he knew all about it. The farm was a place oozing springs and swamps when Jack Waterland bought it, but he would have none of their mischief. He found ways of removing wetness from the land by making drains, you see.'

Mrs Edmunds chipped in. 'Parkgate weren't nowt but a village in them days and just a few shrimpers and fisherfolk living there and a bad, chocky road between the village and Chester.'

Mr Otty scratched the grizzled nap of his head and went on, 'The old master contrived all sorts of drainage machines and sold them all over the kingdom as well. He was desperate keen to get on top of the difficulty of the Dee and make Parkgate a reliable stop for trade.' He paused to remove a well-masticated lump of gristle from his mouth, and lobbed it into the fire before going on. 'He made a powerful penny out of his machines, and levered himself up and Parkgate along with it. When the old quay at Neston was finally jacked in because of the silt, the trade came up here and Jack Waterland found himself in right good buckle.'

Miss Broadbent said, 'Why did the Waterlands' fortunes dwindle then? I wonder.'

'Old Jack Waterland planned to build drains under the Dee, so that Parkgate would not succumb to sludge, but he died before he could realise his design. A committee of Chester men, who were after business themselves, had the New Cut dug in the river instead. That pushed the course of the Dee over to the Welsh side and Parkgate fell into difficulties with the loss of trade.'

Rorke said, 'In any case, the Dee cannot hold a candle to the Mersey. They can ram any amount of two-hundred-tonners up that waterway.'

Mrs Edmunds said, 'You must not dawdle your time away down here, Rorke. They will be wanting the cheese taken from the table.' Rorke slugged the last of his beer and wiped his chops with the back of his hand.

Miss Broadbent said, 'Do you think, Mr Otty, that the present master walks in the shadow of his father?'

'Our master is no dullard, but he wants the ability of his father to convert his brains into brass. Her upstairs, nor her father, didn't know that when they accepted Bernard Waterland. He, of course, had given her to expect that he had the moon in his pocket.'

Mrs Edmunds said with lowered voice, 'He was a different man in them days. He was bowled over by Miss Felling something fierce and it was all right merry at the outset of the marriage. But by the time Master Johnny was born she was coming to see there was nowt but a few shillings rattling round at Sedge Court.'

Miss Broadbent said, 'And the lady was brought up to a certain style, of course.'

'Oh aye, she will want things when she wants them and it is not in her make-up to do without. All credit to her silver tongue though, because she went to her aunt Lady Paine in Derbyshire, who was the older sister of Sir Joseph, God rest her soul, and she coaxed the lady into settling an annuity on her, a good amount of which went into schemes to revive the master's fortunes.'

'They went off travelling hither and yon,' said Mr Otty. 'They were up and down every coast of the kingdom and beyond. The master went to look on the way that tides circulate. He was pondering after the success of his father and the plans for drains that went under the sea. But his studies came to nowt, him not being the type who is much of a manifester, and it is many a year now since he went abroad. Not since they brought young Em back for Miss Eliza to play with.'

'Where did they get you from, Emma?' Abby asked.

'My name is not Emma,' I said. 'It is M for Mary. Eliza coined the name when we were little and she saw M. Smith written on my conduct book.'

Miss Broadbent said, 'Mrs Waterland brought you from London, didn't she?'

Downes said in a lofty manner, 'In point of fact, I have heard quite a different story about the origins of Smith here.'

I stiffened myself against a tale that was bound to mortify me.

'Mrs Waterland got her from Chester,' Downes said darkly, as if Chester were Hades itself, 'in the days when she and Lady Broome went out of charity to pray for prisoners at the assizes. On one such occasion the mistress came across a condemned man who was to be hanged as an incorrigible poacher. This scurvy wretch was lamenting his fate and that of his motherless child, and what do you think the mistress does out of the kindness of her heart?' Downes aimed her beady gaze at me. 'She brought the poacher's daughter to live at Sedge Court.'

Miss Broadbent said crisply, 'What nonsense, Miss Downes.'

'I had the story from the mistress herself!'

'I doubt that very much. If Em were a poacher's daughter we should have heard about it before now. You ought to be ashamed of yourself for impugning the poor child.'

I felt less impugned than reminded how likely it was that I was the progeny of a lowly felon rather than – and this was my sustaining pipe dream at the time – the clandestine child of Mrs Waterland. I had once heard Mrs Heswall ask Hester, with a raised eyebrow, if I had been made 'on the other side of the blanket'. It was the first time I had come across the phrase but its meaning was clear enough to me. In a high tone, Hester rebuked the laundress for her presumption, but when I asked her myself, Hester said that she had never heard anything so batty, which was the same as saying she knew nothing. Sometimes I dared to let myself imagine that Mrs Waterland and I were united by a shared tragedy, where I was the child she could not acknowledge and she the mother I could not claim.

The conversation had rushed on, leaving Downes high and dry, to the topic of Mrs Waterland's aunt, Lady Paine. Hester recalled how deeply grieved the mistress had been when the aunt expired.

'As well she might be,' declared Mrs Edmunds. 'When Lady Paine ceased to exist, so did the annuity that she had put on the mistress. That money has been sore missed in this house. Late-whiles it has been a devil of a business to reconcile the accounts, or the ones I deal with, any road. I have had to codgel and mend just to keep the fires burning.'

Hester said, 'No wonder the master is oft so out of sorts. He was beholden to the mistress all those years to pay the bills and it has preyed on him.'

Miss Broadbent said, 'It is a pity Sir Joseph could not have found it in himself to take up where his sister left off. He might have offered assistance to his relations.'

'Sir Joseph is a heckle-tempered fellow, by Jove,' said Mr Otty. 'He ever opposed Bernard Waterland. He never reckoned our master good enough for a Felling, but the mistress's father was still alive at that time so Sir Joseph could not thwart the marriage. And then the master has been so troubled these last several years, there was nothing in his situation to alter Sir Joseph's low opinion. Sir Joe thought him good for nowt.'

Miss Broadbent said, 'Then it is miraculous that Sir Joseph has agreed to prosper Mr Waterland's son.'

'Mayhappen he sees in the young master something of himself, for isn't Johnny an up-and-comer in the Felling vein?'

Downes said, 'We are all under an obligation to the mistress. She it was who swallowed her pride and begged Sir Joseph to sponsor Johnny Waterland.'

Mr Otty said, 'That's true, I will uphold.'

Mrs Edmunds said, 'Happen it was the begging that did it. Sir Joseph would not be the first man to savour the sight of a high woman lowering herself to him.' She drained her cup, and then observed in a tone that scored a line under the discussion, 'In the long run, families come up and go down like the grass and there's no end to it.'

After supper, I accompanied Miss Broadbent to the door of her chamber to bid her goodnight. She resided in a cramped closet off the schoolroom. She bent to kiss my cheek and then she laid a light hand on my arm. 'Em,' she said, 'do you know that the foundling hospital in London would have made a record of your admission. Perhaps you could ask the mistress if she has the document. It will show your original name, and the date of birth.'

'My original name?' My voice caught in my throat. It had not occurred to me that Mary Smith might not be the name bestowed on me at birth.

Miss Broadbent said in her quiet way, 'Every foundling is baptised with a new name on being admitted to the hospital and they are entered in a register.'

I might have asked Miss Broadbent how she knew such a thing, but there was an unusually closed look in her eye and I did not dare to put the question to her.

I trembled with anticipation at the thought that I could learn my identity from an official record. But did I want to know? To discover that I came from dishonoured stock – my fantasy of belonging to Mrs Waterland was much more appealing. And yet, if it should turn out that my mother was a worthless person, oughtn't I to know that? At the same time I felt that I must tread cautiously. I did not want Mrs Waterland to interpret an interest in my origins as an aspersion on her generosity in supplying me with an alternative life. However one afternoon she called me to her parlour to help work embroideries for one of Eliza's new gowns and I found a way to chisel an opening for the topic. I asked her whether fashions had changed very much since her entry into society. I hoped that talking of her youth might bring her to the subject of parentage, by which I could bring up mine.

Mrs Waterland worked her needle for a minute or so without acknowledging my enquiry, but then she began to describe rather dreamily an ensemble she had once appeared in at a ball: the petticoat of silver tissue worn very bouffant, the stays cut breathtakingly low, the tight sleeves making the most of her slender arms, her headdress a cloud of snowy gauze and falling from her shoulders a train of ice-blue shagreen that imitated sharkskin. She sighed, 'I was seventeen and never was more beautiful, I freely admit. I felled the heart of a young viscount that night. He was terribly handsome. I have always been hopelessly drawn to good looks, you know.'

It was a statement that begged the question of the master's appearance, but of course I could not remark such a thing.

She bent over her tambour and tugged at a thread. I hesitated to ask more about the viscount. Evidently a match had not been made and I feared probing a wound. I said, instead, 'I imagine you were always beset by admirers, madam.' I suppose I expected her to counter with something prettily self-deprecating, but she did not say anything at all for a few minutes. She looked in silence towards a window. Her emotions seemed very near the surface, which was not something in her that I was used to.

She said flatly, 'Beauty is a great benefit, but it is not a reliable currency. He was madly in love with me, but my lack of fortune was a stumbling block. He married an heiress with a shape like a barge. When I saw in the newspaper that he was dead of an accident from his horse quite soon after his marriage, I was glad.' Her smile was tight. She resumed her needle, adding, 'It is pointless to dwell on the past.'

I said, picking my way carefully, 'I must admit that I cannot help wondering about my own past. I am rather curious about my people.'

I thought she stiffened rather as she said, 'But, my dear Em, you know the story. You were abandoned at the hospital.'

'It crossed my mind that you might have been given my certificate of birth.'

She said, 'I believe no such document exists.'

I did not wish to quote Miss Broadbent's assertion that the foundling hospital kept records. I intuited that it would not advantage her. 'Oh. I assumed there must be something on paper. Perhaps we could send away to ask at the hospital. You know, dear madam, that I am not even sure of my correct age.'

Mrs Waterland said, 'Alas, child, the births of foundlings are rarely recorded.'

You see how she did not quite answer the question. I had the impression that she did not want to be pinned down, but it may have been that she was dwelling still on those dashed hopes of her youth. I wondered if Miss Broadbent had been wrong about the records, although it was not like her to be inaccurate.

The mechanism of the clock on the chimney piece whirred loudly and chimed the hour.

Mrs Waterland said, 'You must accept, my love, that you will never know your provenance. Were I in your shoes, I should tell myself that my parents were of high rank and fallen, alas, on hard times. Just because such a tale is the fanciful wish of every foundling does not mean it cannot be true.' She laughed her tinkling laugh and I found myself grateful for the shelter of her regard.

When I told Miss Broadbent some of what had transpired between the mistress and me, largely that there was no certificate of birth, I saw at once by her almost infinitesimal shake of the head that she did not believe this to be the case, but she said only, 'That is rather surprising.' I thought she was about to add something else, but then Eliza came back into the room with some boisterous request or other.

I wished that I could have pursued the subject with Mrs Waterland more zealously, but I lacked the courage. At the same time I was puzzled by her refusal to satisfy what was a natural interest on my part. I felt that she was determined to give me an insufficient response and that piqued my curiosity even more.

Mrs Waterland's Apartment

March, 1758

My slow slide towards an estrangement from Sedge Court can be traced to the watershed of Eliza's and my shared fourteenth birthday. The day began, however, with promise. The moon was in a bright phase, and since it was able to light the way, the Waterlands had decided to leave early and drive to Chester to meet Johnny's coach from London. Eliza and I rose before dawn. When I opened the window of the bedchamber for fresh air, I saw that the sky was still dusty with stars and a carpet of wavering mist concealed the lawn. I was buoyant, looking forward to spreading my wings in the schoolroom without Eliza's distractions. I can almost hear her snort of derision at that.

I rigged us in our warm wadded robes and our felt slippers and we ran downstairs to the next floor and knocked at the mistress's apartment. Downes opened the door brandishing a silver-backed hairbrush like some fabulous weapon.

Mrs Waterland's dressing room, with its intricate wall-papers, its obscuring festoons of tulle, its screens and hangings keeping their secrets, always struck me as the command post of the house, from where she worked the levers of Sedge Court. She was sitting at her toilette in the glow of candlelight, fragrant, fur-wrapped, looking at least partially divine. You are probably tiring of my extravagant descriptions of her – but once one has formed an idea about someone it takes an effort to shift it, don't you think?

She wished us a joyous birthday and added with an arched eyebrow, 'Don't my girls look fetching today!' One was not sure whether she meant it as a jest. But in any case, I was confident that she had at her disposal the means to improve our defects. Her dressing table thronged with silver-topped bottles and cut-glass jars. Glimmers of light ricocheted among the bevelled surfaces of these mysterious receptacles, which contained, surely, all the ingredients needed to beautify the world.

With a mischievous smile, she ordered Downes to retrieve from the closet 'something that might interest Miss Waterland', before returning her attention to her toilette. She dabbed at a cake of lip colour with her little finger, while we helped ourselves to the breakfast set out on a low table.

From the closet came the sound of a struggle, followed by a volley of yelps. Then Downes emerged, grim-eyed, with a tawny young pug squirming against her bosom.

Mrs Waterland rose in a rustle of silk and set the dog on a tuffet. She fondled his sooty face and cried, 'Isn't he a darling? He is all yours, child!' She handed his leash to Eliza with a smile that suggested an outpouring of gratitude was in order.

I could see that it was not love at first sight between Eliza and the pug. They regarded one another with mutual uncertainty, their brows similarly corrugated.

'Do you not adore him?'

'Of course, Mama.'

'You must devise a sweet little name for him.'

Eliza scrutinised the pug, and he backed away from the effort of her stare. After a few seconds of deliberation she announced, 'His name shall be Brownie.'

'Good heavens, darling, could you be less inventive? Why not call him Pug and be done with it.'

Eliza made a gesture of deflation and the leash fell from her hand. The pug seized his chance, bolting for the door, but I managed to reel him in. I said, 'We ought to call him Dasher.'

'Dasher! Oh, clever Em!' Mrs Waterland beamed. 'He is absolutely a Dasher, don't you think, Eliza?'

'I suppose so,' said Eliza lamely. 'Shall he come with us to Chester?'

'Not today, my love. He is too young and disorderly.'

She called Downes to take Eliza away to be dressed. I, however, she detained with a whispered, 'Do not think you have been forgotten, my love.'

Perhaps you can imagine my surprise and delight at that.

She invited me to sit down again and then presented me with a substantial parcel wrapped in dark red linen. A portable writing desk! Well, that was what I hoped to find. But the unbundling revealed instead a rosewood workbox, which contained a plethora of needles and pins and skeins of thread.

Mrs Waterland beamed. 'Cunning, isn't it? Certainly an improvement on the little box you have had all these years.'

I thanked her and she replied after a pause, avoiding my eye, 'Well, of course, a rather more capacious workbox is called for now.'

When a ship is wrecked off our coast, a tolling bell at Parkgate announces the melancholy news. I heard in Mrs Waterland's *of course* a similarly mournful knell. As she patted my hand, foreboding began to steal over me like a sea fog.

'Dear little Em,' she murmured. She spoke in the condoling tone of one who must inform of an accident. 'The moment has come when you must assume the life that is apposite to your rank.'

I was stunned by her words.

They meant a wrenching shift was about to take place for me. But I nodded reflexively in acceptance. Despite my shock, I felt that I was required somehow to reassure Mrs Waterland. I mean to say: the true expression of my own feelings could never be other than secondary. I was habituated to serve her interests.

She sighed. 'It is all because of Eliza, of course. Alas, my dear daughter lacks those natural embellishments that draw a gentleman to look favourably upon a young lady. You, however –' she directed an impish smile at me as if we were in cahoots – 'must take care to keep the fellows at a distance.'

Which fellows? I wished to protest. I had the feeling I was being reproved for something that was not my fault as though I had deprived Eliza of a toy and she must be compensated for her loss.

A current of air rattled the windows and fluttered the candle flames. Drawing her fur more snugly about her shoulders, Mrs Waterland leaned towards me and said, 'Ahead of us lies a great undertaking, and all of us must play our part. Eliza must contract a marriage that will make fast her finances and her place in society. You understand the importance of that, don't you, my love? Your own security depends upon it. You will want, as I do, to see her make an attractive match. After all, whomever Eliza marries shall become your master, too.'

That my fate rested in Eliza's hands was a daunting prospect. I shivered at the thought. Then it occurred to me, clutching wildly at straws, that since a marriage was contingent on Eliza's being able to attract a suitor, perhaps we might never leave Sedge Court. I plucked up the nerve to ask, 'Madam, how should Eliza and I be disposed if it should happen – I mean, in the event that – that Eliza might not marry?'

Was it the raw draught seeping across the windowsill that made me quake or the remote eye that Mrs Waterland turned on me? 'There is no question,' she said icily, 'that Eliza shall not be settled on an estate. And you will strive, as shall I, to make it so. In any case, one day Johnny will have his inheritance and you will not like to be annexed at Sedge Court when he installs his wife here. Eliza must have her own household to command.'

Mrs Waterland came then to the nub of the matter. Henceforth, I was to take up the position of Eliza's waiting woman. My status at Sedge Court had never been formally determined in the past. It had lodged somewhere between companion and cousin, a situation that had allowed me to maintain the illusion that I was a member of the family. Now I was to be designated a lady's maid, a demotion which in one swoop cut off at the knees the fantasy that I belonged to the Waterlands by blood and made clear that my only right to live at Sedge Court was by dint of the master–servant contract.

'It is the way of the world, my love,' said Mrs Waterland with a little squeeze of my hand. 'We are governed by the stations to which we are born.'

I must have looked very staggered, because in order to cheer me up she offered to let me work on her project in the summer house, where her underwater design was to be rendered in shells. However, she made it clear that my principal responsibility, naturally, was to attend to Eliza's toilette. I was also to clean Eliza's apartment, and tend Eliza's fire and bring supplies of fuel, candles and paper. I must launder her laces and fine linens, iron and repair her clothes and undertake white-work, plain-work and the salvation of delicate stuffs as required. I must press her bed linen, draw the figures for her embroideries and make patterns when necessary to refurbish her clothes. I must keep her millinery and her footwear in order. I must manage Dasher. My time apart from that was to be held in reserve in order to assist Mrs Edmunds and Miss Downes in the smooth running of the household and with tasks that arise with the seasons – the putting-up of preserves, for instance, and the beating of rugs and drapes during spring and autumn.

I stared into the empty maw of my workbox. I did not baulk at earning my keep, and certainly it had not escaped my attention that Sedge Court was understaffed, but I could not see that there were enough hours in the day to accomplish my duties and my studies as well. I closed the workbox.

I asked in a weak voice, 'Shall I continue to go to Miss Broadbent?'

Mrs Waterland's expression told me that it pained her to disappoint me, but disappoint me she must. 'I know,' she sighed, 'that you have been a most laborious pupil. Miss Broadbent tells me you have already mastered a syllabus far beyond your years, but . . .' She brushed a stray curl from my face.

'Now is the time for a different kind of guidance – and Miss Downes shall provide it.'

My despair at her answer was hopelessly commingled with the fear of displeasing her, and so I held back my tears and colluded with her vaguely sorrowful smile. It was not only the cancellation of my lessons that grieved me so bitterly, but also the loss of Miss Broadbent's company, which had always been a joy to me. I looked away at the sullen fire in the grate. A rising draught chivvied it and the dank wood began to fume.

Mrs Waterland said in a tone of determined gaiety, which had yet an edge to it, 'Buck up, Em, there's a good girl. You are not the first girl to be harried out of the schoolroom. I will tell you frankly that a woman who loves learning must find her ambition ever frustrated. I had far more genius than either of my brothers, yet there was no question that I should receive the opportunities that they did. One must accept that one is subsidiary.'

'I will follow your instructions diligently, madam.'

She patted my knee. 'That's my girl. Now be a love and find something for the dog to eat. We must shift ourselves to leave for Chester.'

I nodded, suddenly unable to speak. Smoke scratched the back of my throat and pricked my eyes. I felt short of breath, as though something were being snuffed out before I had had the chance to understand what it was.

With Dasher lopsided under my arm, paws dangling, I lighted my way to the basement, every footstep of my descent sounding a knell of doom to my ears. I brought the dog into the scullery to search out scraps for his breakfast and found

Abby scrubbing out a dripping pan. At once the dog lifted his head and stared at her with lovestruck eyes. The whole of his little body strained towards her. 'Oh, it is only the smell of the bacon bones he has got a whiff of,' she said, pleased as Punch. 'It is a great nuisance, but I will settle him down if you like.' I left her dandling him on her knee. I had an appointment with Downes in the laundry, but my feet did not seem to want to take me there.

Hearing the rattle of the chaise in the courtyard, I pulled open the door of the back entry. The sky had lightened grudgingly – a daylight moon still glowed above the stables. The blustery wind was making a sound like someone shaking out a counterpane. I ran along the side path with unfledged thoughts of entreaty churning in my head, of beseeching the mistress to let me stay at my books, but my impetus faltered at the corner of the house.

From the vicinity of the porte cochère, where Mr Otty had stopped to pick up the Waterlands, came the slam of the chaise's doors. The clink of the harness and the grating of wheels on the semicircle of gravel in front of the house announced the family's departure. I watched the black-and-yellow chaise trundle on to the drive. It looked like an overgrown bumblebee, a freak of nature, that dwarfed the rider approaching it from the entrance gates. I recognised the lumpen silhouette of Mr Sutton, astride his horse like a bag of sand.

The chaise pulled up and Mr Waterland alighted. Sutton dismounted and he and the master walked towards the lake, falling into a conference. I could not hear what was said, but the discussion was animated, and I had the impression that something was passed from Mr Sutton's hand to Mr Waterland's. Mr Sutton returned to his mount and rode away at a fast trot. Once he was out of sight, Mr Waterland threw the object he was holding into the lake. Despite my melancholy mood, I could not help being curious about the scene I had just witnessed.

As soon as the chaise had turned on to the road I hurried to the spot where the exchange had taken place, but I could find nothing there but a couple of cockleshells scattered on the damp grass. Perhaps Sutton had brought shells for the mistress. She was in need of large numbers of them for her decoration of the summer house. But in that case why had the master thrown them away, and so angrily, too? I picked up one of the shells and weighed it in the palm of my hand. And why would Sutton ride up here for the sake of a handful of shells? I remembered Rorke telling me that Sutton used to be the master's servant, although he has come up in the world since then. Rorke observed that Theo Sutton owned an uncommon fine house for a fellow of his background, and he did not get that by peddling periwinkles. I think Rorke meant that Sutton dabbled in illegal goods. But of course he, Rorke, would want to be circumspect with that accusation, since there was something brutish about Sutton and one imagined that he would not take kindly to an imputation.

Someone was shouting my name. It was Croft, running across the lawn to fetch me. Although I could have cried a river, it was useless to weep over the ending of my education. Sedge Court supplied me with the necessaries of life and I could do nothing but accept a different way of belonging to the house. Let the staggering reality of things be your lesson now, Mary Smith. How could it be otherwise?

Miss Broadbent's Closet and the Summer House

March, 1758

Downe's elbow worked in and out like a bellows as she demonstrated how to insert a fire slug into the cavity of a smoothing iron. While she droned on, I stared into the ceiling where Eliza's translucent white shifts hung on the drying frame like ghosts at rest. At length I was ordered to winch the frame to earth and to iron the shifts, while Downes set about suppressing a pile of turbulent handkerchiefs. Of course my duties were light compared to the tasks of others. You have only to see the herring girls at Parkgate with their arms dripping oil and their hands nicked by their sharp knives to know that – and Abby's duties were hardly whimsical, scouring with horehound filthy tinware and chamber pots in the freezing scullery. But on that first day at the ironing table I struggled to accept that my life from now on must be measured out in the interminable ruffles of Eliza's apparel. Downes had shown me how the point of the wretched iron must nose into the root of a seam as determined as a terrier down a rathole, without compromising the puffiness of the gathers, but I found it a feat very troublesome to achieve.

'There is no room for a long face in my lady's service, Smith.' Downes's mouth twitched in a vinegary smile and she added, 'Although should the truth be told, you might not have a lady to serve for much longer.' This kitchen gossip startled me, which was Downes's aim.

'They are sending Miss Waterland away to school, you know. That is why they have taken her to Chester. She is to be enrolled at Mrs Ramsay's Academy, beginning after Easter.'

'I find that hard to believe. If Eliza were going away, the mistress would not have asked me expressly to serve her.'

'She has asked you to serve the house, miss. You are to be at the disposal of Mrs Edmunds and me. Do not worry, we will find plenty for you to do – you will soon climb down off your high horse.'

I hunched over the iron, wondering if it were true about the school. Did that mean my post was in jeopardy – and Miss Broadbent's, too? But I would not let Downes meet with the satisfaction of further questions.

After I had finished in the laundry I asked Mrs Edmunds's permission to bring up barley water and a chop to Miss Broadbent. I found her settled in a niche on a night chair next to her bed, which was hardly wider than a slat, with a writing box balanced on her lap and a quill in her hand. She looked up with an abstracted expression as I entered as if interrupted in some thorny mental endeavour. I saw that the few lines she had written were heavily scored through.

'Miss Broadbent,' I began, 'I am sorry for my absence this morning, but—'

She sketched a scribble in the air which overwrote my apology and said, 'No need to explain, Em. Mrs Waterland has informed me of the alteration in your duties. Naturally, one is dismayed on your behalf. To be denied education is a blow, and worse for a child of your capacity, but this was inevitable.'

I was still holding the dinner tray. I put it down on a table of Lilliputian dimensions. Miss Broadbent frowned at it and then hung her head. She said, 'What can I say, child, but that one must accept one's fate?'

I was surprised by her detached tone. I found it rather dispiriting. But then Miss Broadbent's face crumpled a little and I cried, 'You are not leaving Sedge Court, I hope!'

Miss Broadbent made an effort to compose herself. She said, 'I cannot imagine why you would think that. There is a great deal for me to do here.'

Despite her queer manner, I was relieved by her retort. I wanted to believe that there was nothing to the sneery rumour put about by Downes.

Miss Broadbent suddenly said, 'I asked the mistress for your admission number, you know. Perhaps I ought not to have done that, but I have it buzzing around in my mind like some infernal fly that there ought to have been a document attached to you.' Seeing my puzzlement, she added, 'Every foundling given entry to the London hospital has an admission number. Had I mentioned that? If one has the admission number, one can apply for the certificate of birth. You see, Em, I am determined to help you even if I cannot help myself.'

I was grateful that Miss Broadbent was still fixed to the idea of uncovering my identity, but I was rather rattled by it, too. It was out of character for her to bring a matter so determinedly to the attention of the mistress and I had an uneasy feeling that no good would come of it. That is, Mrs Waterland would not be pleased.

'Were you given the number?' I asked.

'No. She says she does not have it.' Miss Broadbent clasped her hands under her chin and looked up at the ceiling like a child about to say its prayers. I followed her gaze, but there was no sign of a benevolent god aloft. There was nothing up there but cracked paint. Miss Broadbent said softly, as if speaking to herself, 'That is untrue, I think.'

'But why should she lie?'

'I do not know.'

I said thoughtlessly, 'Well, it does not matter.'

'Of course it matters!' Miss Broadbent cried. 'Think of the woman who was forced to leave you there with nothing but an anonymous token to say who she was! Wouldn't she always wonder in her heart if you would come to look for her?'

Miss Broadbent had never raised her voice to me before.

'I am sorry,' she said, closing her eyes and pinching her temples. 'I am a little out of humour.'

She would help me *even if she could not help herself*. I wondered what she meant by that. But I was afraid of agitating her further. With a curtsy I murmured, 'I will not keep you, Miss Broadbent, but may I thank you sincerely for everything you have taught me. It was a pleasure to attend your lessons.'

I thought that she had not heard me. She was transferring her writing equipment to the bed, since there was nowhere else to put it. But then she rose, smoothed her petticoat and took a step towards me. She placed a hand on my shoulder. The gesture had a trace of something ceremonial about it. She leaned forward and said in a low voice as if passing on a secret, 'Your wit and your conduct have ever endeared you to me, Mary Smith. They will, I am sure, make your destiny. But take care, child, for you have strong feelings. Do not convert them always into thoughts, otherwise you are liable to be overcharged by melancholy and kept in a state that is improper for the purpose of being useful. Perhaps I have already delivered you such advice. My mind runs on the subject. In any case, I regret that it is not much to give you.'

She turned away abruptly and straightened a volume in her sliver of a bookcase. I noticed that a lock of her mousy hair had come unpinned and I was troubled by its suggestion of quiet disarray. I wished that I could engage her attention further, but her silence and my inability to fill it in any meaningful way gave me no remit to stay. She did not look around as I excused myself from her presence.

I returned to the laundry and tied up my sleeves. A petticoat whose hem had come unstitched awaited my attention and I reached for my rosewood box. As I sewed, my thoughts dwelled on Miss Broadbent and the perilousness of being alone. I chewed over the question of the foundling hospital, too. I considered writing a letter to its secretary to ask for my admission number, but feared that I could not do so without alienating Mrs Waterland. I resolved instead that when I was older I would visit the hospital – surely when Eliza was married, she would have occasion to go to London, and I with her – in order to find out for myself whether I had come from there. I finished hemming the petticoat and took up a pair of stays whose boning channels were frayed. A weak sunbeam fell through the laundry's high window and collapsed briefly across the table. The hours limped on like those beggary old seamen you see at Parkgate hauling their wooden legs along the road. I stitched the loose cords on one of Eliza's stomachers. I picked wadding out of an old quilted petticoat and washed it for reuse. I had never known time to lag so. I assisted Hester in the boiling-up of a mess of candle stubs, and when the tallow was liquefied we poured it into moulds for new lights. Empiricists such as Mr Locke say that all knowledge must arise through the senses and so it does, for I can report that the lower the grade of tallow the more evil the smell, and none more so than the congealing suet of a hog. By the time Hester and I had completed our task we had the stench of carrion about us.

Eliza was ravenous when I brought her breakfast the following morning and she began straight away to pillage the tray. It was an awkward moment. At least, I found it so. Neither of us remarked on my altered role. In fact it has never been explicitly discussed between us, I think because the subject was too charged with potential recrimination – I might say that Eliza patronised me, and she might counter that I made her feel guilty. We liked one another well enough, the inference was, to want to avoid damaging our mutual attachment. On that first morning we both felt self-conscious. Eliza reached for the jug of beef tea and then snatched back her hand uncertainly and glanced at me sideways. Ought I to pour it for her? A waft of discomfort came off her as I leaned in to fill her bowl and I realised that she had not yet come to terms with her new power. I threw open the curtains. The sun had risen with difficulty, its frail rays hardly able to burn off the morning mist. The lake below looked like a lost penny and the road was a white ribbon unspooling towards Parkgate. I said that I would call Miss Broadbent, but Eliza informed me, a little slyly I thought, that the governess was to take breakfast with Mrs Waterland.

'Do you know why?'

She shook her head violently and stuffed a handful of plum cake into her mouth.

I cleared my throat. 'You know of course that I am to be more extensively at your disposal now.'

Eliza narrowed her eyes. 'It is not my fault. I must have an attendant.'

'I did not say it was your fault.'

She sucked the tea down in one swallow and thumped the empty bowl on to the tray. When she acts in that cantankerous banging clanging way it usually indicates that she is ill at ease.

I said, 'Did your brother arrive safely at Chester?'

I knew that Johnny was already in the house, but I thought it might defuse the tension of the situation if Eliza could chatter about him. The reflected glory of Johnny Waterland can always be relied on to bring a sparkle to her eye.

'Oh, he cuts such a figure,' she gushed. 'He came off the coach wearing buckles so bright I was almost blinded by them. Mama says he may now spend near one thousand pounds a year without hurting himself.'

I could not help but think what a difference even fifty of Johnny's profligate pounds might make to Miss Broadbent. Had she such a stipend she might be able to rent a little cottage of her own and have her independence.

I asked Eliza if I should make her ready so that she would not be late for her lesson.

'But I am not obliged to go to the schoolroom today.

Hurrah! Mama has given permission for me to be at leisure. I am to recover from the journey. The road was awfully claggy and we nearly stalled at Shotwick. Do you know what else? Johnny's friend from Cambridge will come here tomorrow in his own chaise.'

I extracted a robe de chambre from Eliza's press and shook it out. 'Will you like to wear this lilac?'

Eliza shrugged. 'As you will. Johnny's friend is called the Honourable Tobias Barfield and his mother is a dowager-countess. Mr Barfield is not a banker like Johnny though. He is too elevated for that.'

'What is it that bankers do?'

'Papa says that one gives a bank money for safekeeping and the bank may lend the money out for a venture.'

'If the money is lent out, how can it be in safekeeping at the same time?'

'Obviously I am not an expert.'

'Obviously.' I unfolded the robe and held it open. I said, 'Was Chester agreeable?'

Eliza stepped into the robe. She said, 'Mama turned over every mercery shop to find a silk that pleased her. She settled on one with a white ground and a running green stalk, and she bought a lace cap hardly as big as my hand with pink ribbons. Then we looked at horrid old houses.' I fastened Eliza's sash and she sat at her dressing table to put on the pale blue stockings I had unfurled for her. 'Johnny says Papa ought to buy a row of houses in one of the old streets and pull them down and put up new ones in the London style.'

'What is the London style?' I handed Eliza the ribbons for her garters.

'If you do not know, I cannot stir to tell you.' She wrapped a ribbon around her stockinged thigh, tied it and made a face at the knot. 'And we are to despise Liverpool.'

'How so?'

'Because we are against it, out of envy. Liverpool men make money hand over fist, Johnny says, because they have the sense to be in the African trade and the plantations. Mr Barfield's family has a sugar plantation in Jamaica. But Chester men only make gloves and hats. They think they are above Liverpool men, but they are not.' Eliza said testily, 'Does that answer your question?'

'Why are you so grumpy?'

She pretended to concentrate on the tying of the second garter.

I said, 'Are you going away to school?'

Eliza tugged at the garter and the knot broke down.

'You *are* going away aren't you?'

'I am not to say.'

'What about Miss Broadbent?'

'Do you know, Smith, that you must not speak to me in such a bold manner. I am your mistress now.'

Despite her lofty tone, Eliza's haughtiness was unconvincing. She looked down at her foot where the unsecured stocking had wilted and then caught my eye. We grinned at one another out of shared anxiety at the onset of change. It would be hard for Eliza to be sent away from home. And I worried about the repercussions of Eliza's departure from Sedge Court for Miss Broadbent and for me.

★

I was always very fond of the summer house. It is constructed on the plan of a pentagon, which lends it the appearance of a temple, and it did seem like a sanctuary of sorts to me. A few days after learning that Eliza was to be sent away, I was dispatched there to work on Mrs Waterland's design. Her drawing had been transferred to a grid scored on the walls and it was my task to affix the shells. I was elevated for the purpose on a trestle that Mr Otty had set up between two ladders. The glue was kept warm in a copper pot on a brazier below. My arms ached from the continual reaching up to press the shells on to the outline of the frieze, but I was not sorry to be out of the way of the basement, which was in a commotion preparing for the arrival of a chum of Johnny's – the fellow Eliza had mentioned with his aristocratic connections.

Every so often I paused and rested my gaze on the leafless trees in the surrounding orchard, the tousled skeins of their branches imprinted against a metallic sky. The trees seemed to lean in, whispering among themselves as I worked. I remember hearing the unmistakable *tee-hee-hee* of a wood-pecker laughing at its own joke and then the crunch of footfalls approaching on the gravel path. I hoped it might be Abby, bringing me something to eat. The feeble sun had clam-bered over its meridian and I was hungry. I patted another shell into place and deposited the glue brush in its pot.

I was wiping my hands on my apron when a sensation of being watched rippled across my back. I swung around to find a slender, spry figure leaning against the frame of the portal with straw-coloured hair rushing away from a pale face. One hand rested on his hip, the other swung a cane.

I almost did not recognise Johnny Waterland, the saviour of Sedge Court. He was turned out very burnished in a brilliant white neck-cloth, a black satin waistcoat, whose silver lacing winked at me, and a mustard riding coat, and yet he reminded me of nothing so much as fantome corn in the umber. Do you know the phrase? It is an expression we use in Cheshire. It means weak corn that has been planted in shade and grows up overlong in the stalk.

I offered a curtsy.

Johnny Waterland lolled, his cane oscillating ever slower like a retarded pendulum. The woodpecker laughed again. Johnny stayed without a word and yet he did not seem lost in his own silence as a person is when under the spell of contemplation. His lingering had something insolent in it, as if it were meant to unsettle. All at once he pivoted on his heel and faded away among the trees. He left behind a surprisingly forceful emanation of his presence.

I climbed down from the trestle just as Mr Otty and Croft arrived, followed by Abby with Dasher on his lead and a basket over her arm. She handed me a slice of pie wrapped in a cloth, and I sat down on a small stone bench near the portal to eat it, while Mr Otty and Croft shifted the trestle. I pushed aside the stems of a milkweed plant that had overpowered the bench and noticed that an early caterpillar was trimming a leaf of the plant to its liking.

Abby said, 'There is a pickled egg and all if you want.' At the squeal of ladders being dragged across the flags of the summer house, she poked her head through the portal and said, 'What is the meaning of that?'

I explained that the mistress had made a design of the underneath of the sea and that the cockleshells represented the crests of waves. Abby frowned. I wondered if all Welsh people were like her – not very impressed by anything much.

I said, 'Actually, Mrs Waterland found those shells in Wales.'

'Where are they from then?'

'She says from Gwynedd.'

'I am from Gwynedd, though. Near as. There is a world under water close by that place. Mayhappen that is where she took the idea.'

I grinned. 'With the gentlemen riding around on their seahorses and the ladies tucking into their sea salads.'

Abby said, 'Are you lampooning me?'

'No, I am not. I am conjuring a scene.'

She shot me with a flat-eyed look.

Mr Otty shouted, 'Go about your work now, wench. You have stayed out too long.'

'All right, Mr Otty, I will be gone in a minute.' Abby tossed her head and said, 'Don't you know it is not a joke, Mary Smith. There are lands under the sea, where people live as we do, only better, you know, and they are free to caper about as they wish. My mother told me so.'

As the light began to fail, I caught a whiff on the air of tarry smoke – the lamps had been lit in the courtyard – and judged it time to leave off my work. I followed the path through the orchard and entered the kitchen garden by the door in the south wall. The layout of the farm was reflected in miniature in the garden's design of repetitive rectangles and I strode past the diligent beds of herbs and vegetables like a giantess. To my left was the village of the poultry, its inhabitants asleep, and to my right the spaniels running up and down outside their kennels. I knelt at the dogs' enclosure and they pushed their snuffling muzzles at me. With one hand I rummaged their foreheads while the other rested on one of the kennel's bars.

All at once I felt a faint vibration pass through the metal and the strings on the empty trellises behind me seemed to hum. The dogs pricked up their ears. At the sound of a distant rumble, they began to bark. Affronted hens appeared in the dim openings of the poultry house, their squawking adding to the racket of the dogs. As I reached the wicket gate leading to the house, an uproarious four-wheeled chaise hurtled into the courtyard. The demented whooping of its postilion brought Mr Otty and Croft running from the coach house, while I took a step backwards into the shelter of the garden.

The horses pulled up with a gasp and the postilion, who was untypically ponderous of figure, slid from his saddle. The door of the still-shuddering chaise sprang open and Mr Otty found himself bowing before two sheepish passengers tricked out in orange and purple livery. The jape became clear then – the postilion was the gentry and the passengers his servants. I instinctively did not like this person, who had brought his pandemonium with him.

Johnny Waterland sauntered from the house into the pool of dirty yellow light thrown by the lamps and greeted the postilion with a mocking bow and a volley of laughter. They strutted through the back entry of the house like dandycocks both.

On coming indoors I found Johnny and his friend Barfield dallying in the servants' hall. Rorke was hovering at Johnny's side in joyful subjugation and they were urging the friend to quaff a tankard of ale. The tankard was a trick one and Barfield was duped by its concealed aperture. The ale deluged his chin and his neck-cloth instead of his mouth, but he was game for the prank and guffawed loudly about it. I remember thinking that he looked as if he had been constructed from the parts of many different forebears, his bulbous head and fleshiness at odds with his pointy nose and girlish eyebrows. At once I made for the laundry, but not without catching the vulpine gleam of his teeth as his eye lighted on me.

PART THREE

The *Seal*, The River Avon, Bristol

April, 1766

The odour of brine and mud clings to my waterlogged hair and there is a smell of resin too, seeping from the rough planks on which I sprawl. My drenched skirts are twisted about my legs. My torso aches as though it has been pummelled. A consequence of my impact with the water. I remember tumbling head over heels in the depths. And shooting to the surface with a gasp. Someone passed a rope under my arms and pulled me through the water. Bruises smart where I bumped against the hull as I was hauled upward.

I blink away salt water and open my eyes. Above me looms a tower of huge, dark sails and beyond them a bronze sky and copper-tinged clouds.

I am on a boat. I have never been aboard one before.

I struggle to come to sitting, energised by a rush of elation. I am on the *Seal*. I have succeeded in my escape.

'You idiot. You might have drowned.'

I turn my head to find a tall, broad figure silhouetted against the grainy light of the early-evening sky. His face is in shadow but I have the impression that he is glaring at me from beneath his slouch hat. His dark hair hangs untied and brushes the epaulettes of his coat. The coat is a buff colour with dark blue facings. It looks like a military uniform, but not one that I have seen before. An indistinct memory flutters in my mind. Am I in the presence of someone I ought to recognise? But I do not know this surly individual.

I ask his name and he retorts in a tone that is quick and hard, 'More to the point, who the devil are you? And what makes you take a leap as bold as bedamned at my vessel? Now I must go to the trouble of putting you off.'

'No! I beg you, sir.' As I lurch to my feet I feel the cut of the wind and a spasm of shivering overtakes me. 'My name is Mary Smith. I was brought to this desperate play because of your ship's boy, Terry Madden. He stole my money – and I am determined to have it back.'

'Madden is no longer a hand on this vessel.' The captain's cold eyes glint in a dark face and I have no way of knowing if he is telling the truth.

'He told me that he belonged to the *Seal*. Then he cut my purse.'

'And is paying heartily for it, I warrant, since we have not seen hide nor hair of him.' The captain's attention lofts towards the rigging and he adds without apparent interest, 'He was likely taken by a press gang for all his brightness, while he was drinking up your coin.'

'Sir, I was bound for France, but now that I am robbed I cannot get my fare. Let me work my passage on board your ship. I am handy for any kind –'

He cuts me off with, 'I have no accommodation to offer, madam,' and turns towards the stern.

'Why bother to save me then?' I shout with a flash of anger – or fear. Those two emotions are always mingled in me.

He offers me no other reply than a look of scorn, but it is

eloquent enough. He calls to the helmsman, 'Mr Guttery, when we come alongside our friends at Marsh dock, will you rustle them up with their wherry, which may return this lady to shore.' Then he shouts, 'Mr Robinson, do not let the wind back out of it!' He is looking up at the luffing edge of the mainsail. A sailor in a short jacket and wide trousers hastens to tighten the sheet. He owns the beefy shoulders and barrel chest of those who work the canvas.

As the boat bounds forward, I stagger to keep my balance, and the captain barks at me, 'Will you hold on to the binnacle and stay there!' He points at a wooden box mounted on a pedestal that stands a few feet before the helm and I steady myself against this article, this 'binnacle', whatever it is, perhaps a housing for the boat's compass, while the cutter skims the surface of a broad channel.

The captain removes from his coat a spy-glass and raises it to his eye.

Despite the chill in the air, sweat breaks out on my upper lip and I have the sensation of things slipping inside. I sink beside the binnacle. Has the shock of my fall arrived belatedly to play out its repertoire of blanchings and tremblings? But I know that it is not the leap into the water that accounts for my sudden state of distress.

It is the sight of the spy-glass; just that.

There was another spy-glass. A cunning glass. It was an instrument that belonged to Eliza's second cousin Arthur Paine. It was an irregular kind of telescope that he called a jealousy glass.

I crouch at the binnacle, watching as the channel we are navigating grows wider. There are lanterns in the distance delineating the shores of the river. They seem to be receding at quite a pace.

I do not know why the thought of the jealousy glass upset me so much just now. There is nothing very mysterious about the thing. It works by means of a slanted mirror. The mirror lets the viewer eye one object while giving the appearance of studying another – a useful function for a suspicious lover, which is how the glass got its name, no doubt. Mr Paine did not enlighten us on that point, but I wondered if he had employed the glass in relation to his wife. Mrs Paine is only ever to be found where Mr Paine is not – this isn't gossip; it is common knowledge – and one senses his chagrin at that division.

Now the *Seal*'s hands are going at their work with greater urgency. There are perhaps ten or twelve crew that I can see, not counting the helmsman. Their appearance is uniformly nefarious. They are dressed in ticking waistcoats and tarred trews, which appear to be stitched from old sails, and they carry sheathed knives in their belts. I glance down at my own battered ensemble. This damp and dirty outfit was once my best gown, have I mentioned that? I used to be very pleased with it. I remember smoothing the skirt as I . . .

As I walked across a square!

I am beginning to remember.

I was on my way to a soirée. In London, surely.

When was it? My mind scrambles after the scrap of recall. If I count back the hours, it was perhaps only three or four days ago. I was walking across Soho Square towards an assembly house. We were going to watch a show. And Eliza brought along the jealousy glass, I remember that now. Mr Paine was in charge of the show's effects – a storm. Thunder and lightning. He had been steered to the undertaking by Johnny Waterland.

I suck in my breath.

Johnny is dressed in his violet coat. In that case it was the evening of his death.

My heart begins to thud. With a great effort of will I try to control my emotions and to face the scene in my head. The soirée was one of Johnny's money-making schemes. He has – he had – fingers in many pies. He had been impressed by the thunder machine when Mr Paine showed it off at Weever Hall last summer and had seen the machine's commercial potential at once as a popular entertainment and also perceived Arthur Paine's weakness. Mr Paine craves recognition. That is how Johnny would have persuaded Mr Paine, who reputes himself to be a lofty man of science, to involve himself in a show that was beneath his dignity and alien to his nature. It was a wanton show. And of course Arthur Paine would not have been difficult to persuade. He has always held Johnny Waterland in high regard. Johnny was a man about town. He knew how to generate admiration even if it were based on nothing. I can understand how Mr Paine, whose applications to the Royal Society have been numerously rejected, might find the applause of the rabble better than nothing.

It is very difficult to accept that Johnny is not alive. It was he who led Eliza and me to the assembly rooms.

I had never been to such a gathering. Dandies surrounded us, their faces powdered as thick as frosting and rouged in a swathe from cheek to jawline as if a bear had raked them.

There were women who wore their robes cut so low they exposed bright nipples. Others had traced the veins beneath their pale décolletages with blue paint. It looked as though the branches of mouldering trees were growing out of their black hearts.

Blackamoors dressed antithetically in white satin rushed about extinguishing the lights and the show began with an ear-splitting clap of thunder made by Mr Paine's machine. The noise was tremendous and the ladies in the hall screamed at every roll of thunder and flash of lightning. As the artificial storm raged, a naked girl sitting on a rock rose out of the floor of the stage and a master of ceremonies announced that any gentleman who was able to win the nymph with a kiss should be permitted to do what he liked with her. Save that the audience must be allowed to watch.

Why did Johnny bring his sister and me to such an indecent show? And where were the Waterland parents, you might ask? They had remained in Cheshire, I know that. They were supposed to accompany us to London, but the day before our departure half of the master's guts fell out of his arse, as Abby put it. The mistress said she was obliged to tend to him. Yet now that I think on it, the cataclysms of Mr Waterland's innards had become commonplace at Sedge Court and it was out of character for Mrs Waterland to stay by his side. Her usual style is to eschew the sickroom and, frankly, to eschew Mr Waterland altogether. Yet she insisted that Eliza and I must not delay and sent us off alone to London.

Eliza's mission was to cultivate Mr Paine, or his money, rather. That is what Mrs Waterland told me. This was at a point when desperation was in the air at Sedge Court, but still, the assignment was flawed at the outset. Eliza's parents had never gone to the trouble of sending her to London before, not even for a season in the marriage market. I could not understand why they thought it worth the expense at this late stage. It seemed futile to task Eliza of all people with soliciting funds from Arthur Paine. He is as tight as an oyster and her powers of persuasion are flimsy at the best of times. If cash was to be extracted from Mr Paine, why couldn't Johnny have performed the operation, since Mr Paine was of the opinion that the sun shone out of him. I wondered if there might be another plan hiding behind the ostensible one.

The wind is swinging around wildly at the water's level and the buffeting alarms me. I press against the binnacle like a calf against its mother, suddenly conscious of the *Seal*'s frailty. How can such a slender boat possibly meet the demands of open seas? What if we should encounter a storm? It won't be Arthur Paine's false thunder and lightning. I think of the blue sparks that flew from the mouth of the nymph on the stage at the Soho assembly rooms. There was no shortage of volunteers bent on kissing her, but each time a man lowered his face to her, lightning crackled from her lips and defeated him. That was the ruse. No matter how determined was the swain, he could not grapple with the electric nymph.

The audience went mad for it and Mr Paine came to our table at the conclusion – I was sitting with Eliza and Johnny – looking pleased with himself. I can see him dabbing at his shiny face with a handkerchief as big as a flag.

Eliza shrieked, 'Upon my soul, I was terrified by the lights and the noise!' and Mr Paine said that it was all accomplished by friction and the cooperation of vapours and electricity. He said the subject needed to be a woman. Apparently we are more atmospheric than men.

I asked him how he had manifested the sparks and he explained that the nymph's rocky seat was insulated in such a way that an operator beneath the stage could charge her body with an electrical machine. Some other people arrived then to congratulate Mr Paine and Johnny on the show.

I turned away and, without thinking about it, picked up the jealousy glass that was sitting on the table in front of Eliza and raised it to my eye. I had forgotten about its trick angle. Instead of fixing on the orchestra as I intended, my gaze veered away and swam into a glittering haze that was the reflection of hundreds of candle flames, I realised, in the wall mirrors. All of a sudden, against this brazen background, a face shot up huge and unexpected. My fright was intense. I knew the horrible features captured in the lens. My blood ran cold at the sight.

In the gloom beyond our rucked-up wake, something has caught the captain's attention and he has ordered the mast lamp to be extinguished. And now a vast shadow falls over the *Seal*. It is cast by a high cliff that makes a miniature of us. We have entered a sublime gorge, whose walls rise to misty heights and provide a funnel for the wind. Its eerie moan makes the hair stand up on the nape of my neck.

The captain says abruptly, 'In fact we cannot stop to place you on to the wherry, madam, we are obliged to make haste. I will put you off as soon as I can.'

My heart leaps at this reprieve, although my gladness is compromised by the fear that we are being followed. My straining eyes make out a blotch beyond our stern that might be another vessel, perhaps. In any case, I am relieved to feel the cutter surge.

The faster we go, the colder it becomes, and I cannot help the chatter of my teeth. That velvet scarf is gone. At the bottom of the harbour now, I suppose. It is the third covering I have lost. You see how my protection comes and goes. I doubt that this captain is moved by my plight – he is more likely to be irritated by my quaking and gasping – but he commands a canvas-covered hatch under the long sweep of the tiller to be opened. There is another larger hatch, I notice, cut into the foredeck, which is straddled by a heavy machine for handling cargo. The captain bellows at me to watch my head and he dispatches me below.

I climb down the steep companionway into a musty hold where space presses hard. The view forward discloses a figure poking at a cauldron on top of a stove. He looks up at my approach, his cropped hat nearly grazing a swaying clutch of game and cured haunches fastened to a beam overhead, and if he is surprised to see a sloven doused in seawater materialise in his domain, he gives no sign of it. He has a tufty beard like a goat's whiskers and a stiff frock and his face is as creased as brown wrapping paper. With his wooden spoon he indicates a bunker. He is as close-mouthed as his master for he will not offer his name or any word at all. I take up a spot on the bunker, which is convenient for the warmth of the stove. I do not mind its film of coal dust. Under the restless light of lanterns that swing from the beams, I take in my surroundings. A strong smell of canvas, hemp and lard, with an undercurrent of night soil, carries from the cutter's forward direction. I glimpse swaying hammocks and bulky shapes which I take to be lockers. The remainder of the hold might be taken up by cargo if there were any.

The cook shuffles towards me. As he bends stiffly to lower on hinges a small table next to the bunker, I see, exposed by his tattered breeches, a shin and foot whose grotesque appearance tell of some ghastly mishap in the past. I dare say it is this impairment that has reduced him to a life below decks.

I ask what name the captain goes by, and he replies, 'What need you care?'

He is right about that. The identity of the *Seal*'s master is peripheral to my principal concern, which is to stay on this cutter until it lands in France. I am beginning to think this objective might be accomplished if only the conditions continue to prevent the captain from offloading me. My gaze strays sternwards to a doorless after-cabin – the captain's quarters, judging by papers, or charts, held fast in slats, and by some sort of instrument sitting in a gimbal on an economical table. A half-drawn curtain discloses the corner of a bed-place, and I turn away from the intimacy of that sight.

The tang of juniper cuts through the sweaty scent of stewing meat. The cook is grinding something in a tumbler.

Waves bang against the hull as loud as drumbeats. A faint vapour rises up from my drying petticoat.

The cook stirs sugar into the tumbler. As he passes me the toddy, the boat bucks violently. I cannot bring the drink to my lips. The lanterns squeak on their hooks and shadows swoop wildly around the hold. One of these shadows dives at me and I flinch and cry out. My hand flies to my mouth.

★

The squall has lost its force and my stomach has ceased its spasms, yet still I crouch at the rail. I am on deck in the lee of one of the *Seal*'s stolid little guns. Doubtless it has not escaped your attention that I do nothing but stoop and duck and cower. This probably says as much about my character as it does about my circumstances. I wish it were not so. I wish I were more admirable. I mean: I should like you to be proud of me and not because of my curly hair or my ability to dance a fetching minuet.

This is an uncomfortable sea, but the waves look beautiful. They prance under the moonlight like small white horses and every so often they join together in a long trail of spume. It reminds me of a stole of cream lace once favoured by Mrs Waterland. I see it surging around her like foam on the grey sea of her petticoat, while her hair billows from her forehead as though she were making her way dauntless against a headwind.

It is painful to think of Sedge Court and yet I cannot stop wandering its rooms in my mind. Every detail is still so present to me. But I know that the house is already beginning its process of retreat. With each day that passes, it will fade a little more until I can no longer claim it as my home even in my memory.

Mrs Waterland wore that cream stole on the evening that Eliza and I were summoned to entertain Barfield in the withdrawing room. When I was very young I thought it was called the *withdrawn* room, which seemed an apt description for an aloof space that was little used. The gelid colour scheme of garter-blue and chalk, the white marble fireplace, the lonesome islands of bandy-legged chairs and tables, the remote ceiling and its haughty chandelier, the acreage of parquet flooring on which the heels of our footwear boomed emptily, these elements conspired to produce an effect of absolute froideur.

When Eliza and I arrived we found Mr Waterland deposed upon the pale sofa. He was sheathed in a drab waistcoat unfashionably long, an earthy velvet coat and an ancient brunette wig – the overall effect was rather like a broken bough in a winter landscape. He acknowledged Eliza's curtsy with a cryptic clearing of the throat, while I kept my gaze low, which enabled him to overlook me.

Barfield was surmounted by a dingy wig with curls as fat as sausages stacked above each ear. The combination of his yellow suit, black facial patches and stockings of a weary green brought to mind a vegetable left overly long in the larder. He seemed determined to be a living lampoon of his class, all roaring opinion and pink-cheeked certitude. As soon as I was introduced as Eliza's attendant, Barfield expounded on his view that waiting girls ought to be got up in livery like footmen, else we could hardly be told apart from the quality. He spread open his arms, his limp hands hanging at their ends like gloves drying on a line, and grouched, 'I was at Shugborough this Christmas last and there was a minx of a lady's maid decked out finer than her mistress. I came perilous close to kissing her and handing her in to supper!' Then he cackled long and hard, giving us all an unimpeded view of the wet workings of his mouth. Johnny Waterland was lounging at the card table with an amused-at-a-distance mien. As usual, he wore his own hair, which he shook out of his eyes and smoothed a great deal as if he enjoyed demonstrating the freedom of it. I cannot remember what he was wearing. Something precious no doubt, and I am sure those buckles that had impressed Eliza so would have been scintillating expensively on his fine shoes.

Mrs Waterland rose to the spinet and played a brisk, introductory arpeggio that was the signal for me to seize Eliza's hand and lead her into a minuet. Imagine us, if you can, in the open ground between a card table and the sofa, with heads a-droop like a couple of cabbage roses buckling under the weight of their beauty, as we set off on our serpentine course. Our display was designed to impress Eliza upon Tobias Barfield and I was as tense as the high-pitched strings, excruciatingly attuned to the potential for a misstep. I thought it likely that Barfield's family would boil itself in oil before it lowered to a girl sullied by mercantile connections, but Mrs Waterland was determined to contract her daughter with an estate, and no avenue should be left untried.

The brittle music hammered on and Eliza and I stepped and bowed and exchanged wistful over-the-shoulder glances, as a girl dancing a minuet should, as if to intimate that we were slightly sorry about the recent death by duel of our twin admirers — and it seemed that we might come through the thing unscathed. But inevitably, the effort of keeping time got the better of Eliza. She stumbled and dropped my hand, so that the shape of the dance was broken. She said, 'Oh dear,' in response to my glare and began to giggle. It was absurd to allow her clumsiness to annoy me so, since I could not care less if Barfield were impressed. Perhaps what upset me was that she was at liberty to make a hash of things, whereas I must be responsible for the success of our performance.

★

At last I feel able to come shakily to my feet – and narrowly miss being brained by the swinging boom. It is the captain who has hauled me by the arm out of its way. He is not interested in my gratitude. He roars instead at the second mate, Mr Robinson, who is at the tiller – 'By almighty God, what kind of shoddy gybe was that, Robinson? The sail was not pulled in!' – and at another hand, small, dark and cat-like – I think his name is Dubois – 'You did not slacken the stays, you dolt! You might have cracked the topmast or the boom.'

The captain's appearance is very stark, a black shape imprinted on the softer dark of the sky. Bareheaded, he stands like a pylon on legs wide apart, braced against the rise and fall of the boat. His hair dives around and about like a collection of innumerable sail ties, his coat swells as he takes a couple of strides towards Dubois, who is fumbling at the boom. The captain seizes Dubois by the front of his shirt and almost lifts him off his feet. 'Drunk are you, by God?' I hear him snarl. In a few brief hours I have already learned that the captain is partial to sarcasm, and so I suppose I expect him to wound the blundering hand with a cutting remark. But he does not. He has walked Dubois back towards the rail and then in one fluid movement he hoists him up and throws him overboard. There is a flat, dead sound of a splash. I cannot believe what I have just seen. 'Break the mast,' the captain shouts, 'and this is what will happen to us all.' He turns on his heel – and catches sight of me with mouth hanging open, appalled.

He says, his tone rough, 'Were it not for the law of hospitality that respects the stranger, you too would be overboard, madam. Next time, close the hatch after you. Or must you baulk at that request, as is your style?'

★

The captain says, 'If I had a glass now I would drink it,' and the cook limps over with a bottle of wine and pours a measure without spilling a drop in spite of the pitching boat. The captain is dining at his table, while I watch from my designated spot – the little fold-down table next to the coal bunker. He looks up suddenly as the dripping Dubois slithers down the companionway and grovels at his master. The *Seal* has been circling this last quarter of an hour and I have been listening to the muffled shouts of the crew's efforts to bring the hapless deckhand from the water. Someone, I gathered, had thrown him an empty cask as a flotation device. The captain has been indifferent to the rescue. The lamp in his quarters throws his face into relief. It is as hard and steep as a cliff, with a steep drop from the cheekbones to the wide ledge of his mouth.

He says, 'Your watch is not finished, Dubois. Go above and see it out or you will not live to enjoy another, by God.'

I am heartily sorry for my own error of failing to shut the hatch, but I think that the captain has treated the deckhand too hard and when Dubois has hauled himself back on deck I cannot help but say, 'No wonder Terry Madden ran off, since you are such a severe master.'

The captain makes a sharp, expulsive sound that might be an attempt at a laugh. 'A dunking is nothing. I've seen a cannonball go through young lads like a hawk through a flock of sparrows and their bodies torn open from luff to leech. The wars of politicians, that's a hard master for you, Miss Smith.' He raises his glass to his lips and finishes it in one draught. His hair is prematurely streaked with grey, I notice. Seeing that my gaze is still on him, he adds with a wry twist of the lip, which seems to be a characteristic of his, 'Please do convince yourself of the quality of my claret, madam. Jim, pour her a glass.' Perhaps he very slightly regrets his sharpness, because he says after a pause, 'The winemaker is known to me. He is a good man, who does not rush his harvest.'

He withdraws to his supper and the contemplation of a chart spread out before him. I think I can discern a compass rose in the top right-hand corner. He wolfs down his stew without noticing it, and when the cook, Jim, has taken our plates away, the captain shifts in his chair, puts one long leg over another and brings out a pair of callipers and other instruments that I do not know. He seems to be calculating the bearings of the *Seal*.

I drain my glass. The claret is indeed excellent. There is a long French summer in the bouquet of it.

The captain's chin lifts in that abrupt way he has and at first I think he has sensed my scrutiny. I am only observing him so closely because, even with the English shore so far behind us, escape from my tormentors depends on him. There is no one else to bring me forward so I must seize the captain's strings like a child and get where I can by my proximity to him.

In fact he is looking past me at the first mate, Mr Guttery. He raises an arm and beckons the man to approach. There is something in the captain's lifting of his arm in that nearly negligent way in order to disguise the urgency of a situation, the hand cupping at the air . . .

The gesture strikes me with such force that I nearly utter a cry out loud. From the time I first laid eyes on the *Seal*'s captain I have had a niggling sense of an acquaintance with him. Now I understand why. I had seen that same unhurried beckoning on the strand at Parkgate when I was a girl.

Can I trust my eyes? Is the captain of the *Seal* the stranger who caught my attention so forcibly that day the master's cargo went under? Eight years have passed since then. But I am certain that it is he! I see him standing on the sands, I see the revenue men approach . . .

And yet, where is the rising tide of delight that so engulfed me then?

The man before me bears an identical physical stamp to that fascinating stranger, but he does not captivate me at all. If anything, he antagonises me with his grudging manners and high-handed attitude.

He has returned his attention to the chart. Won't he be amazed to discover that we have encountered one another before? To come so fortuitously into one another's orbit must signify a meaning – although I cannot tell what. But the novelty of it! It is a connection that might make the captain more disposed to help me.

But as I stare at his lowered head, I find myself becoming reluctant to say anything to him after all. Because I cannot predict his reaction. To disclose that I once watched him escape the customs officer – if this is, indeed, the same man – is nearly the same as declaring that I know him to be a smuggler. There is no advantage to me in that. He is a smuggler still, I realise. Why else does this vessel carry eight swivel guns and a magazine and muskets and such fine claret?

Mr Guttery edges by, light on his thin shoes, and by the time he has settled himself at the captain's table and loosened the buttons of his striped waistcoat, I have quashed the impulse to announce our previous encounter. Instead I stay fast on my bunker.

You see how I am learning to look out for myself. Well, isn't that the way of the world? Nothing must occur but I must ask how it will benefit me.

The captain and Mr Guttery are speaking in low voices with the air of conspirators. I cannot place the captain's accent – and I recall that was true of the stranger at Parkgate, too. At first I took the captain for Irish, but that does not seem absolutely accurate – in any case, did not Terry Madden say his master came from France? I must say that I am curious to know more of this smuggler. I can hardly know less that I do at this moment. He has kept even his name from me.

As I come to bid him and Mr Guttery a good night, I find the boldness to ask, 'Will you do me the courtesy of telling me what you are called, sir?'

Without lifting his gaze from his chart the captain says, 'I am called McDonagh. Now good night to you.'

The *Seal*, Open Sea

April, 1766

In spite of my fatigue, I lie awake in the shifting darkness. My rank, salt-encrusted clothes rub uncomfortably against my bruised skin, and thoughts and images will not leave me alone. Not even the very relative luxury of the captain's berth helps me to sleep. He insisted on donating its use to me, although the courtesy was offered in a most harsh tone.

I find myself rather satisfied to know his name. Captain McDonagh.

I keep going over my first sighting of him at Parkgate: his face takes my attention and holds it. He is in conference with a fisherman on the tide-line. In the distance boatmen shift the master's cargo from a barge to a lopsided punt. Captain McDonagh rows strongly in the surf. Captain McDonagh sets his sail.

He strikes me still as a self-sufficing man and one that is determined to come out of the way of harm. That is a reassuring quality, don't you think?

I continue to marvel at the happenstance that has brought us into proximity. The event cries out for interpretation, but all I can say is that it reinforces my strong sense of being bound by a chain of circumstances whose links I am unable to break. There seems to have been no swerving from anything that has taken place in my life. Is it too far-fetched to believe that my arriving at this spot here on the *Seal* has been decreed? Has Captain McDonagh been sent through time and tide to save me? And by whom or by what force?

Oh, stop, Em. What flagrant nonsense. Did Miss Broadbent teach you nothing in regard to imagination's overbrimming of good sense?

I try to heed her advice, but my nature loves the metaphysical. I am always straining after the immaterial, or listening out for a call, and yet at the same time I know that my hearkening is futile and that the voice I seek to hear lies beyond the frequency of human audition.

I must have slept a little, because I dreamed I was hanging on to the roof of a house in a flood. It has taken me some minutes of puzzling to recall the origin of that image, but I have nailed it down. It belongs to one of those rather admonitory Dutch paintings that hang in the master's library at Sedge Court. I must have seen the picture countless times without paying it any special attention. It shows a town half under water and a scattering of hefty burghers clinging to steeply pitched roofs. In the background a fork of lightning is striking an inundated church.

Why did I dream of that scene?

Because I have been thinking of Sedge Court, and of its library. Johnny and Barfield playing billiards there. Johnny scorning Barfield's shots in that deliberately listless tone he liked to use: 'How pitiful this fellow's game is. He must needs cannon, but instead he fizzed.' And Barfield mock-sulky, bottom lip outthrust, 'Perhaps I meant to fizz.' There was something ritual about their repartee. Johnny pretending to know it all and Barfield pretending to be hopeless. They were always figuratively leaning back on their heels as though to get the full measure of the ironic distance that gaped between them.

There was a brass stand in the library mounted on four clawed feet, half lion, half wading bird, oddly. It was a repository for walking sticks. I can see Mr Waterland bent over the stand examining first one cane and then the other, as if the world depended on his making the correct choice, while Mrs Waterland implored Johnny to treat his guest with greater courtesy. Johnny only made the retort that Barfield was quite stupid and minded nothing but fox hunting. He wiggled his fingers at me, pretending to be a bogeyman, and drawled, 'Watch out, wench, or he will uncouple his beagles and come after you,' and he called me to come to the table and make a shot to demonstrate how facile the game was.

I shrank from the invitation, but Eliza cried, 'I will do it, Johnny.'

Johnny ignored her tremendously.

He began talking to his mother instead about a money-making scheme. He and Mrs Waterland liked to discuss money. I paid attention to those conversations. I knew that many people were frightened of money, of the possibility of its loss, and I wondered if Johnny had discovered how to make money flow. If he had that power, Sedge Court would never be in trouble again. Johnny began telling his mother that he had been to see the dean of the cathedral in Chester. The dean hoped to raise funds for the church by selling a portion of its property at Abbey Square in the town. Mr

Waterland's eyebrow lowered and he muttered something about alienating the ladies with masculine talk, but the mistress impaled him on a pointed look and asked Johnny what he had up his sleeve.

Johnny wanted his father to secure a loan from the bank to buy the land. His idea was that they would build townhouses in the square or in some of the old lanes and sell them on.

Mr Waterland interrupted Johnny's flow again, dismissing the proposal as mere speculation.

'There is nothing mere about it, sir,' Mrs Waterland retorted. 'The improvement of property has made many fortunes.'

'Speculation is all that Chester is good for,' Johnny said. I remember he and his mother smiling at one another out of matching almond eyes.

Mr Waterland remarked that if the difficulty of the Dee could be overcome, Chester might give Liverpool a run for its money once more.

'Oh, the Dee!' Johnny turned to Barfield. 'My esteemed father is infatuated by the river, don't you know, but it is the merchants of Chester who are the difficulty. This is an age of commerce and they are behind the times. The guilds are too much concerned with maintaining their privileges to be capable of mounting a challenge to Liverpool. But Chester's bricks and mortar can be relied on to swell in value. Uncle Felling has shown that.'

I remember Mr Waterland swivelling then towards that painting of the doomed burghers and Barfield remarking with that poorly tuned voice of his that the picture reminded him of wily old Rotterdam.

Mr Waterland said, 'It is not Rotterdam, Mr Barfield. The subject is the drowned land of Reimerswaal in Zeeland.'

'Never heard of it,' Barfield said.

'Most of it vanished in a storm a long time ago. Its loss is blamed on the lord and landowner for his neglect of a creek that scoured at every tide. The town was left marooned on an island for several years until one day it disappeared beneath the waves entirely.'

I am plagued by nightmares. Someone stuffed me into a compartment and filled my head with stones. They kept grinding against one another and banging at my temples. My throat was blocked by debris and it hurt to swallow. I had the feeling that a storm had passed through me, leaving all kinds of wreckage in its wake: broken branches, smashed grasses, a meadow scoured. And then, too, I was sinking in a swamp and no matter how long and hard I screamed for help, nobody came to my assistance. I am afraid to close my eyes again. Has morning arrived? Down here in the hold I cannot tell. My stomach turns and I feel the gripe of nausea. An unpleasant smell of suet hangs in the air. It might have stolen down here from the pot they keep on deck for coating the lanyards. Or perhaps a tallow candle is still burning in one of the lanterns. I pull the berth's curtain aside cautiously.

It is still night, damp and everlasting. The captain is asleep in his chair, his hat pulled down upon his face. I creep from the berth, cesspail in hand, and climb awkwardly above. I mind to close the hatch. A blast of ocean air buffs my face. I can make out a figure at the helm and another forward on his watch, hauling out a line on a sail until it stands flat on the wind. How embarrassing it is to have to do my business in the open like this, but I manage it, grateful for the covering of darkness, with the bucket concealed beneath my petticoat. Then I let down the pail on its rope and rinse it in the spray. There is a terrifying beauty to the scene – a limitless sea of heaving black satin and flashes of spindrift under the moonlight.

Above, the enormous dark sails graze the sky and its breathtaking spill of stars. I notice a sailor swaying at the top of the mast. He is lashing the heel of the topsail, I think. I admire the feat of sailing this touchy vessel. She is forever yawing and pitching and even a landlubber such as I can tell that it is not easy to keep this unsteady creature under rein.

The sound of splashing draws me forward and I grope along the wet deck, wincing at the clang of my pail on the boards. Something luminous arches out of the water. A porpoise! A school of them of them is frolicking at the bows of the cutter, their silhouettes aglow with a pale blue light. What a wonderful sight! My gaze follows them until they disappear and then it swoops up into the starry canopy. I believe that when we see something beautiful in nature it lends us a moment of feeling completely satisfied, which is a state as rare as it is recuperative to most souls. It uplifts me to think that no matter how poor or dispossessed I am, the beauty of the world is not lost to me – and that, if I give myself over to the genius of these spectacles, I may enter, no matter how briefly, the experience of peace.

As if to make a mockery of my pretty sentiment, my stargazing is terminated most abruptly. A grasping hand seizes with great force my shoulder. Straightaway I strike out at the darkness with my fist – and I am mortified to find it has collided with Captain McDonagh's cheek. He releases me at once and we are both of us dismayed. He steps away from me and says with a stiff bow, 'Forgive me, madam.' Then he growls, 'Leaning out like that, you might have gone overboard.'

'I was only looking at the porpoises.' There is a tremble in my voice. 'I am sorry to have struck you, but you startled me.'

'Will you go below, now, please?' His voice is tight.

'The fish were lit up like flares, you know. I have never seen such a sight.'

He says shortly, 'That is not so unusual. Some creatures have the luminescence in themselves, but like most amazements, it does not last.'

His chilly demeanour provokes me to say with some indignation, 'It is not necessary for you take responsibility for my safety, Captain McDonagh. I am quite capable of holding on to a rail.'

He bends down to me and says then in a low but heated tone, 'Safety? For God's sake, girl, you have no notion of the word. Have you any idea what might have befallen you had your impulsive leap brought you among a less disciplined crew? You may treat my protection lightly, madam, but do not expect me to indulge your foolishness.'

In my berth, unable to sleep. Captain McDonagh's admonition lies heavy on me for I do indeed feel foolish. How could I have wound such a mesh of make-believe around that stranger at Parkgate? He and the captain may be one and the same, but there never was a luminary walking the strand that day. It was only a smuggler out for his own gain and, watching him, a girl who seems to have made a bad hash of things.

The past is all chopped up and I struggle to put it back together. The only certainty is that my thoughts, tethered to the place like a ball to its cup, keep returning to Sedge Court.

The House of Kitty Conneely, Connemara

April, 1766

Does the child remember at all her people at home? I wonder. The Blacks and the Lees and my sister, Mary Folan, although that sister has turned her back on me. The Molloys and the Maddens. The Naughtons and the McDonaghs. Galore of them gone now, one way or another. It pierces me to be alone, but so I have been for an age, ever since Mike died, God have mercy on his soul. You had Josey and your child. The dear knows you and Josey were a heart match. I saw the way his eyes would meet yours even when company came at your place and there was a conversation running all around in it. You could have blown the house sky high with that look. I was jealous of your happiness, I will admit.

It was to the stones I went today, Nora. I have a great fancy for that place. What a restless world it is up there with all kinds of sharp gusts shredding the clouds and the gulls hurling themselves about. I came to the stones and petted them as is my habit now and reminded them of their commission.

I turn, and turn again

I turn the dark mass

I turn the charm

I turn the spells

I bestow, I bestow a binding

On the woman of the hat and her daughter.

Let me tell you this, my friend: the daughter who belongs to the woman of the hat has been brought away and she is on the path to her doom. It is only right that she should pay the penalty for her mother's actions and cleanse the ungood. But you know that.

It is a taking and a redeeming.

While I was at the stones the thought of Connla McDonagh came to my mind. Away from us he was for many years but he comes now and then in and out by sea with the wine and the tobacco. You might remember seeing him on the strand when he was a lad, harvesting wrack with his mother, God rest her soul. That was before the great cold came and took his people.

There is silence from you, friend, I have noticed. Ever since I turned the stones. Your voice comes less and less to my mind and I wonder why that is. Don't you want me to bring our child home?

You never said so, but it occurs to me now that you never liked to share her affection with me as much as I thought. Isn't that true? My favouring of your daughter: sometimes you were kicking against it, weren't you?

I think you might have been a little afraid of me, Nora. Lookit, you are right to be so. I did things you never knew, I will confess that now. I made a false charm without a jot of power in it for you when the sickness came on your children and I made a charm against my husband with too much power in it altogether. Filled with fury I was when he looked with a soft eye on my sister and I asked the stones to turn Mary Folan away from him. From his face, from his eyes, from his mouth, from his belly, from his cock, from his anus, from his entire body. From his heart and his soul.

Perhaps you think I am selfish and that I bring back the girl for myself alone and not for you. But she is in need of a mother's love, and it would be hard to find a woman more gifted for the treasuring of a child than myself. Seeing as you cannot. She grips my heart, Nora.

It is not easy to influence events at a distance, but I declare to the devil that I will bring her to me and that fellow McDonagh will help me do it. He is bound to abide by my wishes, although he does not know it. In the roar of the sea his boat will hear my summons.

The Orchard and the Stables, Sedge Court

March, 1758

The day after Eliza and I had danced in the library for Barfield I was in a troubled state of mind. It was clear to me that Mrs Waterland had not been gratified by the clumsy manner in which Eliza and I had brought the minuet to its conclusion, but I felt weary of toiling to be agreeable. I might have appeared on the surface to be a meringue, but if anyone had looked into me, he would have found, in place of sugary froth, any amount of unsweetness, of resentment and envy lique-fying into bitter waters. I worried that before I grew much older, the effort of attractiveness would defeat me and my choler would be exposed – and what should happen to me then? I knew very well that Mrs Waterland owned numerous treasures that had once commanded her eye but now were shelved in dusty storage or banished altogether.

When I received the order the following morning to work in the summer house, the assignment seemed less a boon than a sign that the mistress wished me to be out of sight. I applied myself for several hours to the shellwork, gluing an endless number of cockles, and no one came near me, not even Abby with bread and cheese for my dinner.

I had no sense of foreboding about the tragic event that was taking place while I was pasting shells to the stone walls of the summer house. That, on top of everything else, causes me additional anguish and bewilderment. You have heard me speak probably almost incessantly about my alertness to little signifiers in my surroundings. Why did not an alarm ring for me then?

I did feel nervous on my own account, however, as I set off in the early afternoon to return to the house. I remember looking back over my shoulder at the summer house and noticing that its conical roof poked out of the trees like a witch's hat – but that was not the source of my unease. I had a distinct sensation of being watched as I walked along the path that leads to the kitchen garden. It winds through an old orchard with unkempt pippin and pear trees in a bind of ravelled branches. Behind them taller trees haunted the sky with branches that looked like skeletal arms.

There was a disturbance in the undergrowth that made me pause. It came from a thicket of coppiced ash that encroached on the orchard some thirty yards away. I scanned the trees, but could see nothing. I took a few steps and stopped again at the sound of a sort of snickering. I had the impression of vegetation being pushed aside. Then the insidious rustle sounded again, only closer to hand this time. It was somehow more determined as though a fox or a dog was snuffling about. I walked on, paused again. The sound was louder than a fox and it was no longer rustling . . .

He was not sneaking. He was barging through the trees, making straight for me. The postilion in his ugly livery. Except that it was not the postilion.

He – Barfield – stepped on to the path in front of me and my heart jumped so hard it knocked the breath out of my throat. 'Your servant, lovely,' he said, with a smirking gesture at his livery, and my flesh crawled. I dropped a queasy curtsy and sought to creep on, but he caught my arm. 'What, no how-de-do? Where are your manners, wench?' His humid breath smelled of drink. The pressure of his fingers frightened and angered me and I tried to pull away. He tightened his grip and shoved his hand in the opening of my mantle. I struck at his face. He grabbed my wrist and jerked my arm behind my back with such force I thought the bone would snap. He threw me down then and as soon as I hit the ground he sank on top of me with a crushing weight that made me gasp for air. I realised then that he was serious in his attempt to harm me. At once it was as if all the signs of life in me began to shut down. I felt very cold. Even if I had been able to scream, I do not think I would have done so. I think the thought in my head was to disappear. That if I seemed already to be dead, there would be no point in his prolonging the assault. I also remember thinking that I would do anything as long as it meant that I should survive the attack. I use the word 'thinking', but there was nothing cerebral about my responses. They were primitive, instinctive reactions of self-protection. He grunted something into my hair and began to rub himself against me as he fumbled at my petticoat. He pulled my shift above my thighs and . . . I thought that my ribs would splinter under the mass of him and I would suffocate. Then out of the corner of my eye I saw the movement of a booted foot. The boot wedged against Barfield's shoulder and I heard Johnny Waterland laugh, and say, 'Ain't you a crude beast, man?'

Barfield told him to go hang, but the thrust of Johnny's

boot forced him to loosen his grip on me. I sought frantically to haul myself out from under his bulk.

'Leave her, Barfy,' Johnny ordered in a tone that was almost disinterested. Barfield rolled off me and I wriggled away like an animal into the drift of dead leaves on the path's verge.

'It is only I am in the country and I thought myself to plough,' Barfield giggled.

I groped around for my cap and my mantle and found them lying rumpled further back on the path. They looked humiliated, it seemed to me, and I snatched them up.

'Tidy yourself,' Johnny said in his cool way, 'and be about your work.' He was looking down on me in a superior manner with his arms folded. Tears insisted on spilling over and sliding hot and stinging down my cheeks.

Barfield, dusting off his breeches, said, 'I only meant to have some sport with her, Waterland. I could not help myself. Ain't she a peach—'

'Shut your mouth, sir.'

'You see, though, how a fellow might be tempted by her.'

Johnny turned to me and arched an eyebrow as if amused by a jape. 'Run along now, Em. There is no harm done.'

The stunned expression on my face provoked him to add, 'Say nothing of this and all shall be well. It would be a sad thing to bring my mother's displeasure on yourself.'

At the time I wondered if Johnny demanded my silence so that Mrs Waterland's displeasure would not spill over on to him as well, because it was obvious to anyone that there was a bond of admiration between him and Barfield, but I came to understand that he was immune to censure in that household. As he was keeper of the keys to the family's future, his mother was bound to give credence to whatever Johnny said. He had nothing to check his actions.

I threw my mantle around my shoulders and found the strength to run – without a word of thanks to my rescuer. I had no stomach for gratitude. I plunged between the trees, but I could not outpace the shame that nipped, snivelling, at my heels.

I dared not face the house straight away. There was no one there to whom I could express my outrage at Barfield's offensive, except Miss Broadbent, but I did not wish to burden her. I ran through the wicket gate and pulled up opposite the stable, panting like a coursed hare. My eye fell on a low heap of straw scattered on the cobbles near the door of the stable as Croft emerged with a forkful of staled litter and turned it on to the heap to air. He ducked his ginger head at me and returned to his work. I crept to the doorway and leaned against the jamb with a hanging head. As I slowly recovered my breath, I was overcome by feelings of disgrace and humiliation. Croft was moving around at the rear of the stable under the low-beamed ceiling plying his broom in an empty stall. In the neighbouring stall loomed the hindquarters of our big-shouldered roan mare.

I edged into the stable and lowered myself on to a bench. The wide doors that opened in to the coach house were shut. The light was muted and the air was close. I breathed in the smell of hayseeds and dust and powdery brickwork. A ladder positioned in the middle of the stable led to the hayloft – a place I regarded as a refuge. In the past I had hidden there behind a rampart of hay when I did not feel like bowling a hoop with Eliza or knocking down her skittles.

I raked traces of dried leaf from my hair and pulled on my cap. I listened to the rasping of Croft's broom on the planks and gradually my trembling abated.

Croft towed his sweepings towards the door and cast them out with a flourish. He hung the birch broom on a hook next to the bench where I was sitting and said, 'Beg pardon, miss, will tha give me that hayband? I must brush the mare.' Croft's linen frock was grimy, his breeches frayed at the knees. I found his presence reassuringly benign, his round face as wholesome as an apple. I climbed to my feet. I had been sitting below a honeycomb of cubby-holes in the wall where brushes and lanterns and other tackle were stored.

I said, 'If you please, Croft, may I groom her?'

Croft rocked back on his patched clogs. 'That would be a right mollocky task for a lady's maid.'

'I have no objection to it.' I untied my mantle.

He rubbed at his cheek with a knobbly hand.

I said, 'Do not fret. I will mind what I am doing.'

Croft regarded his fingertips with surprise as if his freckles had come off on them. He wiped his hand on his frock and said, 'Mind tha dunna smudge thyself then.'

The mare was a mild horse, standing about sixteen hands high. She was steady on a halter attached to a ring fixed on the side of the stall. With long, even strokes of the hay-band, I smoothed her milky brown flanks, while in the adjacent stall Croft cleaned out the oat drawer. After some time the mare harrumphed and looked at me with a sideways eye as if to say, Unless you ease up on the polishing, miss, I am in danger of becoming transparent. I left off the hay-band and she allowed me to rest my cheek against her glossy coat. Presently Croft peered over the stall's divider, swiping at the carroty hair plastered on his forehead. He said, 'Heck, it be desperate muggy in here, ain't it, miss?'

I dipped my knees so that I could look up into the space above the hay-rack. 'No wonder,' I said. 'The pitch hole is shut.'

'That is strange.' Croft's brow furrowed. 'Here is me thinking I did open it when I got up.'

I patted the roan's flank. 'I will slip up to loosen the vent and throw down some hay at the same time.'

'There is no need, miss, I will do it.'

But I, reluctant to leave the stable, was already heading towards the ladder. In a trice I climbed the rungs and raised the trapdoor, which flopped on to the floor of the loft with a thud and a puff of dust. I pressed the palms of my hands on the floorboards, ignoring the dart of pain in the arm that Barfield had wrenched, and hauled myself through the opening.

I think that even as I breasted the planked floor I was aware of something abnormal in the stillness of the loft.

The first thing I saw was a big rectangle of white sky framed by the window in the loft's north wall. The contrast between the flaring light and the dimness below made me blink. The frame of the window moved on a pivot and it was opened by a cord running over a pulley in the ceiling and fastened by means of another cord. The reason for the stuffiness in the stable was at once apparent.

Miss Broadbent had closed the pitch hole and then the window, too. She had closed the window by looping the cord around her neck so that as she fell forward she was hanged by her body weight.

There is a stone angel in the churchyard at Great Neston, which I have often noticed. The angel kneels on a grave, slightly leaning forward, wings folded, its gown besmirched by time and the elements. Miss Broadbent was kneeling too or crouching, suspended, sunk into her mournful petticoats. She was listing forward as if in supplication, her arms dangling, only the cord twisted around her neck preventing her from slumping to the floor. The terrible truth of the ligature could not be denied. She was dead – and, shocked as I was, I had to assume by her own hand.

I became practical. I ran to the wall where the rakes and pitchforks hung. I stared at them, trying to recall what I had come for. Oh, a sickle. Its blade looked in need of whetting – but it severed the cord clean enough. At once Miss Broadbent toppled against me, her chin dipping abjectly on her chest, and the window banged open. Cool air rushed into the loft.

I lowered Miss Broadbent gently to the floor – she was as light as a husk – and touched her cheek. It was cold and blue. Her lid was half shut on a bulging eye that I could not look at. I chafed her hands, even though I knew it was useless. Of course they would not come warm. From below came the pitter-patter of rain falling. That made no sense at all, unless Miss Broadbent and I were on the heavenly plane in the clouds where the rain is made. Then I realised it was the sound of Croft pouring oats into the scoured drawer.

I went to the pitch hole and put my face in it. I called down, 'Croft. Miss Broadbent is up here. She is dead. She has hanged herself. Please go to the house and raise the alarm.'

167

Croft gaped at me.

I cleared my throat. I could not seem to get any loudness or urgency into my voice. I could not get my voice to rise to the occasion.

'Tell Mrs Edmunds. Ask her what we should do.'

Without a word, Croft clattered on his clogs out of sight. I returned to Miss Broadbent's side and held her cold hand.

Presently I heard footsteps in the stable and the creak of the ladder, and Rorke's face appeared through the pitch hole. I did not say anything. He scrambled to Miss Broadbent's side and got a view of her face. He said, 'Jesus Lord.'

He ordered me to return to the house, but I did not care to leave Miss Broadbent alone. I was not ready to leave her. I wanted to know why she had taken this action without saying goodbye to me. I was angry with her.

After some time, Mr Otty heaved himself into the hayloft and informed me that Miss Broadbent would have to be moved and that I must go to the servants' hall.

I held Miss Broadbent's hand more tightly. 'Where are you taking her?'

Mr Otty said in a gentle tone, 'It's a dreadful business, Em, but things must be done now according to form.'

'But what is the form? What will happen to her?'

'She must go to Great Neston. The coroner will conduct an inquisition into the cause of death. They always do this when the death is unnatural. Let her go now, child.'

I walked into the kitchen very calm and stood by the table. Only hours before, Miss Broadbent must have passed by this table on her light feet and slipped through the courtyard to the stable. Mrs Edmunds called Abby to bring gin, and she asked me to tell her how I had found Miss Broadbent. She and Hester leaned close to me with an air of expectation.

I did not want to speak about the scene in the hayloft. I said that I expected Mrs Waterland would want to talk to me, but Mrs Edmunds said, 'Her upstairs has plenty enough to occupy her now. It is a pity that Miss Broadbent could not wait until the young master's guest had gone.'

Abby brought the glass of gin. Mrs Edmunds took it from her and handed it to me. I put the glass down on the table.

I said, 'Does Eliza know?'

Mrs Edmunds said, 'Do not concern yourself about Miss Eliza at the minute. Go to the laundry now to your smoothing.'

Perhaps I looked at her then rather stunned, because she added, 'It will make you feel better to have something to do.'

I did not move.

Mrs Edmunds gave me a little push. 'Come along, you must shift yourself. It is better that you do not dwell on this sad event.'

She shooed Abby and Hester away to their work as well. I had the impression that no one other than I was afflicted by the demise of Miss Broadbent. The external drama of the death was uppermost in the minds of the household, but the woman at the centre of it was absent. It was as though she had fallen between the cracks.

In the laundry I loaded the iron with a fire slug and smoothed a sheet or a shift, I do not remember which. Eventually I heard cartwheels grinding on the cobbles. By scrambling on to the ironing table I was able to peer through the lower pane of the laundry window. One of the farm labourers was at the reins of the dray that was used for fetching coal and transporting grain to the mill. Beyond the dray, I saw Mr Otty backing out of the stable in a bent-over position. He was at one end of a burden and a man I did not know, who was wearing a black hat, was stooped at the other end. They were carrying between them a shape wrapped in a winding sheet, which they laid on the bed of straw on the back of the dray. The sight filled me with horror, but I did not weep over it. Despite the evidence before my eyes, I felt that to surrender to tears was to allow the actuality of Miss Broadbent's death.

Twilight arrived, and with it came Abby to the laundry with a bowl of soup, which I could not face, and a candle. Uncharacteristically, she went away without saying anything. I took her silence badly. Could she not think of a single sympathetic remark about Miss Broadbent? I sat before the fire, my ironing long since finished. It seemed that I was in a state of sequestration, but I did not care about that. I preferred to be apart. I was the only person in the house who had loved Miss Broadbent and I wanted the story of her dying to belong me, not to be bandied about the kitchen table. I kept imagining her last actions. She climbs into the hayloft. She winds the cord around her neck. I had the lunatic idea that if I simply tried hard enough, I could change the ending of her story.

But of course I could not keep her to myself. Her death had already passed into the public domain. It saddened me to think that the way Miss Broadbent had died would now take precedence over who she was when she was alive.

Later that evening I was called to the library. A large man with an unshaved chin and mussed hair sat at the map table in an island of light that was lapped by shadows. Mr Waterland was in attendance as an opaque figure in the inky background. Without bothering to introduce himself, the man, whom I guessed was a constable, ordered me to be seated. He announced that he had viewed the body of a woman who had been found hanged in the hayloft of Sedge Court and he was charged to ask me to tell when and how I had discovered her.

I described what had taken place. It never occurred to me to relate the event which had brought me running to the stables. Of course it was pointless to try to bring Barfield to account. As I spoke, I remember wondering why the constable did not write down anything that I said, but I assumed that the questions were a formality. There was nothing suspicious about the death. When I had finished, he regarded me with a sceptical eye. Then he brought out from his coat a leaf of paper, which he unfolded and asked me to read.

I stared numbly at the familiar italic hand:

To Whom It May Concern.
Please find it in your heart to forgive the manner of my death. I could think of no other way to alleviate my sorrows. It is with relief that I commend my soul to Our Merciful Saviour.
I do entreat Miss M. Smith to accept the books I have set aside for her in my closet and to read them in remembrance of me.
Signed Anno Domini 1758 25th day of March.
J. Broadbent.

I put the note aside.

The constable turned to the master and said, 'You see that the wench is unmoved by the note. Do you know why, sir?

Because its contents were already known to her. In my opinion she, and not the governess, was its authoress.'

At that moment the door opened and the mistress entered carrying her own light. She eyed the scene at the table with uptilted chin and lifted eyebrow as if she had chanced upon an unsavoury transaction that must be brought instantly to a halt. She sat down and placed her candle on the table. Its flame pulled the master out of his recess and exposed the constable's face to her gaze. 'Please continue, constable,' she said. 'I am sure you are anxious to be on your way.'

The constable imprisoned Miss Broadbent's poor little note in a stockade made from his heavy hands and offered that I had deprived the governess of her life in order to obtain the valuable books owned by her. He argued that I had written the suicide note myself, employing a skill with letters that was uncanny in a servant and a spur to suspicion. No doubt my state of dry-eyed hostility encouraged him in his belief, but Mrs Waterland, who had been watching him narrowly as he elaborated his highly approximate scenario, cut him off in mid-sentence.

'Sedge Court is a well-governed house –' she drew from the master a confirming twitch – 'and your conjecture is, frankly, an insult to us. Are you actually suggesting that this child made a felonious assault on the governess?'

The master coughed and said, 'This will not do, man.' His intercession startled me. Had he wished to see me gone from the house, here was a perfect opportunity. Instead, he said, 'Mrs Waterland has bred this girl to honesty. My word on it.'

'In fact,' Mrs Waterland continued evenly, 'great apprehensions were always upon our governess. Evidently she came to view her life as an intolerable burden and, wretched though the outcome is, we must accept that she is a victim of herself.'

While the mistress was speaking the constable raised his hands and seemed to push at an invisible membrane that he found to be oddly resistant.

'I will thank you not to dispute with my wife, sir,' Mr Waterland broke in. His tone was surprisingly authoritative and I realised that despite their private disagreements, he was bound to come to the defence of Mrs Waterland and that in any public performance they would present a united front. I feared then that Mrs Waterland's advocacy was only a matter of pragmatism and that her intervention was not for my benefit but for the sake of Sedge Court. Without Eliza at home to give meaning to my existence, my position must needs be shaky.

Having met with the Waterlands' repulse, the constable could do no better than take his leave. Mrs Waterland bustled me off upstairs in a similarly crisp manner. She made only a perfunctory expression of regret at the loss of our governess. Her reaction seemed principally to be one of annoyance. Eliza's emotions were similarly remote. When I arrived in her apartment, where Downes was unlacing her, I found her reluctant to meet my eye.

Downes seemed disappointed to hear that I was not under arrest. She said, 'Miss Broadbent ought to have accepted that she was superfluous. How could Sedge Court be expected to maintain her? And it is not as though the mistress did not try to help. Had Miss Broadbent failed to secure another post, there was no question of her being thrown to the wolves. I know for certain that the mistress offered to install her in a home for indigent servants if it had come to that.'

I said, 'Was Miss Broadbent asked to leave?'

Downes said, 'That is none of our business.'

'Eliza, do you know if Miss Broadbent's post was terminated?'

To my astonishment, Eliza shoved me in the chest with such force that I almost fell. 'How dare you?' she shouted. 'Do you say that my mother is a murderess!'

'Of course not.' I took a step backwards.

But she flew at me with flashing eyes and began flailing with her fists. I backed away from her, stunned by the violence of her response, and found myself turning a defensive shoulder to her.

'It is nothing to do with us!' she cried. 'It was Miss Broadbent's own stupid fault!' She thrust out her lower jaw and her bottom lip.

'Stand still,' Downes snapped. She jerked the ties on Eliza's petticoat and it sagged to the floor.

I said, 'I only wish I knew what brought her to that moment.'

Tears welled in Eliza's eyes. 'Em makes everything out to be my fault.'

'I do not mean to.'

'How should I know if Mama asked her to leave?' Eliza kicked her petticoat aside.

Downes said, 'It has been a wearisome day and we must thank God that it is at an end. Say your prayers now and go to your beds.' She shook out the petticoat brusquely, adding, 'Let this be a lesson to you, Smith. Mind that you do not despise your needle. A person born into the world without a fortune must needs employ her hands rather than her sensibilities.'

Eliza was already on her knees on the Turkey carpet at the foot of the bed, eyes downcast. As I joined her, Downes added in a tone of high righteousness, 'We have no entitlement to spend time in ways that do not benefit our betters.'

I bowed my head, asking our Lord to cherish the soul of Miss Broadbent that she might rest in peace – a request that felt hopelessly insufficient to the tragedy of her death.

The door banged as Downes went out, and immediately Eliza rose and burrowed under her blankets, keeping her back turned to me. I was too exhausted to try to effect a rapprochement with her. I left her there, a wrathful lump in her four-poster, took up the chamberstick and went to my cot in the dressing room.

I shifted around uncomfortably on the mattress. It was bumpy where the woollen flocks inside it had matted. The wind was whistling in the chimney in a maddening way, like a recorder being played badly, and I could not properly sleep. I rolled on to my back to avoid pressure on the hip that Barfield had bruised. As I felt the aching aftermath of his assault, a tremor of relived panic passed through me.

I stared wide-eyed into the darkness of the dressing room. A coal tumbled from behind the fire screen on to the tiles of the hearth, spitting sparks into the gloom. The line of light smouldering at the edges of the screen seemed to hint at an infernal entertainment taking place within. Was it true that Miss Broadbent would go to hell as a punishment for taking her own life?

Why had she killed herself? Was it because she had been asked to leave this house? How terrifying must the world be if hanging were preferable to being abandoned by Sedge Court.

I prayed to God, then, to make me indispensable to the Waterlands. I asked him to keep me under the protection of Sedge Court in any way he could find, so that I would not need to resort to extreme measures. Please let me not be discarded, I beseeched. Please let something happen to forestall that event.

In the days following Miss Broadbent's death I went about my tasks as usual, but I felt detached as though I were only mimicking my customary actions. I had little reaction even to Barfield's sudden departure. During sleepless nights I ransacked through my recollections of Miss Broadbent's behaviour, searching retrospectively for omens and for clues that might have portended her intent had I only paid attention to them. Why hadn't I recognised the desperateness of her state of mind? She had not the habit of despondency — that is what puzzled me so. Like Democritus, who cut up dead beasts in a search for the seat of melancholy in order to cure himself, I anatomised Miss Broadbent's recent conversations; but I was no more successful than he was at finding the mechanism of despair. When I did sleep I had bad dreams of nameless frustration: my feet sank in sucking mud so that I could not get to wherever I was bound, or my shoulders became wedged in a trapdoor that would not let me go either forward or back. On waking I would ask myself again: how was she driven to her fatal decision? I even wondered if it were something to do with her inquisitiveness about where I had come from. She had pressed Mrs Waterland about an admission number to the foundling hospital. Could Miss Broadbent have had a child once whom she left there? Was she my mother? (This is how wild my conjecture became!) But surely that fixation was a symptom and not a cause.

My only certainty was the knowledge that Miss Broadbent would not walk on this earth tomorrow or next week or next year. Her absence was to be eternal.

The verdict brought against Miss Broadbent by the coroner at his inquisition was one of 'felo de se', a felon of herself. As a suicide she was to be buried in disgrace at the crossroads of a public highway. However, Mrs Waterland would not stand for such a thing – she considered it a reproach to Sedge Court – and she succeeded in having the original verdict expunged. It was recorded, instead, that Miss Broadbent had died while of unsound mind, and she was permitted to be laid to rest in hallowed ground. The mistress paid for the internment, but it took place without ceremony late in the evening with no one present but the parson and the sexton. I was expressly forbidden to visit the grave.

Two or three days after Miss Broadbent's burial, I was awoken in the night by such piercing sorrow I could do nothing but sit up, hang my head and weep. I sat for a very long time, consumed by sorrow At length I began to tremble violently with cold – the temperature had dropped dramatically. As I groped for the blanket I had thrown aside, I was startled by the shriek of an owl. It sounded strangely close to hand, almost as though the bird were perched at the window.

I listened with an ear cocked and it seemed to me that the noises of the night were unusually loud. There was a pulsing sound, which I took at first for the wind in the trees, but then I was struck by the notion that it was actually the sound of breakers on the shingle at Parkgate. Of course, that was nonsense. How could I possibly hear the sea, given that the strand was more than a mile away? And yet the sound of surf chafing the sand filled my ears.

As I listened, I began to detect a disturbance in the rhythm of the waves, which lifted the hairs on the nape of my neck and sent a shiver rippling down my spine. I had the very strong sense that something was emerging from the sea.

I climbed out of my bed.

I crept into Eliza's chamber in great trepidation and went to the window. Eliza was still asleep, oblivious to the intense cold. The driveway was a blaze of silver against the dirty purple of the lawn, and the lake glistened like a single dark eye. The only signs of movement in the grounds of the house were the shifting branches of the trees and shreds of mist stealing along the driveway. As I stared at the mist, the blood began to pool in my chest from fright. I believed that an entity was advancing on the house.

I realise now that none of this was anything but a manifestation of exhaustion and grief-stricken nerves, but at the time I was convinced that a wraith was drifting towards the portal of the house. It seeped under the crack of the front door. I divined its excitement as it arrived in the vestibule. My heart was hammering so hard I thought it would crack open my ribs as the ghostly presence wafted up the stairs.

Then it floated into the bedchamber and all at once my

fright evaporated. My straining senses relaxed. There was nothing to be seen, no revenant, no shade, but certainly there was a presence. I remember the atmosphere became a little colder as though a window had been opened and I discerned a person-shape, an outline filled with tepid air that seemed alive. I suppose it was a projection of sorrow that entered the house – and yet, it gave me a feeling of warmth in the end.

I returned to my bed with the distinct sensation of being ushered there and fell asleep. I awoke the following morning in a wash of well-being as though – I don't know how else to express this – as though I had been not only loved, but *succoured*.

I dwelled at length on this incident but I could not wring a satisfactory meaning from it. It is absurd to say I was visited by a ghost, but that is what it felt like. And by whose shade I do not know. I do not think it was Miss Broadbent. I had wished fervently that something might happen that would fortify my position at Sedge Court. As a result of the outlandishly freezing temperature of that night, an ague became lodged in Eliza, which proved hard to budge. It brought her under the sleep of a wasting sickness for more than three weeks and made it impossible for her to attend Mrs Ramsay's Academy in Chester. The school term began without her and I remained by her side at Sedge Court. By the time she had recovered, Lady Broome was in need of a situation for two of her distant relations, and Mrs Waterland, who ever sought to oblige Weever Hall, engaged them as tutors for Eliza.

The *Seal*, The Atlantic Ocean

April, 1766

How raw the air is here. I am looking out on a sea the colour of iron after coming up on deck as a respite from the closeness below. Captain McDonagh has given me a blanket for a mantle, but still I feel the cold. Mr Robinson has just asked me to go below again. By order of the captain, he says, and I am not to come up until I am told. I suppose it does not matter. In any case it has begun to rain. Once more.

Now I am sitting in ignorance on the berth behind the closed curtain as requested, listening to the rain dash against the hull. It makes a noise like gravel hitting a wall. The movement of the cutter has altered significantly – we might even be at anchor. Something is bumping bulkily against us.

Five or ten minutes pass.

Now a scraping sound comes to my ear and an occasional shout of effort. I have the sense that a sustained and difficult undertaking is in progress. Is it possible that cargo is being brought aboard out here on the high seas? Perhaps so, for they are unbattening the wide hatch in the forward part of the vessel.

Yes, it sounds from all the thumping and scraping as if freight is being loaded. I allow myself to peek through a slit in the curtain, and spy dripping barrels being manhandled into the hold. Where have they come from? I have not heard the approach of another vessel.

I am very curious about what has taken place, but it is not until I feel the roll of the waves under us once more and am confident that the *Seal* had resumed her course that I dare to leave my berth. Jim is in the act of swigging from a bottle when he catches sight of me. He wipes his mouth with the back of his hand and offers me a wobbly salute. He tries to put on his habitual scowl but he can't manage it.

'What the dickens is that?' I am referring to a bright bundle of stuffs on the hinged table, which have burst forth voluptuously from an oilcloth bale.

'French favours, they are, and the master says you may furnish yourself from them.' Jim ducks his head at a bulky sack lying on the floor. 'And he says for pity's sake put on shoes, madam. Your feet are not fit for use.'

I can hear the captain's voice in that instruction. The contents of the sack are thrilling, especially in these dour surroundings. I find myself rummaging through a trove of ladies' footwear – satin and velvet slippers and fine shoes in jewel colours with a heady smell of new leather. The bundle on the table is stuffed with bows and feather cockades, silks, laces, stockings, gloves and handkerchiefs. How impossibly exuberant these items seem. I badger Jim until he admits that the finery comes from the barrels that have been brought aboard. He says, 'Silks and brandy and wine galore we have on board now.'

'But where did the barrels come from? You surely did not find them by chance bobbing on the ocean.'

Jim taps his nose and says hoarsely, 'Underneath the sea,

my lady, attached to ropes and weights in a spot that the captain has marked. We keep them barrels all snugly wrapped in oilskins and safe from prying eyes.'

'That is ingenious, but doesn't the liquor spoil for keeping it in the sea?'

'It was touch and go right enough. This time we were obliged to keep them down for fourteen days. Any longer and the wine would have turned and the brandy thickened.'

I have cast aside my fetid garments. Out with the hoyden. In with the fine lady. While the sea crashes and the wind keens, the fur collar of a grass-green velvet mantle sweetly tickles my cheek and soothes my raddled nerves. My chafed skin can hardly believe the softness of the cambric shift I am wearing. The easing of silk stockings over my tormented feet was heaven. And this gown! It is beautiful, the colour of steamed salmon with ruffles of mint-green lace hanging from the sleeves. I am nearly moved to tears by the change of clothes. The relief of them. The ownership of them. A pity that there is no looking glass here. Perhaps Jim may find me Captain McDonagh's shaving glass and – and –

And an alarming thought occurs to me. A mind with the least genius would have lighted on it at once. But I was stupidly mesmerised by the pile of trifles and my swanking in them distracted me, so that I missed their significance until this minute – namely, what contrabander would take on board French goods if he were on his way to France?

Doesn't the raising of these barrels suggest that the *Seal* is headed in quite a different direction?

Oh, Lord! You would think that I might have been able to

tell by the severity of the air and the increasing rain that we are not steering our way towards southern climes at all, but in fact are heading *north*. My hope of landing in France to a new life is dashed. How witless of me not to have seen what was in front of my nose. I would knock my own brains out if I had any.

I arrive on deck to find Captain McDonagh and Mr Guttery conferring at the helm, while belligerent waves try to come aboard. Naturally, it is raining. The captain catches sight of me. He lifts one shoulder in a shrug and says at my approach, 'At any rate you look less of a drowned rat.'

'We are not to land in France, are we?' It comes out as an accusation and a petulant one at that.

Captain McDonagh regards me with ironic weariness. 'Whoever said anything about France, madam? That was your own surmise. And do not bother to thank me for your costume. Consider it a reward for your charming company.'

'I don't care to thank you or anybody else, sir. I have had my fill of gratitude.' Good God, I sound like Eliza in one of her snits, all high dudgeon and hands on hips.

Captain McDonagh observes to Mr Guttery, 'For an uninvited guest this baggage is very full of herself, don't you agree?'

With a start I spy in the distance a headland and Captain McDonagh notices my remarking it.

'We are near land.'

'So it seems,' the captain says drily. 'When the light begins to fall I will send a signal to bring out a lugger to take you ashore.'

'But where are we?'

'Off the coast of Ireland.'

Ireland?! The rain begins to fall more heavily, clattering on the *Seal*'s canvas. I feel a stab of fear. Ireland is ruled by the English – our courts of law prevail there.

Captain McDonagh says not unkindly, 'Do not fret, you will not be stranded. I shall give you money so that you may make your way.'

It is only a remnant of pride that prevents me from sobbing into my hands. I have come all this way by terrifying land and nauseating sea only to circle back into the jurisdiction of the English crown. Everybody knows that Ireland is nothing but wilderness. God's teeth! Must I now hide in a bog instead of walking free in sunny France?

I think there might be a very faint trace of pity in the captain's gaze. He says, 'Indeed, Miss Smith, I will help you to come away.' It is the first time that he has alluded to the possibility that I am a fugitive. I suppose it takes one outlaw to recognise another.

'That is generous of you. I mean that truly.'

'And reckless too, for how do I know that you will not betray the *Seal* for your own interest.'

'I would never do that, I swear.'

Captain McDonagh fixes me with a searching look. His blue eyes have turned grey and unfathomable in this overcast weather. He seems to be satisfied by my sincerity, though, because he allows me the ghost of a smile. Perhaps he does not consider me to be utterly callow.

And then the wind comes to my aid.

Captain McDonagh is alert to the shift straightaway, of course. The air is swinging around to the north-east, blowing the *Seal* away from the headland. He looks up at the sails, cursing the wind for its contrariness, and says, 'God's blood, it would be easier to tear a fee from the hands of a lawyer than be rid of you, Miss Smith!'

It seems that his moment of kindness has passed.

There is no end to dampness below-decks, with mould everywhere. The bilge pump is often at work – I can hear its clappers beating now. I remain melancholy and anxious at the prospect, which has only been delayed, of being offloaded from the *Seal*. If Ireland is not a woebegone barren place, why do endless waves of its people wash up upon the shores of England? I fidget and fret with nothing to do. Jim is making bread, kneading meal, ale and barm in the trough that he has placed on the table. When I offered my help he only looked at me with a refusing stare, although he has let me stay near the warmth of the stove.

This boat is so confining. I miss terribly being able to roam about. I close my eyes and conjure up the beating wings of geese passing overhead in their chevrons, the hum of bees in the air and the soft smack of waves against the rocks. Ah, I am thinking of a place, which lies about five or six miles south of Sedge Court. Burton Point, it is called. The wife of Mr Waterland's wildfowler crony, Georgy Bird Richardson, was a wise-woman and I was sometimes sent down to the Richardsons' cottage at the point for a tincture that would appease the master's belly vengeance. I liked to stand on the rocks and try to spot the line of demarcation in the Dee where the water that runs quick and lively downriver is overcome by the lethargy upstream. But the border between the two waters was always invisible, to my eye at least. I dare say that the alteration from one state to another happens so subtly and infinitesimally it is impossible to know exactly where the flowing water turns to a brown soup until it has already occurred.

I am greatly troubled about how I shall make my way when I am thrown off upon Irish soil – if there is any soil. From what I have glimpsed of this western coast it is nothing but slabs of rock. I will guess that there are few openings for a lady's maid in these parts.

The whiff of sourness rising from Jim's bread dough reminds me of the frightful milk-water that Downes talked Eliza into using in order to take off the spots and scurf from her skin. Downes must have known that the curdled milk would stink – and that Eliza was quite likely to go to her dancing class reeking like a cheese. One felt concern for Eliza at such moments. Her lack of awareness makes her horribly vulnerable to judgments. I swabbed her face at once of the vile milk-water and repaired the damage with rosewater.

The necessity of Eliza's marrying was beginning to loom at Sedge Court at that time. I have no expectation that I should ever marry. I have formed the impression that when nets are cast in the marriage market, they haul up from the cold deep all kinds of distorted beasts. I was deathly afraid even then that Mrs Waterland might try to force a match for Eliza with Tobias Barfield. There was always a faint drone of unease in the background of my existence caused by the fear of Barfield's visits to Sedge Court. I remember an occasion when I was returning from Mrs Richardson's cottage with a tincture for the master. I had climbed up from the point and was crossing a field next to the road. I disturbed a pheasant and it burst out of its covert, bronze feathers flailing, and flew off low over the newly turned earth. As I watched it go, I heard hoof-beats and the rumble of an approaching vehicle.

I recognised the chaise. I turned away and hurried along the verge of the road with the idea of taking a bridle path that I knew was close to hand, but the chaise quickly caught me up. As it came alongside Johnny Waterland leaned from the window with his light hair fluttering. There was a lazy smile in his voice as he offered me a lift to Sedge Court. I shook my head and kept on, but Johnny ordered the driver to pull over. The chaise stopped a few yards ahead and Johnny alighted. He shot his cuffs with a flash of silver buttons and said, 'How thoughtless of me, Em. Of course it would not please you to share a conveyance with Barfield.' He placed a lightly restraining hand on my arm. 'Still, we are miles from home and it is a warm day for walking, by Jove.'

I said, 'The distance is of no concern to me.'

All at once he banged on the side panel of the chaise with his fist – the vehicle flinched and the horses whinnied at the scare. He roared, 'Barfy, you toad! Come out!'

I averted my face, but I heard the chaise creak with relief as Barfield disembarked. I was aware of his barrel shape at the edge of my vision.

Johnny said, 'Miss Smith holds you in abhorrence, sir. For your penance and to spare her feelings, you will walk to Sedge Court, while I escort her in the chaise.'

Barfield hooted with laughter and lisped, 'At your disposal, Waterland. As always.'

'If you have not reached Sedge Court in an hour, I will

send out a search party.' Johnny laughed. 'Come along, Em. We've got rid of that dog.'

I saw that I must ride with Johnny or be left on the road with Barfield. I allowed myself to be handed into the chaise – its interior smelled musty and faintly fermented – but I was uneasy. Johnny leaned back against the seat opposite, one sinuous arm lying along the back of the seat. I could no longer see in him anything of the overshaded cornstalk. There was a sheen on him that must have come from the savoir faire that he cultivated in London.

He said, 'You are quite safe from Barfield now. He knows he made an error.' He might have been referring to a family pet, some old hound that has snapped unexpectedly at a visitor.

I looked out at the fields. The shadows of the trees behind the hedgerows flung themselves at the chaise one after another as we passed by.

Johnny said, 'Do not be a little martyr, Em, you haven't been harmed. Barfy is simply a sporting fellow with a great liking for the hunt. You are not the first little doe he has brought down.'

I turned a cold eye on Johnny, but he only raised his hands palms upwards, lace cuffs drooping in a gesture of laissez-faire, and let them fall again with a rueful smile. He had his mother's rosebud mouth, but it was less suitable on a man. He asked me how old I was and I replied that I was the same age as Eliza.

Of course he could not recall his sister's age.

I said, 'Sixteen and a half.'

He seemed bored. He said, 'It's awfully warm in here, is it not?'

He loosened his neck-cloth and undid a couple of buttons

of his waistcoat. I pulled down the window pane and let in fresh air. It was eighteen months since we had seen Johnny at home. The household bemoaned his absence, but money still flowed in and nobody would argue with its bounty. An army of tradesmen had been renovating the interior of the house for months on end. Eliza's apartment was pasted with the latest wallpaper and lavender borders and she slept now in a mahogany bed hung about with fifty yards of glazed chintz. Mr Otty and Rorke were suave in new livery of blue serge coats and moleskin breeches and there was even a flicker of animation in the master and talk of digging canals and coal mines. None of us below stairs understood exactly what it was that Johnny undertook in London at the bank of Hill & Vezey, but it did seem as if we were in clover, and it was our young master who was the cultivator.

He said, 'Eliza does badger one so. You might point that out to her. Her recent letters are choked with peculiar military metaphors.'

'One of her tutors was an army man.'

'Ah yes, the tutors. I believe I am paying their wages.'

'They ride over from Great Neston four days a week, if the weather allows. They are called Captain Dennison and Dr North.'

'Relations of Lady Broome, ain't they?'

The captain and the doctor of divinity had been engaged as a favour to her ladyship. Captain Dennison was short-tempered with a face like a hunk of corned beef. He habitually wore a soldier's coat, but in an unexpected concession to fashion, he sported gigantic rosettes on his long-snouted shoes. He was missing his left arm, which had been shot off at the

Battle of Fontenoy in 1745. The sacrifice was not in vain because Eliza had been sufficiently impressed to remember the date of the battle, which was an uncommon feat on her part. Dr North had the pallid, damp look of a potato that has been peeled and washed. He hinted that he had once been a curate. There was certainly something starchy in his dress and in his nature. According to Eliza, divinity and pedantry were his strong suits.

Eventually I said, 'Mrs Waterland believes that many lessons germane to domestic life might be drawn from the captain's victories and defeats in the field.' For some reason this made Johnny laugh out loud. Perhaps my tone was drier than I meant it to be. I said, 'Eliza writes you so often because she holds you in high regard.'

'So I gather. I've no idea why.'

I put my face to the window. In the distance I could make out the squat tower of Saint Mary and Saint Helen at Great Neston, where Miss Broadbent was buried. The Sunday after her death the parson there preached a sermon in which he asserted that self-murder is by all agreed to be most unnatural and repugnant to the feelings of mankind. Did I tell you already that it was not until after Miss Broadbent's death that I found out her Christian name – it was revealed during the coroner's inquisition. She was called Juliet. Its poetical nature struck me, and strikes me still, as unbearably affecting. Juliet. A name that suggests an entirely different future had been intended for her than that of a lonely governess. No one came forward to claim her body, you know.

Johnny was saying something to me. I sat back from the window. I had seen enough of the church.

'I did not hear you.'

'I said, you are strange and unaccountable. Do you know, your cool manner is rather agreeable. You ought to teach it to my sister.'

I said, 'Are you going to throw Eliza and me out when you inherit Sedge Court?'

Johnny laughed. 'That depends. I might if you disappoint me. But you won't risk that, will you?'

Jim has left the dough to swell while he gets the beef boiling for the crew's supper. The wind wails and the waves boom. The sound reminds me of Mr Paine's thunder house and his manufactured lightning bolts and my heart gives me a knock. I am at a low ebb now. Here I am stuck, carried along in the dark hold of this miserable vessel towards a destination that has been decided for me. I cannot escape the feeling that I am caught in the operation of an unknowable network. If you can hear my voice, tell me that it is not so!

Weever Hall, Cheshire

June, 1765

Our journey to Weever Hall for Lady Broome's summer dance took place on a lustrous June day. By the time we reached the village of Tarporley on the western edge of the Cheshire plain, it was gone noon and we paused there for refreshment. Mrs Waterland had spotted an old walnut tree favourably contorted for shelter and she instructed Mr Otty to spread a rug and cushions beneath its branches, while I unpacked the provisions. We dined alfresco and afterwards found ourselves inclined to linger in the shade, quite toppled by the heat of the afternoon.

I excused myself and wandered a little way along a hedgerow, looking for a place to make water out of sight. I spied a convenient copse of hawthorn, where I hoisted my petticoat in privacy. But as I emerged from the trees I detected a quiver in the air that suggested the presence of some creature nearby. My imagination bypassed a benevolent explanation and rushed at once to the hair-raising conclusion that I had likely stumbled into the province of a wrathful bull. I fled to the safety of the copse and peeked out from the bushes at the surrounding swards.

There was no sign of a bull – but my eye did light on a queer sight in an adjacent field. Its far reaches had a blackened appearance, which I took at first for a crop that had gone to mould or been burned in a frost. In fact the darkness was due to an infestation of birds – crows, surely. Curiosity drove me from my hiding place then and I skirted the field to gain a closer look. Yes, they were crows, an enormous number of them, hundreds even, standing in an eerie silence. They gave the impression of having been called to muster and seemed to be waiting tensely for a proceeding to commence. I saw that their collective gaze was directed towards a shallow gully, where four crows stood apart. One of these four was cowering before the others in a scene that smacked of menace. It seemed to suggest that a trial was in session or that, in fact, a sentence had already been passed. But my presence had disturbed the birds. One of them looked in my direction with a croak and the next second the entire flock rose as one and beat away into the sky with a great uproar of wings.

I hurried back to report what I had seen – the others must have noticed the birds blotting the blue of the sky – but as I came into our encampment I had a change of heart. Crows were not a good omen. Better not to draw attention to them. One preferred to believe that everything would go well for Eliza at Weever Hall.

'There you are, Em,' Mrs Waterland said. 'I was beginning to think you had absconded.' She stretched slim arms above her head and her cascading bangles tinkled melodiously. 'Isn't it a glorious day? Baron von Boxhagen has chosen a perfect time to visit our little corner of England.'

Eliza was lying curled on her side with one arm draped across her face. She yawned from beneath her armpit and rolled up to sitting. I had rectified her eyebrows with the pincers in preparation for her appearance at Weever Hall, but she retained even in repose the fierce, beetle-browed expression which she had inherited from her father and had never been inclined to banish.

'Do you not think that von Boxhagen is a very comical name?' she chortled.

There was a jangle of jewellery as Mrs Waterland began to brush invisible smuts from her skirts. 'May I remind you, my love, that the baron has a very uncomical fortune. I will thank you to take him seriously.' The violent movement of Mrs Waterland's hand was at odds with the serene lake of her face, but Eliza seemed unaware of her mother's displeasure.

She insisted on saying, 'It is only that his name sounds like carpentry. And anyway, if he is so well off why does he bother to be a dull old botanist?'

'A botanical artist,' Mrs Waterland corrected. 'Like Cousin Arthur, the baron is an investigator of natural philosophy.'

'I am sure there is very little philosophy in Nantwich.'

'His father was acquainted with Sir Henry Broome, Eliza. That is the connection, as you well know.' There was a note of steel in Mrs Waterland's voice.

'Well, I hope the baron proves more amusing than our cousin. Arthur does lecture one so in the most dusty manner.'

Mrs Waterland said with a hint of weariness, 'The point about friends and relations, child, is not that they should delight us, but that they should be of use to us.'

I said in my mollifying way, 'I dare say we are all looking forward to Lady Broome's dance.'

'Oh, the dance,' Eliza groaned. 'I suppose I must play the charmer as usual.' Her sigh suggested Helen of Troy exasperated by the magnitude of her beauty.

'I wonder, my love, is that possible?' Mrs Waterland mused. She waved away a fly and looked off to one side, her face thrown into green shadow by the brim of her bonnet. 'You have made very slender progress as a siren.'

For three seasons Eliza had been produced at public assemblies and every private social in the county without attracting interest. No matter how rigorously Mrs Waterland polished her, Eliza could not be brought to a shine. She affected not to care about her failure as a belle and continued to direct her devotion towards Johnny, or to the idea of him, since he was seldom at Sedge Court, but her mother, as you must know by now, cared very much.

Half an hour later we found ourselves turning down a lane that led to Lady Broome's estate – a sprawling collection of farmhouses, farmland, gardens and a park, surrounding the manor house. Eventually the blue slate roof of Weever hall came into view and we passed through a wrought-iron gateway on to a wide drive that bisects an endless lawn. The lawn looked as if it had been ironed flat. There was a fountain in front of the bulky red-brick mansion hurling water.

As we approached the house we heard a loud bang that sounded like a pistol shot. I was severely jolted by the report. It seemed to reverberate from a reach far beyond the lawn and filled me with inexplicable terror.

We craned towards the windows of the chaise to see what had happened and glimpsed a gentleman rushing from the house, his coat flying. He stumbled along for a few yards and then fell to his knees and seemed to scrabble about in the grass.

'I do believe that is Cousin Arthur,' Mrs Waterland remarked.

A few seconds of anxious silence passed and then Mr Paine staggered to standing apparently intact. He was shortish and of a stringy make. He returned Mrs Waterland's wave and converged with us at the entrance of the house. He was dressed in an informal frockcoat that was, I noticed, nicely cut. I estimated him to be about forty years of age. I thought that his features, eyes wide-set and thin lips placed very low on a long face – sheep-like, to be candid – did not match his character, which was reputed to be cerebral.

'We heard a bang,' Eliza cried.

'Quite. A test, you see.' Mr Paine grinned. He held up a grass-stained ivory ball and a measuring stick. 'I shot a billiard ball from a window upstairs, but the experiment has come out imperfect, I must admit.'

He waded into a monologue about angles and percussion, but it was cut short by Lady Broome's butler, who conducted us into a marbled vestibule and handed us over to a footman in flashy gold livery. We followed the man upstairs in an obedient crocodile, passing through lances of dusty sunlight that struck the portraits of Broome ancestors ascending along the walls. The footman conducted us to an unwelcoming corridor on the second floor where the air was simultaneously clammy and stifling and showed us at last into an apartment. He drew the curtains in the tiny parlour to reveal old-fashioned leaded windows. We peered out of them and I was dismayed to see that yet more crows were about, convening around the chimney pots. The crows aimed black looks in our direction. With a sound like a page being ripped from a book, Mrs Waterland flung open her fan.

'Are you certain,' she said, 'that Lady Broome intended my daughter and me to be lodged here?'

'Quite certain, madam,' the footman replied with a bow.

'Because we are rather accustomed to the view from the south-facing windows.'

The footman said oozily, 'I am sorry, madam, but the house is full and this is the only apartment we are able to offer you.'

At that moment, porters arrived with our luggage. Downes immobilised them with her frosty stare and they bobbed about in the corridor, while the mistress decided whether to escalate the situation.

The footman enquired in a mildly threatening tone, 'Shall I convey your displeasure to her ladyship?'

Mrs Waterland retracted her fan and said with sudden nonchalance, 'Oh, there is no need at all to trouble Lady Broome with such a trivial matter.' She dismissed the man with a smile and said no more about it, but we all knew that our inferior quarters reflected Weever Hall's opinion of us.

I woke the next morning feeling out of sorts. I had been plagued by patchy dreams . . . a red haze . . . the sound of a shot and awful screaming seagulls. It was early and Eliza was still asleep. I got up and laid out her morning costume, although she was not due to coincide with the baron for several hours, and then wondered if I might dare to slip into the gallery where the Broome curiosities were displayed. I was very inquisitive about them.

Weever Hall is designed in the shape of an *H*, the bar of which is the long gallery connecting the two sides of the house where Lady Broome's late husband installed the souvenirs of his expeditions to the East Indies and the Americas. The under-steward had indicated its location the day before as Downes and I and other visiting servants were being shown the back-stairs and covert corridors that allow us to move from one wing of the house to the other without being noticed by our betters.

I recalled the circuitous route to the gallery without difficulty and minutes later entered it from the northern end. Pointed windows along the eastern wall let in a blush of morning light and I paused at one of them to take in a view of flat fields populated by cattle at graze. The mild countryside could not have been in greater contrast to the exotic preserves surrounding me. From the gallery's vaulted ceiling hung all kinds of stuffed creatures – birds and monkeys, a sea creature shaped like a kite, a shark with the head of a hammer, and two extensive serpents. Colossal armoires facing the windows teemed with oddities and kickshaws – fragments of stone, sinister carvings, ceremonial daggers, filigree caskets, branches of red coral, leather puppets on sticks and a cabinet devoted to metal automatons. There was an assortment of old-fashioned chattels in the gallery, too, Jacobean furniture and moody paintings in extravagant gilt frames, which I dare say the Parlia-mentarian Broomes had once confiscated from Royalists. I paused at a cabinet to gaze with appalled interest at two black-ened skulls lolling in an open-weave basket decorated with shells and tassels. As I stared at the tassels, which were constructed, I realised with horror, from wiry human hair, the murmur of voices came to my ear.

My retreat was cut off by the sudden appearance of Lady Broome herself. She was dressed in a wrapping gown secured by a twisted girdle, and her amber hair was packed into a gauze cap. She did not look absolutely pleased to be abroad before breakfast and she stifled a yawn as I curtsied. Her companion by contrast gave the impression of being an early riser. He was attired in a plain but expensive riding coat and a tawny wig that did not make a fuss about itself. He was handsome in a hearty, big-boned way and had the glow on his cheek that arrives after stiff exercise. Had he walked to Nantwich from London? I wondered. I had read that Bavarians – for surely the gentleman was the Baron von Boxhagen – like to propel themselves on foot and think we English soft for our reliance on horses.

Lady Broome stared down her fox's nose at me and said, 'Mrs Waterland's girl, is it? You are out of place, wench.'

I apologised for the intrusion and mumbled something about the fame of the curiosities and my eagerness to see them. To my surprise, the baron said, 'Does the collection answer your expectations?'

I replied, 'The gallery intrigues, sir. How could it not?' I could not help adding, 'Though to tell the truth, it is difficult to sustain the heights of amazement when so many objects compete for attention.'

The baron turned to Lady Broome. 'You see, dear lady, how the girl expects the collection to excite her emotions. This is typical of a lower order of thinking.'

It was pointless to protest that he had misunderstood my observation, since he was determined, I saw, to use me as a spring to his opinion.

He said, 'Gone are the days, Lady Broome, when we gaped at marvels like foolish girls and village yokels. In our reformed, scientific age, specimens must be collected in a spirit of enquiry and presented according to the rules of taxonomy. Allow me to insist, dear lady, that you clarify this mish-mash.' He dismissed the curiosities with a flick of the wrist.

Lady Broome said, 'You are very rational, sir.'

'Of course. Rationality saves us from chaos.'

I wanted to interject, But does not chaos belong to the world as rightfully as order? I was thinking of storms and fire and the meanderings of human minds, but I did not have the temerity to put this question to the baron and he and Lady Broome continued their conversation as if I no longer existed. He glanced about, coolly displeased with the arrangement of the gallery, saying, 'I urge your ladyship to relinquish this childish idea of the marvellous.'

Lady Broome gazed up past the creatures hanging on their wires – they stirred very faintly – into the rafters of the smoked ceiling. She said, 'My husband witnessed many strange things on his travels, do you know? He saw people who walked on fire and others who could make rain. Even magicians who cast spells.'

'Dear Lady Broome, there is no magic in the world but legerdemain tricks.' The baron's gaze rested on my bosom. 'Cosmic order is the true proof of God.'

'Of course,' Lady Broome added hastily, 'you will find no superstitions at Weever Hall.'

At Mrs Waterland's request, Lady Broome had invited the baron to take coffee in the breakfast room. The room looked on to a long garden where the evening's entertainment was to take place. In the distance carpenters hammered at a low stage, for the dancing, I supposed, and an engine watered the lawn. At the baron's entrance, which was briskly made, Lady Broome sprang forth with introductions. My presence went unacknowledged and the baron made no mention of having encountered me earlier. With my netting to hand, I took up a perch slightly behind Eliza's shoulder.

A gnomic footman tiptoed about serving coffee from a loud silver kettle on the sideboard, while opening pleasantries were worked through and then Lady Broome offered that she must attend to the preparations for her soirée. As soon as the door had closed behind her, the slog of the conversation got underway.

The baron made an observation about the topography of Cheshire.

A hush descended as Eliza pondered his remark, but before it could settle, Mrs Waterland prompted her with a terrifying smile.

Eliza said abruptly, 'What is the point of your coming to Nantwich?'

The baron placed his coffee bowl on the enamelled surface of the table beside his chair with a precise click. He leaned back and interlaced long fingers that called tendrils to mind. His wig sat gravely on the rostrum of his high forehead. He said, 'You know, of course, that a very fine botanist stems from Nantwich. His name is John Gerard. He planted an exceptional physic-garden in London and published important catalogues of plants.'

The baron's English was inhumanly faultless.

Mrs Waterland said in a silky tone, 'Oh, we are great admirers of Mr Gerard.'

'And you go about drawing plants?' Eliza broke in.

'I record them and their parts, yes.'

'I suppose it is as good an excuse to travel as any.' Eliza laughed as if she had said something witty. 'And have you a patron, sir?'

'My only master is science. It is on behalf of science that I attend to the task of systemising nature.'

'Heavens, that sounds important,' Eliza said, and made a face whose bared teeth and starting eyes were meant to convey mock-alarm.

Mrs Waterland was quick then to seize the tiller of the conversation and steer it away from Eliza's dangerous reef. She remarked that we were living in an age of great enterprise and extraordinary discoveries where gentlemen of learning, how marvellous, breaking new ground, frightfully rational, the triumph of pragmatism, and so on and so forth . . . While her mother flattered the baron, Eliza quaffed her coffee with the heartiness of a Viking recently home from a successful raid.

Mrs Waterland was saying, 'Inland navigations are the way of the future, so one is told. In fact my husband has recently purchased shares in a canal company.'

'Has he?' the baron said, without a flicker in his static gaze.

'The trick is to sell them on for an immediate profit before the canal is built.'

'I suppose he does not wish to own an actual canal. In England one buys imaginary things with imaginary money, one hears.'

Mrs Waterland laughed deliberately. She said, 'The canal will make its profit. It will charge private operators tolls for its use and the company will use the funds from the tolls to pay back the loans and pay dividends to its shareholders. But I am sure I have no need to explain financial workings to one as astute as you, sir.'

'On the contrary, I know little of these matters. I can only commend your husband on his purchase.'

Mrs Waterland said, 'In fact, it was done on the advice of our son, who has directed us latterly into numerous schemes certain to amplify our fortune.'

'Your family is quite populated by clever fellows. I am told that another relation of yours is the mastermind behind the entertainment we must enjoy this evening.'

'Ha!' Eliza snorted. 'Cousin Arthur is a bubble, if you ask me. The genius in our family is my brother, Johnny Waterland. He lives in London and makes huge amounts of money.'

The baron's eye skewed towards his coffee bowl and he seemed to find something amusing in it.

Eliza pressed on, 'Johnny is a banker and he has a townhouse and—'

'That will do, my love,' Mrs Waterland murmured.

'Is it true, I wonder,' the baron mused, 'that the English economy is fuelled by credit? What a marvel. Now I suppose almost anyone in this land can buy more than he can directly afford.'

The baron did not intend to stay for an answer to his question. Drawing a gold watch from his pocket, he flicked open its lid with a thumbnail and expressed surprise at the revelation of the time. He snapped shut the lid, raised a perfunctory eyebrow and said he had had no idea that he had wasted so much of our time with his tiresome chatter.

'Not at all.' Mrs Waterland was swiftly casual.

The baron rose to his feet. With the sun at his back, he looked like one of those treasured artefacts locked up in Lady Broome's cabinets. He exchanged a stiff bow with Mrs Waterland as if he were peering over a vertiginous parapet and said, 'You are too kind.'

Suddenly he was gone, leaving behind an effulgent afterglow: sunlight poured through the window on to his empty chair.

My thoughts swung towards Eliza and the hopes that had been minced by the baron's cutting condescension. But scarcely had the door closed on him than she jumped up and exclaimed, 'I believe he was much taken by me!'

Do you see why I esteem Eliza in spite of all her blockheadedness? I know she could stand accused of delusion, but there is no gainsaying the mighty engine of her self-belief. It does overrun her obstacles with a roar. I felt a mixture of pity and tenderness towards her, too, especially when I caught the expression of fury on Mrs Waterland's face.

The south side of Weever Hall gives on to a rose garden, enclosed on two sides by high sandstone walls and on the third by a long, shaded walk. That is where people had congregated, the local gentry and visitors from London, under lavish stars and a full moon. The scent of night flowers mingled with the aroma of roasted meat – there were two or three pigs and a flock of chickens rotating on clockwork spits. I watched the scene from the open windows of the breakfast room, where we, the maids and footmen, were stationed. Lady Broome was highly visible in a blatant silver gown and high hair, sweeping through the crowd. She was followed by footmen bearing cordials on glass salvers. Mrs Waterland, sumptuous in blonde silk with pink serpentine ruchings, was sitting at one of the tables under the pergolas with the baron and Eliza. She was not disposed to give up easily.

There was an air of expectation as the gathering awaited Mr Paine's electrical demonstration. I could see him directing the placement of a contraption at the rear of the stage – and with him, to my surprise, Johnny Waterland. I had not known he was expected at Weever Hall. Then I caught sight of Eliza zigzagging towards the house holding her cream silk apron out in front of her like a tray. The apron was marred by a horrible brown blotch. In her excitement at the arrival of her brother, she had dropped a chocolate ice on it. I relieved her of the apron and she hurried back towards the stage.

I found from a passing footman that it was possible to enter the laundry through an external door in the service alley. 'Here,' he said, and handed me his torch – a tallow candle in a wooden holder. 'It is dark along there. Second door on the left.'

I stepped down into a shadowy passageway and paused to let my eyes adjust to the gloom. A huge boom sounded from the garden – it made me jump – and was followed by a noise like splintering ice, and assorted squeals from the ladies gathered. I swung round to see in the distance a yellow flash illuminate the stage and then a rope of blinding white fire leaped into the air with a harsh crackle. At that instant a hand grasped the ties of my apron and yanked me violently backwards.

I screamed so hard I tasted blood in my throat, but the scream was lost amid loud shouts of *Bravo!* and scattered applause commending the electrical display. An arm wrapped around my waist and dragged me struggling into the darkness. I knew at once that it was Barfield. I recognised the rotten smell of him and the rasp of his breathing. From behind he clamped one hand over my mouth and forced the other down the front of my bodice where he clutched at my breast with a savage force, ripping the lace at my neck as he did so. I was still holding the chamberstick, its light reeling wildly. Barfield made a noise at the back of his throat, pushed my face to the passage wall and sank his teeth into my shoulder like a predator that meant to devour me. Grievous fear and outrage surged through my body and at the same time in a still corner of my mind I found the space to know what I must do. I slackened my resistance, which encouraged Barfield to loosen his grip. As I twisted around to face him, he let his hands came free from my mouth and my clothes. I saw his face wavering under the flame of my candle, his eyes glistening. He tangled his fingers in my hair to keep me close and the other hand fumbled at his breeches. The fumbling distracted him. With all my might I struck the side of his head with the chamberstick. He staggered backwards into the darkness, crashing into shrubs and bushes as he went, and I sprang away and fled towards the house.

I stopped on the way by a shrub, a dark solid-looking bush, a laurel perhaps. I was dizzy, the violet sky spun slowly, I remember that, and I had the urge to rest against the shrub for support and at the same time I knew that it was not reliable, that there was nothing to lean on and I would simply sink into its scratchiness. I pulled myself together and reached the safety of the kitchen. I was still clutching the chamberstick. I abandoned it on a sideboard and stepped awayfrom its taint, my heart thudding in my ribs. My hands felt sticky but I hesitated to wipe them on my apron. Incredibly, it was unstained. I expected to see it covered in gouts of blood. That's when with a gasp of panic I remembered Eliza's apron. It must have fallen from my arm when Barfield seized me. I became aware at that point of some of the domestics gawking at the back entry and news of a commotion in the garden. How awkward it would be for Eliza and her mother, especially at such a delicate pass in their pursuit of the baron, if a servant of theirs were found to be involved in a sordid altercation.

I hurried outdoors again as if curious to find what had taken place. I bypassed the knot of people gathered around Barfield. Several men, servants and gentlemen both, were milling about with torches at the entrance of the passageway. I made my way there, crouched down at the step and flailed around until my fingers brushed against silk. As I snatched up Eliza's apron, one of the servants asked me sharply what I was doing. I explained that I was en route to the laundry and I was allowed to pass.

In the laundry I filled a basin with shaking hands and began to soap the apron. Tears pricked at my eyes. I could not stop playing out Barfield's assault in my mind's eye. I was terrified not only by his violence, but by his persistence. Was I to be hounded by this beast until he succeeded in his aim? I felt anger then, burning in my heart. If I had dashed out his brains I would not have felt the least remorse. I imagined raining blow after unstoppable blow on him until he lay lifeless at my feet. I was shocked by the depth of my fury. I had not known that such a savage creature dwelled in the dark core of my nature. I looked down at my hands and shivered. The water was cold and greasy. How long had I been standing at the basin pulping the apron? It floated in the basin looking unpleasantly membraneous, as though it had slithered out of something monstrous.

The Summer House and the Servants' Hall, Sedge Court

June, 1765

It was two or three days after Lady Broome's dance and Mrs Waterland and Eliza were taking tea with Johnny and Mr Paine in the summer house. I was helping Eliza to manage the new samovar. I was glad of any reason to keep my face turned from the conversation, because they were discussing the assault on Barfield at Weever Hall. 'What a terrifying figure he made,' said Mrs Waterland, 'staggering into the garden like that, dripping blood. I would not be surprised if the assailant were one of these Irish harvesters that begin to crowd the countryside this time of year.'

Naturally, I had said nothing to anyone about my part in the scene, and I thought it likely that Barfield would not mention me either, because there was no advantage in it for him. He would bide his time for another attack.

'Is he in order, Johnny, do you think?'

'Of course he is, Mama,' Johnny said testily. 'Barfield is indestructible.'

'How impressive,' Mrs Waterland said, 'to take a ghastly attack in such stride.'

'Oh, it amuses him to meet with a contradiction.'

'But he could have been killed.'

'Actually, the blow was rather feeble, you know.' I felt

Johnny's eyes stray in my direction and I could not help but flush. Of course, I realised then, he knew exactly what had occurred. But he would not say anything about it either, I wagered, for the same reason that I would not. It would not please his mother.

Mrs Waterland said, 'So kind of Lady Broome to put up Mr Barfield while he recovers. We would have him here, you know, were he well enough to go abroad. Although, perhaps he would not get on with Baron von Boxhagen, who shall visit us imminently. I am in quite a mind to hold a dance when he arrives. Is there any chance, Arthur, that Mrs Paine might be persuaded to join us?'

Mr Paine was fiddling with a narrow wooden box that he had brought out of his coat pocket. At Mrs Waterland's question his lips tightened. 'Alas, Mrs Paine is on a pilgrimage to her nieces and nephews in Scotland. You know how very fond she is of her northern relations.'

A cloud passing at that moment across the sun dimmed the interior of the summer house and caused the encrusted walls to heave with grotesque shadows. I felt a pang of regret for the original, simple sandstone now concealed by the layers of shellwork and glass mosaic.

The box that Mr Paine was playing with looked rather like a receptacle for storing quills. He was sliding its cover back and forth with a click-clack sound and fussing with the thing in a manner that suggested he wished it to be a talking point. Eliza inadvertently gave him an opening by enquiring of Johnny, 'Did you arrive in time to see Cousin Arthur's show? I was petrified of the sparks, you know. How on earth does he make them?' This said as if Mr Paine were two hundred miles away in his study at Poland Street instead of perched at the tea table. The Waterlands have quite a genius for taking no notice.

Mr Paine leaned forward, a faint frown of eagerness pulling his ovine eyes closer together, and explained that an electrical charge, generated from a machine, produced the sparks. Johnny, getting wind of his cousin's need for attention, was not disposed to satisfy it – he was looking about his chair as though he had lost something. Mr Paine was obliged to put his shoulder to the topic and launch it himself.

'By the by,' he said, displaying the box, which he had been longing to introduce, 'this particular instrument is an electrometer. It is a device for measuring electricity that exists in the air.'

'Do you mean thunder and lightning?' Eliza asked.

'The operation of lightning is of course a very obvious demonstration of electricity, my dear Eliza, but what interests an experimental philosopher such as myself . . .' Mr Paine paused in order to let the buffed weightiness of *experimental philosopher* sink in, 'is the electricity that is invisible to the eye during fair weather. The purpose of an electrometer is to detect it.' He flipped open the box and two small balls fell from a channel inside and dangled on a fine thread about six inches long. Mr Paine directed a wary '*Voilà!*' at Johnny with the air of a fellow who expected to be disparaged. Johnny was picking at a loose thread on his cuff. He looked tired and hard-eyed.

Mr Paine pressed on. 'One may measure the amount of electrical charge in the atmosphere by the divergence of these balls and their degree of separation.'

Eliza raised her shoulders to her ears with a bored sigh. Mrs Waterland scratched the back of her hand and said, 'But what is the point of this measuring, Cousin?'

'Electricity is connected to the principle of life, dear madam. It has the power to unbind and encourage flow. Do you know, experiments have shown that vegetables can grow considerably faster if they are electrified.'

Mrs Waterland was sweeping at her forearms with long strokes of her ringed fingers.

Mr Paine cleared his throat. 'Which has brought me to wonder if electricity might be used, in fact, to render barren land productive. I am devising a series of experiments to prove such an hypothesis.'

Mrs Waterland lifted her head at an angle and narrowed her eyes at a dark patch of midges near one of the windows.

Johnny drawled, 'We could make a killing with that thunder box of yours at assemblies in London. It's a novel entertainment.'

Mr Paine said, 'I made the entertainment at Weever Hall purely as a favour to Lady Broome. My concerns are rather more scholarly as a rule.' He was about to add something more, but no one was listening to him. The net of midges had fallen on the company and we were forced to abandon the summer house before we were eaten alive.

As I readied Eliza for bed, she declared her disappointment at Johnny's being shut up with their father all night in the library. She had hoped to play cards with him instead of with Arthur, who had turned out to be unappealingly competitive and a poor loser.

'Is Johnny's friend coming to stay, do you know?' I tried to keep my tone light, although I was sickened by the possibility that Barfield would ride on to Sedge Court after leaving Nantwich.

'How should I know?' Eliza said. Then she added, 'Probably not. I am afraid that Johnny intends to go with Papa to Chester. I am furious about it. Why does he always abandon us so quickly?'

Her disappointment was in contrast to my joy, when I found the following morning that Johnny had indeed ridden out with his father. That meant a respite from Barfield. In fact there was an atmosphere of jubilation in general in the house. That the master was well enough to go abroad on his horse to tend to business was greeted with relief in the servants' hall. There was an optimistic discussion around the kitchen table of canals and coal mines and cash flow, which made us feel secure and lively, since where would we be without the master's bulging pocketbook? The esprit of the house climbed higher still when Mrs Waterland received word from Chester that Mr Waterland would not return for at least a fortnight. He had determined to accompany Johnny to London on a matter of business. The knowledge that such a journey was not beyond the master's reach encouraged us, the anxious clan rejoicing at the failing chief's return to vigour.

With Johnny gone, Mr Paine could find no reason to stretch out his visit at Sedge Court. I could not fathom why he was quite so impressed by Johnny Waterland, especially since Johnny treated him with such scorn. But there it was: another of the enigmas of human relations. The afternoon before his departure, I came down to the apothecary's at Parkgate to obtain a phial of vitriolic ether for Mrs Waterland's headache. She was under some pressure of time, trying to hurry along the paperhangers and painters she had contracted to redecorate the withdrawing room. She was determined to have the work completed before Baron von Boxhagen sent his card, which was an event much anticipated.

As I came out of the apothecary's shop, I saw Mr Paine apparently arguing with two or three fishwives at an entrance to a weint. They were having the better of the harangue. I thought to hustle Mr Paine away to safety. 'Best to stay out of the weints, sir,' I said. 'They do not care for outsiders there.'

His intention had been to take a reading with his electrometer of the thick air around the fishing hovels to show that electrical action was inhibited there. It seemed not to have occurred to him that he might be interpreted as an invader and repelled accordingly.

'I work only to benefit mankind,' he said plaintively as we walked back to Sedge Court.

In his view, plants and animals alike are badly affected by vapours and effluvia. When they are subject to moist atmospheres and cloudy days, the electricity within them is stifled and a withering of life occurs. It was his plan to conduct a series of experiments to demonstrate the connection between Ireland's want of atmospheric electricity and her blighted crops. To prove that famines stem from a want of natural electricity was to be his great work and his entrée to the Royal Society.

Then he said that he hoped to persuade Johnny to accompany him on his expedition. I could not imagine anything less likely than Johnny Waterland agreeing to be thrown together with Cousin Arthur in a bog, but then Mr Paine said, 'He has bought a number of Irish mortgages, you know, and he might be interested to inspect the properties at first hand.'

The summer came to a slow boil. By the middle of August the air was so clotted you could throw a barley-spike into it and make it stick, and Lady Broome was drawn to Parkgate to take the sea air. She came on to Sedge Court and was conducted straight away to the drawing room to admire the yellow-and-grey colour scheme and paisley India papers that had supplanted its former glacial blue and white. The new decor gave to the room a moody cast that suggested an impending storm.

The kitchen was heady with the perfume of late-fruiting plums, which Mrs Edmunds was making into pies, and of lush end-of-season roses listing under great velvety heads. Their fallen petals and a general scent of incipient decay hinted at the passing of summer. Downes and I were arranging the roses in vases, when Hester descended into the servants' hall and stood gravid with news from above.

'There will be a right curfuffle now,' she announced, 'going by what her upstairs has just said. Her ladyship's been giving the drawing room the once-over.'

'Has she though?' Abby said.

'But that was just a preamble. I could see she was gloating over something, and so could the mistress.'

Mrs Edmunds growled, 'Mind your glabbering, Mrs Clap-Tongue.'

Hester said, 'It ain't glabber if it's true,' and stared down the housekeeper.

'Get on with it then, if you must,' Mrs Edmunds snapped.

'Whey, I will then. The mistress and her ladyship banter back and forth until finally the mistress comes out with, "How is the baron, by the way?" And guess what her ladyship says?'

I think we all knew the answer to that, but we leaned suspensefully towards Hester and gave her the moment.

'Oh, the baron,' her ladyship says. 'I imagine he has reached Holland by now. He left England two or three weeks ago. But of course you knew that. What a pity he could not manage a sojourn at Sedge Court.'

Abby let out a long, low whistle and Hester went on, 'The mistress don't say quack when she hears that. Just pours the tea as cool as a cucumber. If you ask me, she had too much confidence in that baron.'

'There has been no clamour for your opinion, Hart,' Mrs Edmunds said. 'Now go about your work, and you too, Jenkins. Those pies won't rear theirselves.'

Hester dropped an ironic curtsy and said, 'Any road, everybody knows Miss Eliza is not licksome enough to bag a title, so it was always going to come to naught.' She flounced away into the darkness of the stair.

Mrs Edmunds allowed herself a small sigh and remarked, 'Strike me down if there is not an afterclap to this business.'

But there was one more shock to come before that season of disappointments came to its end.

The Master's Storehouse, Parkgate, and the Parlour

Autumn, 1765 and Winter, 1766

In the first week of September, Sedge Court was woken in the middle of a hot, still night by the tolling of the bell at Parkgate. Groggily I heard footsteps banging down the back stairs and realised it must be Abby and Hester descending from the garrets. I joined Eliza in her bedchamber and we rushed to the window and saw our men cantering along the drive on horseback. After some minutes, while we strained to make out what was happening, two small figures came out on to the drive and scurried and half ran towards the gate – Hester and Abby. In a state of excited curiosity, Eliza and I dressed hurriedly in wrapping gowns and, with our shoes in our hands, ran downstairs to the servants' hall.

There was a great lozenge of moonlight on the flagstones, formed by the open door of the back entry, and a feeling of the hall having been hastily and recently vacated. We could hear Dasher's alarmed yapping in the courtyard and more distantly the hunting dogs barking in their kennels and nervous calls from the horses in the coach house. Then the sound of coal clattering on to iron. Eliza froze and widened her eyes at me. I crept towards the kitchen opening and saw that Mrs Edmunds, with her back to me, was stoking the stove. I indicated to Eliza with a rolling eye that we should sneak outdoors. She nodded; we were of the same mind.

We stole around the corner of the house and hurried to the gate. As we came on to the road, we noticed the gleam of lanterns. They were carried by figures streaming dimly across the fields, all of them hurrying in the direction of Parkgate. We soon smelled on the air the acrid stink of charred corn and I knew at once that the master's granary must be on fire. Eliza knew it, too. She gave a little cry and rushed forward past the drovers' fields. Horses were squealing and stamping their hoofs in the fields — they must have been brought up from the beer-house pens for safety — then, as we reached the slope above Parkgate, we could hear the crackle of flames feasting on timbers and presently a fiery glow came into view.

Eliza gasped. Her father's storehouse was crowned by an orange halo and the burned-out door on the upper storey gave it the appearance of a Cyclops. Evidently it was beyond saving.

Eliza and I ran towards the conflagration. There were two fire engines at work pumping water from the Dee to douse the beer-house and its outbuildings. We could hear the effortful grunting of the men who were working the clanking levers and treadles to draw water into the cisterns, and the belching of the hoses. Lines of people stretched from the water's edge to the beer-house, passing pails of seawater from hand to hand.

All of a sudden there was a report like the crack of a whip — and all eyes turned to the stricken storehouse. With an agonised sound of joints tearing free of their fixtures, the beams fell in. Flames leaped up from the howling interior and people ran about beating out the singeing smuts that rained down.

★

The following afternoon as I brought smoke-saturated clothing to the laundry, Hester stopped me and asked if I had heard about the dreadful discovery that had been made in the storehouse. Croft had seen with his own eyes mutilated remains being brought out of the burned-out cellar. At supper time, Mr Otty came back from Parkgate with the news that the body was that of Theo Sutton. The master had confirmed to the watchmen raking through the ruins that the day before he had asked Sutton to examine a consignment of linen that was in the basement of the storehouse. His grain was kept in the floors above. Mr Otty said, 'Mayhappen it was an overturned candle or a spark from his pipe that started the blaze.' Hester remarked with bright, rimless eyes that the thought of burning to death was horrifying. Mr Otty said that Sutton would have suffocated from the smoke and probably expired long before the floor fell in and smothered him with tons of corn. I remember failing to feel, on any level, the least bit sorry for Sutton. I note that in passing – there is a coldness inside me.

In November news came that Sir Joseph Felling was dead of the dropsy. You can imagine the rejoicing that swept through Sedge Court even as we pinned on our mourning crêpe and prayed for the repose of the patriarch's soul. The mistress was quietly gay at the prospect of the inheritance. You could sense her keeping a tight lid on the effervescence within. But there was to be no deliverance for Sedge Court. Mrs Waterland's expectations were annihilated in December by an apocalyptic communiqué from the Fellings' lawyer. Sir Joseph had named as his heir his sister's son, Arthur Paine, whose already considerable pockets were to swell like blown bladders with the

Felling goods, chattels, husbandry and personal estate. To his great-nephew, John Waterland, Sir Joseph bequeathed ten shillings and a feather bed. To his niece, Henrietta Waterland, he left his best bedclothes; only that.

There was not one of us who did not feel the sour hostility of the legacy. I would go so far as to describe the overwhelming feeling at Sedge Court as one of embarrassment. It was as if we had been swanning about in a fine new gown at a public assembly only to be informed after the event that the skirt had been rucked up in the nether regions and the focus of much ribald remark.

'It is not fair,' Eliza cried. 'Arthur already has so much. He came early into his money on the death of his father and he is swimming in it. No one tells him he must marry, for he is married already. He may spend his days fiddling with electricity or blowing up his Leyden jar, or whatever it is he does while he lives on his rents, and everyone is very pleased with him.'

Mrs Waterland would not retrench. She carried on spending money, ordering goods and provisions and contracting workmen with a brittle nonchalance as if the distribution of her uncle's fortune had been a huge mistake soon to be rectified. In the meantime, she averred, Johnny must cultivate Mr Paine and perhaps something would come our way. Mr Paine had no children and an absent wife. He was besotted with Johnny – that is the word the mistress used, *besotted* – and that affection was the only advantage the Waterlands had. You see how desperate things had become at Sedge Court despite the pretending otherwise: the mistress at a tilt to reason; the master incapacitated.

Mr Waterland has become more withdrawn than before, if such a thing were possible. He was not disposed to do anything about the blackened skeleton of the storehouse. At first people were respectful of the ruin, which stood as a grim memorial to poor Sutton. But as the year turned and Mr Waterland made no effort to pull it down and build over the disaster, rumours began to arise. It was said he lacked the means to replace the building or to import goods to store in it. A coal mine opened near the village of Ness and we heard that the master had missed an opportunity to invest in it and again it was whispered that his enterprises had failed.

Winter pressed us hard that January. Gauzy shadows hung around the corners of the house and darkness prowled at the windows. One afternoon, I was playing a hand of loo with Eliza and Mrs Waterland in the parlour, when Hester came in with a bag that Croft had collected from the booking office at the beer-house. It had arrived on one of the Parkgate coaches. It was a freezing, grey day, and for the first time that I could recall, the parlour was a place of gloom and umbrage. The consumed candles in the chandelier had not been replaced and the want of light had forced us to abandon our needle-work. Hester's coming in and going out had let a gust of chilly air into the parlour. We shifted the card table closer to the hearth, where a dull little fire sputtered in the grate. The bag contained a set of mohair buttons ordered from Chester and half a pound of the alkanet roots that Mrs Waterland uses to influence the colour of her lip salve. She was surprised to find an additional packet. She unwrapped it and held up a luxurious-looking canister decorated with pink satin ribbon.

'Chocolate from Greek Street in Soho,' Mrs Waterland

announced in a tone that suggested she could take it or leave it. Slipped under the ribbon was a note.

'From Johnny, I expect,' Eliza said hopefully. Taking a cue from her mother's deliberate indifference, she began shuffling the deck of cards as though the chocolate were of no moment. (Do you know, sometimes the tension that springs from pretence makes me want to hurl myself into – into, I don't know – hurl myself out into the *open* so that I can breathe.) A disturbingly speculative expression stole across Mrs Waterland's face as she read the note.

'It is from Mr Barfield,' she said.

At the mention of that name my heart flushed with hatred, cringing, at the same time, like a cuffed dog.

'He says, "Please be so good as to accept from me this gift. It is by way of apology for detaining your son in London."'

Eliza pouted, 'So it is old tub-guts Toby who prevented Johnny from coming to us at Christmas.'

A ball of apprehension began to pulse inside me and I wished Eliza would leave off mashing the cards.

'He also says, "I beg the indulgence of asking after the charming Miss Waterland. I am told that she has a sweet tooth, therefore let this confection show that I consider her interests –"' and here Mrs Waterland paused, before continuing in a significant tone – 'while I hope that in return she will consider mine."'

The cards spurted from Eliza's fingers and tumbled at the feet of the brooding Delft vases. 'Confound it! Em, do pick those up, won't you?'

With their pockets empty of blooms the vases looked glum and useless. I dropped to my knees before them and gathered the scattered cards as though impelled to restore the integrity of something that had burst.

Mrs Waterland said, 'Do you understand the meaning, Eliza? Mr Barfield intimates that you might consider him.'

Surely the man could not be serious about asking leave to court Eliza. What could possibly be in it for him? In any case, wasn't his mother titled? She would never agree to an approach. Eliza's pedigree is paltry and her want of a fortune an insurmountable obstacle.

'Consider Mr Barfield?' Eliza turned down the corners of her mouth. 'Why should I, when I would not consider Baron von Boxhagen, who is at least half handsome?'

A quiver seemed to pass through the parlour and the candle flames quailed. I noticed that the fringes on Mrs Waterland's gown were trembling slightly. She raised her hand and I blinked at the flash of the brilliants in her rings. It was only as she pointed a finger of accusation at Eliza that I realised the throb in the room was caused by her fury. She fixed Eliza with an awful blue glare and spat, 'You don't consider the baron, do you? You illusionist! You stupid fool! The baron does not consider *you*!'

Eliza blanched and her mouth fell open.

'*You* did not catch his eye!' Mrs Waterland cried. 'He rejects *you*!' She pressed a hand against her gem-encrusted bosom and her mouth twisted as if in pain. Eliza added a glazed stare to her hanging jaw, which made her look doltish and supplied her mother with fresh ammunition. 'It defies belief,' Mrs Waterland hissed, 'that you could turn out to be as addled as you are ill-favoured. My God, what have I done to deserve such an unprofitable child?'

Eliza rose to her feet. I stood up as well, the cards clutched in my hands. The clock chimed the half-hour. Its conceited bells sounded absurd in the violent atmosphere of the room, but Eliza seemed to take heart from the interruption. She thrust out her bottom lip and declared with defiance, 'But I do not care to entertain Mr Barfield.'

Mrs Waterland smacked Eliza's face hard. Eliza gasped and put her hand to her cheek.

Mrs Waterland's voice was low but it trembled with anger, 'Do you never think how the bread comes to your mouth or the gown to your closet? If you wish to live life as you please, you must make a match that gives you the means to do so. And you must do it soon. Let me inform you, Miss Waterland, since it seems you are too dull to see the truth in your looking glass: you have worn off your bloom, such as it was, and you are not in a position to discriminate.'

Eliza's eyes began to brim, but her mother was relentless. She went on, 'If Em were in your place, she could have her pick of swells. We should be celebrating a contract with the baron now . . . yes, I saw how he riveted his eye fast on you, Miss Smith.' She directed at me a smile that had something sly in it and I felt a flash of unambiguous dislike that made me recoil. She turned back to Eliza and commanded her to retire to her apartment and write a letter of thanks to Mr Barfield.

'Why doesn't Em write it? After all, Barfield is another one who slavers over her.' Eliza's taunt shocked me. It made me feel that tawdry doings of mine had been exposed – and worse, Eliza looked at me with an accusing eye as though a shameful deed stood between us.

Mrs Waterland was very crisp then. She said, 'In that case, perhaps Miss Smith will advise you how to detain Mr Barfield's fancy.'

It was this remark that forced my hand. Many times I had wound myself up to the task of telling Mrs Waterland about Barfield, but I felt such a magnitude of shame I could not go through with it. However, I was filled with anger and revulsion at her view of me, even it were only a flippant one, as someone who might lure Barfield like a goat staked out in a clearing. When Eliza stomped out of the parlour with her cheek still glowing red from her mother's slap, I did not follow at once.

Mrs Waterland sat down at her little secretary-desk and began flipping noisily through a catalogue as if she needed to absorb the energy released by the scene with Eliza. I took several steps nearer until I was quite close to her and waited in silence while she briskly turned the pages. She was still compensating at that time for the lack of a legacy from Sir Joseph Felling by ordering streams of goods from establishments all over the land.

'Madam,' I said, my voice tight with anxiety, 'I have something to tell you about Tobias Barfield.'

She took her time turning to face me, and her expression was sceptical.

'I beg you, do not permit him by any means to pay court to Eliza.'

Mrs Waterland said shortly, 'I do not follow you.'

'The man is a beast and she will not be safe with him.'

'Those are strong words. What on earth are you talking about?'

Her impatient expression made me feel even more over-wrought. I cried, 'I can hardly bring myself to disclose what has happened!' I remember I almost said *confess* instead of *disclose*, as though it were I who was at fault and in need of forgiveness. Mrs Waterland closed the catalogue and stared at me.

'Well?' she said coldly.

It came out then in a torrent – an account of the assaults in the orchard and at Weever Hall. The effort of the description taxed me dreadfully. I stammered through it in a bitter passion, swept by emotions of humiliation and inexplicable guilt. As I came to the end of my statement, Mrs Waterland pressed a hand to her temple and cried, 'My God, you might have murdered him!'

I had expected that she would leap to a position of moral indignation on my behalf; instead, it was the vigour of my defence that appalled her.

'You little idiot,' she groaned. 'Don't you see how close you came to being arrested for assault yourself? You might have been hanged for that blow.'

'But he treated me with such savagery! And he would try me again if he could seize his chance, I know he would – he has said so. I beg you to keep him away from us.'

The look on Mrs Waterland's face was one of exasperation. She said, 'Have you told anyone else of these events? Does Eliza know? Is that why she made such a fuss just now?'

'No – no, I have told no one.'

She heaved a sigh of relief. 'Thank heavens for that. I implore you not to say a word about this to another soul, especially not to Eliza.' She went on, 'You will only damage her chances if this is brought into the open. Perhaps you think me unsympathetic, but in any whiff of a scandal of this nature, it is you and, by extension, Eliza who will suffer. It is unjust, of course, but that is how it is.'

I bit my lip, wondering how I had come to be so defeated by a situation in which I hoped to find encouragement and concern. I was enormously crushed by Mrs Waterland's failure to see my side. I tried another tack. 'Do you not wonder, madam, why Barfield has never entertained Eliza before? I believe he may have done something so hateful that his people are unable to . . . to—'

'To palm him off on anyone else?' Mrs Waterland said evenly. 'Well, I dare say you and I are agreed that Eliza is a poor catch. That makes it even more imperative to keep her opportunities open, few and far between as they are.'

My interview with Mrs Waterland seemed to me like a runaway horse, which I could not bring under control. How had the lumpen but innocent Eliza come to be a subject of slur, while Barfield escaped condemnation?

'Madam,' I pressed, 'the devil is in this fellow. It truly is!' My voice cracked with emotion.

'Of course I take your feelings seriously,' Mrs Waterland said with a distracted air. Silence fell and she seemed to drift into thought. I was reminded all at once of that milk crock and the jagged sound of its crash on the flagstones. Then Mrs Waterland said, with a gaze that looked past my shoulder, 'Everyone has something odious in his past. But time passes on and one recovers.'

She stood up. 'What a wretched cold day it is. Mrs Edmunds might make a hot toddy, I think.'

I said in a low voice, 'I will tell her.'

'No need.' Mrs Waterland bestowed a bright smile on me. 'I will do it.'

As she went to the bell-pull, I noticed a letter that had been exposed by the closing of the catalogue. It bore the flashy mark of Hill & Vezey. I turned my head away, feeling that it was improper to stare at Mrs Waterland's private papers. Perhaps I suspected that they held secrets, things that would shatter my faith in her. I was shocked by our exchange on the subject of Barfield, but I could not yet admit to myself that that faith had already been shattered. More terrifying still, I could not begin to look at a future where Barfield and Eliza would be married and I would be at his disposal by day and by night.

The Day Coach from Chester to London

April, 1766

Three months after that scene in Mrs Waterland's parlour, Eliza and I were put into a fast day coach bound for London. The coach was called the *Sprinter* and it managed the journey in only four days, but it seemed never-ending to me. We had hardly got out of Chester before Eliza was taken by the gripes. I was obliged to hang out of the door window and beg the driver to throw on the drag. We slithered to a stop, the undergear groaning and Eliza purged the morning's eggs and toast in a ditch. It was a beautiful day with rosebuds swelling in the hedgerows and fields of yellow rape that flowed towards the horizon and lapped against a bank of bunchy clouds. I recall a solitary labourer at a hedgerow gazing at the skid marks of the coach before he bent again to his badging-hook.

I came to Eliza's side, handkerchief deployed, and swabbed at her riding habit, while the coach panted at our backs like a waiting mastiff. At length the coachman grew impatient and shouted, 'Hie now, ladies! In with you and let us step on!'

I felt nauseated too, but it was not the fault of the pitching machine or the outrageous reek of our fellow travellers' pomades. It was the fear of what I would find when we reached our destination. During the month in which arrangements were made for our journey south, I felt as though I were standing in a room divided by a curtain. I was aware by dint of muffled noises, a door opening and closing, that something was going on behind the hanging, but I could not make out what it was. I strained to put it all together. I even hazarded the possibility that a contract had been contrived backstage, as it were, between Eliza and Barfield, in spite of everything I had told Mrs Waterland. But I could not make that postulation stick. It was too outlandish. Even if her parents did not hold Eliza in very high regard, I could not imagine that they would throw her to that wolf.

As I mull over that journey, I recall how vexed Eliza seemed to be throughout. Was it just the discomfort of the road? She was very terse in Coventry, but then again, Coventry was a disagreeable, gloomy place with houses canted closely overhead, their foreheads almost touching, as though they were trying to hold one another up. There was a tumultuous yard at the Dolphin Inn, churning with horses, vehicles and travellers. I negotiated ineptly for a night's accommodation, then fought off all comers for the remnants of a greasy bacon supper, which I conveyed to our damp-walled chamber. Eliza said little while we dined, or afterwards. Thoughts were thickening upon her, I could see.

She stood at the warped window with her back to me, her shoulders huffy. I sent down for a sixpenny pint of hock to cheer our spirits. Eliza settled on the bed with a magazine and made a show of reading while she sipped the acidy wine. I remarked the rot that was eating away a corner of the ceiling and she grunted in reply from behind the shield of her periodical.

I asked her then about Barfield. I said, 'There is no plan to meet him in London, is there?'

She threw the magazine aside and said, 'Will you stop mewling about Barfield, for heaven's sake.' She pulled the eiderdown up to her chin. 'It has got cold. These walls are awfully flawed. Perhaps you might be able to do something about the fire.' She flung herself on her side, again with her back to me.

I encouraged the fire with the few nuggets of coal remaining. As I was folding Eliza's clothes, I unearthed from one of her pockets a familiar creased piece of paper, a note for two guineas to be drawn on the bank of Hill & Vezey. It had been a gift from Johnny, doubtless at the behest of their mother, on the occasion of Eliza's sixteenth birthday. She had been carrying it around for years. How pitiful it was that this withered promissory was all that she really had of her brother.

As I climbed into bed, I was struck by the feeling that these scenes were preordained. There was a compelling sense of inevitability about the Dolphin Inn, the terrible wine, and Eliza's turning away.

As we ground on, the highway altered for the worse. The wheels slipped under hissing rain as the *Sprinter* strained against a strong headwind that seemed to be trying to blow us back to Chester. One was left in the murk of the coach's interior with one's own thoughts.

I understood that the wellspring for Mrs Waterland's outburst at Eliza was the state of the economy at Sedge Court. Anyone could tell that we were in an unsteady condition. I did not wish a new and unpredictable mistress in the house, but I could not comprehend why Johnny did not marry and save the estate. He had reached the age of thirty years without bothering to rake in a moneyed bride. Was not London awash in them? In fact there were many things I did not understand about our recession and the master's inability to pay his debts. The mistress had told Baron von Boxhagen that Mr Waterland had invested in canals. They were being dug everywhere now. Surely something must come of such perceptive speculation. And what about the houses in Chester that Johnny had persuaded the master to buy? I had overheard Mrs Edmunds asking Mr Otty the same question and he had replied, 'The Chester houses? Mayhappen they are mightily encumbered with mortgages or we would have seen them turned into brass by now.' What had become of Johnny's once bountiful schemes?

At each change of horses we managed a glimpse of sky before we were shut up again with a new intake of passengers. Most of them were zealous carpers. The miles unrolled to complaints about deficient friends and servants, perverse weather, shoddy harpsichords, bad butchery, and the perfidy of paper-stainers. Scraps of woodland rushed past the windows. Presently someone claimed to recognise parts of Buckinghamshire. Then we were tipped into the yard of another inn, and our used-up leaders taken away.

At the Highgate turnpike we were stuck for aeons in a traffic jam. Eliza wiped at the window and moaned, 'Will we never arrive?' The turnpike was mobbed by every kind of wheeled conveyance as well as travellers on foot and horseback, but once we were through, the congestion eased and we began a long descent to London down a dirty lane.

Presently hedgerows gave way to buildings closely clustered and an astonishing press of people. I expected our last dash to be made with an air of triumph, blasts of the horn trumpeting the *Sprinter*'s achievement – the scores of miles and dozens of horses vanquished. But so thick was the throng, our coach was only able to slouch towards its terminus, a bedraggled lumberer, drained of its sprinterness.

We alighted into a sea of nagging paupers – *spare any change, madam, a penny, madam* – who looked as if they would slit your throat for a farthing. The guard was obliged to dislodge a ball-faced boy from the hem of Eliza's petticoat and he knocked aside a toothless crone who could no more lift a mist than the portmanteau she was scrabbling at. She was one of a horde fighting to carry our luggage. At my request the guard whistled up a lad with a lantern on a pole, who deployed it to get by the beggars and the yelping dogs as though he were hacking through undergrowth.

Five minutes later we were in a hackney carriage feeling its way on to the Oxford Road. The instant our driver paused to give way, a screaming bung-eyed baby reared up at one of the windows, assisted by some unseen agent, while at the other, a skeletal figure dragged shrieking fingernails on the glaze. In spite of these apparitions, I felt a rush of excitement, for I sensed the mighty engine of this great town turning on its gears and one felt somehow joined to an epic enterprise simply by being there. This gust of energy lifted me up and away from the grubby little feeling of dread that had hung over me on the long journey down.

We arrived in a matter of minutes at a narrow street in Soho and halted before a townhouse, barely two windows wide, but very tall and haughty with a pinched air about it. Under the wavering light of a street lantern, I hammered on the door. It was opened by a footman who seemed pleased with himself. Flicking the sides of his frock away to reveal red plush breeches, he conveyed our luggage into an entrance hall whose outmoded wainscoting was slightly illuminated by a single candle in a sconce. To our right a cramped flight of stairs built around a narrow well ascended into darkness. My first impression was that Arthur Paine was not likely to run through Sir Joseph Felling's fortune in a hurry. There was a sense of skimping about the house – and we had not even reached the parlour.

A butler leaning heavily on a walking stick made a delayed appearance, limping from the shadows behind the staircase, and led us in a time-consuming procession to the far reaches of the hall. After a struggle with the door handle, he at last breached his master's study, as the chamber proved to be, and waved us in. Mr Paine rose bareheaded in a damask gown from behind a large table, looking startled to see us, and then, collecting himself, he came to take Eliza's hand and offered me a bow. He apologised for his informality, explaining that he had scorched his best wig while studying close to a lamp. He ordered Samuels, the butler, to send up tea. With a disgruntled expression, Eliza assessed her surroundings. The dozens of prints infesting the walls and the muddle of papers and books gave to Mr Paine's study an air of dogged profusion.

Eliza said with a pout, 'The house does not look very commodious, Cousin. I hope we may be fitted in.'

Mr Paine grimaced. 'I am sorry that Poland Street is not what it was. The address was fashionable when my late mother bought the place thirty or forty years ago, but now we have been rather left in the lurch. The quality has moved west, you see.'

Eliza poked at one of the baffling apparatuses strewn about the table, a scioptic projector, according to Mr Paine, and announced that she was hungry enough to eat a horse and chase the rider. I was sent below to command her supper.

Despite its modest dimensions, the house managed to accommodate a servants' staircase at its rear, which I descended on vertiginous steps. The kitchen was bathed in blue smoke produced from the pipe of an ample woman seated before the hearth, who introduced herself as the housekeeper, Mrs Jellicoat. At her back a less lardy, younger woman laboured over a concoction boiling loudly on the hob. The footman loomed out of the haze with a tray holding the tea equipage and winked at me. Mrs Jellicoat wheezed, 'Granger will fuck you as soon as look at you, so keep on your toes, lady's maid.' Granger laughed like a drain and swaggered towards the stairs.

After supper we were settled in an apartment on the first floor that had been used formerly by Cousin Arthur's mother, Lady Paine. Some trace of her lingered still in the stuffy chambers, a suggestion of stale lavender water and unwashed hair. Of Mr Paine's wife there was not a trace and I wondered if it were true that she and her husband lived apart, as I had heard.

I was to sleep in the dressing room. Having tucked Eliza into her bed, I locked the door against the footman and padded to the window. I raised the sash and leaned out, wondering if I might glimpse the famous Thames. But I could see only countless buildings with fuming chimneys. The air smelled of cinders and it was difficult to see into the distance. The town was enveloped in a dark haze.

I lay awake listening to noises rising from the street. Cats yowling, dogs howling. A horrible grinding sound of something being dragged. An argument, a song. The hollow roll of endless traffic. It was excitement, too, that kept me from sleep. I was afraid of London and the uncertainties it harboured, but my arrival there also put me within striking distance of the foundling hospital. I had not given up the possibility that I might find out who my parents were and where I had come from. It was a hope that I had hugged close to my chest all the way from Chester.

The Paine Townhouse, Soho, London

April, 1766

The morning is well advanced by the time breakfast is served in Mr Paine's house. 'In town we rise late,' the kitchen wench informed me flatly when I tried to obtain hot water from her at seven on that first morning. I was itching to go abroad. I tended to my tasks, unpacking, smoothing, folding, airing, and drafted a letter for Eliza to send to her mother confirming our safe arrival. After cooling my heels upstairs for another hour, I descended to the hall and hung about like a dog waiting for its walk. It says a great deal about the tight bonds of propriety that in spite of my fizzing curiosity I felt unable to open the front door of the house and step out to see what I could see. The restrictions by which virtuous women must live are designed to shield us from vicissitudes or at least to mitigate their effects on us, but we must exist at the same time in a quarantine. I had always interpreted that quarantine as security, and yet I found myself chafing like a captive in Mr Paine's hall – I, who had always bridled so well.

Eventually, from the parlour came the bossy chimes of a clock reminding the world that it ought to be getting on and at last Eliza and I were brought out by Mr Paine to accompany him to his peruke-maker. I had not proceeded five yards along the street when I had every kind of fright for my life. Coaches and hackneys and pedestrians alike seemed determined to bowl us over and we had constantly to step smartly out of their way. Mr Paine paid the hurly-burly no heed and we strode on, Eliza and I keeping our alarm and amazement to ourselves. We turned into a wider street flanked by large dwellings that might once have been grand but were fallen to lodging houses and rookeries. Numbers of raggedy irregular individuals were crying their wares of second-hand clothes, old bottles and nails and cracked pots, which they had set out on the stones along with their squalling children. 'You see,' Mr Paine said, steering us away, 'how the world so fatally degrades and breaks down.'

We edged along a squalid thoroughfare, which looked as though it might provide a convenient ambuscade for cutpurses or footpads, but Mr Paine seemed impervious to the potential for danger, his mind being so immersed in knotty thoughts, I presume, that he could not fully take in what lay before him. That is a kind of protection in its way, for he passed men with unquiet eyes as if they did not exist and they, having been rendered invisible, lost their power to threaten. Perhaps this is a common tactic for avoiding trouble in the metropolis, because I noticed that a beplumed young man, crossing in high heels and a showy coat towards a tavern, seemed deaf to the insults that his Frenchified dress attracted from fellows clustered about outside a print shop, where we had stopped so that I could buy a plan of London.

Perhaps I would ask Johnny if he could indicate on the plan where he lived. He had recently moved house, apparently, and no one seemed able to say what his new address was. I had begun to form the idea that Johnny was untruthful about his circumstances – which gave me a sense of dismay.

As Mr Paine led us towards Piccadilly, where his peruke-maker kept a shop, I was greatly diverted by the sights around me. It was clear even to a novice visitor that London could easily mince one's soul without giving a hoot, so enormously absorbed is it in its own interests, but at the same time there was something exhilarating about the indifference of those humming streets. There was a freedom in them that made one feel anything was possible and that one could do anything.

We came eventually to a wide, racing thoroughfare beset by speeding conveyances and men on horseback, all of whom seemed to be dashing to an emergency. You have already followed me along this route on a later occasion. There was the peruke-maker's establishment across the road in a range of shops with bowed windows. There was the White Bear Inn.

While Mr Paine was having his wig fitted, Eliza, who rarely exhibits any interest in *la mode*, as I am sure you know by now, decided to inspect a pair of sleeves displayed next door in the window of a mantua-maker's establishment. 'I might wear them when I go out with Johnny,' she said, and bit her lip. So: they had been in communication. But I knew better than to enquire after details at that moment. Eliza is never forthcoming when she feels she has been caught out. Instead, I asked to be shown the sleeves. The mantua-maker spread them upon the counter. They were dove-grey satin embroidered with silver thread. As she bent her sleek head over them, I caught the fragrance of her hair powder – oranges or perhaps bergamot.

Eliza declared in a faintly defiant tone that she would take the sleeves and pay with a promissory note. She drew from her pocketbook the note Johnny had given her. It was limp with overhandling, reduced almost to the consistency of tissue.

The mantua-maker examined the note carefully. She directed a thoughtful gaze at the floor and Eliza shifted her feet. Then the woman said, 'I am afraid we are not able to encash this, madam.'

'Is there a disorder?'

A hesitation. 'Only it is in rather poor condition.'

'I cannot agree with you,' Eliza said in a huff. But she picked up the note and tucked it into the pocket of her coat. All at once I saw in my mind's eye that letter from Hill & Vezey that had lain hidden under the catalogue on Mrs Waterland's desk. Was it a routine communication or something more ominous in nature?

Once Eliza and I were in the street again, I whispered to her, 'Do you think we ought to be concerned about the condition of Johnny's bank?'

Eliza tossed her head. 'Why don't you ask him yourself? He is coming for tea this afternoon.'

You can imagine the bellow of delight from Eliza as Samuels leaned creakily around the door of Mr Paine's parlour and announced the arrival of Mr Waterland. Johnny sauntered in on the end of a silver-topped walking stick as long as a barge pole. To my monumental surprise, Eliza's enthusiasm was matched by a similar show from Johnny, who slapped his thigh with his glove and exclaimed, 'By Jove, never was a brother so well pleased to see his sister. Welcome to London, my dear.'

I could see that Johnny was altered. His bonhomie could not hide the fact that he did not look well. His skin was as pale as wax and his eyes were hollow.

Eliza flushed to a shade of cerise that matched the extreme suit Johnny was wearing. I had never known him to make a folly of his costume, but his appearance was in general much intensified with a toupee brushed up and raised on pads so that it resembled a loaf upon his head. It made me think that his judgement was wanting.

Mr Paine entered then with an expression of welcome nearly as enraptured as Eliza's. He beamed and patted at his own new wig as though it deserved its share of praise. The foretop and the sides were smooth and plain, with one hori- zontal roll of curls projecting above the ears. It was a style favoured by naval men and explorers, he reported. Johnny thumped the tuffet at his feet by way of inviting Eliza to sit and she sank on to it and gazed at him shining-eyed. In spite of my reservations about her brother, one was glad to see her so happy. Tea arrived, and gin for Johnny. I busied myself with the service, while a rackety exchange went on between brother and sister about how thrilling it was to be in London.

Mr Paine went away and returned again with an electrometer – I surmised so from the shape of the case. He sat down and leaned towards Johnny with a look, it hit me, of Dasher in relation to Abby. Good heavens, I exclaimed inwardly. Given that moist gaze, anyone would think that Mr Paine was in love with Johnny. I began to turn that thought over in my mind.

'Will you remark this, sir,' he said eagerly, proffering the mahogany case. More elaborate than the one he had shown us at Sedge Court, it was decorated with gleaming brass cartouches. 'I've just had it made by my apothecary.'

A spark of irritation crossed Johnny's face. 'Oh, the marvellous electrometer,' he said. 'The key to all our fortunes, I am sure.'

'How so?' Eliza asked.

Mr Paine said, 'As all the world knows, Eliza, I am an improver. It has ever been my intent to reverse processes of decline. With this useful instrument, I shall undertake a course of experiments that will ultimately bring about a boost to the value of your brother's properties in Ireland.'

I looked up at that. What had happened to Mr Paine's lifting of the famines? How corrupting was Johnny's influence, I thought then. I could not imagine who else could have persuaded Mr Paine to cheapen his ambition until its only concern was the enlarging of an investment. If Mr Paine noticed my surprise he gave no sign of it.

Johnny said, 'You would be mad, Arthur, to go to Ireland these days. Haven't you heard that all manner of terrorists are ravaging the countryside there? They will stab an Englishman as quick as look at him.'

Mr Paine blinked. 'Terrorists?' he said.

'I am only thinking of you,' Johnny said with a grin. 'I should be rather amused to encounter one of those wild fellows. But given the political situation it is hardly the ideal time to go jaunting in the bogs with your instruments, is it?'

'I should think it might still be possible if you were with me, to keep a lookout, as it were.'

Johnny slugged his drink, slapped the arm of his chair and changed the subject. 'Now then, Arthur, have you sent your man over to Soho Square with the paraphernalia? You must have your electricals set up tomorrow and assure our hostess that the mechanics are sound. Don't disappoint her or she will try to wriggle out of paying us our full amount.'

Mr Paine was crestfallen. 'I wish you could give me a firm

answer about Ireland,' he said. 'I have already planned much of our trip there.'

Johnny said, 'Ireland is not the sort of place that offers a firm answer, Arthur. Why must you be such a miser, I do not know. You could easily lend me a little to give me a respite from worrying about those mortgages without my having to go in person to inspect the properties.'

Mr Paine looked away. But it was easy to read his thoughts. His money was the only ace he held. Once he gave it up to Johnny, he was out of the game and it was likely he should not see Johnny for dust.

Johnny stood up and adjusted his toupee. 'Em,' he said, 'we shall include you in our party at Soho Square on Friday. You know that my dear sister cannot manage without you. Please do your best to rig her out in a blazing style.' He winked at me.

I said, 'Do you know, she tried to buy sleeves today with your bill, but the shopkeeper would not take it.'

'Em!' Eliza was aghast. 'How dare you!'

Johnny laughed easily. 'Did you really try to use that note after all this time?' He shook his head as though transcendentally unperturbed by the promissory's rejection. 'No matter. I shall buy Eliza a pair of sleeves myself, the more splendid the better. What do you think of that?'

Eliza gave a squeal like a combusting kettle.

To my astonishment, Johnny was as good as his word. The next morning he sent a chair for Eliza. We came down to find it standing in the hall like a portable sepulchre with two brawny porters stationed at either end. I tied Eliza's mantle, straightened her hat, she stepped into the chair and was borne away. She was still annoyed with me for embarrassing her brother, as she saw it, with that remark about the promissory note. Her irritation would turn to anger if she saw that I was wearing her coat, which I had run upstairs to put on, along with one of her hats, as soon as her chair was out of sight. I hoped that I would manage to return to Mr Paine's house before she did and she would be none the wiser. It was a risk I was willing to take in order to appear at the foundling hospital looking as though I had risen in the world and had a right to information.

My plan of London showed that Lamb's Conduit Fields, the location of the hospital, was not a great distance from Poland Street. I walked up to the Oxford Road and then east to a junction. The cross street was not named. I asked a woman in a fur hat for directions to the Fields. She pointed tersely north and said I might take a lane on the right off Tottenham Court Road and then ask someone else with more time on his hands. I pressed on in a state of nervousness, consulting alternately the plan and passers-by.

It struck me as I walked that there must be a great call for fancy needlework in London, judging by the purse-proud turn-outs on the streets, for even on a brief acquaintance, I could say that the people of that town are in love with their attire. Even the muck-shufflers sported a nosegay in a tattered coat or some rag about the neck that tried to make a distinction of itself.

Eventually I sighted in the distance treeless, open fields surrounding a dun-coloured building. My footsteps slowed and I came to a halt. I looked at the plan. I was in the right place. A tremor passed through me and my hands shook in anticipation of what I might find out. I folded the plan and put it away in the pocket of my – actually, Eliza's – coat. As I did so, my fingers brushed something that felt dry and flimsy. I drew out the object and found that it was the faithless promissory note. I thrust it back into the pocket and strode towards the clearing in front of the hospital. The architecture of the forecourt's entrance is severe and I saw that watchmen patrolled back and forth, perhaps to prevent desperate women from leaving their infants. I applied to the gatekeeper to pass through. He asked me my business and I found myself saying quite fluently that I was desirous of having a girl out of the hospital to be in service to me. He allowed me admission.

A long, windswept driveway led to a deep portico at the front of the hospital, where I hovered while I marshalled my thoughts. I was not sure how to go about my mission, but I was at least determined. I wanted to know more of the life I might have lived had fate not intervened. I knew that my material circumstances would have been dreadful had I stayed with you, my mother, but the possibility of belonging to a person or a place by right – that had a powerful appeal for me. I realised that the odds of finding out who you were, and who I was, were doubtless stacked against me. But I had to try.

Three or four ladies of quality were also waiting in the portico. They were grandly cloaked and wore lavish hats. When a manservant came to conduct them inside, I attached myself to the tail of the group and followed the ladies into a hall without attracting notice. They were met by a short woman in black taffeta, with frizzy grey hair and a sheepish expression, whom they greeted by name as Mrs Collingwood. She conducted them to another room, leaving me alone in the hall with its muddy shadows and walls lined with portraits of worthies.

The halo-haired Mrs Collingwood reappeared in the hall. I approached her and launched my petition straight away.

'My name is Mary Smith,' I said, 'and I am in search of my mother. I was taken as a foster child from this hospital by a family called the Waterlands, who live in Cheshire. They brought me up in comfortable circumstances and I hold them in great affection. Since I have had advantages, it occurs to me that perhaps I might be of assistance to my mother, but I do not know how to find her.'

Mrs Collingwood said briskly, 'I am afraid your curiosity cannot be satisfied at this time, madam, but you are at leave to fill in a form petitioning to know the details of your admission. The committee of governors meets each Saturday morning to deliberate on requests received.'

'I see. Where shall I find the form?'

'You will need to see the registrar.'

'I suppose there is no doubt that you would have a record of my admission?'

'No doubt at all. Our records are meticulous. When an infant is admitted, he is numbered, baptised and sent to a nurse in the country. He generally stays with the foster family for several years before being returned to us. Each of these steps is recorded in our billet books in the event that a parent later makes enquiries about a particular child. You fill in your admission number on the form and if the governors agree to release the information, the registrar will consult the billet book for the year of your birth. You will find the registrar down there.' She pointed at a door on the left-hand side of the hallway.

'Unfortunately I do not have my admission number. I am not even sure of the year of my birth.'

Mrs Collingwood said, 'Well, your birth certificate will be able to tell you that.'

'My foster family never had one for me.'

'Of course you have a birth certificate. We do not take foundlings without one. We must ascertain that they are not more than twelve months old on admission.'

I felt a rush of optimism. 'Perhaps the certificate is held in your records.'

'I could not say. You must make an appointment with the registrar.' She excused herself and bustled away.

I knocked at the registrar's office and a clerk in a coat that was too big for him came to the door and told me that the registrar was indisposed and probably would not return until the next day. I asked him if I could make an appointment, but he said that must be done with the registrar directly. Oh, the frustration of it! I breathed in a huge sigh. Now that I was there, I could not stand to walk away, not knowing whether I'd even be able to come back another day.

'Excuse me,' I said, and stepped uninvited into the office. It contained a large table covered in papers, a couple of chairs and a tall glass-fronted cabinet tight with folios. A sickly odour of sealing wax hung in the air.

'Madam? Are you in order?'

The clerk was a dumpy man in middle age. Encouraged by the mild expression on his face, I asked him if I might sit down. His hand dangled in the direction of a chair and I sank on to it, my gaze downcast.

He cleared his throat and said, 'Beg pardon, madam, but I am not in charge here. The registrar . . .' The sentence trailed away. His voice was soft and disheartened.

'I am only trying to find my mother,' I burst out. 'But I don't have an admission number and I am not even sure when I was born. I was fostered to Mr and Mrs Waterland of Cheshire in 1749, I think it was, from this hospital. I believe I was about four years old.'

Almost before I knew what I was doing I had risen to my feet and was leaning towards the clerk in the manner of a supplicant. My heart was beating hard. He blinked rapidly. His face had turned pink.

He must have recognised that I was an unstoppable force, because he suddenly said, 'If you were fostered in 1749, there will be a record of that in the general register along with your admission number. Your foster parents would have been given a receipt as proof of the transaction. The hospital is always careful about that.'

'Thank you,' I said.

He pulled at his plump lower lip and then offered me a sorrowful expression. 'But it does not seem to me that we would release a child to permanent fosterage unless there was proof that the child's parents were dead.'

I said, 'Even if I could only know that, I should be grateful. Is there any way I might consult the register now? My stay in London may be short and I am not at leisure to return and then wait for the governors' meeting.'

The clerk shook his head. 'No, no, I am afraid I am not at liberty to show you the register.'

I thought of the shilling I had brought with me in case I was pressed for time and needed to take a hackney back to Poland Street. It wasn't much of a douceur, but still. I reached into my pocket, but the clerk said quickly, 'I cannot take anything from you.'

I said, 'I understand.' But I put the shilling on the table in any case. I had already decided that I would not leave that room until I had looked at the register. It was what I had come to do and I meant to do it. I am often a quaking, cowering milksop with a surfeit of nerves and feelings, but there is iron inside me, too.

I thought of you. I thought how saddened you would be if I crept away without doing everything I could to find you. And I was thinking of myself, too. Perhaps I had divined that the Waterlands could not be relied on as much as I had always hoped and that it was time to look elsewhere for a refuge. And to know this one inconvertible thing alone – the date of my birth – would shore me up amid the shaky circumstances in which I found myself.

Was it the expression on my face? I am sure it was fierce enough. But the clerk turned without a word and went to the cabinet. As he walked by the table he swept the shilling into his hand. He took a key from a chain on his belt, unlocked the cabinet and returned with a folio. He opened it on the table.

The register gave the day of a foundling's reception, the admission number, the baptismal name bestowed by the found-ling hospital, any significant illnesses and the date of death or discharge.

The clerk said, 'The reason for discharge is almost always

that a child has reached an age to be apprenticed. The register will say where and to whom the child has been sent. In your case it will say you were fostered. That will give me your admission number and I can find you in the billet book. Please tell me your name.'

I told him and he said, 'Mary Smith will not be the name your mother gave you. Infants admitted to the hospital are immediately baptised with new names and the register does not record your birth name or your mother's name. That information was written on your birth certificate. The certificate would have been given to your foster parents. Nowadays the billet book holds a record of the mother's name, because she must make a formal petition for admission, but in the early years of the hospital the child could be left at the door with no questions asked. Still, your mother might have left something to mark her connection with you. If that is so, the billet book will have a record. The book is an inventory of such things as the clothes you were wearing when you arrived here and physical details of identification. Do you have a birthmark? I wonder.'

'No.'

'A pity. You might find your birth name if your mother wrote it down in a poem or a letter addressed to you. That is not uncommon, and such papers are kept in the billet book.'

The clerk turned a page of the register and began to read. He did not object when I came to his side. I felt my pulse quicken as I scrutinised the lists. They were detailed: male child 14 days old gone to nurse, Eunice Smith returned to the Hospital from nurse, Sidcup, 3rd April, James Sooley apprenticed to engraver 28th October and so on. There were receipts for children's clothes: linsey sleeves 6d, white baize blankets 9d each, three caps 6d each, and records of smallpox inoculation, infirmities recorded, watery breach, thrush, excoriations, names, addresses, parishes, dinner menus and even petitions for the return of a child.

The clerk said, 'Here is a Mary Smith. Ah, not you, unless you were apprenticed to a milliner.' Then he found another Mary Smith, but she had died, and another, apprenticed to a lace-maker. Several pages later he found a Maria Smith, but she had gone to service in Kent. Then a Mary Smithie, dead of consumption, and a Mary Smyth, also dead.

Finally, the clerk said, 'I can't find a Mary Smith who matches you, or even a single child discharged permanently to foster parents.'

Disappointment flooded through me and I felt the chagrin of having dared to hope for an easy result from the register.

The clerk said, 'Of course, it is conceivable that a mistake could have been made in the record-keeping. Or I may have missed something . . .'

But I had seen for myself the careful entries: the admission numbers, the inventories, the ruled columns, the minutiae.

The clerk closed the folio and slipped it back into place in the cabinet. He said, 'I am sorry, but without your admission number I cannot even direct you to make a petition for your birth certificate.'

I said, 'It puzzles me that you have no record of a permanent fosterage to Cheshire.'

The clerk said, 'I think, perhaps, that it is likely you were not a foundling of this hospital and that your foster parents obtained you from elsewhere.'

'Is there another institution such as this?'

'No, we are the only foundling hospital. But I cannot speak for the actions of private individuals who may make a business of such transactions.'

'Perhaps my name might be recorded somewhere else here, on a list, say, of children inoculated against smallpox or – or . . .' I struggled to think of some other record where I could discover myself.

'Madam,' the clerk said with some firmness, 'you must accept that our records show no trace of you.'

I left the foundling hospital in a daze. I crossed the forecourt and strode along a street until the sensation of my knees buckling forced me to halt. I sought to gather my thoughts – but how could my disquiet abate? Mrs Waterland's assertion that I had been admitted to the foundling hospital in London without a birth certificate had been incorrect. There was no mistake about it. The hospital, I had learned, was scrupulous about its documentation.

Mrs Waterland had not told me the truth – and that discovery made me feel that my situation at Sedge Court was even more precarious. I was shaken by her dishonesty. Had she obtained me privately in some way that was not absolutely legal? Perhaps she had fabricated the story about the foundling hospital because my provenance was too tawdry to be disclosed. But it did not make sense that someone of the mistress's sensibilities would go looking for a companion for her daughter among lowlifes. Or was it rather, that on some visit to a town, her pity had been aroused by a pathetic little child living on the street and she had struck a bargain with the child's indigent mother? But why wouldn't she have told me so? Such a story would have reflected well on her charitable nature. Then I recalled that time Downes had said I was a poacher's daughter. Was that the truth? Perhaps Mrs Waterland had not told me a sincere account of my origins because she wished to spare my feelings.

So my speculations churned on as I walked and beneath them disappointment flowed. I had been soundly baulked in my search for you, and now my confidence in Mrs Waterland was undermined.

I arrived at an ill-kept jostling intersection and here it came to me that I had been proceeding without direction for some time. As a result, I had lost my way. There were no signs to tell me the name of the streets where I stood. What a hemmed-in feeling one gets from this continuous press of buildings and when one looks to the sky there is nothing but roofs coated with pigeons.

I brought out my plan from the pocket of Eliza's coat – and that wretched promissory note came with it and fell to the ground as though I needed reminding of things that were hopeless and useless. I picked it up and stuffed it back in the pocket. I stared at the plan, seeking to trace the path I had taken since I had left the hospital. I might have come south instead of veering westwards as I ought to have done – and I now lacked a shilling to get me back to Mr Paine's house in good time.

Amid the clamour of the street, I puzzled over the plan. There were two men dragging a sled loaded with broken furniture. The iron runners scraping over the cobbles were making a hellish din. At the same time a pair of milk-sellers on the corner were trying to drum up custom by banging the pails that hung from their yokes. I flagged down a woman toiling towards me with a basket of oranges over her arm and found from her that I was at a place where Fleet Street becomes the Strand. I squinted again at my plan. Fleet Street: I had a flare of recognition at hearing that name. But when I located the street on the map, I saw that I was far from Soho, where Mr Paine's house was. I would need to walk to the west along the Strand.

But some little recollection to do with Fleet Street tugged at me. I closed my eyes, pinching the bridge of my nose. One always had so much to think about. I plunged my hand into my pocket and brought out the note belonging to Johnny's bank.

It said: We promise to pay the bearer on demand the sum of Two Guineas. Fleet Street, London, the 2nd day of July, 1761. The Governors of the Bank of Hill & Vezey.

I was bothered by the mantua-maker's disdaining the note at that shop in Piccadilly and I wondered if there were more to her refusal than a scruple about the note's condition. I happened to be feeling particularly thwarted by my lack of knowledge – and since I could not satisfy my curiosity about two gaping subjects, my parentage and the nature of Eliza's mission in London, I thought to wander towards the bank and to see what I could see. Why should I not? I was at Fleet Street and in an investigative mood. And I was already very late to go to Mr Paine's. What would another an hour matter now?

I had never encountered a banking house before, but my state of suspicion disposed me to boldness. I asked a passing gentleman for directions to Hill & Vezey. Was it my imagination or was there a slight raising of his eyebrows when I mentioned the bank? The place was not difficult to find. I had only to walk twenty yards along Fleet Street before I came to a building with a facade punctuated by an ecclesiastical-looking bay window behind a grille on one side. The bank's name was engraved on a brass plaque at the portal. The door itself was guarded by a bulldoggish figure in black with a long staff. I met his challenge with a request to encash one of the bank's promissory notes. The guard barred my way, saying that no cash transactions were taking place that day.

I took my courage in my hands and said that I insisted on cashing the note. Perhaps the guard did not like the way my raised voice attracted the attention of passers-by, because he turned and banged with his staff on the door. Presently it opened and a footman in maroon livery appeared.

'She's making a to-do about encashing her note,' the guard said.

The footman admitted me to a gaunt antechamber with the dusty smell of old stone. I could sense by his emollient air that he did not intend to let me go further and that his task was to manage my expectations. He said that the bank was not at that time converting its notes into coin, because it had been overrun with counterfeits, which were threatening the credibility of its promissories.

'I can assure you that my note is genuine,' I said. 'Shall you like to see it?'

The footman raised a hand of protest. A very fine lace cuff flopped from beneath his coat sleeve.

'If only you will be patient, dear lady —' here he offered

me a shifty bow, 'you may convert the note in a week or two more and no harm done.'

The footman's tone was bland, but tension fizzed underneath it, I thought. He could hardly wait to bundle me out into the street, which he did with another bow that was rather more cursory.

I began slowly to make my way along the raucous street, pondering on the bank of Hill & Vezey. I passed numerous coffee-houses as I went. It was hard to miss them. To the pungent aroma of coffee was added the racket made by the lads at their entrances shouting and waving bills of fare – or were they hawking news sheets?

Do you know, over the course of time, listening to conversations at Sedge Court about investments and mortgages and shareholdings and profits and losses, I have absorbed some faint notion of the workings of money. It did not seem right to me that one could only redeem one's banknote at the bank's leisure. What had happened to the gold and silver coin someone would have given to the bank in the first place in exchange for a promise to pay on them? Had it all been paid out on counterfeit promissories? In which case, wouldn't one feel a great lack of confidence in the bank's ability to redeem a genuine note? Evidently the bank could not pay. Or else I should have been able to encash the note. Could it be, I wondered with a start, that Hill & Vezey was bankrupt?

Out of the corner of my eye I saw one of the coffee-house striplings leap forward and thrust a leaf of paper at a gentleman wearing the sober dress of a merchant. The merchant took the paper and perused it with keen interest. In fact, most of the patrons of those coffee-houses looked like merchants – or were they bankers? The stripling's establishment was called Percy's. A slate hung on the door and chalked on it was some kind of list. Of commodities, I saw, as I edged closer – cotton, sugar, tea and so on. I understood then that these lads were handing out the latest stock prices and the coffee-house was likely frequented by traders. The lad squinted at me with a face in which you could see already the future curmudgeon and offered me a sheet with an ironic smirk. As I took his list, it occurred to me to ask him if he knew of Hill & Vezey's bank. He expressed a knowing snort.

I remarked that the bank was unable to encash my promissory note, and he said, 'It is unable to issue them neither. You can set that name down on the blacklist. A crowd has already withdrawn their investments and the bank ain't got the wherewithal now to carry on its business. You'll be lucky if you can ever get your money back, missus. Everyone in the city knows that H&V is done for.'

For the price of a silver button from Eliza's coat, which was all I had to give, he was prepared to tell me why and how Hill & Vezey had come to rupture.

As I pushed through the crowds along the Strand I pondered the news I had been given by the stockbroker's lad. According to him, the bank's reserves of gold had been ruinously depleted and it had effectively ceased trading. Its promissory notes were worthless. I thought of the many bills that had piled up at Sedge Court in response to the mania of refurbishment that had taken place the previous summer and the compensatory spree, ordering fripperies from catalogues, that had blown up in the wake of Sir Joseph Felling's death. I thought of the ruins of Mr Waterland's storehouse. I knew from Mrs Edmunds's account-keeping that Sedge Court had been run on credit for a long time and that Johnny's bank was the source of that credit.

If Johnny was insolvent, so was Sedge Court. The Waterlands needed cash to pay their bills. If cash did not come their way, I could see that they were likely to succumb to an economic infirmity that threatened their way of life. If there were ever a moment when Mr and Mrs Waterland needed one or both of their children to haul in a generous annuity, then here it was.

Had I been right to think that Eliza had been sent to London on covert marriage business? A shiver ran down my spine. Surely, surely, Barfield could not be a part of it.

By the time I reached Poland Street my apprehension had ballooned and I was impatient to warn Eliza that a stratagem might be in play. She had not yet come home from shopping with Johnny. I was obliged to wait another two or three hours in the apartment before she returned with her new sleeves. I barely glanced at them. When I said I must speak to her about a weighty matter, she began to conduct herself evasively. She bustled about, thrusting a needless poker in the fire. She fiddled with her neckerchief. I seized her arm to force her to attend to me, but she immediately shook me off.

I said, 'The promissory note that Johnny gave you, the one that you could not use in Piccadilly—'

'What about it?'

'I tried to cash it at Hill & Vezey today, but the bank would not honour it. They *could* not honour it.'

Eliza said with an attempt at a ringing tone, 'What on earth were you doing with my promissory? How dare you go delving into Johnny's business?'

'I thought you ought to know: the note is worthless.'

'Oh, fiddle. Johnny said as much yesterday when you made a fuss about it in the parlour. The note is old. That does not mean the bank has failed. In fact Johnny has just spent a fortune on my new sleeves, so there!'

'I am only repeating what I was told. The coffee-houses around that part of Fleet Street are frequented by men of the stock exchange. It is their business to know about these things. I asked at one of them for news of Hill & Vezey and I was told that the bank has nearly collapsed.'

Eliza gave me one of her bulbous stares. 'I don't believe you.'

'All right, don't believe me. But will you do me the favour of listening to what I have to say. You may castigate me afterwards if you decide that I am in error.'

'Who told you this balderdash?'

'It was a stockbroker's lad.'

Eliza gave a snort of derision.

'He makes his living among traders.' I brought out from underneath my cuff the folded commodities list from the lad at Percy's. 'Look, you can see, here is a list of commodity prices the boy gives out for his master.'

Eliza ignored the list. She sat down and kicked off her slippers.

On I pressed. 'He said that things started to go wrong for Hill & Vezey last autumn when one of their trading partners in Rotterdam was reported to be overstretched. The partner might have come out of the difficulty, but rivals of the bank made a hue and cry about it. The rumours they spread created doubts about the solvency of the banking house.'

Eliza bent down to straighten the clocks of her stockings – but she was paying attention to my words, I sensed.

'At the same time, so I was told, the bank had a problem with counterfeit notes. There was such a proliferation of them it undermined confidence in the bank and that made investors nervous. A number of them began to withdraw their funds because they feared that the bank might be compromised. Then the trickle of withdrawals turned into a flood. The boy I spoke to says that confidence in Hill & Vezey had ebbed completely by the end of February and now the bank's bills of exchange are no longer accepted for the payment of debts.'

Eliza shook her head. She said, 'I have no idea what you are talking about, and I do not believe that you do either.' She looked up with an air of defiance. 'Have you ever had more than five shillings of your own to rub together? What makes you such a know-it-all about the ins and outs of finance all of a sudden? You will be slipping on a wig and gown next and preaching the law to me.'

I said as mildly as I could – Eliza does not respond well to stridency, from me at any rate – 'The mechanism of the breakdown is not hard to understand. People who had given Hill & Vezey their funds to hold came to fear that the bank might be unable to meet its liabilities. Once the bank became suspect, it experienced a run by its noteholders. But its reserves were not sufficient to meet the demand for withdrawals. Now it is on the verge of closing its doors.'

Eliza stood up and went to the window and said, 'I should like some hot chocolate.'

I said sharply, 'Eliza, don't you see what this means? Your parents may be in a precarious situation.'

'My parents? What do they have to do with it?' She gave a little false laugh. 'Upon my soul, Em, you are the most awful scaremonger.'

I said, 'Your parents have made investments on Johnny's advice. I fear that they were funded by promissory notes that cannot now be honoured.'

It seemed to me that if a great deal of money was owed, wasn't the master in danger of losing his estate or even of being thrown into a debtors' prison? And what should happen to us then – not only Eliza and me, but the servants and the labourers attached to Sedge Court?

Eliza said haughtily, 'As far as I am aware, my father has not confided his business affairs in you. I can tell you one thing that is truly observed – you are forever dinning my ears with problems and perplexities. Even if the bank is in a temporary difficulty, my parents are very far from its consequences.'

I cried, 'But Mr and Mrs Waterland have been bound up in Johnny's dealings for years! Think of the canal companies! Your father gave Johnny funds to invest in them – you know he did, because your mother spoke of it quite publically at Lady Broome's. And now the canals are booming – and yet your father shows no sign of benefiting from his investment. Where has the money gone? Don't you think it is possible that Johnny used it to make an investment of high risk elsewhere. Perhaps he hoped to turn a quick profit for himself and then return your father's stake to its original account at Hill & Vezey.'

Except that his get-rich-quick scheme had evaporated. Was

it to do with those Irish mortgages that Mr Paine had mentioned? And then the bank had crashed. As a result, Mr Waterland no longer had the funds to pay his debts to the extent of the bills of exchange borrowed by his son. I imagined that Johnny's creditors were already breathing down his neck.

Eliza was eyeing me with stony forbearance. I saw I would not convince her that Johnny was in error – the indestructibility of his genius was fundamental to her creed – but how could she not suspect that her father was in difficulty? His negligent appearance alone seemed to bear out the supposition. Ever since the fire at Parkgate he had given up any pretence of maintaining appearances. We glimpsed him from time to time, going about in an old sludge shooting coat. He had left off wearing his wig, so that his wispy hair blew about like a cobweb. There was nothing in his countenance that was well-seeming. It seemed clear to me that Mr Waterland's consuming illness was connected to the despair he must be feeling as the interest on his debts mounted.

'I do not care for your suggestion that my parents are in danger of ruin,' Eliza said.

'But you *must* care! If your parents are ruined, how shall we live otherwise?'

I felt faint at the thought that Sedge Court might be lost to creditors, but my panic was nothing compared to the humiliation and despair that Mrs Waterland would feel. If there ever was a woman who could meet desperate times with desperate measures, it was she. Again, a marriage contract came into my thoughts. Were we here to contract a contract so abhorrent that Eliza could not be told of it until the thing was in train?

I crept close to Eliza and took her reluctant hand in mine.

She tried to pull away but I would not let her. 'Eliza,' I said softly, 'don't you wonder why you have been sent here to press Mr Paine for a portion of his money? Johnny is much better placed to do that than you. Has it not occurred to you that there may be some scheme attached to this visit to London that was not told to us at the outset?'

She succeeded in withdrawing her hand. 'No, it has not. Why should it?' She placed her hands on her hips. 'Johnny is solvent, you know. You said yourself that speculation about the bank is based on rumour. In fact, only today Johnny observed that the greatest danger to his enterprises lies in unfounded gossip.'

'But this is not gossip. People have withdrawn their money. Hill & Vezey will go out of business and take your father's investments along with it, I fear.'

Eliza offered me a remote smile tinged with pity. 'Poor Em. How peevish you are of your station in life, despite everything we have done for you.'

'What do you mean?' I was thrown off balance by her remark.

'You are not a Waterland. More than that, you cannot bear that Johnny is so very partial to me. I see where this maligning of him comes from. Its wellspring is your jealousy.'

I was struck dumb by the utter wrongness of this interpretation, and Eliza allowed herself a chuckle of victory. She said, 'Will you fetch my drink or must I see to it myself?'

I went downstairs to make her damned hot chocolate. I was confounded by our exchange. How was it that we had come to be so at odds over our shared predicament?

The House of Kitty Conneely, Connemara

April, 1766

Nora, friend of my heart, are you there? It is a few long days since I sensed anything of you and I'm talking to myself, so it seems. A freezing wind came down from the mountain in a great swagger today and I kicked up against going out into the coldness. I should have gone to the stones, but a storm might be about to rise, I think. Nothing would do me today but to stay put at the hearth, blankets and all, with a smoke of the pipe to my hand. Soon I will lie down on my mat. Doubtless you can see the tired look on me. I am weak in myself and I find I cannot do the work of the house. The effort of my powers takes it out of me. The dreams I have bring me away at night and it's not a sker-rick of rest I have.

But you will want to know that the penalised daughter is coming under my sway. On the waves she is now, I see that. There are some people it is unlucky to meet and that is true of the fellow she is travelling with. A bad one he is, but bring him on to my turf, I say. The monster may come flying in with a monster's face on him, but I will be pleased to catch him in my trap.

They have a boat and they pursue their quarry. That was two days ago. In a fearful rush they are. The penalised girl is on a wild goose chase, but she does not know it. Oh, it may be that she feels some heavy thing come on her and she will wonder what it is, but she will not know. That is my curse. No one is able to take it off her but me – and that I will not do.

This is how it will be, Nora: that penalised girl will come here and she'll be after falling in a hole and she'll be after disappearing, never to be seen again. The woman of the hat will hear a cry in the air over her head, and she will think it is a gull or some other bird, but it will be the cry of the daughter being carried away from her.

And do you know what I am going to tell you? This is it: our girl is forceful in her mind and she is become hard to bend to my will. She and Connla McDonagh are a very strong article when they are together and they will try to do as they wish and not as I want. He has no right to captivate her, Nora. She is *my* darling. I will try to throw the McDonagh off. It is a difficult enough task as it is to draw our girl home without his interference. He has got into her mind, Nora, and made it cloudy and sometimes now the picture is not clear to me. And the devil of it is, he does not know himself that he is in love with her.

By the blood of Brigid, I wish a hand might come and seize our child right now and let her down into my arms. Why can I not make that happen in a hurry, instead of being in the grip of this long waiting? Still and all, when she comes to live with me I will never be troubled after that.

The *Seal*, South of Galway Bay

April, 1766

We are bumping over the ridges of a hard sea now and there is an air about the crew of reaching a journey's end. The faces of massive cliffs stare out at us from a bold coast on our starboard side. They do not look at all welcoming, but soon I will be landed at their rocky feet. Captain McDonagh is about to send out a signal for a boat that will bring me away to the shore. We are somewhere near the mouth of Galway Bay, apparently. The only thing I know about the town of Galway is that it is supposed to be a grim kind of citadel and the last outpost of the western world.

When I made this mournful remark to Captain McDonagh he said, 'The afternoon men of London and Paris might run from the rigours of Galway town, but it will suit you well enough, Miss Smith.'

I dare say it would suit him, too. You only have to look at him planted firmly on the deck, vigilant of eye and granite of jaw, to know he is very far from being an afternoon man. He is always performing a task or anticipating an incident. Not a quarter of an hour must pass on deck without his scrutinising the sky or raising his spy-glass to scan the sea and then he prowls from stern to fo'c'sle attending every nuance of his vessel's behaviour.

I am strained at the thought of my impending departure from the *Seal*. In spite of its discomforts, this voyage has lulled me into a false security. It has released me from the terror that clawed at me on my flight to Bristol, but Galway is a military outpost and I foresee many opportunities to be stopped and questioned by constables and militiamen. I cannot bear the thought of returning to that everyday fearfulness, the looking over my shoulder, the constant wondering about what will happen to me.

I worry about English news sheets. Are they sold in Galway's print shops? Will my likeness turn up on a pamphlet advertising wanted felons? If I am arrested for murder, I doubt there will be any trial at all. They will haul me through the streets tied to a sledge and hang me in a public place. Then my body will be given to the anatomists to tear apart. I ought not to stay in the town, only I fear I may not know how to survive in the countryside outside its walls.

Captain McDonagh has been partly obliging, but I see he is not sorry to put me off. My presence has been an inconvenience at best, requiring him to go on with his unlawful business under the nose of a stranger. Still, I wonder if he has managed to form enough sympathy for my plight to stretch out the help he has already given me. I am summoning up my courage to ask him a favour. I regard it as my last hope.

'Captain McDonagh, may I speak with you?'

He glances at me without saying anything.

'Sir, as you know, my aim has always been to reach France. I will tell you frankly that I am in danger of coming under arrest, and Galway—'

The captain takes a step towards me with such suddenness

I flinch. He leans to my ear and says forcefully, 'A word of advice, Miss Smith. Don't ever volunteer information that can be used against you. Only a fool does such a thing.'

'Mayn't I trust you?'

'I know what you are after. You see that I engage in a little trade with France and it occurs to you that the *Seal* must be headed that way sooner or later. Why, you wonder, don't I let you stay on board until we reach French waters.'

'That is exactly it.'

'I must disappoint you.'

'You are unkind! How can you leave me behind to face mortal danger?'

'Because you would have me grapple with your sentiments and in one way or another pay attention to you.' He sees that I am about to protest and he cuts me off. 'What am I doing now but contending with you? I have a ship to run and business to attend to. Any additional element endangers my very simple objective, which is to stay alive and to earn my coin. Yes, your fate is uncertain – but so is the fate of every man on the *Seal*. You are right, Miss Smith. I am unkind. I do not want to have to think about you.'

I am crushed by his blunt refusal.

'Captain!' The cry comes aloft from the masthead. 'Sails astern!'

No wonder Terry Madden betrayed me. Doubtless he learned at his captain's knee how to harden his heart. What an idiot I was to think that Captain McDonagh might be a decent man, even a rugged gallant.

I gaze with despair into the dingy evening light.

And gradually my eyes begin to pick out a vessel off our stern. It lies about a third of a league away. At that distance it looks as flimsy as a leaf blowing across a pond, but the sight of it spurs Captain McDonagh to action. He shouts at Mr Guttery to tack away at once to the west.

My pulse races with fear. I will never see anything come up behind us without thinking that it means to pounce on me.

The *Seal* trembles as she is brought across the wind. She leans into her new course with urgency and I find myself willing her on as if she were in need of self-belief. I grip again the mahogany binnacle for support. Upon my soul, this binnacle and I have forged a close connection, you must have noticed. I am reassured by its undulant yet dependable shape and by the firm base on which it rests. It does not mind to be imposed upon.

My eye swivels towards the vessel behind, heavily canvassed like the *Seal* – and a cutter, surely, given its quick lines. Captain McDonagh orders a jib to be set at the masthead and the *Seal*'s hands spring to the complicated business of controlling the topsail's lines. 'Sheet it as hard as you can, Dubois,' the captain roars. 'Put some beef into it!'

In spite of her heavy cargo, the *Seal* fizzes along, pointing an eager bow high into the wind. But the cutter astern piles on the sail, too, and I see by the bulge of the mainsail that it has caught a favourable breeze. In fact, it seems to be gaining on us. Is that possible? We ought to have the advantage still. The *Seal*'s high jib is scooping wind out of the sky. And yet, we do not leap as sprightly as before. Our pursuer, on the other hand, is rushing at us with such speed it is not long before I am able to catch a glimpse of the crew.

They are specks of scarlet moving around on deck. I know what that means. I have seen those red shirts and the blue breeches that go with them on seamen at Parkgate. It is the livery of His Majesty's revenue service.

I will the *Seal* to bear away. Away, away from the chasing men. But something ails the boat. Despite a large press of canvas, her tail drags in the water and we cannot get on. Captain McDonagh has already detected the lag, of course, and has called for the bilge man. Has the pump failed? There are men working it hard, but the way the *Seal* is flopping in the swell I fear the revenue cutter must overpower us.

The captain sends the bilge man below with a mechanic and then lifts his spy-glass once more. 'Damn his eyes,' he growls.

'An old friend of ours, is it, Captain?' Mr Guttery, who is at the helm, glances over his shoulder with a show of uncon-cern.

'It's the shape of the *Vindicator*, Mr Guttery, if I am not mistaken.'

Captain McDonagh lowers the glass and narrows his gaze at the western sky. Scowling clouds have assembled on the horizon around the embers of the day and the wind has grown blustery. There is a sharp, salty smell in the air. The captain shouts up at the masthead man to loosen the foresail and shake out the reefs.

The chasing cutter draws ever nearer.

All at once a derisory little noise like a fan being cracked open sounds from her port side and a puff of smoke blooms like the head of a dandelion. Something whistles overhead and clatters among our rigging. We are under fire.

'Take cover below,' Captain McDonagh shouts at me, 'unless you want to be killed!'

A second volley whines across our foredeck and tears holes in the jib that Dubois is busy reefing.

I skitter down the companionway, more wary of the captain's wrath than I am of the *Vindicator*'s iron shot, and crouch between the stove and the coal bunker. I sense the *Seal* continuing to double and tack. Every so often her timbers shudder at the impact of the *Vindicator*'s guns. She still feels sluggish, not at all like her usual racy self, and I can hear the gasping action of the valves in the bilge pump amid the tumult above. Jim is not at his post. He has gone aft where the mechanics are at work at the foot of a bulkhead.

A shot lands directly overhead, showering my head with dust and splinters. I scramble away from the debris, squeezing past the barrels and bales in the hold towards the forepeak, although there is no reason why it should be any safer there. In fact the movement of the boat is more tumultuous in the bows. I tip up and down as if on a rocking horse as the *Seal* shakes with each strike of the big waves and seems to reel.

By God, I believe she is listing. And what is that seeping across the floor?

'Jim!' I cry, retreating from the dark stain at my feet. 'We are taking on water!'

'A stop-water has rotted,' he shouts. 'It has let water in the hull and we cannot repair it on the run like this.'

'Will the cutter take us? They are revenue men.'

'So they are.' Jim shrugs.

It had not occurred to me that Captain McDonagh might not carry the day. Am I to fall now with such ease into the hands of the law? Damnation, but this life of mine is a cross-grained one!

Jim says, 'Our master and the *Vindicator* have a history, they do. You can be sure that Captain McDonagh will parley to give himself up afore he loses the *Seal* – and the *Vindicator* will be pleased enough to clap him in irons, in particular if it cause no risk to themselves. Lieutenant Blake may run a quick vessel but he don't have the stomach for a stoush, not with the McDonagh, he don't.'

Making an effort to suspend my anxiety, I hoist myself through the hatch. The decking has been peppered by shot – and the black-hulled *Vindicator* is standing off to starboard of the wallowing *Seal*.

Captain McDonagh salutes the revenue commander, who has struck a triumphant pose on his foredeck in a tight-wrapped blue coat. The revenue boat has lit its lanterns in the gloaming, which adds to its aura of celebration. Fearful of being seen, I observe from the shadows.

Captain McDonagh calls across the strait between the two vessels, 'My compliments, Lieutenant. You see our vessel is in disorder.' He makes a flourish with his hat. I notice then that the *Seal*'s crew are at their battle stations. Each of the swivels is manned and Mr Guttery and Mr Robinson have their pistols crooked in their arms. Jim was right. The captain is offering to surrender himself to the *Vindicator*'s commander in lieu of a fight. 'Think on it,' Captain McDonagh booms. 'You may take the *Seal*, but not before we've blasted a good few holes in your vessel and your crew. Or I will come across now in my tender.'

The lieutenant shouts something in reply, but his words are

blown away by the wind and Captain McDonagh responds with a showy open-palmed shrug. Now the lieutenant confers with his first mate and they crane their heads at the sky. A great crowd of bleating seagulls is flying overhead, making for the coast, and the furious clouds have formed a thunderhead.

All at once, Captain McDonagh pulls me forward.

My alarm at being touched by him is confused with some other undefined feeling, that makes me grow turbulent – and I try to shake myself free. But he grips my arm more fiercely, and shouts, 'Let me sweeten my offer with this little runaway! She has been up to no good, I warrant, and it will reflect well on you to bring her to justice!'

I gasp in amazement at this cruel and utterly unexpected betrayal.

'What are you saying?' I cry. It must be a ploy, surely. He of all people would not hand me to the custody of the preventives. But without a glance at me, although he holds me fast, the captain orders the *Seal*'s tender to be lowered. He bows in the direction of the *Vindicator*'s commander to acknowledge that the deal has de facto been struck.

'The devil take you, you dog!' I gasp, struggling violently, kicking and flailing, to get away. But his hand circles my wrist like an iron manacle.

Captain McDonagh lowers his head to mine and says in a hoarse voice, 'I told you, I have not escaped the noose all these years by being a man of sentiment. I will do what I must to win through.'

'Rot in hell, McDonagh!' I shout.

Suddenly sheet lightning blanches the sky. Gulls shriek in panic and whirl in confused circles. The darkened air fills with a ticking sound. It builds, tick-tick-tick, and erupts in a bone-shaking crash of thunder.

Captain McDonagh turns to Mr Guttery, who has been watching us with his impassive stare, and says, 'With luck on your side, you will manage to reach Inishmore, man. The preventives will want to run for shelter and will not send a prize-master after you.'

Then he chivvies me towards the rope ladder that has been hung from the gunwale.

I quail at the prospect of capture, yet where is there to go but down. I climb the rail and find a handhold on the swaying ladder and descend, my feet groping for a hold on the rungs, my silks waving madly in the gusts as if trying, uselessly, to signal for help. Below, the rowboat bounces up and down on its tether.

Captain McDonagh arrives close on my heels, and as he leans forward to set the oars in the rowlocks he looks into my face with a strange, frank expression and says, 'Have no illusions. This is the villain I am.'

'Yes,' I hiss in anger, 'I see who you are.'

The captain lays into the oars with a short, hard action, and away we go. I am angry, but more than that I feel forsaken. I watch the *Seal* begin to limp away and with it the possibility of some kind of freedom. I know myself at this moment to be completely alone in the world.

The *Vindicator* is near. Its lieutenant stands at the rail of the foredeck with a pistol in his hand, although the deteriorating weather, full of misty spray and imminent rain, must be a deterrent to his powder and to the ammunition of the guns trained on us.

We rise up and crash down uncomfortably in the choppy sea, but Captain McDonagh has a way of varying his stroke to get over the waves. Through a combination of pull and drift he brings us alongside the *Vindicator*. He ships the oars, and deckhands reach down with their grappling hooks and push our bow in against the hull. The lieutenant leans over to get a look at us. He has a screwed-up face and the darting ogle of a nervy man. As the rope ladder drops down from the cutter, he aims his pistol at Captain McDonagh – or alternately at the captain and at me, since the sea is tossing us around and the distance between the crests is becoming shorter. The wind clamours and complains, and the lieutenant twitches at the frequent streaks of lightning. As I begin my ascent, an almighty clap of thunder makes my ears ring. My skirts are fluttering so hard they sound as though they are beating a tattoo against the air, and I find it an effort to progress up the ladder. I tighten my grip on the ropes for fear of being thrown off into the sea, while thunder rolls in the sky and blue lightning flashes with fury.

Good God, what was *that*? The most awful crack of light and sound as though the gods had tossed a grenade at us from behind their black bastion of clouds. Has the boat been struck by lightning? Something has caused consternation on the deck of the *Vindicator*. Difficult to make out anything with my hair flying in my eyes and my petticoat threatening to tear itself to pieces in the gusts. I almost wonder if I might slide down the ladder and plead with the captain to take our chances in the rowboat. The thought is accompanied by a quick glance below. What is that shape in the gloom? It almost looks as though the captain has cast off. I twist around to get a better look. Yes, he has! There is the tender on a crest, all whipped by spray and mist, and now it has sunk out of sight into a trough.

What a rotten deluder. What a cowardly cheat he is to leave me stuck on this punishment vessel. Damn him, by God!

I clamber over the rail to the accompaniment of a report from the lieutenant's pistol. Then comes the boom of the *Vindicator*'s swivel guns. I turn to see Captain McDonagh's rowboat rising out of a trough, badly exposed to his foes. The lieutenant pulls a second pistol from his belt and aims again, but the weather has dampened his powder and his pulling of the trigger yields only a flash in the pan. In a fit of petulance he flings the errant pistol on the deck. It fires belatedly with a cracking loud *bang*! There is a volley of shouts – the ball seems to have narrowly missed someone's foot – and in those few seconds, Captain McDonagh, who is rowing hard, makes valuable ground. The guns swivel and let loose their shot, but the captain, bobbing up and down in the building sea, is not an easy target. Despite his perfidy, I find I do not wish to see him killed. I believe he will get away, for now it is beginning to rain, but can there be any hope for him in a rowboat on a stormy sea?

The detonation of a gun towards the port bow makes me jump. Smoke rises lazily from the mouth of the gun. And this time when the rowboat surges up on the crest of the big, grey swell, I cannot see Captain McDonagh. Or is that a glimpse of him lying wounded, perhaps, in the bottom of the boat? He does not ply the oars at all. Where are the oars? How will he propel himself without them?

The lieutenant orders another round to be fired. The shot splatters in the sea. I do not know the range of these swivels

– could it be a quarter of a mile? But what does it matter, for Captain McDonagh does not sit up. I am galled with him all over again – and then I must admit that it is not anger but distress.

Captain! Sit up! If you do not start to row, you will be swamped. With my heart in my mouth I watch the tender swing around broadside to the waves.

Pouring down now in a determined way, rods of rain pit the water. The lieutenant commands his helmsman to pursue the tender to confirm the captain's death, but it is a course of action that grows more impossible by the second. The storm has come blustering in upon us with its mayhem, and waves are exploding around the *Vindicator*'s bows. The master of this vessel must stir himself to reef his sails.

I can see nothing of the rowboat.

Surely Captain McDonagh is feigning death in order to throw off the *Vindicator*. Surely that is what he is doing. Would not it be just like him to dissemble so? I creep forward, no one paying me any heed – the men on the foredeck are struggling with the jib. The lieutenant is leaning out amidships looking into the chaotic gloom, but even when another flash of lightning illuminates the convulsing sea, he cannot see any trace of the captain either. With an expression of irritation he turns away – there is a contretemps in the bow and he must attend to the messiness of the jib. The men brought the canvas down just as the cutter tunnelled into a wave and now the sail has slumped into the sea. Captain McDonagh, I cannot but think, would never have allowed such incompetence. Woe betide the man who let tackle drag in the water when the *Seal* heeled in a breeze.

I flail at a line that is tied to the mast below the boom and hold on tight against the wild movements of the boat. It occurs to me that I could not have chosen a worse place to ride out a lightning storm. Were the captain here, he would say, 'Do you want to go to blazes, madam? Go below or must you baulk at my every command?' I look for a binnacle but there is none. However, I will not go below. I do not trust the seamanship of this commander or his crew. The bow has come up again, but still the hands are unable to bring in the sodden jib before the next wave hits. They must hack at the rigging in order to cut the sail free.

I am concentrated on the detail of these actions – I cannot pretend to care about the wretched jib! – because I do not wish to turn my thoughts to the fate of Captain McDonagh. And yet my thoughts insist on going towards him, damn it. He is a cur, but it distresses me to think of him killed by the preventives' shot. And the alternative is almost worse: that he is wounded and beyond rescue and bleeding to death, that is, if the flimsy tender remains afloat. The seas have risen from five to ten feet in less than twenty minutes – and the light is going now.

The elements have compelled the *Vindicator* on to a reckless course. I cannot see what is happening outside now. The lieutenant ordered me taken below-decks and one of his crew pushed me into this squalid hold. The hatch above wants a lid, and each time the boat hurtles off the top of one wave and buries its bow into the backside of the next, seawater washes through the grating. I am numb with cold, although I cannot bother myself about it, not when I consider Captain McDonagh's fate. Senseless to reprehend him now.

The thought of his piteous death — and the waste of his life — grieves me in spite of his treachery. He was a commander as resolute and weatherly as the *Seal* herself and his practicality could be trusted. I remember how he liked a ship's rigging to have a little give in it as an aid to speed. He liked a loose-footed mainsail to fly freely with plenty of draught and power in it, although he would not abide carelessness. Yet he was not averse to granting a liberty either. And if a difficulty arose, he sprang to propose a remedy. I suppose I was just such an answer.

I am babbling to you out of fear — but you guessed that, no doubt. I am also under the influence of a peculiar calm, which accepts that I shall likely join Captain McDonagh at the bottom of the ocean before much longer. In my short life I have discovered that human beings have the capacity to entertain many different, often conflicting strands of their characters at the same time. I am reconciled to my fate. At the same time I am deathly afraid. My hands tremble, my heart races. Each assault by the sea, each roll of the battered vessel, terrifies me. Yet, when the wave has passed, optimism, incredibly, rushes into the void. I think, as death approaches, that we must keep believing, until the very last second, that we will get out of the jam.

I never knew I had such buoyancy.

It is pitch black down here. The lanterns went out almost as soon as I was cast down due to the wind and the wet and their antic movements. I sense that there is another prisoner in the hold, or a member of the crew. I keep my distance from him and cling to the companionway below the hatch. I can see nothing through the grating but a churn of greyness. How long has the *Vindicator* been battling this storm? More than an hour, I conject, but it seems to me that the lieutenant is losing the fight. As far as I can tell, he has tried to wrest control of his vessel from the storm by changing direction, heading into the wind. He has been hindered, however, by a mighty cross swell that bats the hull and sends the *Vindicator* yawing like a guzzler too drunk to stand. I fear that the swell is pushing us at a dangerous angle to the wind.

Oh, Lord, listen to that roar. I know before it breaks that this wave is calamitous. It falls upon us like a hammer on an anvil. The *Vindicator* reverberates from the force and tips forward at a frightening angle, her bow stuck into the sea like a skewer. Then the sea scoops us up and, among the pandemonium, objects tumbling, wild shouts, it slews us around at a desperate tilt and I nearly drop from the companionway. We are in danger of capsizing.

I must get out now!

Clawing at the grating over the hatch, although I know it has been battened, screwed down as surely as any fastening of an early coffin, I fail to make headway. My cries evaporate in the shrieking air – and are overtaken then by the hollow sound of the keel scraping on rock and the splintering of timbers. Have we arrived at a shore or are we on a reef? Amid the crew's frantic hubbub and the cacophony of the sea and the groaning vessel, someone calls the order to abandon ship. I hammer my fist against the grating.

All of a sudden a hand grabs my ankle. An elbow knocks me aside.

I crash from my perch and bang up hard on slimy boards. Who is it here? A cook or a carpenter – I don't know, but he has a hatchet and is slashing at the wooden grating.

I force my way from the hold and grasp one of the mast hoops.

The *Vindicator* is heeling badly, the crew is fumbling with a tender to make good their escape, when all at once an eerie lull comes over the storm, as though it has lowered its head and is gathering itself for a final charge.

And, here it comes, now – the big, galloping wave that will overwhelm us.

A shudder passes through the cutter as it submits to its fate.

It is a shock to find myself thrown into the frigid sea, my mantle and skirts inflating around me like some sudden fungus.

I fear that the weight of them will drag me beneath the surface and it is with relief I hear in the darkness and confusion men's voices and the rattle of rowlocks. I glimpse the outline of the tender and – is that a second, smaller rowboat? Yet my cries for help do not bring them near. Why do they not hear me?!

I have no idea how to keep afloat. My feet kick madly – and my shoes are lost. One hand makes a circular motion as if stirring laundry, the other fumbles at the strings of my mantle and my top petticoat and they fall away.

A wave slaps my face. I scream for help and swallow a mouthful of choking salt water. I scream again. The crew's voices sound greatly more distant. They are rowing away and I am sinking like a stone. The percussion in my ears is the pounding of my frantic heart.

My higher self looks down in sorrow on the poor, panicked creature thrashing in the sea and can do nothing but regret that she is so very ill-equipped for her ordeal.

And then: the herring girls of Parkgate swim into my mind.

I see them waist deep in the Dee, washing the fish oil from their arms. Some of them liked to frolic in the water, driving themselves quite a long way out. How did they do it?

With head up, I reach forward and drag a hand through the sea, and repeat the action with my other arm. Yes, they turned their arms like a windmill.

Again, I reach up, reach over and pull. And again, and again, and again . . . My shoulders burn with the effort, but I plough onward. Onward, onward, onward. Sweating and freezing at the same time. I cannot go on, but I must. I do not want to die in this lonesome way, I do not.

I alter the movement of my desperate arms, pushing the water away from my breast. The propulsion is less effective, but I lack the strength to do otherwise. How very tired I am, and the thought of the dark, silent fathoms beneath, the malign profundity of them, is dangerously paralysing. I force myself to crane my neck as far as I can out of the water and it is then that the moonlight shows me a shape in the swells, rising and falling. I do not know what it is. My eyes are stinging from the salt.

Something grazes against my leg, something finny, and its slithery touch so appals me I find the energy to kick out and continue.

The only thing anchoring me to life is the screaming pain in my muscles. Overarm again. Rotate right arm, slap into water, slap and scoop, now the left arm. An object is bobbing nearby. With a cry I seize hold of it and find myself clinging to a wooden grid about the size of a small door. It is one of the *Vindicator*'s hatch covers!

I begin to cry then, out of gratitude for the hatch cover,

and there is even some fleeting comfort in the heat of my welling tears. Oh, this beautiful raft. Surely it will save my life. Very cautiously, I wriggle on to it, lying on my stomach. The thing dips a little, but it holds my weight. My entire body is shaking with cold and I dare say I might freeze to death, but it is bliss to rest my cramping arms. For a long while I simply drift, with frozen fingers clamped to the grid. It occurs to me eventually that I am being carried on a current.

And then I wonder if I am drifting further out to sea into the great abyss of the Atlantic.

I beat away the thought, silently shouting at it to leave me alone.

But what can I do except drift?

The noise of the sea is one unceasing roar.

Who can say how many minutes or even hours I have been dawdling on this sea? I rise up and down the swells in a trance. Up and down. My feet and my hands grow numb. What a pity that the elegant mantle the captain gave me has gone to its doom. And I lament my poor French slippers, drifting down on their long journey to the bottom of the sea.

There is something amiss. My raft is waterlogged. It is sinking! In a panic I slide off the hatch cover and begin to kick. I kick desperately, hanging on to the cover. I am pure will, for to give up is to go under. I pretend there is nothing in my mind, no fear of death, no horror of annihilation. I am nothing but kicking feet. I hang on to the hatch cover and I kick my feet.

I am exhausted and the raft is exhausted too. It wants to go under.

I manoeuvre around the thing so that I am lying on my

back, clutching the raft to my chest as though in an encouraging embrace. The raft and I stay afloat, but now I have a view of the black sky and the pitiless beauty of its stars. They glitter at a distance that is so terribly remote it seems the definition of loneliness.

I turn away from the stars and take up the grind of pushing the raft and kicking.

And then, up ahead, something shining! Oh, thank God, there are lights, yellow and a strange blue-green. With a last burst, I drive towards the brightness.

I discover a sight as hopeless as it is enchanting. The lights are only the glowing emanation of a school of fish. At my approach, the luminous creatures swim away, fanning out in a glittering formation of green brilliants, like a gorgeous necklace ornamenting the vast body of the sea. As though cast down by this disappointment, the raft decides it is unable to go on and it submerges itself – not entirely, but enough so that I cannot make use of it except to hang on to a corner of it as I watch the phosphorescence fade.

I am in a state of isolation that it is beyond me to bear. I tread water slowly, wearily, spent now. My limbs feel as though they are broken. All that is keeping my head above the surface is the thought, delirious though it is, that you wait for me on a shore somewhere, near or far. The thought of you is the same thing as life itself.

Ah, is there anything left in you, Em? Just try. *Go on.*

A tugging in the sea passes over the skin of my legs. The current wants to push me.

The raft has gone, but I float, somehow I stay afloat, and the current draws me onward into an underwater forest.

Fronds of seaweed rise and fall around my legs. I had no idea that seaweed could grow so tall from the bottom of the ocean. I wonder if there truly are miracles under the waves. Sea-gardens and mansions made of coral and shells. Abby's world under water. Where people live as we do, only better. I am very curious now to see such a place. It is just a case, surely, of letting go and drifting downwards in order to find myself in a palace made of pearls.

My feet seem to brush something fixed, grainy, but then a wave lifts me up and the firmness underfoot recedes. But my salt-stung eyes have made out a sort of blackish stripe at the base of the inky sky, and a little moonlit frill.

Waves washing against rocks.

That distant sound is the whisper of breakers.

A flowing tide has washed me ashore. I crawled through rushing surf, I clawed through heaving shingle, and lie now on my bed of sand, one cheek pressing into cold softness, one eye open, listening to the waves clasp the shore and then cleave from it. The smell of brine is very strong. Turning my tired head, I see that I am surrounded by collapsed kelp, flung up fresh from the sea, strung with sprinkles of blue and green, glowing like ghost seaweed. What a night for creatures being alight. I am, too. Alight and alive. Spasms of cold shake me, but I understand in every fibre of my being that just to be alive is enough.

PART FOUR

The Long Strand, Connemara

April, 1766

The air smells of smoke and there is a pearly cast to the sand that stretches away towards a scattering of low rocks. I haul myself to sitting and vomit up salt water. The light is flushing pink. It illuminates a bank of scant grass above the strand where I have washed up. At my back the tide is retreating, exposing long fingers of rock and glistening red seaweed. Out to sea a line of tall, jagged rocks – is that where the *Vindicator* came aground? – and further towards the horizon a violet smudge, which may be an island. I turn over a speckled stone and a dank green crab scuttles away from under it. My limbs feel sluggish. As I watch the waves expend themselves against the outcrops I must fight the urge to stretch out again on my sandy bed. I begin to make my way on hands and knees towards the narrow strip of land that slopes down to the sand. It is occupied by sombre hillocks, shaped somewhat like haycocks, and at its foot numbers of small, sleek black boats lie upturned like giant beetles. A cloud slides in front of the sun and subdues the light and I feel a shivering in my skin as if some bad thing is near, but it only prefaces another bout of vomiting.

As I look up from my retching, I seem to glimpse shadowy indistinct figures moving among the brooding hillocks – and presently I detect a low murmur of voices in the distance. The approaching creatures seem peculiar, misshapen. Ah, I see that many of them are carrying tall baskets on their backs and others are transporting upside-down boats on their heads, which lend them the look of fabulous beasts. I watch their advance as though in a reverie, my mind enjoying the hope that my arduous journey will end in deliverance.

A fisherman in cap and wide-legged breeches rolled up to his knees has noticed me. I wave him onward with a weak hand, but he has halted as though frozen in fear at the sight of me in my soaking rags and dripping hair. He stretches out his arms like a barricade, and gradually the people clustering at his back fall silent. They have a wild look about them, a stark look, especially the women dressed in black and red like emblems.

I manage to get to my feet. The action causes a collective intake of breath among the watchers. As I take a staggering step forward, I sense that these people are mortally frightened. Some of them are making the sign of the cross. A large fellow clutching a long sort of pike calls to someone in the thick of the crowd and the people stir and mutter among themselves. They are armed with implements, I see, with pikes and knives and little sickles.

I wait patiently.

Seabirds are flying all around.

I turn my gaze towards the complication of islets and sker-ries that lies beyond the slopping low waters and a feeling of giddiness comes over me. The huddle of people parts, allowing a tall, bony woman to pass through. She is in her fifties, perhaps, barefoot, raggedly attired like her fellows with a knitted mantle criss-crossed over her bosom. Her broad face has evidently been much buffeted by wind and sea spray. She regards me with hooded pale eyes full of misgiving and addresses me in a language I do not recognise.

'Forgive me, madam, I cannot understand you.' My voice is hoarse, little more than a whisper.

She clears her throat. To my surprise she says, 'I have a little English, if that is what you speak now. I had it from Mike, don't you remember?'

What does she mean by *Do I remember?*

I croak that my ship was wrecked, but I do not think she hears me. She says, 'I beg you to leave us alone! I know that Kitty must have called you back, but you have come to the wrong place. She does not live at us these days. She means only mischief now.'

I stare at the woman, blinking with incomprehension. 'We cannot let you come back,' she cries. 'It is a terrible thing when people like you come walking about among us!'

I am mystified by her meaning. I feel befuddled, as if I might faint, but somehow I raise an arm to point at this lady, who looks so hardy and yet so improbably terrified. 'Who are you?' I ask with great weariness.

'You know very well that my name is Mary Folan.'

It has not escaped my notice that the people on the strand have begun to inch forward in a stealthy manner that makes me uneasy. The woman before me, Mrs Folan, gives the impression she is screwing up her courage – it is the squaring of her shoulders, the narrowing of her eyes. She leans forward and shows to me the palms of her hands. For a second I expect to see something there, a gushing from those sacred wounds that Papists believe in or some such. But she pushes her hands at me with a loud shriek. 'Go back, Nora,' she cries. 'Go back.'

'Who is Nora?' I mumble.

'Yourself, of course.' Mrs Folan gives a snort of grim laughter.

My mouth opens to tell her who I am, but I hear Captain McDonagh's words ringing in my ears. Do not volunteer information about yourself that can be used against you. Then it strikes me: is this not a wonderful opportunity to escape the identity of Mary Smith and her taint of crime? If Miss Smith is traced to the *Vindicator*, it will be assumed that she drowned when the vessel foundered. And even if these grim peasants are questioned, what can they say about a drenched creature discovered on their strand, but that she was a person called Nora. A marvellous feeling of letting go comes over me then at being released from the burden of Mary Smith. I feel euphoric all of a sudden. I escaped the sea with my life and now I have a new one!

It seems that Mrs Folan has lost interest in questioning me, because she turns to her people with one shoulder raised, as if to suggest that there is nothing more that she can do, and pivots on her heel and strides towards the embankment. What a strange, desolate place this is, but with a wild beauty, too. The land is low and the sky is awfully high. I watch Mrs Folan pass among the odd hillocks, which stand like morose sentinels guarding the shore, and set off along a path. Far beyond her diminishing figure, huge clouds are floating on the horizon. Or are they hills? I cannot quite make them out for there are splinters of light in my eyes.

At first the hissing seems to belong to the sea. The waves have been washing up sibilantly in the background, but that sound is gentle, lulling. This is a noise that is made to deter an intruder or a predator. The people on the strand are hissing between their teeth. They press towards me, making flicking motions with their fingers as though shaking off something unwelcome.

One of the fisherwomen springs forward and pushes me hard on to the sand, and all at once hands are reaching for me in a tumult of haste and grunting. Someone seizes my arm and begins to drag me through the sand.

I realise with horror that they mean to drive me back into the sea.

I am outraged. This treatment is *undeserved*!

A roar of protest rises from my core and rumbles out of my mouth. Frightfulness is all that I have for a defence against these people. The awful noise shocks them, and in the split second of their faltering I fight free and run towards the rocks. I have no idea of a route of escape, except to follow the direction taken by Mrs Folan. Perhaps it leads to a road or to woodland, where I can hide. I hardly know what I am doing, except that I must flee. This has become the condition of my life.

I turn towards the embankment. Somehow I have the wit to know that I will make quicker progress leaping from rock to rock than labouring through the sand. I am amazed at the surefootedness of my bare feet. It is as though they know exactly where to place themselves. But surely my pursuers are equally fleet of foot. With a glance over my shoulder I see that the people are coming at me, but they do so in a crowded little knot, which makes me think they are sticking together for safety.

They are afraid of me!

Encouraged by this advantage, I scramble up the embankment and zigzag among the hillocks, which reek of rotting seaweed, and duck behind one of them to catch my breath. There is no other cover.

I peer out from behind the seaweed cock and finding that the people hesitate to pursue me, seize my chance and continue inland, staggering across a stony field. I do not know where I find the strength for this. I climb over a stone wall draped with drying loops of seaweed and enter a smaller field of tough grass studded with mottled stones and boulders. The field drops away into a ragged inlet with a narrow channel of water surrounded by hanks of kelp and on the far shore of the inlet there is a handful of whitewashed cottages dispersed among tiny fields. I can make out small children at play in front of some of them. My eye alights on a figure striding the lane that passes along the line of the shore. Impossible to say if it is Mrs Folan.

My throat hurts as a consequence of the seawater I have swallowed and I am dreadfully thirsty. I ask myself how I will find shelter and sustenance in this austere place. Casting many anxious looks around me, I negotiate the rocks below the field and descend into the inlet. I have no scheme to put in play, only the hope of eventually finding a stream to drink from and a barn where I can sleep. There must be a village somewhere in this county or even a town.

Each footstep sinks deeply into the inlet's muddy sand floor and the hem of my smuggled silk gown is soon weighted with mud, but at last I reach the other side of the inlet and begin to pick my way among rock pools. There is a dark cloud hanging overhead like an enormous straining bag, and within seconds its bulging underside bursts and the rain teems down. I labour on as best I can, shivering, with dripping hair, but managing to catch some raindrops in my mouth.

There is a donkey honking somewhere. Perhaps it has a byre I may share. I find myself hurrying through sheaves of slippery greenish-black kelp, its bladders popping underfoot, until I gain a hummocky piece of land. It gives me a view of a low cottage on the edge of a blunt point. A donkey, snuffling at thin turf, stands under a sod awning attached to the cottage. He looks up in surprise as I approach. The cottage overlooks another rocky, seaweedy inlet. Through the sheets of rain, I see that someone is pushing aside the hide that covers the entrance of the cottage.

Her mantle discarded and with faded hair hanging like skeins of seaweed, Mrs Folan fills the frame of her doorway. I hesitate – will she call on her people to attack me? But there is a good chance I will die in any case if I remain exposed to the conditions of this place, and so I creep forward in my bedraggled clothes. I have, oddly enough, the impression Mrs Folan is expecting me. She raises a hand and lets it fall as though powerless in the face of whatever the Fates may bring her.

The floor of the cottage is set a little below ground level, which gives the feeling of being in a cave. The only light comes from the glow of the hearth and a lamp of rushes burning in a scallop shell. The table is made from a tea chest. I can make out some sort of bed on the floor and a wooden churn in a corner and a barrel. On one of the walls lobster pots and nets hang from hooks. I am drawn at once to the heat of the stone hearth with its bricks of burning turf.

Without a word, Mrs Folan removes the cover from a tin pail and hands me a wooden dipper.

When I have drunk my fill, she says, 'Will you tell me what it is that you want, Nora, and then I beg you to go.'

I note the quaver in her voice. She is terribly frightened of me or of the woman she calls Nora. I confess that my spirits lift at that. I see that it may benefit me to manipulate Mrs Folan's fear. I, Mary Smith, have no power at all, but the baleful Nora seems to wield a great deal.

I ask her whether she has a husband or children and she replies sharply, 'Would I still bear the name of Folan if I did?' Then she looks wary. 'Is it a riddle you mean to try me with?'

'I only wish to know if you live alone.'

'I do.'

'Then I will ask one small favour of you, and you will never hear from me again. You see I am soaking wet. Let me rest a night or two with you and dry my clothes. Only you must swear not to tell a soul that I am here.'

I can tell that Mrs Folan is loathe to have me under her roof, but she says at last, 'Very well, so you may, but I beg you to be on your way to Cashel just as soon as you can.'

Then she adds, 'That is where Kitty has put herself away these days, which is all I will say of her.'

I mean to ask her why I should want to go to this person called Kitty, but my head swims and will not form the question. In the chamber's smoky fug, everything seems misty. As if from a distance I hear Mrs Folan say, 'I will shelter you, although it is many others who would not. I will put myself under the protection of the Holy Mother for it.'

The House of Mary Folan, Connemara

May, 1766

Still half-asleep, I listen to the sound of the sea as it surges and falls away, surges and falls away, just as it does in my dreams: sea-surge and bird-scream and a disappearing boat. Is it Captain McDonagh's boat? Ah, Captain, I mourn your death still. I press my ear to my mattress and listen to the faint whispers of its mossy stuffing. My blanket smells faintly of kelp. Presently my eyes open fully without heaviness and I realise that my ague has dispersed. I sit up with a feeling of clarity. I am in Mrs Folan's cottage. As my gaze travels around an interior of flaking, limed walls, I remark my feeling of contentment. In some way that I cannot absolutely comprehend, I am soothed by the earthy smells of moss and peat which pervade everything, including the shift I am wearing. It is my French cambric shift that was a gift from Captain McDonagh. Mrs Folan must have laundered it and dried it in front of her turf fire. Its particular smoky smell seems intensely familiar to me. I sense recollection rising and shaking its feathers at the edge of my understanding, but then it retreats into the shadows.

I get myself up, stretch, yawn, a little light-headed. I peep through the gap of the window covering. In the arm of the sea beneath Mrs Folan's cottage there are people cutting seaweed and bearing it ashore. Old women raking the weed to dry on the blond sand, their white hair in turmoil, and men standing in the swell up to their waists and sometimes up to their necks in order to gather the kelp. It looks like an arduous business.

My gaze comes to rest on a small figure by the shoreline. I contemplate her for some time, quite fascinated, although it is only a girl stamping her feet in the shallows. Watching her, I have a strong sense of having been here before. I remember asking Abby once if she ever had the experience of having lived through a thing more than once and she told me that she had. Sometimes she would see a commonplace phenomenon like an ear of corn waving in the field or a sack of shrimps falling from a cart and she would know that in another time she had stood in that spot and witnessed that event, outwardly unremarkable though it was. She explained it then as a memory of the other world where we live before our births and after our deaths as spirits.

'You are on your two feet at last.' It is Mrs Folan in the doorway. 'No one saw you at the window, I hope.' She peers through the chink of the flap, then turns to me with an accusing look and says, 'A great fright it was that your crowd gave me once. I was coming home one night when I saw lights galore on those rocks down there and a terrible chattering going on. It was a band of the good people – I saw them with my own eyes – with their tiny lanterns, and they were kicking up their heels and having the time of their lives.'

Good heavens, does she think that I am some sort of supernatural creature?

She says, 'It has been a devil of a business to keep you hidden all this time. A fortnight you have lain here.'

'A fortnight! How is that?'

'You were in a fever, just like any human soul. I fed you with mash and water, I did, and kept you going.'

'I was not aware that so much time had passed. I am awfully grateful to you.'

'What choice did I have?' She says anxiously, 'Will you be going now, Nora?'

My heart sinks. Each time I attain a respite from my relentless flight, I cannot make it last. I say with a sigh, 'May I trouble you for a bite to eat, if you don't mind, to put me on the road.'

Mrs Folan is mightily relieved to know that my departure is imminent, because she says with something approaching a smile, 'It is a wonder that you can eat our food at all. You are not used to it, so. After all, you live on air by the look of you.'

She scoops a fillet of preserved fish from a barrel in the corner and puts it on a wooden platter, then takes up a seat on her stool near the doorway, while I repose on the mattress with my breakfast. My stomach has shrunk so that I have almost got out of the way of eating solid food and I must go tentatively with the fish on my plate. Mrs Folan begins to plait straw with nimble fingers, while glancing at me from under a mistrustful brow from time to time. I think I have come to understand the source of her fear. She has mistaken me for a woman from these parts who died — did she recently drown? I wonder. I suppose I must resemble her. I dare say these people are as superstitious as any of our country folk at home, who are more than willing to believe in spirits returned from the dead. That would explain why they raised such a temper at the sight of me and tried to throw me into the sea. No doubt they fear I have an evil eye that will cause the milk of their cows to sour or the fish to flee their nets – and it is unlikely that I could convince them otherwise. There is no refuge for me here, alas. I ask Mrs Folan if we are near Galway.

She narrows her eyes as though it were a trick question, and says, 'Not so near, but not too far either.'

'What is the name of this place? I wonder.'

Again a puzzled look. 'Are you trying to trick me?' she says.

A few fat raindrops spatter through the smoke hole in the roof and hiss on the stone of the hearth. The fair skies have fled already. How changeable is this weather. I wish I were not obliged to go out into it, but what can I do but ask for my gown and my stays.

Mrs Folan suspends her plaiting. She says, 'I have burned them.'

'Burned them?'

'Was I to hang your fancy silk out to dry like a signal to the parish that a faerie-woman was biding her time in the house of Folan?' She climbs to her feet, her bones creaking, upends the tea-chest table and brings out a bundle that was concealed beneath. 'Here,' she says, 'these belonged to my mother. A small woman she was such as yourself. You may put them on and take them to the other side with you, and if you see her there, she will be glad to have them back.'

The rusty black shirt and the faded crimson petticoat are made of a homespun stuff. There is a thin woven girdle to wind around the waist of the petticoat, and a dark knitted mantle. I understand that poor though she is, Mrs Folan would give up these few possessions if that is what it would take to see the back of me.

It is a simple matter to put on the clothes. There is none of the complication of tying stays or pinning a stomacher. Humble though this costume is, I appreciate its usefulness. It will be convenient to play the part of a peasant woman as I haunt the countryside. Given the lack of a looking glass in which to inspect my appearance, I must rake my fingers through my curls as best I can. Apparently exasperated by the slowness of my toilette, Mrs Folan comes forward and ties back my hair with a piece of twine. I settle the mantle upon my head and turn to face her. Will I pass muster as an Irish woman?

'Holy God!' Mrs Folan exclaims, her eyes staring. A hand flies to her mouth.

The atmosphere in the cottage seems to grow more dense as she gapes at me. I am sure that rest and sustenance have transfigured me and banished the barely human creature that came out of the sea. I suppose that Mrs Folan realises at last that she has made a mistake. I am not the frightful Nora at all. Certainly she is powerfully affected by the restoration of my vigour. Her head shakes as though she cannot believe her eyes, she presses her palms on either side of her face. I lower my head to shake out the wrinkles in the petticoat as a distraction from the intensity of her gaze. As I do so, a shivery sensation passes through me and I have one of those happened-once-before experiences: it is a momentary sense of smoothing a similar petticoat in a similar manner in a similar place.

'Argh!' Mrs Folan cries with a crack in her voice. 'Why did I not see it at once?' She holds out her hands to me. 'You are the child, faith!'

Her words puzzle me. 'As you can see, I am not a child and I am not Nora either. I have no idea who she is.'

Mrs Folan cries, 'Now that is a very strange thing to say.'

I raise my hands in bewilderment. What does she mean?

Mrs Folan says, 'I do not know what name she goes by where you live now, but in this place, Nora Mulkerrin was your mother!'

My heart stops.

Nora Mulkerrin was my mother.

Then a bad temper rises in me. What an absurd thing for this woman to say. It is cruel, too, even if she does not know that I am motherless. She has jabbed a wound that never seems to heal.

And yet, I must wonder if her words could possibly be true – that is, I *want* them to be true. Haven't I remarked on my strong feelings of familiarity about this place? Does that signify an actual connection? Have I been brought here by fate? Oh, stop it. It's all nonsense.

I release a great sigh, as of effort. I feel as though I have had thrust into my hands an immense object of great import. I have no idea what to do with it, but now I find I cannot put it down and must walk on with the burden of it.

Gathering my composure, I say, 'Tell me about Nora. What happened to her?'

Mrs Folan shakes her head. 'I will not speak any more of this, nor do I need to. It will cause me bad luck, you know it will. I have done what you asked and you must go to Kitty now. She it was who called you. Who else would do so but Kitty Conneely?'

'I do not understand who Kitty is.'

Mrs Folan is losing patience with me. 'She is my sister and the heart-friend of Nora Mulkerrin. Sure, you know that very well. And if there was a child that Kitty loved more than you, I do not know it.'

'But how did she call me? What do you mean by that?'

'She turned the stones, no doubt, and that is a very bad business.' Mrs Folan makes the sign of the cross on herself. Then she looks at me with a peculiar sort of deference. 'I know you can fly to her without any help from me.'

I say slowly, 'Who am I? I wonder.'

There comes a bewildered knitting of Mrs Folan's brow. She says, 'Have you forgotten your own name?'

My knees feel weak at the prospect of another shock.

She says, 'Don't you know that you are Molly O'Halloran?'

I turn this name over in my mind with a sense of wonder. Molly O'Halloran. I find I must burst out laughing. I do not know how else to express the new dimension of amazement that has come upon me – although perhaps I ought not to be so surprised by Mrs Folan's make-believe. Are not people of this land known for their knotted fancies and their compulsive inventions? In her view I am a returned spirit whom no one wants anything to do with save for a woman called Kitty Conneely with peculiar and possibly unwelcome powers.

Pull yourself together, Em. None of this accords with reality.

Mrs Folan sighs deeply and her shoulders sag. She says, 'I do not say anything against you for being what you are, but for pity's sake, will you leave me alone now?' She presses her lips tight and everything about her indicates that she is closed and nothing else shall be forthcoming.

Perhaps she is right and I *am* the dead daughter of a dead mother – because that is how I feel: as though the self I once was has vaporised.

Dressed in the clothes of Mrs Folan's deceased mother, I set off in the rain. I take the only path that I can see and I trust that it will bring me eventually to the place called Cashel where Mrs Folan's sister lives. My prevailing mood is one of bafflement tinged with scepticism, but I am eager to question Kitty Conneely. Though my understanding is frustrated, I believe I have stumbled across something momentous. I feel like an adventuresome excavator, who has unearthed an ancient structure only to discover that the glyphs are unreadable, the gods and goddesses unknown. I need to find out more. Mrs Folan will not say another word, but she seems to think her sister will. I hope that Mrs Conneely can tell me the fate of Nora Mulkerrin and her daughter, Molly O'Halloran. And if, as Mrs Folan says, I am loved by Kitty, might I find with her an ultimate refuge from my woes?

Is this what you intended all along?

I have stopped once or twice on the path and anyone who saw me might think I was unhinged, because my ear is cocked as if listening to the air. I am listening out for you. Is there a vibration of your spirit in this place? You see, you are still alive to me. But no one looks up from his labours in the bumpy fields or detains me as I trudge inland. Occasionally I pass women bent nearly double under the waterlogged ribbons of laminaria that they carry on their backs and others heaping seaweed at the foot of a huge stack, as though offering votives to a giant vegetable deity, but they are too burdened to pay me any heed.

It occurs to me as I walk along that I am on an island. Presently, my arrival at a narrow strait of water confirms this impression. There is a scattering of people on a strand a little distance away, but I hang back from them and edge behind a line of glossy, black rocks. I am startled to catch sight of myself in a pool of water. I do not recognise my likeness shrouded in the mantle. My face seems to have little to do with the person I think I am. There is something wedged in a cleft next to the pool and I pull it free. It looks like one of those egg cases called a mermaid's purse that dogfish or skate leave behind. I turn the gritty thing over in my hands, again with a sensation of having done this before. But there is nothing strange about that. There are mermaid's purses at Parkgate, too.

Someone is watching me. A thin-limbed child in ancient breeches and a short, darned cape of sacking eyes me frankly from a perch on the rocks further upshore. The child – I think it is a girl, despite the breeches – jumps down from the rock and begins to drag a kind of coracle composed of hides towards the shallows. I run after her with a cry and she looks up and shouts something that sounds friendly to my ear.

The obliging girl is ferrying me across the low waters. I look back at the island. It is rather prostrate in appearance. I cannot take in Mrs Folan's inference that this might have been my home. The thought of it is too huge, like a colossus of such astounding dimensions that even when you tip your head so far back that the sky reels, you still cannot see where it ends. My mind is not expansive enough to contain it.

The rain lifts as we approach the far shore, although not for long, I fear. I can see a flotilla of clouds streaming towards the mountains that loom in the distance. My young pilot puts me out on a muddy landing in front of a sparse belt of stunted little trees. They seem to stagger backwards against the onslaught of the prevailing wind as though their feet were slipping out from under them. Behind the trees there is a string of battered dwellings. The pilot and a barefoot band of wretchedly clad urchins hanging around the shore are entertained by my intermittent utterances of the word Cashel. I sound like a demented bird, I will admit. Eventually, when they have had their fun, the girl points to a smooth conical hill, which is not as far as the mountains, and then at a track, which runs westwards out of the settlement on the shore. She sends me off with a friendly wave.

Proceeding as directed, I pass a hill-sized lump of crumpled granite. It wears a lacy cape of yellow lichen above a skirt of grass. Where its slopes come to soil men are digging out sods with their spades and women are loading them into wicker baskets, which are strapped to their backs. I join the stream of women on the rutted trail that serves for a road. One or two of them call a greeting to which I reply with a nod. Gradually they peel off into poor little fields, among a network of low walls, where the stones have been cleared. I suppose the fields must be made by hand with transported sods and the seaweed for fertiliser.

On this imperfect bridle path studded with primroses I sense you everywhere and these heathery meadows of marsh and stones tug at me. I am prepared to admit that I have an inclination to the place.

Dense black rushes now and the pitiful calls of waterfowl. The sheen of water up ahead – which turns out to be a broad, desolate lake scattered with islets. The sky is trying to get the lake's attention, throwing all sorts of reflections on to the still, dark surface, but the lake keeps its inscrutable beauty to itself. It is hard going here on my tender feet. Leaving the lake behind, I enter a confusing tract where the water and the land are all mixed up. What a contrary place this is – stern granite on one hand; on the other, a wallowing softness that might sink you to your armpits. I fear I have lost my way among this down-flowing, dropping terrain, and I cannot help but think of the great dread rivers that are said to lie between the worlds of the living and the dead.

I have edged towards the coast under darkening clouds in the hope of coming on to a more certain footing. A long slope brings me to a crescent strand, where big boulders have been flung by the tides above the fawn sands. A few spots of rain have begun to fall. There are women on the upper shore bending to the rocks. A frisky black-and-white dog draws my eye to a young woman, who is frying an egg in a seashell over embers in the sand, but it is the tent that she has fashioned from her scarlet petticoat – a sheltering child peeks out from it – that causes my breath to catch in my throat. The sight of it affects me terribly. I cannot rid myself of the heart-rending feeling that something dreadful is about to happen to the child. I do not know what it could be. There must be something peculiar about my expression because the egg-fryer has risen to her feet with a look of concern. She passes the egg to the child and turns to me, her forehead buckled up in a frown.

'Cashel?' I point towards the hill.

The rain has faltered and the women on the rocks have interrupted their work to watch me. The young woman says something with a dip of her head in the direction of the interior. She has a long upper lip, which gives her an air of vulnerability, I think. She plucks the cover from the child, now eggy of face, steps into the petticoat, ties it fast, settles the child on her hip and beckons me to follow her. The child, I notice now, clutches a doll that has been manufactured out of seaweed and shells and dressed in a scrap of scarlet frieze for its petticoat. I am fascinated by the doll, I have the feeling that it holds some meaning for me, but the child does not want to let me look closely at it.

The woman is indicating that I should follow her and so I walk on in her wake. We stride up the slope above the strand, the dog bouncing around us, my feet smarting on the stones. Under a light rain we reach a trail, which I might have missed altogether in its obscurity. It gradually becomes apparent that the trail is marked by a series of cairns, but I am not sure they would be obvious to an outsider. The woman lowers the child to the ground and bends to impress in the mud at her callused feet four dots in a vertical line – they are bodies of water, I believe – and she sketches the way for me. She swoops to pick up the child, and leaves me behind to face the moor, which stretches before me like a lumpy, green sea and gives off a bleak, creeping dampness.

★

I am seated now at rest on a cold boulder that time has scribbled all over with several colours of lichen. It sits at the corner of a dismal allotment, rye pushing up among its stones. The toes at the end of my bare legs are digging into the few inches of soil that lie like a threadbare cover on the stone bed of this country. I cannot see how the farmers here have anything much to work with. I have lost the piece of twine Mrs Folan gave me to secure my hair and the wind keeps blowing it into my face. In the background there is the occasional boom of a big wave striking rocks. I am not certain of the way, but Cashel Hill has grown larger in my field of sight. In one of those rapid changes that I associate with the weather here, the light makes off and an unearthly whine begins to rise and fall. It is the wind blowing through countless holes in countless stone walls.

A horse whinnies in the distance.

The wind croons.

And then the muffled clip-clop of hoof-beats. And the swell of voices. I come to my feet, alert, straining to hear. Habitual caution leads me to crouch behind the wall where I may watch through one of its chinks without being seen.

A cavalcade is approaching.

My stomach contracts at the thought of my pursuer, that devil I last saw in plain sight at the George Inn in Reading. But then the man leading the string of ponies and mules comes into clearer view. He is a tall, hatless figure in the dark blue garb worn by the men of these parts. A big man, he sits light in the saddle. He rides straight as a candle, controlling his mount on the rough terrain with deliberate, rather graceful movements that seem familiar to me.

God almighty, is this a vision?

I stare with amazement.

He ought by all reason to be a ghost, and yet he could not look more alive. My heart leaps like a hare – the man passing not ten feet away is unmistakably Captain McDonagh! He is not drowned! But my delight is quickly doused by the recollection of his treachery and rage breaks through in its place. Damn your eyes, you perfidious man.

This unexpected and jaunty manifestation of his, ambling along with a train of ill-gotten goods, is it not a doubling of betrayal? First he gave me over to the *Vindicator* and then he wrenched sympathy from my heart for his supposed demise.

I abhor you, deceiver!

It takes an effort of will not to spring from my hiding place and confront the rogue. Instead I manage to quiet my fury, although it continues to smoulder as I watch the ponies plod by. There are perhaps a dozen of them connected by halters and they are laden with kegs and ankers and oilskin-wrapped bales. Mr Guttery and Mr Robinson are among the convoy. At the tail of the caravan a crowd of ragtag children is following. I slip in among them with the expectation that they will bring me to a village where I may find directions to Mrs Conneely. I comfort myself with the thought that Captain McDonagh has been brought back to life so that I may have the use of him, just as he sought to get an advantage from me.

As I scuff along at the back of the procession, I ponder what I may get from the captain as a recompense for the way he deceived me. I am furious with him for making me furious. I detest the way he triggers a tumult of emotions in me. I ought to demand that he allows me aboard his ship – evidently he has found another. Surely he is bound, this time, to go to France with goods he will have got here in exchange for his brandy and tea and silk. But even if I could bear to ask, and even if he should agree, is that any kind of reprieve? I may as well hide in this storm-tossed corner of the world as well as anywhere else, although French is more penetrable than the language that is spoken here. In any case, a rope is probably intended for the captain's neck as well as for mine, therefore it would not be clever to hook my fate to his.

I wish that someone could tell me why it is that life has so many goings-out and so few comings-in.

The Stormy Peninsula, Connemara

May, 1766

The cavalcade has reached a settlement of a couple of dozen cabins with peeling walls and moulting thatch. It is not difficult to keep out of the captain's sight, since there is a huge jam of humanity in this little place. The arrival of the convoy is greeted with a great cheer by the wild-haired crowd in their homespun clothes. Some of them are unloading what look like woolpacks from battered mule-drawn carts and others are stacking the packs in front of the largest dwelling in the place, which for all its prominence is hardly three chambers wide. Women press around a weighing table, watching as their casks, containing I know not what – butter? meat? – are marked by a man in an archaic frock coat, and there are a good many children and hounds running about in a state of enthusiasm.

The people fall back as two of Captain McDonagh's smugglers carry between them a chest reinforced with iron into the principal dwelling. They are followed by the captain himself. Then the two smugglers come out and stand on either side of the doorway with their pistols to hand. Evidently this village is a transfer station for smuggled wares and a point of payment for those who have brought their goods for export. I am hazy about the reason for this. Perhaps there are restrictions on trade in Irish wool. I imagine the growers are only permitted to make legal export of their fleeces to England. As a consequence they have taken matters into their own hands.

The English language is spoken in this place, I hear, which makes me feel less conspicuous approaching likely candidates, women mostly, who may be able to set me on the path to Kitty Conneely. But none of my enquiries yields a helpful result. I go about in the background, my antic cries of 'Cashel? Conneely?' ignored. The people are convivial, but their clustering with one another increases my sense of aloneness.

A queue has formed outside the house of business – the exporters are to receive their payments, I assume. When Captain McDonagh appears at the door of the house, I will him to look my way. Why do this? I cannot say. Perhaps I fantasise that he will catch sight of me and offer the abject apology that I deserve. Perhaps I simply want his attention, as he remarked to me on the deck of the *Seal*. But of course he does not look my way. It would be quite out of character for him to be so obliging.

He sets out at a stroll, hat in hand, in the direction of his pony. I find myself striding towards him with a recriminatory flashing eye. At first he does not recognise the tattered peasant in his path, but then he slows his step with a knitted brow and rubs the stubble on his chin.

As I reach him, he says casually, 'By God, Miss Smith, you are quite the one for coming in my way.'

'How dare you?' I cry, and push him hard in the chest with my accusing finger. 'How can you look me in the face after what you have done? You betrayed me and I would be dead now if it were not for the grace of God.'

He must be startled, but he will not show it. He steps around me to arrive at his pony. He stands there with his weight on one leg, one hand on his saddle to steady his mount, and regards me with an inscrutable stare. My first flush of anger has ebbed somewhat, but it irks me that he refuses to admit the least amazement at our encounter. He does begin to say something, but I cut him off. 'Nothing that you can say will overcome my distrust of you.'

He says infuriatingly, 'What is wrong with you that you are surprised, madam? Did you think I would let a revenue man take me?' He lets a pause occur, then he adds, 'I told you I was a villain.'

'And you have the devil's luck, it seems. I thought you were shot.'

'I feigned the injury and got away.'

'The revenue cutter was wrecked on a reef, do you know that?'

'So I heard. Naturally I am glad that you survived.' His face seems more than ever like a stern cliff. He says, 'I will find someone to take you to Galway. You do not want to wander around in this backwater.'

'Yes, I do, Captain. In fact I have business here. Perhaps you can assist me.'

The bow he offers me has an ironical tinge, as usual. I suppose it is the captain's savage opinion of the world that compromises his sincerity.

'I see you are well acquainted with these people. I am in search of a Mrs Conneely, who dwells, I am told, near Cashel Hill.' There might have been a glint of interest in his face at that. Or perhaps it is only his habitually watchful air and the impression he gives of staying his hand against the right opportunity. 'Will you find someone to lead me to her? I believe that is not too great a favour to ask.' He gives no sign of having registered the latent grievance in that last sentence.

He says, 'Who is Kitty Conneely to you?'

'She is the sister of the woman who took me in when I came ashore. The people tried to put me back in the water, you know.'

'I would not doubt it. They fear those who escape from the sea. They think they are in cahoots with the crowd on the other side and that the only reason they have been spared is to snatch some fine person and take him away.'

'So I have gathered.'

'Kathleen Conneely keeps her own company and she has been made strange by it. The people do not like to meddle with her and nor should you.'

'How do you know that?'

'Two or three fellows here that you may trust on my honour are returning to Galway imminently. I will furnish you with funds and with apparel, so that you may make your way there with them.' He adds, shortly, 'My father was a man of this place. I was born to boats.'

'I do not wish to go to Galway. What would I do there?' Not for the first time during an exchange with Captain McDonagh, I have to restrain myself from stamping my foot. This man has an unerring knack for bringing out in me the vexed child. 'I will find Mrs Conneely with or without your help.'

He shrugs. 'I cannot stand here disputing with you. There is a French ship at anchor in the bay waiting to receive our cargo.' He frowns at the sky and then consults an improbably glamorous pocket watch, which he brings out from his rough coat. 'Very well,' he says with a sigh of irritation, as if I have forced him to a position, 'since you are determined to turn your back on Galway, I dare say we can manage to take you to France. But you must come now. I have a task to be getting on with and it will stay with me until it is finished. We rendez-vous with our ship at midnight.'

I am completely taken by surprise. Is the captain capable of compassion after all? I sense the abrupt stalling of my mission in the face of this tempting offer. In the cold light of this mercantile little village it seems preposterous that I should continue stumbling through bogland that will swallow me if I put a foot wrong on the off-chance that a barbarous hermit woman, who by all accounts of her is hopelessly touched, and to whom I have been directed in the first instance by a peasant who mistook me for a ghost, should be able to tell me anything at all about my long-disappeared people. Face the truth of it, Em: despite all your longing and projecting and the intense mental effort you have expended in order to make her your familiar, your mother, child, does not exist. The wrongheadedness of my storytelling hardly differs, except in its degree of elaboration, to those hollow tales Eliza used to tell when we were young of her adventures with Johnny. And weren't they a bleakly inadvertent demonstration of what was not? Only a fool would continue this wild goose chase instead of sailing to asylum in France. Certainly the captain has assumed that the matter is settled. He is in discussion now with one of his men. Good heavens, didn't I throw myself at the *Seal* for exactly this – to be rescued and carried away? To choose a wraith over a place where safety may give me leave to breathe easy again . . . there is no sense at all in clutching at phantoms.

'Captain.' He half turns from his conversation and glances at me with a you-still-here? expression. 'Captain, I think . . . I think, on reflection, I must refuse your kind offer. I am bound to find Mrs Conneely.'

Dear God, what have I said? How the course of one's life hinges upon such moments. But against all reason I cannot ignore the powerfully insinuating nature of this coast and the insistent feeling that it has significance for me. I find that I cannot walk away from any possibility of you.

Captain McDonagh regards me at length, weighing my reply. Perhaps he sees that sorrow fuels my lunacy, because he says with almost a trace of kindness, 'You have a drop of brave blood in you, Miss Smith.'

At that a foolish flush comes to my cheek.

My mule is a shaggy brown beast with a white nose, my guide a youth who goes by the name of Tag, who has dusty ropes of black hair hanging down his back and a habit of cracking his knuckles. When Captain McDonagh asked him to take me to the house of Kitty Conneely, Tag said with eagerness that he would do so; but he has developed a dull-eyed look since our meeting the hour previous and I wonder if he has been pouring strong-waters down his throat, for there is a torrent of them in the village. Or perhaps his rolling gait comes naturally to him.

North of the settlement, the landscape turns out to be, against all probability, even starker and we travel on a trail that becomes, in short order, imperceptible. My braying mule refuses to go on and I must dismount and pull at its halter to persuade the beast forward. Then I discover that Tag has disappeared. I find him nearby in a dip in the ground, snoring on a bed of tussock, and no amount of shaking his shoulder or shouting his name will rouse him. Since the mule is a native of this place, I decide to trust its knowledge. It must have a little inkling of the way to a cabbage dinner, surely. I urge the animal on and indeed it plods patiently for a while, but eventually it dwindles to a very slow walk and then stops as though its mechanism has wound down completely. Must I get down and carry this animal across country myself? And is it even worth mentioning that it has begun to rain again?

We have reached a spot that is irredeemably cryptic. All around, hillocks of granite merge with the wet sky and I cannot figure how to get out nor even how I got here. I am surrounded by a great deal of stubborn silence. The silence has a quality of misgiving, too, as though a lull between an event and a consequence. I have had the whole day ahead of me for hours, but now I am in danger of darkness.

I have the feeling that I am being followed or watched. It is because of this overwrought landscape, I tell myself – it ripples with import. One can come to believe anything out here, I am sure. I resolve to press on, one footstep at a time, but the wretched mule is of an alternative mind and digs in with a desperate hee-hawing. Yet I ought not to say anything against it because if it had not been for its racket, Captain McDonagh might never have unearthed me. Tag, it transpired, made a dazed reappearance in the settlement that alerted the captain to the lad's dereliction of duty and he came to find me. He regarded me with an air of weary inevitability, then without a word he bent over and made a stirrup of his hands.

I raised a filthy foot and placed it in his palm and with one hand against his shoulder to steady myself, I let him hoist me on to the back of the mule.

The rain had become a relentless downpour now, making our passage thoroughly miserable. Captain McDonagh shouts over his shoulder, 'It will not hurt to shelter until the weather passes,' then veers away and urges his horse over a slight rise. Where the land beyond falls away into shadow, I can make out the shape of a tired-looking cabin hunched against the elements. Captain McDonagh leads his pony directly through the empty doorway and I follow suit with the mule. The place is derelict, its single chamber damp and dark with a floor that inclines slightly downhill towards the remains of a byre. The captain settles our mounts there before a drinking trough that is supplied with rainwater, and then glances at me with a frown and says, 'Will you make yourself comfortable or will you stand like a post?' He indicates a rotting mattress in the corner. 'Hell's bells, girl, sit before you fall down.' At my collapse on to the flaccid mattress, a displaced mouse scurries into the squally outdoors. I ask the captain if his rendezvous is in jeopardy, but he says that the bad weather has led to a change of plans and the French ship will not leave until noon the following day. He does not repeat his offer to bring me with him.

Captain McDonagh travels well supplied with victuals and a fire-making bag. He moves to and fro establishing order: feed for the animals, a fire kindled on the sooty hearthstone, potatoes quartered with his knife and put to roast and water to boil in a makeshift kettle. Gusts batter the walls of the cabin.

Raindrops go astray in the fire with a hiss. The water gurgles in the kettle . . . a picture of Mrs Waterland comes to mind. She is unlocking her tea caddy, while glinting crystals watch secretively from behind the glass doors of their mirrored palace on the chimney piece. Her image is awfully distant as though painted as a miniature.

The pony twitches as a gust of wind enters at a lurch and sets about worrying the fire. Captain McDonagh crosses to the byre and mutters something to the animal. He glances in my direction and says, 'I will admit I am curious to know what has set you on your course and what Kitty has to do with it.'

He returns with the saddlebags and brings out from one of them a twist of tea. He cocks an eyebrow at me as if to say, 'Well then?'

I ask him if he has ever heard of a woman from these parts by the name of Nora Mulkerrin or O'Halloran.

'I have not, although Mulkerrin is a common name here. What do you want of her?'

I hesitate to explain why she is important to me. An imaginary mother is not a subject that I wish to expose to Captain McDonagh's scorn. I ask instead, 'What kind of person is Mrs Conneely? Her own sister seems daunted by her.'

'Kitty is a woman of unpredictable humours and many people prefer to avoid her. She was a wise-woman in the old days, but after the year of the slaughter she stopped doing cures, I have heard.'

'Who was it came to slaughter?'

The captain's gaze ebbs inwards like a man searching for a way to summarise a long and branching story. At length he says, 'A great frost, it was. It fell on us with a cold so bad it would snap your arm off. Afterwards many of our settled people were forced by their losses to disperse. My father's home could not provide for me and I was sent to the French army like plenty of our lads.'

A soft nicker from the drowsing pony causes Captain McDonagh to rise abruptly. He glances at the animals – the mule is asleep on its feet with a drooping lip – and then strides to the doorway and stands with his hands on his hips regarding the fall of darkness. It is only when he says, 'We will go abroad at first light,' that I realise I am to stay here with him overnight.

As though to forestall a thing that I cannot name, I say in a strangled voice, 'I shall be awake all night. It is too uncomfortable to sleep.'

'If you require a feather bed before you can rest, you will never refresh yourself at all.'

'You have a cutting style of speech, Captain McDonagh. It makes a person feel very mown down.'

He looks taken aback, which is not a view of him that I have had before. In silence he pours tea from the kettle into the single tin cup at our disposal. Did he make the tea by sleight of hand? Somehow it was concocted without drawing attention to the undertaking. He passes the cup to me, then sits down with his back against the scaly wall, his legs bent, his arms loosely folded, and gives me a plain sort of look.

'It was never my intention to disparage you, Miss Smith. I am sometimes inclined to bitter, bad manners as you can tell from the poor apology that I am squeezing out, but I hope it will do to reconcile us.'

'It will do.' There is that pouty tone at work again, which

I suppose I employ to mask the delight that floods through me at hearing the captain's apology. I do not want him to know how much I esteem him for it.

Captain McDonagh says, 'We can be a hard people, those of us who come from these parts. There is nothing much to soften the terrain, or those who live in it, but a scattering of heather and furze. They say it wasn't always so. There was a time long ago when the forest in these parts was so thick you could walk on the top of the trees from Letterfrack all the way to Galway town.'

'I can hardly imagine such a thing.' I sound as if I have been running. It is the effort of trying to stifle a recollection that insists on intruding.

The captain says, 'I suppose there is a memory of Eden even in the most unlikely of places. Give any old boy a couple of jars and he will start telling you how in the old days all our geese were swans. How the lads could shoulder a load of weed the size of Cashel Hill and snare gigantic fish on a hand line alone. Not to mention the galore of cattle that belonged to us. Your unicorns could not pass them by without stabbing themselves out of jealousy.' He leans forward, his elbows resting on his knees, and says in a level voice, 'You may tell me what brought you here and I will listen to it.'

My mouth opens and closes. I do not register my tears until I feel their heat on my cheeks.

Captain McDonagh regards me with calm attention.

Carlisle House, Soho Square, London

April, 1766

Throughout the day following my revelation about Hill & Vessey, Eliza hardly spoke to me, but early in the evening she announced that we were to dress for an outing to a pleasure garden. A little later, around eight o'clock, Johnny arrived at Poland Street and I found that we were to go abroad with him and Mr Paine. The journey was rather uncomfortable, squashed as we all were on seats in Mr Paine's carriage that had lost their spring, while listening to Mr Paine lecture on the subject of medical electricity. He posited a machine that would allow people to administer electric shocks to themselves in order to cure aches and pains. It was strange, I thought, that he spent his time in close observations of the natural world and yet he could not see Johnny's insincerity.

'What do you think of Cousin Arthur's notions?' Johnny addressed the question to me, then grinned at Mr Paine. 'She may be only a waiting woman, but she is quite fascinated by all sorts of things above her station.'

I knew then that Eliza must have reported to him the allegations I had made about the bank. I said nothing in reply, only staring at the pale blob of my face reflected in the black window. The carriage had picked up speed and the horses' hoofs rang on the cobbles. One of the lamps flickered and went out. I could sense Johnny eyeing me and could feel Eliza stiff and subdued at my side.

Eventually Mr Paine's driver dropped us at a sentry box at the gate of a grand avenue bordered by trees. Johnny paid an entrance fee and we passed into the avenue. Immediately a young woman in a feathered hat accosted Mr Paine and without ceremony offered him her arm. Mr Paine started, and Johnny laughed. 'Everyone is equal here, Arthur. You see?' And he took my arm.

Although he flashed a smile at me, I thought there was some malice in the firmness with which he gripped me. My great fear as always was that Barfield awaited us. If that turned out to be the case, I meant to take to my heels and run as fast as I could into the night. And then what? I felt the constriction of my lack of choices.

Mr Paine shook off his accoster and took Eliza as his escort. I caught a glimpse of Eliza's face, intent and watchful as Johnny led us into an elaborate garden gleaming by moonlight. There was the sound of plashing water and faint music in the air and the murmur of conversation. We crossed a shimmering canal by means of a Chinese bridge and passed through a bottleneck of people in an arcade. I glanced over my shoulder at Eliza. How uncharacteristic of her not to make a single remark. In fact had Eliza been unlike herself ever since we left Sedge Court for London?

We entered a rotunda whose cavernous splendour took my breath away. The scale of it! A gargantuan chimney in the middle of the structure seemingly held up the roof as well as warming the immense space. A multitude of persons in brilliant costumes ambulated around a concourse that was illuminated by hundreds of candles in glass globes. And all of this activity was accompanied by the sweet airs of an enchanting orchestra. Johnny led us to a supper box in the gallery on the first floor and a boy brought us tea and bread and butter.

For several minutes we watched the people circling below, then Johnny urged Mr Paine to take Eliza down for a promenade. Eliza stood up at once as if at a prearranged signal.

When they were gone Johnny sat at his ease without speaking. I think he meant to prolong my discomfort. Presently he said, 'You are very clever to have found out about the bank's difficulties, Em. But I wish you had not seen the need to alarm my sister.'

I said, 'Do you think it is better to keep Eliza, and all of us, in ignorance? How much greater the shock would be if we should discover without warning that all is lost and Sedge Court must be sold.'

'Oh, it is not that bad.'

'I cannot believe that.'

Johnny laughed. 'Very well, I will admit it is rather bad. But we have a way out. Actually I have seen this disaster coming for some little while. I warned my father that things in Rotterdam were out of control and he wrote to Arthur after Christmas and asked frankly for help in regard to our bills. No doubt I do not need to tell you how hard it is to prise a coin from Mr Paine's grasp. It has taken me these many weeks to soften him, but he has agreed to lend us a substantial sum and finally we will meet next week with the conveyancer and all will be well.'

I had been right to think that it was Johnny and not Eliza who must persuade Mr Paine, despite what Mrs Waterland had told me about the reasons for Eliza's coming to London. That had turned out to be another of the mistress's inaccuracies. I said, 'But why are Eliza and I here?'

'Arthur likes you, Em. He thinks you appreciate his genius. So it does not hurt to have you around to keep him in good cheer. But the chief reason for bringing Eliza to London concerns a marriage. You have probably guessed that, haven't you?'

'Marriage with whom?'

'With a kinsman of Lady Broome's.'

'Eliza has said nothing about it.'

'Eliza did not know. She has only just been told.'

I suppose that news may have answered for her subdued demeanour, if I could believe that Johnny was telling the truth.

'But nothing has been settled yet. We are still in negotiation. I am telling you this so that you understand that although we face difficulties, we do not court catastrophe.'

'When will Eliza and I go back to Sedge Court?'

'I cannot say. I am telling you how things are in order to put your mind at ease. After all, you are almost one of the family.'

His gaze flicked towards the perambulating crowd below, and he said, 'There's Eliza making her contribution to the beau monde.' He pointed at a plodding scrap of yellow among the glittering whirl. 'Why don't you join her now, Em? I am sure you will find it amusing to inspect the lords and ladies at close quarters.'

'Why did you bring us here? You could have said what you had to say to me at Poland Street.'

His sloe eyes played over me. 'How suspicious you are.' The way he gave a soft little sigh reminded me of his mother. 'I am no different to Mr Paine, who likes events to be verifiable. And if I am suspicious it is because your dishonourable friend and his assaults have stolen my peace.'

Of course Johnny side-stepped the subject of Barfield, although it lifted my spirits to bring my accusation out into the open. Johnny reached out and I flinched as he took my hand.

'Poor little Em.' I thought that was exactly what Mrs Waterland would have said. *Poor little Em*. 'I could have spoken to you at Poland Street, but I decided it would be agreeable to go out. Feel free to hold that against me if you must.'

A waiter appeared out of the shadows and I pulled my hand away from Johnny's grip. Johnny, coldly smiling, said we did not want anything more.

Later in the night, as I prepared Eliza for bed, I said that Johnny had mentioned the possibility of contracting with a relative of Lady Broome's. Eliza said shortly, 'So I have been told.'

But now I am sure that Johnny was lying to me. Nothing had been fixed. Mr Paine had not agreed to lend his money. There was no Broome kinsman waiting in the wings with an annuity for Eliza.

On the Friday evening, we went to the assembly rooms in Carlisle House. I see it now: Johnny manoeuvres Eliza and me through crowds of coquettes and sparks in silver heels and coloured hair powder and aggressively fashionable turn-outs. He is in a suit of violet taffeta and his hair new-curled. He steers us through an enormous supper room with vivid carpets underfoot and tall windows hung with crimson drapes and leads us up a flight of marble stairs into a hall. It is scattered with tables and hung with chandeliers whose candles cast a seductive light. At the far end of the hall in front of a stage a small orchestra appears to be playing silently, its music smothered by the din of hundreds of babbling people. Parties of howling rowdies wear the universal grin of the carouser.

Our table is near the stage. As Johnny pulls back my chair, a courtesy that makes me uncomfortable since he is not obliged to offer it to me, his eye lights on my throat. Perhaps he notes that the necklace I am wearing does not belong to me. Eliza has let me wear it tonight to improve my appearance. She has brought the jealousy glass along and is amusing herself with it. Her spirits are much more lively tonight although that may be due to the wine she drank at Poland Street while we were getting ready. Johnny opens a bottle of champagne, but I refuse the glass he offers me. Gazing at the spicy attire on display is enough to set one's senses reeling.

'Oh, for goodness sake take a glass,' Eliza cries. 'It's very uncivil of you not to, Em, when Johnny has gone to so much trouble to entertain us. Go on.'

A sudden clap of thunder makes her scream. It's the electrical show, the curtain rising on a young woman in Grecian garb. At her back a painted backdrop of hill and sky. 'Behold Mount Olympus,' cries the master of ceremonies, 'and the fair Aphrodite.'

After the show is over Mr Paine joins our table, dabbing at his face with a handkerchief, and tells us it is all accomplished by frictions, you know.

I raise the jealousy glass to my eyes, unheedful of its trick angle. Swimming golden sequins. Bring them into focus to find they are quivering candle flames. A pink pastille becomes a face – an abhorrent face. No!

I lay down the glass. Turn my head away.

Eliza is gawping at me with shining eyes and shining teeth.

The champagne is very potent. Even the little I have sipped makes my head spin. I bring myself to standing and the room swirls. It is sickly and close in here. It feels dangerous. I turn with a stagger, pick up my skirts, stumble through the squawking masses towards the stairs. I aim myself at the door, longing for fresh air.

'Careful, child, or you will fall.' Johnny takes my arm. 'It would be a great pity to break that pretty neck and an even greater one to lose my sister's pearls.'

My account of the soirée at Soho Square has left me feeling drained and confused. I say, 'I am not sure what happened after that.'

'If you are not privy to all the facts, it can be difficult to get at the truth of a thing.' Captain McDonagh motions to the wall behind as though to indicate everything that is beyond us and outside of us.

I nod dumbly.

He says, 'I remember when I was a lad and out sailing with my father, we came upon tall, stormy waves breaking in the middle of the sea with an awful boom. It was a sight that scared the bejesus out of me, but I kept my fear to myself because I was ashamed by my weakness. On the next occasion that my father went fishing in that quarter, I hid myself at home, although I liked nothing more than to be at sea with him.' He slants towards the fire to poke at the potatoes in the embers and blows on his fingertips to cool them. He says, 'My father was the kind of man who was always alert to the signs of things. When he got out of me the reason for my dread, he explained that it was the shallowness of the sea near the head, and a reef in the vicinity, that forced the waves to stand up like giants and crash into the open sea, and that was all there was to it. But when I did not know that, my ignorance caused me great distress. It is a blessed relief to find out how things are. It releases you from fear.' He catches my eye. 'Is that the reason for your journey here? To find out how things are?'

Oh, that wind pulsing in and out of the doorway, will it never stop? Staring out into the wild, black night I feel the prickle of fear that has ever dogged me on my flight. 'Are you all right?' the captain asks shortly. 'You look like you have seen a ghost.'

'Have you ever seen one? A ghost, that is.'

'I never saw anything worse than myself.'

'I am not as certain as I used to be that ghosts do not exist.'

The captain says, 'I do not discount the force of physical sensations, especially when they combine with thoughts.'

That is the sort of thing Miss Broadbent would have said. As if down a long corridor, I see the figure of my dear governess turn and look over her shoulder at me before walking away into darkness. She leaves behind an echoing silence.

'Mrs Conneely's sister, Mary Folan, has seen ghosts – faeries, she calls them. She saw the lights of their lanterns and heard their chattering.'

Captain McDonagh says, 'Those lights would have been nothing more than the shine that comes on starfish and jelly-fish in the night. You have seen that glow yourself on creatures in the sea in the dark. As for the chattering, don't the shells rolling over one another in the breakers make a sound like a hundred little voices?'

His rationalising is a comfort, yet there is something about the captain himself that brings to mind the mythic and the fabulous. I see him on the deck of the *Seal* with the black of the sea and the sky at his back. Droplets of sea spray glitter on his cheeks. He raises an arm and dries off his face with his sleeve. He seems monumental, like a hero of some ancient cycle of tall tales – and flawed too, as I well know.

'But if supernatural events do not exist, why are there so many ghost stories in the world?'

'I dare say we have an urge to make reasons for things that are beyond our understanding. We to want to know that our ideas and emotions add up to something, especially when we have been exposed to suffering. It is in our nature to invent stories to make sense of events that are at heart senseless.'

'What about the will of God? It seems that every ghastly incident is attributed to his caprice.'

'To my mind the will of God is just another version of a ghost story. But I am not punctilious in matters of religion.'

He smiles at me out of a corner of his face and pulls a potato from the embers and squeezes it. It splits open with a steamy hiss. For some minutes we are silent, eating. It is good to feel the starchy warmth of the potato in my stomach. Captain McDonagh remains on his feet while he consumes his portion, eating the soft centre of the potato out of the charred skin. He feeds the skins to the pony and dusts off his hands. He takes up his seat once more against the wall and says, 'It is the central dilemma of being human, in my opinion: how to keep going in the face of suffering – and not only suffering as a result of unspeakable evil or of a random tragedy. Repeated common-place casualties are more than capable of eroding hope and happiness if they are persistent enough.' His expression is mild and experienced; its intentional blandness is a cover, I suspect.

He remarks, 'You have an air of being burdened, Miss Smith, but surely you are not plagued by a ghost.' He offers me the gesture of an open hand. 'You have too much spirit yourself for that, I warrant. You are quite a shining one – anyone can see that.'

I am flummoxed by his compliment. I remain on guard, pike raised at the ready against him, but he strolls across my drawbridge in an untroubled manner and beckons my story to come forward – 'Let's have it,' he says, 'the account of your ghost' – and settles back against the wall to listen.

'I am in service to a family called the Waterlands, and in particular to their daughter, Eliza, and I had known no other home. When Eliza's parents decided to send her away to school, I felt terribly threatened. I was afraid that Eliza's depar-ture would mean my tenure in the house and that I would be turned out to fend for myself. I wished desperately that some-thing, anything, would happen to prevent Eliza from going away. One night I became convinced that some sort of inhuman entity had come into the chamber I shared with Eliza and that this presence had come to help me. In fact I felt that the ghost, if I can call it that, cared very much about me. It brought with it a freezing temperature and that caused Eliza to succumb to a serious ague. So it seemed that my petition was answered, you see. Eliza was badly ill for many weeks and had to depend on me more than ever. The plan to send her away was put aside and my position was saved. My rational mind tells me that I could not possibly have been visited by a spectre and yet the episode was so vivid and consequential I still struggle to disavow it.'

The captain says, 'Has it occurred to you that we might invent ghosts in order to cover up something in ourselves that we do not wish to acknowledge?'

'Yes, it has. A part of me has always envied Eliza. I fear that the ghost that came to harm her was a projection of my own wishes – wishes that were too ugly to admit to.'

Captain McDonagh reaches for the cup that I have left on the floor, and settles against the wall again, his face and shoulders swallowed by shadows. Presently he says, 'I can tell you one thing about getting older, Miss Smith – you become more aware not only of the double-dealing of other people, but of the darkness in yourself. The task then is to face up to your own callousness.' He clears his throat and opens his mouth as if about to utter something else, but then only drinks down the last mouthful of the tea and leans back against the wall, engrossed in a thought.

He says suddenly, 'That business with the *Vindicator* – I am heartily sorry for it. I used you badly.'

I half expect a throwaway quip to follow this declaration – 'So hang me for it,' or some such astringency. Instead he says with an effort, 'My conduct was dishonourable.'

I can feel my heart beating. He expects a response, but it comes to me with a start that I am reluctant to dispatch the wrong that lies between us. To continue hugging his treachery close to me is very much my wish. The captain is the offender and I am the casualty. That gives me the upper hand and I feel a base thrill at foiling his apology. I cannot like myself for it, but that does not detract from the exhilaration of thwarting him. You see how the little injured party comes stealthily to lord it over the master and the malefactor?

'Why do you make your living the way you do?' I speak in the high tone that destroys the atmosphere of confidence between the captain and me. I cannot say why I must do such a thing. Is it about clutching to my bosom a sense of power? The drive to do so is irresistible. I go on, stupidly, 'It is quite dangerous, you know, and leads you to hostile situations. You will be caught one day by a revenue man and hanged or transported.'

The captain shifts his position with a creaking of boot-leather before replying, in a voice so low it seems that he is speaking to himself, 'That is the fate that is designed for me, of course. I harbour the hope, though, that I shall continue to step around it.' He offers himself a grim chuckle. 'You see? Delusion is a hard habit to break.'

In the silence that follows, the smoke dies away and a chill seeps in through the countless chinks in our shelter.

A Trail to Cashel, Connemara

May, 1766

Captain McDonagh and I left our refuge before dawn and have been slogging along in semi-darkness. We have exchanged very few words this morning. There is a gleam on the horizon now where the sun is being dragged from its bed, and the puddles left by last night's rain are beginning to reflect the lightening sky. I am weary of the gloom and of my shivering. How consoling it was yesterday afternoon to place my ruined foot into the stirrup of Captain McDonagh's hands as he assisted me on to the back of the mule. I can still feel the warmth of them as my toes nestled into the cave of his interlinked fingers.

My face feels as though it is on fire all of a sudden, but it is only that the sun has come up at last and suddenly everything is alight. The dew on the bog is glittering and the mountains ahead glow like massive ingots of gold.

It discomforts me that the thought of the captain lingers. I must remind myself that although his touch felt tender in passing yesterday, when I was temporarily lost, it is not illustrative of his character by any means. He is a hard man and a lawless one, and he cares only for his own gain. He said as much last night. His life is difficult and open to danger. As is mine.

You see how quickly the brightness fades here. All at once the appearance of the mountains has altered and they are now crouched on the horizon like humped brown beasts, grazing behind distant veils of rain. I remark anew the paradox of this landscape – so mutable and at the same time fixed. On the one hand openness and the grand range, the huge sky, the unrolling moor; on the other, things closing in on themselves – the tight, tiny stone-walled fields that became smaller and smaller with each passing mile, the sudden withdrawal of light as some housekeeper in the heavens throws a heavy drop-cloth of clouds over our heads. I can see how Captain McDonagh has echoed the spirit of these surroundings in his life at sea. I mean, the tension between the close confines of his sailing vessel and the awesome and unpredictable sweep of the ocean. My own existence by contrast has been a flimsy thing lived under the spell of Sedge Court and the allure of its mistress. But am I capable of inhabiting this aloof heath? I fear I may not have the pluck for it.

At length the trail stutters until it is not much more than a narrow track glimpsed through ropey brambles and soon Captain McDonagh pulls up his pony. He indicates a spot some hundred yards to the east.

There it is, a ruinous dwelling, outlined against the mottled sky, with a wind-whipped tree leaning over the thatch. The cottage is wedged into a shallow slope like a chock tasked with preventing a slippage.

This blasted mule. It will not budge. Captain McDonagh dismounts and without a word takes the mule's halter and leads me, and his pony, towards Mrs Conneely's cottage. A goat bleats from behind a stone-walled enclosure next to the cottage. A guttural wheezing, which comes from the same direction, belongs to a grubby white donkey. All at once a ragged collie shoots from the doorway of the cottage and charges at us, showing its teeth. Captain McDonagh orders it to hush and it does. At a shout from within the cottage, the dog casts a wary glance behind.

A woman has thrust aside the door hanging. The words she cries could be either a warning or a welcome, I cannot tell which, but there is no question that the onset of Mrs Conneely makes me prey to all kinds of excitable feelings as I dismount from the mule.

She is a bony woman like her sister, but her limbs are more crooked. She looks as if she might have been taller once. She leans on a stick, dragging a stiff leg along in a scruffy patch of dirt. Her garments are of such decrepitude they have fallen to strips, but she is yet a formidable figure. Invisible eddies like the swirling updraughts that sometimes manifest on the road during a hot, dry summer seem to spin around her as though she were the eye of a vortex. She is bareheaded and her long wispy plaits fly off to one side. Her apron flaps and her petticoat, its crimson colour drained by aeons of wear, flutters like a collection of pennants.

Throughout her slow advance, Mrs Conneely remains riveted to me as though I were a lodestone. And I, stumbling forward, am drawn towards her outstretched arm. She engulfs me in a musky embrace of surprising force and cries an incomprehensible greeting in a voice that sounds like a rusty door being heaved open after decades of disuse.

She gazes into my face with an unnerving sea-green eye and a tremor passes through her body. She croaks words I cannot understand as her speckled hand reaches to stroke my hair and she begins to laugh. She radiates glee – or even a kind of rapture – that leaves me in no doubt of the significance my presence holds for her.

'Hold your horses, Kitty,' Captain McDonagh says. 'Miss Smith has only the English.'

'Miss Smith is it?' She slaps a thigh as if in the throes of unstoppable merriment. 'No, it is not, by God. This girl here, the name on her is Molly O'Halloran.'

Molly O'Halloran again. I cannot seem to affix myself to this name. Yet I feel my blood flooding with excitement at the prospect of what I will learn from this old woman, and if she chooses to call me Molly O'Halloran then I shall answer to it.

I offer Mrs Conneely a curtsy and start to explain, 'I came here—'

She breaks in with, 'Summonsed, Molly. Summonsed here by me you were, and though you will find it a queer bit of news, it is the truth. Ah, Molleen, do you know how you came to be here? I saw you in all classes of situations that were no good to you at all and I put it on myself to bring you home.'

I do not think that Mrs Conneely can be entirely in her right mind. Surely she cannot think that she has cast a spell on me which has pulled me to this spot.

She says, 'Things will move along in great style now that you are here. How will you like that?' Then she remarks to Captain McDonagh, 'She has something of her father in the shape of her face, but if you ever saw Nora Mulkerrin, it would frighten you to look at the child, for she is the spitting image of her mother. Those black curls and eyes as blue-green as a heron's egg and the sleepy eyelids – you would not mix her up with another.'

'My parents . . .' Those are words that snag on my tongue for lack of demand. My voice cracks with emotion. 'They are dead, I suppose.'

Captain McDonagh says, 'You see the girl is in a state of anxiousness, Kitty. Did you know her people at all or do you intend to spin a yarn? You're well known for that, friend.'

Mrs Conneely turns a truculent eye on him. 'Will you have a bit of sense, Mac. Would I ever mistake the daughter of Josey O'Halloran and Nora Mulkerrin? Hang me high if I would. As for the story, I will satisfy her in the matter, but I will not speak of it outdoors, I won't so. It is unlucky.'

Standing here being worried by this wind, which throws our hair all around like an irritating prankster, I have the sense of being split in two. I cannot incorporate myself with this unexpected Molly O'Halloran and enter her life – the life that was not lived, the language I do not speak. I can only watch her accompany Mrs Conneely into the cottage and bide my time until something happens that will cause Molly and me to merge or to part definitively. But it is disconcerting, this intense feeling of separation from oneself. It is like walking through a construction that is out of true.

As we enter the cottage, the dog barks at the doorway and a hen squawks in the corner and flaps its wings and settles itself. A rather fetid, intimate smell rises up to meet us, a years-long distillation of Mrs Conneely concentrated in the single dusky chamber. There is something a little discreditable about our intrusion, I think, as though the old woman has been unwittingly laid bare. Mrs Conneely lets the straw mat hang down in the doorway to keep the wind out and invites us to sit on the low stones near her glowering fire. A cauldron on the boil emits the mealy smell of potatoes.

Mrs Conneely climbs stiffly on to her knees, lights a twist of rushes in a slit stick and rams the stick into a sod of turf. 'How's yourself, Connla?' she asks. 'Keeping one step ahead of trouble?'

It gives me a jolt to hear the captain's given name disclosed. Connla. A curious, melodious sound.

'I'm not too bad, Kitty, all that's left of me.'

'Don't let me delay you now. Sure you must get on about your business. Molly and I can manage without you.'

'I will do so, Kitty, but let me house a load of turf for you before I go, if that creel can be trusted.' He is referring to a derelict basket hanging next to a low pyramid of sods.

I am eager to question Mrs Conneely, but despite the extraordinary nature of our meeting, I gather that preliminaries must be paid their due and so I sit quietly listening to the muffled thud outside the cottage of Captain McDonagh at work, while Mrs Conneely kindles a long-shanked pipe. In no hurry to speak, she draws on her pipe with soft popping sounds and squints at me, grinning through the smoke. Something scampers overhead, mice, I suppose, coming and going among the rafters. The cottage throngs with stones, hanks of dried seaweed, a pile of potatoes, some driftwood piled against a soot-furred wall. In the corner a mattress is covered with an exhausted piece of homespun for a blanket.

Mrs Conneely serves tea to me in a scallop shell, but it does little to dissolve the knot of nerves in my stomach. And I am unsettled too by the way in which this woman feasts her eyes on me. It compels me to break the silence.

'Captain McDonagh tells me that your husband was a scholar. What an esteemed gentleman he must have been.'

Mrs Conneely cackles. 'Mike Conneely was that lazy he would not stir to knock a burning ember off his foot, but you could not beat him for brains.' She is a woman rather mobile in her moods, for her laughter quickly fades and she seems overtaken by melancholy.

Captain McDonagh shoulders his way through the doorway with the laden basket and tips the sods against one of the gable walls. I am glad when he removes himself to a corner, where there is a plank balanced on a couple of flat stones, and seats himself with his long legs stretched out. There is a trace of regret in my mood at the prospect of his departure, but I know he must press on to the bay where Mr Guttery has left a boat for him. He brings a brace of pistols and a powder horn from his bag, and a lead ball, which he rolls in the palm of his hand. He looks up in my direction or at something past my shoulder – the nervous mat, perhaps, that is used for a windbreak. It was slapping itself against the door jamb just now, but it has fallen still. The scratchings and skitterings in the cottage have ceased, too, and the smoke hangs limply above our heads. I have a feeling of breathlessness. It seems as if all the air has rushed outside under the pressure of unsaid things.

Eventually Kitty breaks her silence. 'I will tell you this about Nora,' she says. 'It was an awful ardent temperament that was in her. She thought the world of Josey, you know.' She frowns up at the wreaths of pipe smoke and bats them away, and says, 'But that's no way to begin. I will tell you about those days from the start. It was a time, Molly, when we were all in it – myself and Nora and Josey, and you, of course. You were always a great girl for the wonders of the world.'

Something shifts in my memory like the insects kicking their way through the dried sedge strewn over Kitty's floor. It is that mattress of Kitty's slumped in the shadows. I see myself, I believe, tucked under a blanket on just such a mattress, watching dim figures move about in the shadows. A woman reaches behind her back and unties her apron and a man dips a corner of the apron into a bowl of water and scrubs at his face. Sleepily I embrace a thing that smells grassy and salty, a little effigy with two small hard shells for eyes.

I sit up straight in a rush of recollection. 'Did I ever have a doll made of straw?'

Kitty's face splits open in a gappy smile. 'By Our Lady, you did so! But that morning there, when we came to the long strand, you lost your footing. Your basket went flying and the doll with it. A state of disintegration went on it then. What a to-do you made!'

Seaweed and shells and blades of straw scattering across sand. Is it the wreckage of a plaything? I cannot say precisely that my memory retrieves this image. It could be my imagination that watches shreds of crimson – from the doll's tiny petticoat? – blow towards the weed sprawled at the water's edge.

'And you will remember,' Kitty says, 'the necklace of heather I twisted for you that day.'

But that is something I cannot recall. Kitty is disappointed. She says, 'It seems like yesterday to me. Nora I knew since she was a girl. I was older by some years. You should have seen us in the vigour of our youth. Nora with her sweet face and myself with the long tail of hair as bright as the mayweed, can you believe it, hanging down the back of me.'

Indeed, an image of the younger Kitty Conneely does appear to me then, with a creaturely twitching and tossing of her mane of red hair.

She goes on. 'There is a well we have here that has always been partial to the words of women. The well of the seven daughters it is called. You may reach it on a path that passes above the long strand and the kiln.'

Perhaps I look puzzled because Kitty says impatiently, 'The kiln for burning wrack of course.'

Captain McDonagh explains, 'It is the industry of the place, Miss Smith.' I note the 'Miss Smith'. He does not believe that I am Molly O'Halloran. 'The people gather kelp and dry it and burn it in a long trough in the ground. It can take days to melt the stuff. Then it cools into a blue slab as hard as a rock, and the men break it up with mallets.'

'I will say they are a sight, those men,' Kitty remarks, 'working all night to top up the kilns. If you could see them stripped to the waist in the glow of the pit, stirring the molten mass at their feet with their ash poles, you would say that they looked like every class of red devil.'

'What do they do with it?'

Captain McDonagh says, 'The kelp clinker? It's sent to Glasgow and rendered into soap and glass.'

'Listen to what I am going to tell you,' Kitty says, 'and you keep out of it, Mac.' Captain McDonagh tips his hand to her with a rueful smile. 'It is the meeting between Nora and Josey O'Halloran.'

My *father*. Josey O'Halloran. My *mother*. Nora Mulkerrin. Is any of this true?

'Nora and I went to the well one day, each of us with a particular request. Nora wished to be released from the house of her father, Tommy Mulkerrin. Her mother was dead four or five years and Tommy had a second wife taken. The woman was not to Nora's liking. As for me – ' Something hardens in Kitty's face. 'The pain of being without a child was eating away at me. So we walked our rounds at the well and cast our pebbles into it. Nine times it was that we circled the stones and each time in went a pebble and we asked the well to grant our wishes – for Nora a husband and for myself an end to my barren state.'

Kitty sits nursing a silence. The sudden cry of the goat in the distance adds a plaintive note to the atmosphere in the cottage. The bleating sounds again and it brings to my mind the memory of a crisp morning and the pungent smell of goat's milk. If I close my eyes I can see the goat – and I see myself. I am a little cold and sleepy. Has someone chucked me under the chin? I see myself in a fit of giggles, pressing my chin into the hollow of my shoulder to escape the tickle, while the goat backs away in consternation. Did this happen? Since I trust myself as little as I trust others, I am unable to slough off the suspicion that I am making things up.

The House of Kitty Conneely, Connemara

May, 1766

Kitty's outburst of coughing rattles the rafters. She tamps it down with a pull on her pipe and says, 'I will tell you this much: not more than a fortnight after Nora and I were to the well, there came along the boreen a stranger. It was on a day when we were in the field of Tommy Mulkerrin and sharpening our knives with a stone. The stranger was a well-knit young man with a crest of brown hair standing up against the gusts and a shape made from hard work. In his hand he held a spade. Faith, I can see him now. There was heartbreak on his face and determination in the gripping of the spade.

'I will never forget it, the way Nora came straight up to standing with the squared shoulders and a clear eye, and the young man bringing himself to a halt and his gaze traversing the field and she with the black curly hair leaping all around her head and the wind going mad in the sky in its excitement. There was no use in him walking on, was there? He was bound to stop.'

Kitty reddens her pipe. 'That was Josey O'Halloran himself, come down from the upland.' She glances over her shoulder, which gives me to understand she is referring to the mountains in the north. 'Sickness had his people taken, God rest their souls. A fever went on the father, and on the mother, too. After that, Josey was all alone in the world.'

'I suppose he was evicted then,' Captain McDonagh says. He glances at me sideways all of a sudden with a look that seems awfully tired. There is more to his expression, too, but I cannot think how to explain it. I am tired also, and temperamental, and he is darkly difficult to comprehend. Perhaps he, like me, is in need of remembering and that is why he stays to hear Kitty's story.

'He had nothing but his father's spade and he was frightened out of his life.'

'I would not doubt that,' the captain adds. It is still very early and his tide will be caught, but I wonder why he did not leave at once after bringing me to Kitty. I suppose he wants to satisfy himself that she is telling the truth. He is the sort of man who is inclined to see a thing through to the end, I warrant, even if it should come to a disagreeable conclusion.

Kitty tells us that Tommy Mulkerrin would not have been inclined to welcome a penniless wanderer from the hills into his house, but it happened that the Mulkerrin was brooding at the time on the wrongdoing of a kelp agent in Galway. The agent was a very bad bit of work and a towering disappointment to the kelpers. He alone determined the worth of the kelp and oftentimes he rejected out of hand a fine load that had taken weeks of backbreaking toil to produce. The kelpers were expected to do nothing about it but grit their teeth and swallow down the aggravation, while the agent was living on the pig's back.

For some time Tommy Mulkerrin had been composing in his head a letter of complaint to the governor of Galway about the egregious practices of the agent. He was keen to bring a compelling lilt to the prose, but he conceded that a talent for persuasion was marginally beyond his reach. The obvious candidate for the task was the schoolmaster of the parish, Kitty's own husband, Michael Conneely, but Tommy had fallen out with Mike and the rift had not been mended. So it was that Tommy brought himself to ask the mountainy man, Josey O'Halloran, if he had it in him to plead the case of the disgruntled men.

Josey replied at once, 'Sure, I can so,' and his confident tone reassured Tommy that there would be no hard straining in the matter.

'And what does Josey do,' says Kitty, 'but write the letter three ways, do you know that? In the Latin and the English and the old tongue. Wasn't that a marvel in all fairness?'

'But how had Josey O'Halloran learned his letters in such a remote place?' I asked.

Captain McDonagh says, 'Wandering schoolmasters and friars with the Latin and the Greek. That is how we come by learning in these parts, Miss Smith.'

Kitty jerks a thumb at Captain McDonagh. 'This one was a fierce boy for Latin.'

Captain McDonagh waves the observation away. 'I was off the flank of the Bens before I learned much at all. Now get on with it, Kitty.'

'I will thank you not hurry me to my end, Connla. This story will be finished before you are much older.'

Captain McDonagh laughs. I like the sound of his little-heard laugh, a lazy roll of bass notes that reminds me of an easygoing sort of day. Hearing that laugh, you would not think that he had violence in him.

'You will like to know,' Kitty says, 'that Tommy Mulkerrin took his time reading the letter, but finally he found it in himself to say, "That is to your credit, O'Halloran," and he took up the quill and signed the letter 'Myself Mulkerrin'. That same day the wife sewed the letter into an envelope made of rawhide and it was sent away by sea to Galway.'

Kitty pulls the pot from the fire without minding the heat of the iron and hands the potatoes around. I am beset by familiarity – the clink of a cauldron against its hook, the splash of water pouring from a pitcher, the swish of a petticoat, the patter of bare feet on the earth floor.

No reply to Josey's letter ever came, apparently. 'But,' Kitty says, 'it was no great surprise on us to hear what happened at Kilkieran Bay at the end of that particular time. It was a mild day and the kelp agent was out fishing. All of a sudden a squall blew up out of nowhere. In the blink of an eye the boat of the agent was overturned and the waters were seen to drown him in a determined manner. When the news reached us, Tommy Mulkerrin pondered on the incident. And then he said that in his opinion the letter had served its purpose.'

The match between Nora and Josey, she tells us, did not please Nora's brother, Colman Mulkerrin. It did not help that his father marked off a few perches of his holding, thus lessening Colman's share, in order to accommodate a house for the young couple.

The minutes lengthen and Kitty adds, 'Do not worry, there is worse coming.' She looks meaningfully at Captain McDonagh.

He tucks one of his pistols into his belt and places the other next to him on the bench. He stares at the pistol with a frown as if it is a conundrum. My mouth tastes as if something has burned in it. It is the bitterness of the tea leaves, no doubt.

I wonder aloud, 'Am I the only child of my parents, can you say?'

'Ah,' Kitty sighs, distantly. Then she remarks, 'Nora was awful fond of her children.'

Children. Brothers and sisters.

The elation that I feel is swallowed immediately by alarm as Kitty says, 'She was warned by the women of the place about it. It does the children no good but harm to be always talking of them. The dear knows who might be listening. It is well known that the other crowd takes the brightest and best and spirits them away. Everyone knows of a handsome boy at the top of it for dancing or a lovely girl who could do what she liked with a song – and one day they are never seen again. But Nora was forever petting the little ones and mooning over them. The things Pat could do with himself, she would say, and he not even three years old. Lookit, Kitty, he can balance on one leg on that tall stone in the field of Martin Lee and he is the steadiest boy that is in it. And Bridie is the class of girl who is not afraid to walk the whole world with herself. And Luke, isn't he the sweetest little packet? By the Holy Mother, I cautioned her, dim your rapture for fear of tempting fate.'

Two brothers and a sister. I am swamped by the vast idea of them and I feel a deep pain within my breast, because I can tell by the sadness that has gathered in Kitty's face what is coming next.

'The great cold arrived,' she says, 'and the children died in it.'

There is an overwhelming tear at my heart for what might have been. I grieve for my disappeared siblings and for the stillborn hope of finding someone alive of my blood to whom I may cleave. But as my gaze rests on Captain McDonagh, I sense that I am not alone in my sadness.

'It was a pitiless year,' he says suddenly. 'For the first time in living memory, the islands were shrouded in ice. The fisheries vanished and birds fell from the sky and the cold gave birth to famine. A dank spring rotted the crops in their beds and left nothing to harvest, and when the frost returned in the autumn it found people weakened by hunger and fever. It was no trouble at all to take their lives.'

Kitty says, 'Bridie was the last to go. She had nearly six years on her by then. She was a fighter, too, by God. She did not want to leave. The grief had Nora and Josey nearly destroyed.'

I crane my neck to stare up at the filmy circle in the roof where the smoke passes into the sky. I suppose that a soul might look like that – a small, blurry radiance in the midst of shadows.

Oh, Bridie! Oh, Pat! Oh, Luke! Taken and they could not save you.

'Nora did not want to believe the children were dead. Taken by the other crowd, that is what she hoped.'

'Then she hoped in vain,' Captain McDonagh says. 'When our people are gone, it is certain we will never hear from them again.'

'You are a fellow cut from the same cloth as Josey

O'Halloran. He would not have a bar of the other crowd at all,' Kitty harrumphs. 'Lookit, man, those lads will spirit you away easy enough. Nab you when you're asleep in the bed and it's off to live in one of their mansions under the loughs. You must watch that you do not cause bad luck for yourself, Conn. Many's the good man has had the life taken from him out of spite.'

Captain McDonagh stretches his legs. Is he getting ready to depart? I find I do not want him to leave. He says, 'Hang it, Kitty, there is more than enough to grapple with in the world without taking on the invisible realms as well.'

She retorts, 'What do you know, Connla McDonagh, you are only a man. You do not understand the power of the other side. That belongs to women.'

She raps her pipe violently on a stone to knock the ash from it.

After a pause, she says, 'Do you know, Molly, that although some people die, they don't go out of the world at all? Sometimes when you look at a person it is not himself that is there, but a fetch, we call it, a good-for-nothing that has been put in his place by the faeries. "I would not mind," Nora said, "if that had happened. To be left some sort of likeness of the children would be better than nothing." At any rate, it is said that on a certain wind you can hear their cries from the other side and that is what Nora's ear listened for. Are you all right, Molleen? It's very white you're looking.'

I nod dumbly at Kitty, but I am not all right. My heart has sunk down under the heavy lading of this tale. The more Kitty reveals to me of those fatal days, the more I find myself discovered in them. Distinctly in my head, Nora and Josey speak and they are alive to me with such vividness I can picture it all.

Here is my third and final leap: it is an internal movement of belief that sends me in one precipitous bound over the gulf of time – and with that, I land in the cottage of the O'Hallorans.

It is an unseasonably warm autumn evening. I find myself curled on a mattress with a little doll clasped to my chest. My eyes are closed, but I am only pretending to sleep. In fact, I hear everything.

Kitty says, 'Do you know what I am going to tell you now?'

I do, Kitty. I do know for I was there and I will tell it back to you and to Captain McDonagh in my own voice.

The House of O'Halloran, Connemara

October, 1749

The autumn that year was hot and dry and it seemed likely that the season would stretch itself out as a boon to the O'Hallorans. For all its toilsome effort, the kelp fetched barely one pound for the ton, but if the burning could be made to last through October, Josey O'Halloran might put his supplementary earnings towards the purchase of timber for a boat. The O'Hallorans and Kitty Conneely, the heart-friend who was always in Nora O'Halloran's company, were laying into talk on this subject when there was a rustle at the doorpost. Martin Lee, an old neighbour, edged himself into the cottage and announced he was not stopping, only he had a skerrick of news to pass on.

He had come to tell Nora and Josey that the sacred well on the saint's island was flowing for the first time in living memory. A crowd would sail the following morning to collect the holy water and Martin urged the O'Hallorans to do all in their power to join the throng. 'There is not a man, woman nor child who would not go to Saint MacDara's Island in the morning,' he said.

Josey said, 'Thank you kindly, Martin, but my work is already cut out for me.'

'Faith, man,' Martin pressed, 'the saint's island is the place to be on the morrow.'

'The kiln must be cleaned and I have agreed to do it. I can be of some use to yourselves as a lookout while I am at it.'

'God preserve your honour,' Martin said. 'I will drink to that.'

Devotions were against the law of the land. There were always bluecoats snooping about and the people must hide from them their patterns and priests and the sacred apparatus. Moreover, there was an additional force at work on Josey O'Halloran that prevented him from reneging on his pledge to clean the kiln.

Despite the passing of years and his coming to know Nora's island home backwards, every sprawl stone and grass blade of it, Josey could never be other than set apart from the men born of the place. To their islander eyes he would always be O'Halloran the hill man. Nevertheless, he strived perpetually to prove the worth of himself in order to overcome the divide. It vexed Nora badly, though, that he felt bound to take on more than his share.

The night was drawing in. Nora said, 'O'Halloran, if you do not lay down your head you will be no good for your work in the morning,' and at last Martin and Kitty took the hint and shifted themselves.

As Nora rose to see them out, she noticed a sultry little breeze intruding through the doorway. It reminded her of the fug of body heat that strikes one when entering into a house packed with roisterers. That kind of thickening in the air is regarded as a warning. It is the sign of a band of faeries travelling from one fort to another and you will want to be on your guard against them.

And God with me, were there other signs, too, she

wondered, that should be minded? The marvel of the flowing well and the blessing of the exceptional weather, for instance, and Martin Lee coming by to make a point of urging them to celebrate the miracle. Should she and Josey take little Molly and sail to the saint's island in the morning after all? Col would say that his boat was full, but they could find someone else to make room for them. Nora wished she had not been so sharp to Martin Lee. She had put a sour mouth on her, she was ashamed to say.

Josey called, 'I can hear you thinking, Noreen.'

'It is only that I wonder why you must be at labour on the morrow when everyone else will sail to the saint's island. Let us go, too.'

'I gave my word to stay at my work.'

'Josey, my heart, you too often sacrifice your own convenience to others.'

'I cannot be other than I am.'

'Stubborn, you mean, and righteous.'

Josey took Nora in his arms and she mock-pushed him away, laughing, and said, 'Am I not a terrible harridan?'

'You're well known for it.' Josey pulled her back into his closeness and Nora sighed and pressed her hands against the muscles in his back. His life was hard, but his spirit was light. There seemed to be no end to Josey's light, even in the darkest moments, and Nora could not have enough of it. It was difficult to believe that a circuit around MacDara's well could be an action of greater virtue than the cleaning of the kiln by a man who would stay behind for the benefit of others.

★

Turning her head in its nest of curls, Nora watched as the cat rose from warming his backside at the fire and put his nose to the doorway. Josey made a grumbling sound, flung up an arm and began to stir. Climbing to her feet, Nora donned her petticoats and tied up her fall of hair. She reached for the cauldron, hung it on a hook and filled it with water from a pitcher.

There was an edge to the morning as sharp as an oyster shell. The earth of the floor felt especially smooth and cool underfoot. She noticed that the spade resting against a wall and the kelp hooks hung nearby were limned with light that had squeezed in under the door flap. It gave the impression that there was more to these humble objects than met the eye.

As she went about her customary tasks – the settling of the fire, the fanning of the embers with an apron, the putting of the potatoes to boil – Nora had the peculiar sensation that some kind of import was attached to them. She felt, as she picked up the bowl with the animals' feed and the pail, as though she were acting her part in a mysterious, intricate pattern. They were all part of it, she and Josey and myself, Molly, and the tall two-year-old pig in the yard, and the goat.

At the sound of Nora's step, the goat brought herself at once to the milking stool and waited while Nora threw potato peelings and seaweed mash into the pig's trough. The pig shifted its stance, its hoofs making a sucking noise in the mud, and began to nose through the peelings. No sooner had Nora squeezed the first spurt of greyish milk from the goat, than the cat arrived to lick the drops that fell on the ground. Nora pushed him out of the way with her foot without breaking the rhythm of wringing the teats. The milk made its racket against the side of the pail, while the inevitable gulls cried overhead.

She could hear the rise and fall of voices, and laughter, which came from the people bound for the saint's island. She recalled the queer breeze that had stirred the dust in the doorway the night before, and wished she had said a prayer against it.

I stumbled into the yard, tousle-haired and heavy-eyed with sleep and cried, 'Brr, it's cold, Mama!' The goat lurched and Nora placed her hand on the beast's flank to calm it. She said, 'Shush, Molleen. You've given her a start. Put your hand on her now like this and give her a stroke and you will feel warm altogether as well.'

I pressed my hands against the goat's hide and Nora went on with the milking, watching with satisfaction as the frothy level in the pail climbed higher. I yawned and flopped against my mother. When the goat was empty, Nora moved the pail of milk out of the way and scratched the goat underneath her chin. She said, 'Your turn,' and chucked me in the same way. I twisted away, laughing, pressing my chin into the hollow of my shoulder to escape the tickle, and the goat backed away in consternation.

While Nora mashed the potatoes with the milk for breakfast, Josey dressed and pegged back the door flap to release smoke from the house. The still air carried voices from the strand, and they heard the clunk and splash of boats being launched. 'They will want to hurry to catch the tide,' Josey said, and sat down to his breakfast.

The O'Hallorans ate without speaking. She and Josey both, Nora observed, seemed to be in a reverie of attentiveness:

Josey was watching me toss from hand to hand a ball he had made for me from the dried holdfast of a sea-rod and Nora found herself aiming at the cat an unswerving gaze that made him shift uncomfortably and frown over his striped shoulder at her.

Presently, Josey stood up and said, 'Well, my pretty girls, there's been that much loitering you wouldn't credit. It's about time I went to my work.'

Nora followed him out of the house with a basin of laundry on her hip. She noticed the beginning of a stoop in his posture, influenced by the loads both manifest and unseen that were persistently set upon his shoulders. She was aware of her own alterations, too. Many parts of her had coarsened – her once lissom waist, her hands, her feet, and the Lord knew what in her interior.

They came out into a morning of impossibly limpid light, and Nora exclaimed, 'Isn't it a pet of a day?' There were a few clouds folded on top of one another near the horizon, but an otherwise faultless pale pink sky streamed over their heads. Out on the flat golden sea, shouts of excitement and the splash of oars rose from the fleet of boats swarming towards the saint's island. Josey's gaze, however, lingered on a hut in the field across the boreen that belonged to Liam Black. On the slope of its roof, a dozen or more big flatfish were laid out to dry in a dovetail pattern.

Nora could almost see the boat-shaped thought that occupied Josey's mind. He was exasperated by the want of his own vessel. The O'Hallorans' drying hut had nothing better in it than a score of pouting, a desperate, meagre fish at the best of times, but beggars could not be choosers. His brother-in-law, Colman Mulkerrin, was a gentleman who did not care to be bested in any arena, and on the intermittent occasions that he permitted Josey to come fishing with him, the good cod with its wide mouth went as a matter of course to the house of Mulkerrin, while Josey took home the cod's lesser relations.

Josey said, 'Right-oh, jewel, might as well make the most of this weather,' and the earnestness of his smile reminded Nora of that heartbreaking spade he had carried on his arrival at the island. He set off at a lope in the direction of the kiln and Nora turned to the basin, which she had set down on the wall of the boreen, and began to wring Josey's shirt. Although he worked at his limit, the kelp and the turf earned little, which left the O'Hallorans vulnerable to the outbreak of hard times. A man with a boat might pursue the fat shoals of herrings and mackerel that flooded the bays twice a year, and sink lobster pots and dredge for oysters in the autumn. He might fish for wrasse to put up for the winter at his own convenience, and there was always work to be had rowing woolpacks out to the illegal French ships. It was a secretive coastline and the contrabanders who anchored in its hideaway harbours easily bore away the wool from under the noses of the revenue men in exchange for tea and silks, wine and brandy. Had Colman Mulkerrin been a decent character he would have made his brother-in-law a partner in his fishing boat, but it gratified him to keep Josey at a disadvantage. And since the passing of his father there was no one to rebuke his conduct. As Josey could only go to sea at Colman's whim – no other crew would invite him for fear of aggravating the disputatious Mulkerrin – possessing a boat of his name was an aspiration that gnawed at him with increasing bite, although the getting of wood for a boat in this treeless place was as troublesome a prospect as the amassing of a fee for the boat-wright.

Just as Nora shook out the folds of the wrung shirt with a snap, a shadow darted at her and made her jump.

'God be with you, Noreen. Did I frighten you?'

It was Kitty Conneely with her black mantle drawn low over her head and a wicker creel strapped to her back. She raised a hand – there were links of dried heather wound around one of her wrists – and pushed behind her ear a lock or two that had strayed from beneath her mantle. Her hair had lost its brilliant colour and was faded to the same russet tone as her petticoat. The vividness had gone out of her since the losses of the great cold, although she was not alone in that.

Nora said, 'I am only surprised to see you, friend. Did you not think to go to the saint's island yourself?'

'Ah, no, it's the quietness of the shore will suit me more.' Kitty lifted her head at an angle like a bird and cried, 'Molleen! How's yourself?'

I was a little shy of Kitty, but I tried to oblige her by coming forward and allowing myself to be petted. 'Look, jewel,' Kitty released from her wrist the twist of heather. 'I have something for you.'

'Have you no use for such a pretty thing yourself?'

'Ah, it is only coming in my way, Noreen. Let the child have it.'

With the necklace in place, I peered down my nose to view the tiny purple-pink blooms. Kitty never rested but she obliged the O'Hallorans with an over-brimming fondness that seemed to find no other outlet than to dote upon the little family.

Nora anchored Josey's shirt on the wall with a stone, and said, 'What is wrong with me I do not know. I have not yet made up a bundle for our dinner.'

'I have potatoes galore at me. They will do for all of us.'

'That is a great help, Kitty.'

Nora found my basket and a knife whose blade was sunk into a piece of sea-rod for its handle. I settled my doll into the basket and waited with an impatient jiggling foot while Nora gathered herself. As soon as I left the house I raced ahead and Kitty strode after me. Nora paused, however. She felt compelled to cast a backward look at the house – it seemed to loom at her in a clinging way, as if it thought she was about to abandon it, and a shiver passed through her. What a fierce morning for feelings it was. She turned away from the house and walked down the path, trying to shake the sense of misgiving.

Nora passed among the seaweed cocks above the strand, hurrying to catch up with Kitty and me. Josey was at work near the kiln, preparing a beacon, and Nora stopped to watch him as he raised a knee and broke a piece of kindling across his thigh. In the event that men of the militia put in an appearance, he would light the beacon to signal the people on MacDara's Island that their pattern was in danger of discovery. He looked up and caught sight of Nora. He waved his cap and Nora lifted an arm in reply. She pressed a hand against her breast to quiet the thud of her heart. She could feel Josey's love running through her like her own rivers of blood. She watched as Josey picked up his ash pole and began to saw it back and forth as he teased apart tangles of weed. She could not seem to tear her eyes from her man.

A shriek sounded from the bank nearby. I had tumbled on to the flat of the strand and my doll had flown from my basket. I began wailing over its wreckage. Kitty tried to distract me by asking me if I would help cut a load of weed that would do as food for the potatoes. As Kitty hurried me to the lower shore, Nora felt, and not for the first time either, a twinge of irritation at her friend's covetousness towards me — then she reminded herself that Kitty could not be faulted for an impulse that came out of loneliness.

Nora joined us on the shelves of rock where clumps of yellow-brown sea thong were heaped damp and heavy like clippings dropped by a titan's hairdresser. Kitty's hand rested on my shoulder. She bent to me, saying, 'It would be a great help to us if you would fill a basket, jewel.'

Nora added, 'We might get the yellow out of it, too, and use it to colour our cloth.'

I brought out the knife and crouched down with a purposeful air. 'Mind that blade,' Kitty cautioned. 'It is that sharp you could shave a sleeping kitten with it.'

As I hacked a bunch of long, sappy, branching thongs from the rock, Nora cried, 'Harvest it, child, don't murder it.' She pointed to the succulent discs dribbling at the ends of the stalks I was holding and said, 'See? You have torn away the holdfasts and now the weed cannot sprout for another day.'

I tried again, my tongue working in the corner of my mouth with the effort of concentration, and made a meticulously executed stroke through a single thong. I laid it carefully in the well of my basket.

Nora laughed. 'That's a start, at least.'

Leaving me to my harvest, Nora and Kitty hung from their

shoulders the goatskins that they used to protect themselves from the chafing ropes of the creels. As they wriggled the bulky creels into place again, Nora looked towards the kiln. Josey was putting his back into his labour, going at a few big chunks of kelp clinker with a mallet.

'God bless your work,' Kitty said.

'And yours too, friend.'

They splashed through the eddies until they drew parallel with the craggier reaches of rock, where the low tide had laid bare ruffs of glistening brown oarweed. They began to strip the laminate blades from the clawed holdfasts, working quickly while the water was low.

On occasion Nora glanced heavenwards to note the progress of the sun. What a morning. You would not want to swap it for Paris. A canopy of marvellous blue sheltered a shore that was more used to having its ears boxed by the savage winds and sullen clouds that stormed in from the Atlantic. Instead, the breeze was a caress and the sky compassion itself. And would you look at the rippling oarweed there, gilded by the sun like a meadow of liquid gold.

All morning Nora and Kitty waded ashore with creel after dripping creel of the stuff. When they tipped it on to the sand the weed sprang from its confines with a gasp as though shocked at its dislocation.

Eventually, swells of the incoming tide began to flood the rocks and the water rose until it was slapping at Nora's thighs. Undulating tangleweeds wrapped themselves around her legs as though determined to pull her off her feet. The weeds came alive once they were submerged. When they were severed they gave out a groan that boomed eerily from beneath the water.

Nora hoisted a foot on to a shelf of rock and hauled herself and her streaming petticoats from the grasp of the sea. She cupped her stinging fingers around her mouth – they had been nearly rubbed raw by her work – and called to me. I was canted over a cleft in the rock watching ribbons of black weed as they stirred languidly in the sun-dappled water of a pool. I picked up a mermaid's purse that I had found and waved it at my mother.

Bold waves were scrambling up the face of the rocks, and Nora shouted at me to retreat to the sand. Then she shrugged her shoulders to ease the groaning load on her back. 'Kitty!' she sang out. Kitty was returning from the shore with her umpteenth emptied creel. 'It would not hurt to stop for a bite, I think.'

Kitty lifted a hand in assent.

The mermaid's purse was lying where I had dropped it next to the rock pool. I had not gone far. I was sitting on a boulder waggling in the air a foot that had got something sharp and niggling in it. Nora gathered me up with an effort – I was nearly too big to carry – and brought me to the sand at the high-water mark, where Kitty had already laid out on her mantle a heaping of cold roast potatoes as well as the mussels that she and Nora had pulled from the rocks. Josey had scooped from the sand a bed for a fire and was filling it with stones and filaments of dried wrack.

'Will you look at Molly's foot, Josey? She has a prickle in it,' Nora said, setting me down. Then it was every kind of relief to let slip the creel from her shoulders. Josey lit the wrack in the fireplace with his flint, and turned to inspect my foot. Nora emptied the creel and wrung the seawater from the hem of her petticoat.

'There's the devil,' Josey said. He squeezed the prickle from my toe to the accompaniment of my squeals and ordered me to hop down to the sea on my good foot and to give the other one a dunking. 'Go on, hop as quick as you can, and if you fall, don't wait to get up.'

While I bounded on one spindly leg towards the shallows, Josey fed the fire, and when the flames had calmed down, Nora threw the mussels among the smouldering wrack. She watched me stamp my foot in the lacy foam at the water's edge. It was uncanny to find the sea so deserted. On such a fair day the waves ought to have been crowded with men rowing to their lobster pots or further out to lift their nets. I returned at a skip and Josey said, 'You will be right as rain now.'

While we ate the potatoes and drank the water Kitty had brought with her, the wind dropped almost completely until there was hardly enough strength in it to trouble the air. In the strand's muffled hush you could hear a sort of faint whistle, which was the sound of the mussel shells springing open. Josey snatched them from the embers and set them down to cool.

Kitty said, 'What have you in your basket, jewel?' I showed her a snarl of sea thong and soft straps of bladderwrack.

After we had eaten, we stretched out and watched the lazy, curling waves slide on to the shore and break and roll back, while gulls and terns swooped over the rush of foam, their cries falling and fading. Nora's aching back and shoulders were glad of the rest. Josey wondered how the holy pattern was unfolding on the saint's island and Kitty said she hoped the water from the well was abundant enough to duck those who came to it with afflictions, God bless them.

Nora began singing a song, but she went astray in it, distracted by her thoughts. Oh, the gorgeousness of a quiet, sunny day. The unquenchable delight of it was almost enough to make up for all the freezing, depriving days of which there were no shortage. It was the kind of day you sought to keep alive in your memory by making a song or a story of it as a counterblast to hardship. In that way the soul of yourself and your people would be unforgotten. On a day such as this you almost could not recall drudgery and the toil of gathering weed in a numbing rain and the icy winds that raced down from the north, and the discomfort of clothes that were always damp and salted so that they chafed the skin and sowed disease in the lungs. What could you do when faced with the heavy burdens of life but bend to them? Either that or surrender your life – and God knew there were those who did that through despair and drink.

I crawled on to my mother's lap and looked up at her with a steady, soulful gaze. The colour of her eyes shifted between blue and green like the sea. She looked back at me and saw a clean, sunny world reflected in mine with not a bad thing in them. She stroked my hair.

For people such as us, my heart, she said in a silent communication to me, the spark of ourselves is all that we own and we must not give it up without a fight. The landlords of this world will try to extort rent from our spirits as well as our purses, because it is in their nature to accumulate, but their grasp cannot come inside us if we will not let it.

What was it that Kitty was saying? Nora turned to her friend. The salty light had a sort of scouring effect on Kitty, Nora observed. It rendered her almost transparent, like one of those relic jars filled with frightening, agonised components that the occasional wandering priest would bring out from underneath his bog-spattered cloak to amaze the people. Kitty repeated herself. Ah, she had a thought to cross to the inlet at the western end of the strand to cut the yellow weed and bladderwrack for fertiliser.

Nora was reluctant. Strictly speaking, the inlet was not their ground. For as long as anyone could remember, the shore was divided among the people as far down as the bottom of a low spring tide according to their landholding. People veered now and then across one another's territory, but still, it would be a discourtesy to the Molloys and the Maddens, who had the lion's share of the inlet. But it would have mortified Nora to be picking limpets here and there, like an idler afraid of work, while another was all industry with the creel and the hook, and she found herself falling in with Kitty's plan.

There was Kitty even now up on her feet, shaking crumbs from her mantle, smothering the fire with handfuls of sand. She had always been a propulsive woman – and the more despondent her mood, the more urgent were her deeds. Nora, however, tended latterly to dreaminess as if she wished things to stand still and even to evade the perturbing forward thrust of time and its spiteful surprises. Ah, to be a lingerer in the beauty of small moments, like this one . . . watching adorable Molleen as she popped the air sacs of the bladderwrack, the girl gurgling with delight. A smile unfurled across Nora's face. That *pop* sounded just like the soft report of the kisses she liked to plant on her daughter's plump cheek. She sighed and marvelled anew at the way in which love refreshed the world.

Having exhausted the wrack, I tossed one of the straps in

the direction of the murmuring waves. A gull snatched it up and dropped it again with a yelp of disappointment. The bird flung itself into the air and beat towards the tall stone that stood on one of the southward fingers of rock. The people used the stone to measure the ebb and flow of the tide.

Nora said, 'There is that much of a dazzle I cannot make out where the sea has arrived at the marker.'

Josey lifted a callused hand to shade his eyes from the sharp light. He said, 'I would say we have a little more than two hours before the tide turns.'

Nora led me to the dry sand below the kiln, where Josey could mind me, and said, 'Stay back from the sea, won't you, my heart? We do not want a water horse to come and take you.'

I brandished my knife. 'If a water horse came I would kill it, so I would.'

Josey laughed. 'That's the spirit.'

Kitty said, 'You are a fine, brave girl, God bless you. There would be nothing left of the creature but a pool of water.'

All at once Josey's chin went up like a hound on the scent and he narrowed his eyes against the glare of the sea. 'Who is that now?' he wondered.

There was a solitary sail in the shimmering distance. They watched for several minutes as a single-masted vessel tacked with difficulty in the light air. It was not rigged like a smuggler's cutter or one belonging to militia or revenue men, but Josey said it would suit him to keep an eye on it. He smiled at Nora as if to say, do not concern yourself, and yet, what way it came Nora did not know, but for the second time that day she was touched by a sudden chill, as though the wind had got up, although it had not. It made her want to press close to Josey and never leave him – yet her work she must do, of course. It was with a sense of unease that she turned from her beloved and climbed with Kitty the rocky spur that hid the inlet from the big strand.

The granite jetties of the inlet enclosed a pocket of white sand that was still exposed when Nora and Kitty arrived. Time passed as they gathered the weeds on the rocks and eventually the tide ran up and began jumping at Nora and Kitty's legs. The women carried their loads away to the bank near the kiln and emptied them. I was making a nuisance of myself – I was tired and tempestuous – and Josey complained that I was coming under his feet. Nora pulled me away on to the soft sand beneath the bank and made a roof for me to sleep under. It was done using Nora's under-petticoat, which she slipped off and draped like a tent over a couple of sea-rods that Kitty rammed into the sand. A pushy little breeze made an abrupt arrival onshore and insisted on ballooning the petticoat, so that it pulsed like a sea anemone. Nora anchored the tent with a stone, lifted up the hem and I crawled inside. She reached in and stroked my hair. 'Are you comfortable, my heart?' I closed my eyes against the rosy light filtering through the frieze and snuggled into myself.

Nora got to her feet and called, 'Hie, Josey!' He appeared on the bank with his ash pole in his hand. 'We are off once more. Molly is asleep.'

'Right, so!' Josey saluted.

On their return to the inlet, Nora and Kitty stationed themselves on the uppermost reach of the shore, where a population of spiral wrack remained exposed. It was a poor sort of wrack, but worth harvesting to make caps to protect the seaweed cocks.

'What is it?' Kitty asked, looking up from the curly leaves.

'Ah, it is maddening me, this skin.' Nora reached behind to adjust the irksome goatskin, which had bunched up under her creel.

At that moment, a wedge of whooper swans, necks outstretched, cleaved the air overhead with long, strong wings and flew on into the western sky. As Nora's gaze pursued them, scudding over the dark fringe of underwater rocks and a wide stripe of teal-coloured current, a ruffle of white water and the glimmer of an object caught her attention. At first she took it for a porpoise with the sunlight bouncing off its back. Then she realised what it was.

'Kitty! Is that wreck-wood out there?'

Nora did not stay for a reply. She was already flinging off the creel. Kitty stood up and made an awning of her hand, the better to make out what lay in the blue distance. Nora untied her waist-cord, let her soggy woollen petticoat drop and wound the cord around her head like a diadem. She said, 'I will get that wood, if the wind stays in this quarter. The tide will bring me in.'

Kitty offered to give her a hand to tow it and she too stripped to her shift. The two women picked their way off the rocks and stepped into the churning shallows.

Kitty said, 'Be careful, won't you? Good luck.'

'We will be back in a flash. Good luck to you!'

They slogged through the sea's floating gardens until the sandy bottom fell away and then they were able to kick free of the weeds. Nora propelled herself forward, pushing the water away with powerful sweeps of her arms. The timber was at a greater distance than she had calculated and she was panting by the time she approached the nearest log. It skidded from her reach, but she threw herself at it with determination and managed to drape an arm over it in an awkward embrace. She had not realised that the log was so long. It was the trimmed trunk of a tall tree about twenty feet in length and more than a foot in diameter. How long it had been at sea who could say – it might have floated loose from the cargo of a foundered ship hundreds of miles away, but it was in good condition with none of the tiny pin marks that indicate borer. The tree must have been a handsome sight when it was rooted in its home.

Treading water, she looked around and saw that Kitty was heading for another log that was bobbing two or three yards behind the first. There were others congregating in the distance, but the current was already hustling them out of reach. Josey would be over the moon if they could land even one of these beauties.

Kitty grasped her log and cried, 'Both of them we can bring in, I am sure! Or will I come and help you to manage the one?'

Nora shook her head. 'Don't worry, friend. You know I am able for swimming.'

Kitty shouted, 'The tide will ebb soon, Noreen. We must not tarry.'

Nora wished she had a decent length of rope by her, but the waist-cord would have to do. She tugged it from her head, passed the working end around the log and secured it with a bowline knot. She could see that Kitty was doing the same.

Nora tightened the knot against the log. Would she have the strength to tow the thing? The log was awfully extensive – but that meant there was a deal of wood in it. She imagined the elation that would fill Josey when she brought this prize ashore. A boat might be made from it by the time the November starlings arrived. The image of a curvaceous vessel filled to the gunwales with glistening heaps of cod and haddock glided into Nora's mind.

With the end of the cord in one hand, she turned and struck out for the shore. At once the log bunted her between the shoulder blades. Nora spluttered out a mouthful of water and pushed her hair from her eyes. She tried to shove forward, but the log yawed inconveniently. Mother of God, this thing was a devil, wasn't it? She wondered if it might be easier to paddle the log to shore. Of course, the beast did not want to let her on at first. It rolled and spun and insisted on much wearisome effort before she could haul herself astride. The wood dipped into the sea under her weight, but when the following swell lofted her up, Nora was able to pinpoint Kitty, some distance behind, joggling along like a determined retriever with her catch.

Nora's thighs gripped the log as though she were riding an irascible donkey, and making an oar of her hands she drove it onward. It was a tiring business, though, on top of the day's kelping. She altered her position, flopping on to her belly, with splayed legs providing a grip, one hand hanging on, the other sweeping strongly in the sea. She swivelled her head and warm water trickled from her left ear. The throb of the sea sounded very loud. Or was that the beating of her blood? She drew up her arms, resting her left cheek on them.

It was a relief to float for a moment without striving, feeling the sun's heat on her back, and watching her indolent hair trailing on the surface of the sea. She could see almost to the sandy floor below. Shafts of sunlight cut through the clear water like a loy through turf, picking out a haze of restless, translucent infant lobsters and schools of tiny silver fish twitching among the dancing fronds of weed. She rose and fell on the swell, pacified by the lazy rhythm of the waves, and began to drowse . . .

What was that?

That sound – wasn't it the clunk of oars turning in their rowlocks and the creak of timbers?

Nora pushed herself up to sitting and saw a rowboat not far away that did not belong to these parts. It had not the shape of a *púcán* bringing seaweed from one of the islands or a load of potatoes. Where are those people all going? Nora asked herself.

There were three people in the boat, the oarsman and a couple of the gentry, by the look of their headgear. The man sported an authoritative three-cornered hat, while the lady was repressing the brim of a sizeable bonnet whose ribbons snapped in the breeze. They had not noticed Nora.

She cast about for Kitty and was disquieted to find that her friend's course was going one way while hers went another, so that a separation had come between them. Nora stifled a warning cry for fear that it would draw the strangers' attention. Who knew what manner of people they were. They might inform the militia that women of the island had been seen purloining wreck-wood that belonged by rights to the landlord – he was an awful tyrant for staking his claim to the sea's bounty. Galore of people had been marched away in manacles to Galway for less. If she could only get this brute of a log ashore, then it would be no hard matter for Josey and her to carry it home in the dead of night.

Nora slipped from the log and quietly entered the sea. She was lying off the point of the spur that divided the inlet from the strand. With a turn of her head she could discern the crimson blob of her tent-petticoat on the shore. The thought of Molly folded up inside like the nub of a flower lifted her spirits. She hauled on the cord that was attached to the log and, with her legs scissoring under the water to provide momentum, she paddled and hauled, paddled and hauled. But the shore would not come closer. She detected some opposition in the sea, a reluctance to let her go forward.

She realised then that she no longer had the tide in her favour. The blasted thing had begun to ebb. No matter how vigorously she laboured, she could not advance. She felt the undertow tugging at her legs, and a stiff offshore breeze was making the sea lumpy and obstructive. Nora found herself drifting away.

She looked again towards the strand and was rattled to find that the strangers' boat had pulled up on the shingle and the people had disembarked. How had that happened so quickly? The woman was strolling along with her mantle and flashing white skirts billowing like sails. Her neck was bent and her head obscured by the hat. Was she searching for something to eat in the sand – scallops or gapers or razor shells? However, the men with her were agitated, Nora sensed that.

Nora's heart flopped over cold and heavy as the interlopers registered the red tent. The woman looked up and drew closer to the man in the masterful hat as though she were afraid. Yes, Nora urged, fear the wild natives. Go away, go away, back, back from whence you came! The other man pointed at the pile of oarweed that the tide had washed up near the bank. The tension in Nora wound tighter as he approached the heap and kicked at it and pulled some of the fronds away. Josey would not have him meddling with the wrack, not when he was responsible for it. Nora felt a sinking sensation in her stomach like a stone at the end of a long, long line dropping into one of the ocean's terrifying chasms.

She began to swim with desperate, thrashing strokes towards the shore, not caring now how much commotion she made, intending, in fact, to distract the intruders so that the events that were about to occur would stall and fail to go forward and life would go on as it was and not be changed violently and for ever – for Nora knew with horror-stricken certainty that death was walking on the strand and nothing would satisfy him more than to spring his trap.

The House of Kitty Conneely, Connemara

May, 1766

As the boat beached on the strand, Kitty's first thought was that the people had lost their way. The man of the hat and his oarsman hung back at first near the water's edge and she sensed their trepidation. But the fancy woman was bold at the outset. The instant she stepped ashore, she took a great interest in whatever it was at her feet, for she set off with her nose down, fossicking.

With that detail, memory strikes me like a thunderbolt.

I recognise the fossicking woman, of course. She is Mrs Waterland – with her great hat and her wilful sense of entitlement and her unsatisfactory little daughter at home.

I recognise, too, with ghastly foreboding, that her stroll along the strand will devastate Nora and Josey O'Halloran, and I marvel at the relentless sequence of events that has driven me to this place. Kitty Conneely insists that she summonsed me here, which is an impossible and absurd thing to say, yet here I am with the truth rushing at me. It bursts into the room like some long-delayed messenger gasping out the news of a terrible rout. There was no foundling hospital or penitent poacher in the cells at Chester. Nor was there a merciful rescue or a lucky escape.

I was stolen.

I might have been a specimen of lichen or a curious shell that happened to catch Mrs Waterland's eye. She simply wrenched me away and left behind havoc in my place.

My eyes fix on Kitty in heavy silence. My world has broken free of its axle and gone reeling off the path.

Far away on the moor the wind is moaning. The outcome of this tale sits between the three of us in the cottage like some huge, unmanageable bale that has split open from its fastenings. Kitty coughs and sniffs and leans forward with sweeping gestures of her arms as if she intends to gather up the invisible mess at her feet.

'The woman of the hat picked you up,' she says at length. Her face darkens and a sigh catches in her throat. 'Nora left off the wreck-wood, I saw then, and she started to swim for the shore. At the same time up jumped Josey from behind the kiln and he sprang on to the strand to protect his child. I will admit it is frightening that he looked with the ash pole brandished high, but it was only Josey running to his daughter, and there was no need for the oarsman to shoot. And yet shoot he did. A flash came out of the hand of that man, may a red devil take him and use him.'

A sound it was like stone falling on stone. My blood runs cold and somewhere inside me a child's voice begins to wail in panic.

For a few seconds Josey stood on his feet with the people on the strand gawking at him . . .

I should like to quit this cottage and this story at this instant, leaving my father yet alive. If I do not hear what comes next, he will live still! But then Kitty speaks and Josey O'Halloran falls down on the white sand. My hands are already pressed to my mouth to stifle a cry and yet it seems to me that a scream sounds in the hush of the cottage. I think it must have travelled a great distance from the past because it arrives at my ear with a sound as thin as a wire.

It is Nora's scream of anguish.

Mrs Waterland was unmoved by the screams, if she heard them at all above the sound of the wind and the waves. I doubt she noticed the desperate soul struggling in the sea. She would have been preoccupied, carrying away to the boat the little girl. Mrs Waterland held the child fast on her lap, Kitty tells us, and the men cast off and they hurried away on the convenient tide.

All of this happened on the spur of the moment. There was no planned design.

Kitty cannot fathom the impulse behind Mrs Waterland's heartless theft. 'Why would she do so?' she cries, her eyes sparking with anger. 'The cruelty of it, on top of the wicked shooting.'

'For God's sake, you know the answer to that.' Captain McDonagh, his shoulders bunched under his coat, presses his hands on his knees as though he must physically restrain himself. 'Such people never think that they are cruel. They are blinded and deafened by the privilege of themselves. They tell themselves that others do not feel pain and loss to the same degree that they do. That is how they think, and they must hold fast to their views to avoid despising themselves.'

'Had our men been at home,' Kitty says, 'they would have launched the boats and been after the child in a flash. But there was no one to help, and the ebbing tide and the freshening wind were against us. They helped the devils get away.'

Another long, terrible silence. Then she says thickly, 'Ah, Molleen, Nora swam the life out of herself to try to bring you back.'

My heart collapses, felled by grief at the thought of my parents. I believe in them now, absolutely, I do, and their loss a second time over is unbearable. Hot, salty tears slide down my cheeks. A soundless torrent of them drips from my chin.

Captain McDonagh passes to me from his pocket a hand-kerchief and I bury my face in it to muffle my sobs. He murmurs, 'Has Kitty got it right? Do you remember it all?'

The scene is vividly excruciating to me: my father bleeding on the strand, my mother beating through the sea in the ever-widening distance between us. I covered it over with a haze of crimson and the cry of gulls, which sounded as an echo in my head until this day.

I turn to the captain. I straighten myself as much as I am able and tell him, 'You may address me as Molly O'Halloran, if you please. It is my name and I will use it.'

He acknowledges me with a grave bow.

Afterwards it was said that it was not people who had come but that brigade from the other side, Kitty tells us, and that I had been taken by a *bán sí*, a faeriewoman, for a hostage. The wife of Liam Black said that when she and her husband went to their boat that morning they saw a puff of dust moving along the path and they recognised it as a sign that a band of faeries was travelling on the way to the long strand. They said that Josey or Nora must have done something to offend the other crowd. Martin Lee let it be known that he had warned Josey and Nora not to stay behind. Had the O'Hallorans only sailed to the holy well on the saint's island, the dreadful fatalities never would have occurred. It was fate, by God, and that is the way the incident was left.

'But I knew,' Kitty hisses, 'that those devils were flesh and blood.'

'Was anything ever seen of Nora again?' My voice trembles. What a hopeless question. She was swept out to sea – how could it be otherwise? But it agitates me to find Kitty answering me with a nod. 'When the starlings arrived later that month I saw her, faith. On Josey's mountain she was, looking backwards to her home. Others saw her, too. She was seen riding a sea horse across the bay, going as fast as the wind in the sky.'

I am driven to climb to my feet then in order to take upon myself the weight of my emotions – grief on the one hand; wrath on the other. They dangle with equal heaviness like brimming pails suspended from the chains of a yoke.

Captain McDonagh is standing, too, his cloak on his shoulders. He says, 'I am sorry for the loss of good people, God rest their souls.'

'The outrage has been on me these many years,' Kitty says, 'but I did not have the mastery of myself until now to avenge the O'Hallorans and return Molly to her rightful place. Only as I have grown older has a marvel come in my way and my powers have swelled. When I look into a pool of water, do I see my own reflection? I do not. I see things. Scenes from places far away show themselves to me just as surely as if I were looking in on them from a window. You, Molly, I saw you. Weren't you walking out of the light into the dark with a man in a coat the colour of heather? I saw how tight he held your arm, and a crowd around you.'

I am shocked to my core. She cannot possibly know of

Johnny Waterland in his violet suit and of his bringing me from the assembly rooms in Soho and walking me through the shoals of gawpers and the scroungers in the square.

Kitty reaches out a scrawny hand to me and I help her to her feet. 'Don't you worry now about the she-devil who hurried you off,' she growls. 'The greed of her! Hadn't she a daughter already when she took you from us?'

Oh, Lord! How does Kitty Conneely know of Eliza? Perhaps it is true that she possesses weird powers, although I know that Captain McDonagh will not credit it. But in my state of wonderment I am disposed to believe her. Who is not to say that our feelings and thoughts may be portals to prodigious insights if only we are awakened to them?

Kitty offers me a grim smile. 'Let me tell you a good one, Molly. That woman of the hat will pay a penalty for the wrong that was done and I will see that she pays. I must do so, for I owe Nora a debt.'

Captain McDonagh with an abrupt movement turns to me and says, 'Molly.' At the sound of this name on his lips my heart swells. It sounds easy and right and my qualms about its use slip away. 'Molly,' he says, 'you may come away from this melancholy, now, if you wish, but I must be on my way.'

'You hound, McDonagh!' Kitty cries. 'Do not try to spirit the child away a second time or you will feel the heat of my wrath, so you will!'

'Why do you ask me such a thing?' I will say that I feel a tremor of excitement – dare I call it that? – at Captain McDonagh's invitation.

Instead of replying to me directly, he turns to Kitty and

says, 'She is not used to a place such as this. And you would have her live here with a crowd of ghosts.'

I bristle at his deciding what must answer for my well-being without weighing my own opinion, and yet I feel a pull towards him. But Kitty's red-rimmed eyes well suddenly with tears. She has a terrible raw look about her as she turns to me in wordless appeal. How can I leave her now, even though the thought of saying farewell to Captain McDonagh saddens me more than I can say? I must bow to the influence of my conscience.

'I meant to come to Mrs Conneely and here I will stay, if she will have me.'

'As you wish.' Captain McDonagh puts on his hat. He gathers up his saddlebag and lodges one of his pistols in it. 'I am off now, Kitty,' he says. 'The morning is half spent and I have much to do.'

'And here's me thinking not a quarter of an hour had passed since you stepped in.' Kitty has brightened now that she knows that I will remain with her.

The captain says distantly, as if he is thinking of something else, 'It's a tricky thing is time.'

'You are right there, Mac. We will never get to the bottom of it.'

The captain takes one or two steps towards the doorway and then he pauses. Is he about to say something to me? I steel myself to resist him. But he looks past me at Kitty, and says, 'What is the debt, I wonder?' Kitty regards him with a careful look on her face. 'What,' he presses, 'is the debt that you owe Nora Mulkerrin?'

Kitty places the back of her wrist to her forehead as if her head hurts and closes her eyes against an onslaught of pain, it seems. 'Mike and I were never favoured with a child, have I told you that?' She opens her eyes and grimaces at the rafters. 'At any rate, it preyed on my mind. Do you know it destroyed me sometimes to see Nora dandling the babies upon her knee?' She sighs. 'It was to the holy well I went again one day and my purpose was to make a vow. I swore I would give up my powers. I would never do cures for others again, if I would only get a little babe in return. That was my solemn promise. I told nobody about this, not even Nora. But from that time onward, do you know –' Kitty's mouth twists bitterly – 'sure, there was no good at all in anything. The killing season came with its cold and the O'Halloran children fell to pining.' Kitty shakes her head. 'Nora wanted help from me, of course, to take the sickness off them. She gave me no peace until I would make a cure with *lus-mór*. It is a plant, Molly, well known to influence evil spirits. I made a cure, but it had not a jot of power in it. And do you know why? I would not say over it the words that cause a spell to bind. God forgive me, I did not tell Nora that my cure was useless, and for my sin her children were brought away one after the other. My blazing Mike was taken too for good measure and my heart was shattered.'

Captain McDonagh says, 'Kitty, I will tell you that there is no human blame in those deaths, and if you think me wrong, then you have a conceit on you beyond all pity. Thousands died in that year through cold and hunger and disease.' He breaks off with an intake of breath and I can see the marks of sorrow on his face among other untold hardships.

Kitty snaps, 'You have no understanding of things, Connla

McDonagh, since you do not live among your people any more. In any case, the woman must forfeit her daughter. That is the penalty.'

There is nothing in this cottage but an endless series of shocks. What does Kitty mean by *forfeit her daughter*? Surely she cannot be referring to Eliza. I cannot say whether I have come to this place because of a fateful personal contract driven by a supernatural force, but truly I do not wish Eliza harm. I doubt that Kitty's powers, whatever they are, will stretch across the sea in their hunt for revenge, but in any case I say to her, 'Mrs Conneely, I do not wish to play a part in your penalty, however you mean to manifest it. Will you give it up, for my sake, at least?'

'Yes, give it up, Kitty,' the captain adds. 'A curse is an awful thing to take upon yourself.'

Kitty looks at me and speaks with a voice that is hard. 'You have been influenced by Connla, so you have.' She grimaces at him and says, 'I see where your eye lands and what you want to take for yourself.' Her gaze passes from the captain to me and I flush at her words. 'But I am more powerful than you, McDonagh. I have turned the stones. I have said all I mean to say, and there's no use in it any more. That girl there will die and she is meant to die – and Molly will be at home once more.' Kitty's face closes.

'Vengefulness will not bring my family back.' I sigh. 'Eliza Waterland and I grew up together, Kitty, and I hold her in affection. Let her alone, please, I beg you.'

Kitty says, 'It's strange to our ways you have become, my jewel, like Connla here. He is an outsider now. Nor do you know how things are done. When a heart is killed it must be avenged. It is a chain of consequence. Sure, it is simple enough to understand – just as earth is to wood and wood is to fire and fire is to stone and stone is to wind and wind is to sky and sky is to rain and rain is to earth. The chain must be closed, faith, or danger and death will attend you. The stones have been turned.'

My head reels with Kitty's spiralling words.

Captain McDonagh says, 'Do not let her mesmerise you, Molly. Make a bargain with her instead and she will bend your way.'

'What do you care, man, for you do not believe me?' Kitty is standing a little straighter and there is a glitter in her eye that looks as if it could equally blast or bless its object. She says to me, 'I am all that remains of your people, jewel.'

That is true. She is the keeper of their stories. She knows from whence I came and who I am supposed to be. And I do not wish to abandon her to renewed sorrow. But I cannot let Eliza be harmed. I don't know if I believe in Kitty's curse, but she does and I plead with her to overthrow it. 'Please, Kitty, I cannot stay with you under such a shadow.'

'You don't know what you are asking, child! The words that bind a curse are irrevocable. I will not back down from it.'

Captain McDonagh regards her for a long moment. He says, 'Then you will lose Molly for a second time. Or will you curse me, too, for taking her away?'

Kitty gazes at him with a look that is shrewd as well as anguished. And I – I have the feeling of reaching for something and giving it up all at the same time.

Captain McDonagh says in a deceptively light tone, 'But

you know that it is pointless to curse me, don't you, Kitty? Because it is unjustified and it will come back on you. You love this girl more than your own life. Ask her now what you must do to keep her here.'

'Kitty –' I turn to the old woman, who is kneading her hands with pent-up emotion – 'I implore you: unturn the stones.'

The Cove of the Curlew, Connemara

May, 1766

Captain McDonagh proceeds on foot in the forefront, leading
the pony. He finds the way with a blackthorn stick, which he
prods into the unreliable terrain. I lead the mule and Kitty
rides astride her donkey at my back. The stones on which she
bound the curse are on the flank of Cashel Hill, she says. She
has withdrawn into herself and hunches moodily inside a black
mantle that is so threadbare it resembles a large cobweb.
Captain McDonagh will accompany us part of the way before
diverging to his rendezvous with the French ship.

As we feel our way among the hummocks and the intercon-
necting flushes of the bog, I play the scene on the strand over
and again in my head. I see Mrs Waterland step through the
shingle with her discriminating eye searching for what she can
find. I can imagine the wanting coming off her like the steam
of a melting frost. Did the oarsman mistake Josey's ash pole
for a musket? Did he shoot him out of panic? When Kitty
described his stooped shoulders and a small head that thrust
out of them like a turtle's, I recognised Theodore Sutton. I
suppose Mr Waterland must have paid him well to forget what
took place on that island strand. How else came Sutton by his
unlikely house in Parkgate?

Guilt must have been at the root of those gnawings in the

master's guts and the retchings that have plagued him all these years. I recall the protest of his that I overheard on the stairs at Sedge Court: "Nothing has gone right since you brought that child here!" Now I wonder whether Sutton's death in the fire was an accident. I wonder if Miss Broadbent's death was an accident, too. Our governess had a clever mind and she was an acute observer. Perhaps she had guessed that Mrs Waterland's story about the foundling home was not true. She certainly pressed the mistress on the subject of the admission number, I remember. It was unlike her to be so bold with her employer. But she was distressed in those last weeks of her life at the prospect of losing her post. She might have thought that there was enough at stake to risk bargaining with the mistress in order to keep a roof over her head.

I cannot imagine Mrs Waterland going so far as to take Miss Broadbent's life in a premeditated way, but she was capable of behaving monstrously on impulse, I know that now. She compounded the wickedness of killing an unarmed man with the snatching of his child. Why did she do such a thing? I believe I know her well enough to be able to say that she did so because the opportunity presented itself. She is a collector, a harvester of objects, and the getting of an object has always meant more to her than the thing possessed. I can attest that there are plenty of gewgaws shelved in Sedge Court's cupboards that were crowed over in the acquisition and now never see the light of day.

I can understand how it might have excited her to give way to impetuousness. What a relief to disperse the tension of wanting a thing by taking an action no matter how reprehensible. Would not such an act — that is, the decisive assertion of her will — wouldn't that have made her feel terribly alive? If she felt the need at all to justify the abduction, I can hear her arguing that the child would be rather better turned out in her new circumstances — and that a person could not be chided for undertaking what was only, in the end, a form of improvement.

I have no memory of travelling in the boat with the Waterlands or of the journey to Sedge Court, or my arrival there. Terror extinguished time and place in my mind. Molly O'Halloran fell into the void, a state without sea and sky, nor form nor matter. Mary Smith — Em— came out of it.

I was severed from you, but my holdfast clung to the rocks. Isn't it amazing, the power of regeneration? Now Mary Smith is not. But Molly O'Halloran is once more.

We are making our way through shreds of mist. I suppose we are not very far from the shore now. In fact, Captain McDonagh has brought us to a pause, his hand in the air. All at once a scalp-prickling sensation comes upon me of being watched. Does someone stalk us on the moor? But I can see nothing out of the ordinary in the scrubby vegetation around us.

Captain McDonagh says, 'I will leave you and Kitty here, Molly.'

I am dismayed by his announcement. I do not want him to go. Dear God, I so badly do not want him to go.

The captain mistakes my feelings for trepidation, for he says, 'Don't worry, Molly. Harm is unlikely to visit you here. But shall I leave you a pistol and a charge? You may have it for show in any case to frighten off any soul you do not like the look of. Will that put you at your ease?'

Captain McDonagh hands me the pistol and begins to tell me how the mechanism works. The piece feels heavy in my hands. The captain shows me where the ramrod is stored underneath the barrel. My gaze lingers on his hands with their dirt under the fingernails. He indicates the hammer and the trigger.

I suddenly find that I am standing in a moment of amazing clarity. It is as though my eyes have been unsealed and I am looking on an entirely new universe. I see that I am in love with Captain McDonagh.

'A pistol, is it?' Kitty breaks her long silence. 'Sure, there is no use in that article at all.' She begins to cackle as though nothing in the world has ever amused her so.

'Thank you, Captain, but I believe you need your weapons more than I do.' My voice is so soft he must bow his head to hear my words.

'As you please,' he says, but he seems in no hurry to take the pistol from my hand.

I do not dare to look at him. I hardly let myself breathe for fear that I might startle this fledgling love into darting away. The captain removes the pistol from me, his fingers almost brushing mine, and tucks it into the pocket of his coat. I long to linger in this moment, but I know that I must put my feelings away. I am in love with Captain McDonagh and it grieves my soul to be torn from him, but torn I must be. Duty and compassion oblige me to stay with Mrs Conneely. I gave her my word. I do so in memory of Nora Mulkerrin and Josey O'Halloran. Surrounding them is a much more ancient grief, and to take up a life in the place where they birthed me is the only proper monument I can erect. I want them to know that. I want them to know how my story ends.

For a few minutes I feel that everything around has receded and that I am left in a tight circle of consciousness that encompasses only Captain McDonagh and me. What a haven it is, a safe harbour. But then, I register a faint sound beneath or beyond the wind. I do not recognise exactly what it is, but misgiving turns my innards to water.

Suddenly Captain McDonagh cocks an ear and asks, more of himself than of me, 'Is that a child lost on the bog?' Clearly audible now is a shrill kind of whimpering. It almost resembles a curlew's call, but I cannot persuade myself that it belongs to a bird. I look to Kitty and she lifts her hands in a slow gesture that seems to signify acceptance of the inevitable.

A figure has appeared, pushing through a scrappy stand of undersized alder or birch – I do not know which, all of the vegetation here is stunted and altered. The flaring mist makes it difficult to make out the encroacher at first, but I can guess her identity and somehow I am not even surprised. The air seems to have congealed in order to resist her approach, but what can the air do, what can any of us do, to keep at bay an event that is inexorable? Kitty is laughing away. Even the captain must blanch at the sight of the convulsed creature stumbling towards us in a bedraggled riding habit. She has the appearance of a pitiful child, hopelessly out of her element, and there is something calamitous, fateful, about her, too.

'Captain,' my voice quavers, 'that is Eliza Waterland. It is she whom Kitty means to harm.'

'Good God,' he says quietly. 'I do not like this.'

Eliza has caught sight of us. Her eyes widen and she stands immobilised with mouth agape and arms dangling.

She has not recognised me. I let go the mule's halter, push the mantle from my head and run to her.

'Em?' She cannot believe her eyes. She begins to wail.

'It's me, Eliza. You are safe now.' I do not know if that is exactly true. To come across her in this place fills me with foreboding as much as amazement and I am afraid that Kitty's design may come to pass.

Eliza sags against me, racked by spasms of shivering.

Barfield springs into my mind. Eliza was travelling with him. If she is here, so is he. The thought makes me giddy with fear.

'Eliza.' I look into her face. 'Where is Barfield?'

She stares at me as if she does not comprehend. I shake her a little to bring her out of her abstraction. 'Surely you are not on the moor all alone?'

Eliza stiffens in my arms. She has seen something over my shoulder that she does not like. I turn and follow her gaze. It lights on Kitty, sitting still on her donkey, with a remote air as if she is reposed in some faraway place, inside one of those pools or bubbles where she sees things. The way she is bent over, with her black mantle drawn low over her forehead, makes her look like a large crow.

Now Captain McDonagh steps forward. His orderly, practical demeanour steadies me. Surely Barfield cannot get at me while I have Kitty's powers and the captain's pistols to hand. He says to me, 'What do you want to do with this lady? Keep her with you or send her with me?'

Eliza gulps back her tears and stammers, 'Who is this?'

'Captain McDonagh. He will help you.'

'But where is Johnny? What have you done with him?'

'Johnny? What do you mean?'

She pushes at me and frees herself from my arms. She has no strength in her, but I can feel the force of her anger. 'Where is he?'

In the tone he uses to command his crew, Captain McDonagh advises Eliza to calm herself. He says, 'If your companions have gone astray, we will ask men in the locality to search for them.'

Eliza cries at me, 'You and your scheming! You tricked my brother into coming away with you. You ever wished to thwart us, I see that now.'

Captain McDonagh says, 'You and Kitty may go on, Molly, and I will carry her to the cove. I will find someone to return her to Galway, where she may find passage to her home.'

Eliza pays no attention to the captain's offer. She whimpers, 'I do not like that creature.' She means Kitty. 'Tell her to go away.'

'Eliza, hush.' I pull the mantle from my head and settle it around her shoulders, but she hardly seems aware of me.

She cries, 'Such dreadful things have happened! Mr Barfield has disappeared, too!'

'If Barfield is close by,' I gasp, 'then I am in danger.'

The captain says, 'Who are you talking about?'

But seeing the agonised expression on my face, he does not wait for an answer. He says to Eliza. 'Where did you last see this person?'

'I do not know! He said he was going to judge the lie of the land. We were in a bog. I waited all night for his return. There was no shelter and nothing to eat or drink and it was so dark and I was *terrified*!'

'Kitty —' the captain is brisk — 'the stones must wait. I will not leave you and Molly alone while she is under threat.'

'Do as you please, man,' Kitty rasps. 'I am not in it now at all, for it will end as it is meant to.'

Eliza sobs, 'I fear that he fell into a sinkhole and was swallowed.'

And *I* fear that Barfield is indestructible.

Each time that Johnny knocked him down with a scornful remark or a humiliating prank, Barfield rose up again as enduring as a cockroach. Johnny made a show of being the more dominant of the two, but I never saw Barfield cowed by Johnny's superciliousness — there is too much violence in him for that. If Johnny acted the master, it was only because Barfield allowed him to. I imagine that nothing would arouse Barfield's perverse humour more than to watch Johnny Waterland strut about so very mistaken about the degree of authority at his disposal.

Eliza will not let me comfort her. She shouts once more, 'Where is Johnny?!'

I ask her in bewilderment, 'How could Johnny be here?'

'You bewitched him,' Eliza hisses. 'You took him away from me.' She appeals to the captain. 'Barfield told me. She made Johnny run away with her and now she has ditched him.'

Captain McDonagh is looking at me with an air of enquiry and I worry that he has begun to doubt me. If only I could tell him the events that led to my escape, but I cannot bring them to light. Why can I not do so? Is it because I am a dissembler and my forgetting is only a ruse to board up the truth in its guilty chamber?

'It is not true,' I cry. 'I was never in agreement with Johnny Waterland.'

Eliza pushes at me a bitter face that has broken out into sweat. 'You liar. People in Bristol told Mr Barfield you were with a gentleman who matched Johnny's appearance. He told me so.'

'Why should you believe what Barfield says?'

'Why shouldn't I?'

Because . . . because I am waking up in a noisome bedchamber that reeks of piss and brandy . . . and if I can say what happened there, Barfield will be exposed for the rakehell that he is.

All at once some spark seems to go out of Eliza and she falls to the ground in a faint. The captain props her up and revives her with a pinch of snuff to her nose. He says to me, 'We must go on now. We have wasted enough time.'

Kitty begins to cackle again. She croaks, 'Too late, Molly, my jewel. Too late to take the curse back from the stones.'

The hill of Cashel looks down on us as we descend in a column towards a cove. Captain McDonagh holds the drooping Eliza upright on his pony. We are on a track bordered by a long chocolate-coloured turf wall, its sods piled on one another at an oblique angle. The wall looks in danger of collapse, but I dare say it intends to endure, held up by the mutual binding of its components. On either side of the track lie endless iterations of gorse and granite boulders. The cove below is sheltered by a tongue of grey-green land and crumpled rocks that are heaped about with yellow seaweed. The tide is full and a boat with distinctive curved lines bobs at anchor close inshore. I assume it is a tender that Captain McDonagh has arranged to take himself, and now Eliza as well, to the French ship that is anchored in the bay. I watch his tall back as I follow him on my mule. I am overcome with sorrow at the loss of him.

He has not looked my way since we set off from the misty clearing where we encountered Eliza. I sense that some warm feeling that he came to have for me is already fading. Perhaps he believes Eliza's accusation – that I eloped with her brother and have now abandoned him.

I glance over my shoulder at Kitty, plodding along behind me. She looks very frail. I know she loves me. It is my duty to stay with her even if her end of the bargain has not held up. There is no time now to go with her to the place where she would lift the curse she placed on the Waterlands – as though that would have made any difference to Eliza. Her state of harm is to do with Barfield rather than any hocus-pocus dreamed up by an old hermit woman half deranged by loneliness.

At that instant there is a bang. Kitty grunts softly, and tries to say something. She tugs at her mantle as if to hold herself together.

'Captain!' I cry, pulling up my mule. A dark rosette is forming on Kitty's washed-out shirt. 'Captain! Hurry!'

I have reached Kitty – she has pressed an inadequate hand to her breast, but blood spills between her fingers. Captain McDonagh has pulled Eliza from the pony – she is collapsed in a heap against the wall – and he rushes towards Kitty and me with his pistol in his hand. I understand that Kitty has been shot by mistake. Barfield is close by and means to kill me. The donkey brays as the weight shifts on its back and Kitty topples to one side. All of this happens terribly slowly.

I catch Kitty in my arms, staggering under the impact of her fall, and drag her to the ground. There is a hole in her chest where the shot has torn up her flesh and her breath makes a rattling sound as though her throat were filled with gravel.

Bent low under the cover of the wall, Captain McDonagh commands me to sit Kitty up against the turf. He snatches the mule's rope halter before the animal can abscond. The donkey is out of reach, backing away along the track. Kitty's eyes flutter shut, her crimson hands are folded in her crimson lap. Her face is waxy and she seems already to belong to a place far away. The captain whispers in her ear and makes the sign of the cross on her forehead. She groans faintly and her head droops as life pours out of her on its river of red.

I press my lips to her cool cheek and ask God to commend her soul. She utters a shallow sigh and then she is gone. The captain bends to me with a hoarse whisper. 'Come away!' He seizes my wrist.

There is no time to contemplate the passing of Kitty Conneely – for we are in danger. Barfield will kill me if he can. Because he is a man of violence. Is it the blood pooling around Kitty that speaks to my understanding?

I do, I understand.

The door of Barfield's bedchamber swings open and I see the figures within: Barfield, Johnny, me. But I cannot examine the scene in this present mayhem. We are scuttling at a crouch, Captain McDonagh and I, with the mule for a shield. The animal reaches Eliza. The pony stands patiently at her side, its nose snuffling in the weeds at the foot of the wall.

A second shot thwacks into the turf.

The captain glances at his sleeve, which has been torn by

the shot's trajectory. Scarlet spurts at the ripped cloth. 'It is nothing,' he growls, and pulls the pony away from its grazing. 'Keep your heads down,' he says. 'We have a minute while he loads another charge.'

He urges us forward, screened by the animals. Eliza stumbles along, dazed, in a state of shock. At the point where the turf runs out, a short, grassy slope gives way to rocks and the waves. Beyond, the captain's boat sways on the tide. Between the terminus of the wall and the sea, three or four tallish, squarish boulders lying roughly in a row provide some small cover.

The captain says, 'Tie my neck-cloth around my arm, will you, to staunch the blood. Don't be frightened – the wound is superficial.'

As I lean close to wind the strip of cloth around his upper arm I can see a pulse jumping in his throat. It is the only sign of his tension.

'What are you doing?' I ask. He is pulling off his boots.

'Preparing for a dunking. I will draw him out, while you and Miss Waterland reach the shore using the mounts for protection. I will cover you, while you bring the girl through the waves to the boat.'

'But you will be a sitting duck. And there is no sign of Mr Guttery to reinforce you.'

The captain shrugs and ties his boots together. 'I took my time getting here, and Mr Guttery is flash enough to find his way back to France on his own.' He drapes the boots around his neck.

'Captain, listen to me! It is no business of yours to be shot by Barfield. Where is the pistol you offered me?'

'Do as I ask, Molly. Let me fight this out. I am used to it.'

'I do not wish you to be killed! I have already witnessed that once before and it did not please me.'

His sardonic grin appears. 'Doubtless I deserve to die, for I have more bad deeds to my name than I should like you to know. There will be nothing lost then if it should come to pass.'

'Cannot the three of us go into the water between the mounts and swim the animals out to the boat as a screen.'

'That will not answer. There is a surfeit of us and the pony and the mule are small as it is. A pair of camels would be ideal, but they come thin on the ground in Connaught.'

Eliza groans. She is sunk on the ground, her face a clammy grey. 'You see,' I press, 'she cannot proceed unaided and I have not the strength to carry her. Give me the pistol, for you have not hands enough to manage Eliza, the animals and two weapons.'

He does not want to do it, but he cannot argue against my logic. He brings out the pistol from his pocket and says, 'You must keep the hammer half-cocked. Should you need to fire, pull it all the way back, like this. You have only one shot.' My hands are sticky. I wipe them on my petticoat, take the pistol and secure it beneath my waist-cord.

I am well acquainted enough with him to know that Captain McDonagh will not complicate a hazardous undertaking by admitting emotions into it — and, sure enough, without so much as a 'Godspeed', he assembles us between the shifting animals and springs forth, half dragging Eliza, and we stagger away between the twin shields of the mule and the pony towards the slopping breakers. The boulders cast shadows like crooked teeth on the open ground. My heart is in my mouth as I barely prevent myself from stumbling over Eliza's lagging heels – and then I do trip upon them.

'Go on!' I cry, trying to scramble to my feet in a tangle of cloth. I have stepped on Mrs Folan's ancient mantle and it is torn and I must leave it behind as I run to the shelter of one of the boulders.

I crouch against it with my breath coming and going as effortful as a bellows. There is silence all around save for the soft thump of the animals' hoofs on the sand and the squawk of seabirds. I steal a peek around the corner of the boulder and see that Captain McDonagh has reached the shallows. He glances towards me and I can sense his concern. That glance revives my spirits and spurs me to dash to the neighbouring boulder. I gesture in the captain's direction to signal that I am in order and he gathers up the burden of Eliza to carry her through the water.

My confidence rises. I am sure I can make a successful run to the next boulder, which is three or four yards distant. I reach the lee of that boulder, and the next one, too. Only one more frantic sprint and I will come to the sea. My blood fizzes with intent. I will dive under the waves and use them as cover to reach the boat.

My hair is blowing in my face. As I raise a hand to subdue it, I realise with a chill that without the disguise of the mantle my identity is completely apparent to Barfield.

The surrounding quiet is punctuated by the distinct sound of a pistol being cocked. I glimpse a shadow at the edge of my vision. With tremorous hands I jump up and at the same time yank at the stiff hammer on the pistol.

Nothing happens. My pistol fails.

A shot clangs on the face of the stone. I see the puff of grit rise from the striking-point and my courage almost forsakes me.

Only then do I realise that the shot came from the direction of the sea. Has Captain McDonagh fired on me? He has come forward into range – but he is making a sign . . . he wants me to lie low. Oh God, he was firing to protect me, but now he is hopelessly exposed. My breathing is shallow, my heart squeezed tight by fear. There is a sound in my ears of wind, of waves, of my own blood washing in and out.

I sink on to my haunches and stare at the useless pistol. Did it jam? And then I hear once more – this time with startling clarity – the heavy click of the pistol's hammer. He is aiming at my back, I sense that.

In the distance, but not very far away, Captain McDonagh is shouting in order to attract Barfield's attention. The mule and the pony are wandering about with an air of confusion.

I feel very quiet. I anticipate an explosion, a tearing apart of my innards, a splintering of bone. I have the absurd notion that the effect of this outburst will be somehow countered if I remain utterly, quietly composed. Perhaps my amazing stillness will persuade him that time, and by extension the trigger, have been stopped.

I do not move, but Barfield does, coming from around the wall of turf to smirk into my face. At last I am face to face with him as I always knew I would have to be, even as I fled from him through the English countryside. He looks like hell. Sweating. Mud-streaked. There is a raw-looking cut on his cheek. And yet he retains the power to provoke in me a feeling of ignominy. He has a terrible lunatic eye. I know that look of his. I have seen it before.

He laughs, in fact, and pipes in that voice whose littleness always takes me by surprise, 'Put it away, little peach. Don't you know better than to threaten your elders and betters?'

I look down at the pistol. My hand is stuck to the grip with Kitty's blood. Now I see what is wrong. The hammer is only half-cocked. I had not pulled it back far enough. I pull it back. It is fully cocked.

Barfield giggles again. 'You will not—' I do not know what he meant to say, because I squeeze the trigger and shoot him before he can finish his sentence. The sound of the *boom* hurts my ears.

I climb to my feet and run towards the sea.

The *Cliona*, Bertraghboy Bay

May, 1766

Captain McDonagh hauls in the mooring stone and launches us on the turning tide. As we pass over the continents of weed shifting beneath the sea, he sets the dark brown mainsail, his back straining with the effort. The boat is called the *Cliona*. It heels beneath a westerly, and the sail bellies fatly between the booms. The sea swarms with a tangled mass of kelp, but the *Cliona* beats through it under the captain's navigation and we sail forth among twisting channels. The boat is decked forward of the mast and I have made Eliza as comfortable as I can in the low cabin that lies beneath.

None of us speaks of what has occurred. I direct my attention to tasks — lighting a fire in the stone hearth outside of the cabin, bringing Eliza water from the keg that is stored under the aft platform.

At first it seems that we will achieve our rendezvous with the French ship before it weighs anchor, but quite quickly, while Captain McDonagh is piloting us towards the lee of one of the numerous small islands in the bay, the air darkens and dampens and the breeze begins to die.

Fog reaches out from the confusion of islets and rocks and a curtain of mist comes down on us. We slop to a halt.

In the muffled hush I can hear Eliza babbling with fever. I

mash a little of the dried fish with water, and crawl into the cabin.

'Eliza,' I whisper, 'be a good girl and open your mouth a little. It is time for your supper.' The spoon is too clumsy to use. I pinch the mash in my fingers and feed it to her. She manages to swallow a little, lapping it on her tongue like an infant, but her teeth keep chattering with cold and I can see that the effort of eating is too much for her.

I stretch myself out as well as I can and pull her to me in an embrace to warm her.

'Em,' she says into the hollow of my collarbone.

I stroke her hair. 'I saw you at the George Inn in Reading,' I tell her.

She nods and sighs.

'I was shocked to see you with Barfield. Did he tell you that you were the only one who could make Johnny see sense and come back home?'

She coughs hoarsely.

'You looked very frightened, I remember.'

She nods again. Her breathing is noisy. I think of her in the schoolroom, making a mess of her quill.

We rest without speaking for some while, listening to the cry of curlews and the lapping of the water against the hull of the boat.

I say, 'I suppose it was not difficult, once Barfield had found out that I had bought a ticket to Reading on the night coach, to guess that I was on my way to Bristol. He knew I was travelling with funds enough to buy a passage abroad.' There it is in my mind's eye: a suede moneybag lying on the floor of a bedchamber, where it has fallen from Barfield's coat. 'How did you follow me to Ireland, though?

Eliza stirs against me and opens her eyes. She whispers, 'A boy directed us in exchange for half a crown and then some chairmen told us about a tavern. There was a barmaid there. She was wearing my pearls.'

The Breeze and Feather. Where I sold the necklace cheap.

'The barmaid's son saw you try to drown yourself. Only a guilty person would do something like that.'

'But they must have told Barfield that I was alone.'

There is a long pause before Eliza answers. 'I do not know. Mr Barfield conducted the interviews. They told him you had been picked up by a smuggler's cutter. He tried to buy a place on a patrol of the revenue service to chase the cutter, but it could not be done.'

'Still, he did not give up.'

'He said that Sedge Court would be sold if Johnny could not be found.' Eliza sighs heavily. 'We could not lose Sedge Court, could we? You understand that. The Bristol revenue men, the bluecoats, told us that the master of your cutter came from Connaught. Mr Barfield hired a boat to chase you, but we were stopped by a revenue cutter not far from a coast and ordered to turn back. It had its own business with your boat. But we couldn't turn back. There was a storm approaching and we had to go for shelter in a harbour town. Galway.'

Was it the *Vindicator* that ordered Barfield's boat to desist? It was an interception that probably saved his and Eliza's lives. Had they been hard on the *Seal*'s tail, they would have suffered the full blast of the storm that destroyed the *Vindicator*. I am sure it was easy enough in Galway for Barfield to find informants who could tell him where the master of the *Seal* conducted his business. Poor Eliza. She would have had to travel into Connaught on bridle paths that were rotten in places and broken down. I can imagine her dwindling spirits.

I stroke Eliza's damp hair. Her eyelids flutter and she heaves another huge sigh. 'I was afraid that Johnny might have drowned in the storm. Is that why he is not here? Is he dead?'

'He . . . did not drown.' She does not notice my hesitation. I cannot tell her that he was killed. Not while she is in such a state of weakness.

She says, 'Mr Barfield frightened me. He said he would not be sorry to be relieved of the burden of me. I was afraid of our guides, too. They were wild men. They fell into a dispute with us about money and left us alone. But we could see the outline of a hill that we had been told was near the settlement where the smuggler and you and Johnny could be found. Mr Barfield decided we should strike out for it. It took a long time to walk to the hill and I began to lose my strength. I felt a distemper come on me with painful cramps of the stomach and I could not stay on my pony. Then the pony ran away. It was only the thought of Johnny that kept me going. And then Mr Barfield said he was going to look for the way and did not come back.'

She swallows and grimaces as though her throat hurts. Her face has grown very pale and she has a withdrawn cast about her.

'Rest now, Eliza. I will take care of you.'

The captain's face appears in the doorway of the cabin. 'How is she?' he asks.

'She is feeling cold.'

'It is this damned fog. I cannot make out my outstretched hand in it.' He stands up so that all I can see are his legs and then bends down again and says, 'Here. Put this over her.' It is his coat.

I come out on to the misty deck, shivering in the cold. Captain McDonagh says, 'You know there is nothing supernatural about this, Molly. She contracted a fever in the bog. That is not unusual.'

I do not know what to think about the nature of Eliza's illness. I say, 'We will miss the ship, I suppose.'

He aims a rueful look at me and nods.

There is a sudden flurry of bumps against the bottom of the boat.

'Do not be alarmed,' Captain McDonagh says softly. 'That is only some creature of the sea nosing about.'

He seats himself on the platform in the stern of the boat and blows on his cupped hands to warm them. He says in a disarming, easy way, 'Why don't you sit down here next to me, Molly, and if it occurs to you to mention the burden that has been on you, I shall not be sorry.'

I sit down slowly next to him. I am comforted by his presence.

He says, 'I should like to know who it was that brought poor Kitty to her death. Will you give me that?'

I asked Johnny in a whisper to help me. Barfield was sprawled in a fat armchair at the end of the divan on which I was displayed, his bulging body like a sack of waste matter waiting to be thrown on to the night-soil dray. Behind his shaven head there was a window with curtains drawn. His breeches were unbuttoned and there was a smarting pain between my legs and blotches on my thighs. My shift was pulled up around my waist and I felt with my fingertips that my stomach and arms were bruised and scratched. I had a stabbing headache. Was it caused by the champagne? Could one glass of champagne cause me to black out? Or had I been given a potion to render me insensible? It was with a sensation of nausea that I suspected I must have been ravished, too. My feelings about that I put carefully to one side in a neat pile, like clothes left folded on a riverbank while one attends to the laundering of oneself in cold, clear water. I had wit enough to know that nothing could be repaired or avenged without escaping from that chamber.

'Johnny,' I whispered, 'help me.'

He came towards the divan at an oblique angle and said, 'Now, my little wanton, I will certainly stir to assist you and nor will I say one word about it. We will go on as before with not a dicky bird the wiser.'

'My head hurts very badly.'

'That is because you were drunk. I took you from the assembly rooms to prevent you from making a spectacle of yourself and we had the good fortune to encounter our old chum here, who took us into his equipage. I must blush for you, Em. I always took you for an innocent, but your antics in the carriage were –' Johnny laughed – 'let us say that any whoremaster in Covent Garden would have delighted in your persistence. But then Cousin Arthur came to my mind, unlikely though that sounds. He's quite a prude, you know, and I was concerned that in your heated state you might . . . you know what I am saying . . . when he came home, you might *embarrass* him, and so it occurred to me to bring you here to sleep it off. I intended to have you sent back to Poland Street, and no harm done. Alas, I had not taken properly into account that Barfy too had been imbibing heavily. It was, I am afraid, a case of a fuse and a powder keg. You implored him and he could not refuse. Isn't that right, Barfy?'

Barfield hauled himself to standing, walked to the vicinity of the bed and kicked at something. A chamber pot. I turned away as he fumbled in his breeches. There was the sound of urine hitting the porcelain. He whined, 'Couldn't get the fucker up her, Johnny. Couldn't for the life of me, and I thought I would fit it in as easy as a glove.'

'You will have another shot. Plenty of time for that.'

'Do you know,' Barfield said in a voice whose languidness sounded as though it meant to provoke, 'I can't be arsed now? Lost interest. You might get rid of her now, there's a good fellow.'

Johnny said, 'Of course you haven't lost interest. Look, man, you've been after her for years.'

'All in the chase, Johnny, all in the frolic, ain't it? Now I've bagged her, I don't want her.' He wandered back in the direction of the divan and belched and yawned.

Barfield had not ravished me. He had tried and failed. Some life came back into me as I apprehended that. Johnny hunkered down next to me and spoke into my ear with a hot, alcoholic breath. Even in my foggy state I sensed his frustration and anxiety. He said, 'You may be wondering, Em, why I intend to sweep this unfortunate incident under the carpet. Of course, a certain amount of gallantry is involved – I would hate to see your name soiled – but largely, it is because of my sister.'

He looked up at Barfield and then he stood up. 'Barfield will marry Eliza. He intends to provide for her very handsomely. Isn't that right, Barfy? He will present himself to her this evening. Tomorrow she will attend church with Barfield's esteemed mother and walk with her in St James's Park. Monday at noon a meeting is to take place in Temple Bar at the lawyer's office to sign the marriage contract. We have already sent for the conveyancer to draw articles for the marriage and they are by my father's order ready for signing.'

'Steady on, Johnny,' Barfield said.

'The wedding will be celebrated within a fortnight. The countess is hardly cock-a-hoop, but she will not object for reasons that Barfield knows well. The Waterlands cannot expect to be received with cordiality, but the money we will receive from the marriage will make up for the humiliation, won't it, Barfy?'

Barfield opened a box on a table next to the divan and made a prolonged business out of snorting snuff from his fist. I managed to sit up and pull down my shift to cover myself. My eye travelled to the door.

'God's bones,' Barfield said, 'I feel like shite. You might take this little jade home with you now, Waterland, and let a fellow get some sleep.'

Johnny took a step towards Barfield and I could hear the placating smile in his voice. 'Nonsense, Toby,' he said. 'Do not disoblige me, friend. You are not a man to go back on your word.'

Barfield guffawed, 'But I am, Waterland, you should know that, and I am not of a mood this afternoon to be hampered by a wife and her considerable number of hangers-on.'

Johnny tried to laugh. He said, 'I am in rather a fix, Em. There have been opportunities that slipped away and I do not have time to wait for fortune to bring another advantage to me. If I do not pay my debts, I will go to jail or be sent out of England. Sedge Court will be lost.'

'Dear me,' Barfield laughed, 'ain't you bubbled? It is a problem of such a convoluted nature I wonder if you will escape it. I might put on a bet at my club that you will. You are the type to go very near in your dealing. Out of my way now, and let me call for my valet.'

Johnny seized Barfield's arm, making no pretence now of his desperation. He called Barfield a graceless bollock and said, 'I will not have you renege on me. I promised you this girl in exchange for an offer on Eliza.'

Barfield lost patience then. He said coldly, 'Why, you fop, did your mother really think that I would marry her poxy, ugly daughter? Thank God I have given myself a reprieve, but please do thank her for sending this coy little cunt to me so expeditiously.'

At last I lug this heavy knowledge from disbelief's dim recesses into the glare of public view: the Waterlands are a cabal and they conspired to have their servant raped for a favour. I will exclude Eliza from the plot. Treachery is not her style. But her mother . . .

It causes me pain and shame to think that I once adored and admired her. What a waste of love. If only it had occurred to me, while she was preening herself in her looking glass, to come around the back of the structure, where it was propped up among the cobwebs and the dust. I might have found the unfeigned Henrietta Waterland there, on the other side of the glass, in her awful actuality, her creamy satin stomacher bulging and tearing, her necklace of brilliants shattering, her rosebud mouth ripping open as the monster, which had always dwelled within, burst free from its confinement. Look at her now: a blackened incubus with blood on her hands.

Johnny bowed his head and I thought at first that he was giggling or weeping. Suddenly he straightened up and walked away. I heard a door open – was he entering a closet? Barfield raised his fluting voice that Johnny might hear, and piped, 'Come, Waterland, do not be in a huff. Let us only say that I have won this round.'

Johnny's heels clattered on the floorboards as he returned. He made a movement with his hand and at first I thought that he had slapped Barfield's face or had even opened a fan. But Barfield made a startled sound and I saw that blood was dripping from his cheek.

Johnny was startled, too, and that was his undoing. I think at the sight of the blood, at the reality of it, his intention drained out of him. He was a wastrel and a coward, but he did not possess Barfield's lust for brutality.

Barfield kicked Johnny between the legs and Johnny fell on the floor with a howl. Barfield laughed and said, 'A rout is only good when shared, eh, Johnny? Now give me that.' He picked up the razor, and in a gesture that seemed almost casual he slashed Johnny's face and a scarlet line opened up across Johnny's eyebrow. It was as if Barfield had become suddenly animated like some terrible automaton.

Johnny was flailing with his arms, but Barfield went at him

like a frenzied gamecock, sinking the razor into his chest and arms, slashing back and forth as if he were scything wheat. Johnny tried to scramble away, but Barfield had the advantage of heft and Johnny could not counter him. He made the mistake of holding up a hand and Barfield nearly severed his wrist. The iron smell of blood was thick in the air.

I was at the door by this time in a terror. I did not make a sound. Something told me that other young women had screamed in this bedchamber, at this locked door, to no effect, and I was afraid of provoking Barfield to turn his attention on me.

Johnny whimpered and then began to cough. His violet coat was covered in scribbles of blood. Barfield came at him again – there was a sense of his making a thorough job of the attack. Johnny made an effort to stop the razor with his undamaged arm, but Barfield easily sliced it open. Johnny kicked at Barfield, but he did not have the strength to land a blow and he fell down again and tried to defend himself with his hands, but one of them was entirely useless and the other arm was pumping blood. Barfield stood over Johnny and watched him make a weak thrust. Then he knelt down again and – and I do not know why, but I thought he was about to help Johnny up or make a quip. Isn't that what men do? They half kill each other and then slap one another on the back and quaff a pint of ale. But Barfield took the razor and very slowly drew it across Johnny's throat.

I cannot imagine what depths of hate and fury it took to do that. Johnny's feet in their high heels and fancy buckles began to spasm as he choked on his blood.

The walls of the chamber seemed to close in and I pressed

against the door to try to stay upright. I remember Barfield turned and ogled at me with surprise as though he had forgotten I was there. He began to walk towards me, wiping his hands on his breeches, and I backed away, along one of the walls, towards the door of the closet.

He piped, 'Don't look so put out, peach. You have had all your maintenance from the Waterlands, haven't you? It was not too much to ask you to open your legs in return. You were their little ace in the hole, or so they thought.' He feints at me with the razor and I retreat, so that the divan is between us. 'Your shape is such an invitation. I am sorely vexed that my poor afflicted cock baulks at prosecuting a desire that has been dammed up these many years, but we will try again, won't we, and this time I shall have you for nothing.'

I think I started to babble pathetically then, begging him to let me go.

One of his hands circled my neck and the other hit hard the side of my head. He enjoyed inflicting the blow on me, I could tell that. He liked it so much he did it again, only much harder this time and knocked me unconscious. He would have gone out then to find help from his servants to move Johnny's body or . . . or I do not know what. I don't know what was in his mind. It was as black and fathomless as a sinkhole.

Captain McDonagh has been listening with his head raised. I sense that he maintains this slight distance out of consideration for me. It has been easier to pour this muck into his ear without bringing myself to his eye. Now, here I sit, feeling nauseous with disgust.

The captain says, 'I can help you. I rent a vineyard near

Bordeaux and you may be sequestered there safe from harm. Or I can bring you to any shore, according to your wish. I am at your service.' His calm tone soothes me deeply. He stands up and stretches his legs and looks out over the gunwale. 'The fog is thinning, I believe. I think it is time I brought us out of this place, Molly, don't you?'

I wish I could get Eliza to eat more of the mash, but when I proffer it to her she screws up her face like she did when she was a child. I see myself as her rescuer now, bringing her away from her gruesome family, leaving the muck of Sedge Court to sink into the cistern of the past.

I rest my fingers against the pulse at the side of her neck. It seems faint – and her skin continues burning hot. She is agitated, restless. She pushes Captain McDonagh's coat to one side and mutters something unintelligible.

I moisten her lips with water and stroke her cheek with the crook of my fingers. Suddenly she opens wide her eyes. Her face is chalky white save for two blotches of hectic pink that stand out on her cheeks. She looks exactly as she did at the age of fourteen when she came into the grip of the ague that kept her home from school. I could almost believe that this is a return of the same affliction. Has it lain dormant all these years, biding its time, like some lingerling in the bottom of a slough?

I feel terribly afraid for her. I have the impression that her spirit is winding inwards.

All of a sudden she calls my name with unexpected force. 'Em! I must tell you –'

'What is it?'

'Put down the glass!'

She is delirious. I try to settle her by assuring her that we are sailing to a wonderful place. 'You will find it very agreeable. It is warm and sunny and Captain McDonagh has a house at a vineyard where you will recover your health.'

As I speak I can feel our boat rushing through the lively waters and hear the sail snapping in the breeze and the creak of the busy rigging. It consoles me to know that Captain McDonagh stands at the helm.

Eliza cries again, 'Em!'

'Shhh,' I soothe her.

'Put down your glass! Don't drink the champagne!'

I recoil from her as if I have been slapped.

Eliza's eyes flutter open. Shock reverberates through every part of me.

I gasp, 'The champagne!'

Eliza pants to catch her breath. The effort of bringing out this revelation has exhausted her.

'Johnny put something in my glass at the assembly house in London.'

She offers me a barely discernible nod and closes her eyes again.

Eliza betrayed me. She was part of it. She was one of the plotters. She played her part in the Waterlands' scheme to sell me to Barfield. She knew that Johnny had adulterated my glass. In fact, she urged me to drink the champagne. *Take a glass. It's very uncivil of you not to, Em, when Johnny has gone to so much trouble to entertain us.*

A quiver passes across her white lips, but she cannot or will not look at me. I do not revile her. She could not help herself. She was always obliged to fulfil the demands of her insatiable mother and brother.

'Eliza, did you know that Johnny had taken me to Barfield that night of the soirée?'

A nearly imperceptible nod.

'The plan was decided at Sedge Court,' I say.

She whispers, 'You were right about the bank. The debts must be paid or we will lose our home. What would we do without it? What would Mama do? Barfield offered a bargain. He would marry me if he could have you first. As if you were a douceur.'

A tear drips down her cheek.

'Johnny took you to Barfield. I was to come the following evening to Barfield's house to meet the lawyer. There was a marriage contract. It was worth a lot of money to us. But I never met the lawyer. I came to the house, and Barfield was already in the street with his carriage and his footman. He told me you had run away with Johnny. I was hysterical about it. Screaming and screaming. It wasn't fair. You would be with Johnny and I would be left with Barfield. He threw me into the carriage and told me to stop my noise and I suppose he did not know what to do with me at first, because he was eager to get to a posting house in Piccadilly. His footman had the information that you had gone to Piccadilly. And what would you possibly do there, except get a coach from the White Bear?'

'And he guessed that I was Mrs Ann Jones.'

'We described you to the book-keeper. So we knew then that you were heading for Bristol. I expected Mr Barfield to throw me out, but he changed his mind and said we would find Johnny. Perhaps he thought I might be useful in some way that he hadn't yet figured. And then we drove on all the way to Reading. By then I wanted to accompany him on the chase. I thought I was running after Johnny.' She presses her hand to her mouth to stifle her sobs.

Barfield would have realised that Eliza's distress reinforced his lying story: that Johnny had disappeared with me. Her presence drew attention away from London and gave credence to the belief that Johnny was still alive.

'Does your mother know that the plan miscarried?'

Eliza shakes her head. 'I do not know. I would be very afraid to return to Sedge Court having failed. I had some hope, you see, as I ran on with Barfield, that we would find Johnny and he would conjure a way for us to live.' Her voice falters. 'Mama frightens me. She is capable of nearly anything.'

Eliza's face twists in pain. I slide my arms around her shoulders — her shift is drenched with sweat — and raise the cup of water to her lips again. With an effort she swallows a few drops.

I take her damp hand in mine. As I sit with her, listening to the harsh sound of her breathing, I am aware that something has been finished with.

We have emerged from between two chains of islands into the open sea, where we are forcefully rocked upon the breaking waves. Captain McDonagh orders me to take the bailer and throw out the water that we have taken on. I can see that it would take only one nasty wave to swamp our low-lying vessel, but the *Cliona* is sturdy and easy to manoeuvre, especially to windward. She points into the waves with a good turn of speed, spray flying from underneath the bow like two wings, and keeps her head up. Captain McDonagh must give me a precipitate lesson in sailing, since it requires the two of us to work the boat in these conditions, but I have already absorbed a surprising amount from my passage on the *Seal*. In any case, the captain and I have a shared willingness to dare. Since I know him to be a bold man on the sea, I have faith in his ability to bring us safely to our destination.

Eliza has elapsed into a state of suspension that has remained unchanged these last hours. She breathes and yet she seems hardly alive. As the sun sinks, I duck my head into the cabin in order to remark the light that beams at us from the western horizon. Eliza gives no sign of hearing, but speaking to her is a ploy to keep her attached to life.

None of this would have happened had there not been such unquenchable desire in Mrs Waterland's heart. From her river-head of need flowed the waters that sank so many lives. I do not know how else to explain her actions. The opportune snatching of a child. The exploitation of those who loved her. The moral void. Why do people do the things that they do? I realise now that sometimes we do not know why. Sometimes there is no answer, no matter how desperately we wish to supply meaning to a villain's chaotic acts.

I do know that none of us was ever truly alive to her. In that oversight – and its dearth of empathy – lay her crime. It appals me that I mistook this most negligent of women for an ideal mother. Isn't it terrifying that we take so long to come to the truth of things? And that if we are disposed to believe something, we will not notice the duplicity that lies under our noses.

An intense crimson cast fills the little cabin. I watch as the fiery eye of the sun sinks into the sea.

I murmur, 'It is a wonderful sunset, Eliza.'

Has she suddenly come awake? Her eyes are shining and her cheeks glow. But I see in the next second that her eyes are only a reflection of the light for they are glazed in death.

I cling to Eliza's hand for a long time, feeling it grow cold and light and then Captain McDonagh draws me out of the cabin and invites me to sit with him on the transom and to cry my tears into the spray.

Eliza could never have argued against the force of her family, I tell him. She never could have admitted that Sedge Court had been brought to financial downfall by the hubris of her beloved brother. Eliza and I were sent down to London to repair the damage. Johnny brokered the trade, of course. He would supply me to Barfield and in return Barfield would marry Eliza and the debts could be discharged and her family would have the ease of her new money and status. Barfield would have the use of me in perpetuity if he so desired. I still could not understand, though, why Barfield's mother would allow the marriage.

Captain McDonagh says, 'Because he was rotten with the pox, I wager. He could not be married to anyone.'

Then he would have – he would have infected both of us. I gaze up into the sky at the sparkle of the stars. They say there is a pattern of constellations up there, but it is difficult to make them out. They look like nothing so much as an arbitrary scattering.

Captain McDonagh lifts his chin towards the sky and says, 'Do you see that speck?'

'The very bright one?'

'That is our pilot star. Shall I show you how we find our way by it?'

I nod my head, too bursting with emotion to speak. He stands up then and says gently, 'But first we must help Miss Waterland to take the step that isn't there.'

I should like to wrap Eliza in cloth, but Captain McDonagh says that our need of a spare sail is greater than that of Eliza's for a shroud. I dress her hair and button her habit and the captain carries her on to the deck, just as she is. He recites words from the scriptures over her body and then he gently gathers her up and gives her into the custody of the sea. There is a splash and she is gone.

As Captain McDonagh and I stand in the stern watching the wake fan out behind us, I weep for Eliza. The captain says gently, 'She is in the place of truth now, Molly.' Then he places his hands on my shoulders and turns me around to face the bow. 'Go forward,' he says, and I do as he bids, climbing on to the foredeck and crouching in the V of the boat with my sorrow.

I awake to the smell of fuming turf. Although I thought I could not possibly sleep, I have done so, dreamlessly. I emerge from the cabin to find that the captain has a few sods burning in a bucket.

'Do you ever sleep?' I ask.

'I am like a horse,' he says, 'I snatch my rest when I can. Are you hungry?' He eyes the birds that hover behind our stern as if they are part of our procession. 'I would say there is a pretty shoal out there, wouldn't you?'

He ferrets around under the aft platform – there is turf

stored there and provisions, dried fish and seaweed and potatoes, and fishing paraphernalia – and brings out a line, hooks
and a basket of limpets. We bait the line with the limpets and
Captain McDonagh trails it in the water with one hand while
the other lies on the tiller. After some while, he draws in the
line and discovers three spiky gurnard twitching on it.

As we feast on our catch, cooked on the smouldering sods,
the captain bats at the gulls, which are loitering above our
meal. He flicks a fishbone away, and says, 'Why don't you call
me by the name my friends use and we will get along a little
better.'

I watch the clouds charge along the highway of the sky and
the waves flow past. 'Are you ever afraid?' My question takes
in the entirety of the ocean and the uncertainty of our voyage.

'Only a fool is without fear, but let us do our best to survive.
As my father liked to say, a good run is better than a bad
stand.' I like the glint of amusement in Connla McDonagh's
eye. It stirs in me a swift rush of ardour.

'Connla –' his name sounds strange on my tongue, but I
shall become used to it – 'there is something I should like to
say. It concerns the *Vindicator*. It is only – may I say that I
accept the apology you offered me?'

Connla leans a little way forward and meets my eye with a
gladdened expression and something eases between us. Then
he and I look out past ourselves at the open vista.

The foam curls from our bow and the sea and wind rush
by. My mother, Nora, and my father, Josey, are alive in me,
and Henrietta Waterland has shrivelled away to nothing at all.

I imagine you racing across the waves on your sea horse.
Your long, black hair streams in the wind and your crimson

petticoat flutters. Are you coming with me? Ah, no, you have ridden out this far only to see me off. You certainly have a marvellous sky for a playground today. There is nothing much left of those clouds. They are little more than teasings of fleece. And now I would like to ask you, with all the love in my heart, to watch me out of sight with a blessing.

Author's Note

I would very much like to thank my generous and insightful agent, Clare Conville, who has always believed in me. I owe a great debt to the friends who so kindly put me up when I was teetering on the brink and offered me a place to write, particularly Markie and Ian and Greg and Gill. And without my excellent and supportive publisher, Susan Watt, and the team at Heron there would be no book.

I overhauled the first draft of *Turning the Stones* after attending Theresa Rebeck's inspiring masterclass at Hedgebrook women writers' retreat on Whidbey Island. I am very grateful to Theresa and to the writers I met while I was there.

I am always charmed by the hospitality of County Galway. My thanks go to a stranger I encountered on Mweenish Island who brought to my attention Séamus Mac an Iomaire's wonderful mixture of memoir and natural history, *The Shores of Connemara,* whose translation by Padraic de Bhaldraithe was published by Tír Eolas in 2000. The descriptions of kelp-making in this book proved indispensable to me. Also, an anecdote about obtaining wood from shipwrecks for boat-building gave me the idea to have Nora O'Halloran spot useful logs floating in the sea.

Among many books and maps consulted in numbers of

libraries and museums, I am indebted to the following: Anne Buck, *Dress in Eighteenth Century England*, Homes & Meier, 1979; Katherine Cahill, *Mrs Delany's Menus, Medicines and Manners*, New Island, 2005; E. Keble Chatterton, *King's Cutters and Smugglers 1700–1855*, J.B. Lippincott, 1912; Cheshire County Council, *Cheshire Historic Town Survey*, Chester, 2003; Louis M. Cullen's various essays on eighteenth-century Irish smuggling, privateering and mercantile networks, published in numerous academic journals; Lady Gregory, *Visions and Beliefs in the West of Ireland*, G.P. Putnam's Sons, 1920; Stanley Harris, *Old Coaching Days*, R. Bentley, 1882; Bridget Hill, *Servants: English Domestics in the Eighteenth Century*, Clarendon Press, 1996; G.H. Kinahan, 'Connemara Folk-Lore', *The Folk-Lore Journal*, Vol. 2 Sept. 1884; M.E. Marker, *The Dee Estuary – its progressive silting and saltmarsh development*, Transactions of the Institute of British Geographers 41, 1967; Bernard Mees, *Celtic Curses*, Boydell and Brewer, 2009; Amanda Vickery, *Behind Closed Doors: At Home in Georgian England*, Yale University Press, 2010